ANGEL'S PEAK

This Large Print Book carries the
Seal of Approval of N.A.V.H.

A VIRGIN RIVER NOVEL

ANGEL'S PEAK

ROBYN CARR

WHEELER PUBLISHING
A part of Gale, Cengage Learning

GALE
CENGAGE Learning

Detroit • New York • San Francisco • New Haven, Conn • Waterville, Maine • London

GALE
CENGAGE Learning

LIBRARY OF CONGRESS CATALOGING-IN-PUBLICATION DATA

Carr, Robyn.
    Angel's Peak / by Robyn Carr. — Large print ed.
        p. cm.
    Originally published: Don Mills, Ont. : Mira, 2010.
    "A Virgin River novel" —T.p. verso.
    ISBN-13: 978-1-4104-2405-1 (alk. paper)
    ISBN-10: 1-4104-2405-7 (alk. paper)
    1. California, Northern—Fiction. 2. Large type books. I. Title.
PS3553.A76334A85 2010
813'.54—dc22   2009052166

Published in 2010 by arrangement with Harlequin Books S.A.

Printed in Mexico
4 5 6 7 14 13 12 11 10

For Beki Keene, who remembers every detail. Thank you for your lovely, committed, loyal friendship. I treasure every e-mail and visit.

ONE

Once the sun went down in Virgin River there wasn't a whole lot of entertainment for Sean Riordan, unless he wanted to sit by the fire at his brother Luke's house. But sitting all quiet and cozy while Luke and his new wife, Shelby, snuggled and said sweet little things to each other was a special kind of torment he could do without. Sometimes they just faked being tired so they could slip off to bed at eight o'clock at night. More often than not Sean just made it easy on them — he'd head over to a larger town on the coast where he could enjoy the sights and do a little window-shopping, maybe meet a woman of his own.

Sean was a U-2 pilot stationed at Beale Air Force Base in Northern California, a few hours south of Virgin River. He had accumulated a ton of vacation and could only carry over ninety days to the next fiscal year, so he had a couple of months to kill. His brother had just gotten married and Sean had been his best man. After the wedding, Sean decided to stay on in Virgin River and use up some of his leave. Given the fact that Luke and Shelby had been together about a year, Sean didn't feel as if he was interfering with the honeymoon by hanging around. All that lovey-dovey stuff was not so much about them sealing the deal, as it was about them still being hot to trot, as if they'd just met.

And there was a lot of talk about baby making, something that surprised Sean about Luke. However, Luke's willingness to step up and try to nail that egg, night after night after night, that did *not* surprise Sean in the slightest.

During the daytime, Sean always had lots to do. There was plenty of upkeep on the cabins Luke and Sean had bought together as an investment and which Luke now managed and rented full-time. There was hunting and fishing — it was still deer season — and the salmon and trout were fat; the river ran practically outside the front door. Luke and his helper, Art, were catching so many fish that Luke had to buy a shed, run some wiring to it from the house and invest in a big freezer.

There was no denying the appeal of the

Virgin River area for a guy with time on his hands. Sean was an outdoorsman at heart and the October colors in the mountains were awesome. It wouldn't be all that long before the first snowfall, and soon after that he would have to get back to Beale. So, in the meantime, all he wanted to do was find a nice bar with a fireplace to relax next to — one without his brother and sister-in-law cuddling up in front of it.

"Ready for another drink, pal?" the bartender asked him.

"I'm good, thanks. I didn't come in here to check out the architecture, but the detailed carving in this place is impressive," Sean replied.

The bartender laughed. "Two things are obvious about you. You're not from around here and you're military."

"Okay, I admit the haircut is a giveaway. But the rest — ?"

"This is lumber country and this bar is wall-to-wall oak. When it was built, the wood was probably cheaper than the nails. The craftsmanship? Common around here. So, what brings you to town?"

Sean took a sip of his beer. "Burning off some leave. Visiting my brother. I have a little over six weeks of leave left. I used to hit the bars with my brother, but his running days are over."

"War injury?" the bartender asked.

"Battle of the sexes. He just got married."

The bartender whistled. "My condolences."

Tonight Sean had landed in a large upscale bar and restaurant in Arcata. He occupied a spot at the end of the bar where he could get a one-hundred-and-eighty-degree view of the place. So far it appeared as if all the women were with husbands or dates, but that didn't diminish his pleasure — Sean wasn't always looking for a pickup. Sometimes it was nice to simply appreciate the view. Since he was going to be spending some time in this part of the world, he wasn't opposed to the idea of getting to know a girl, take her out, maybe even get a little up close and personal.

All such thoughts were suddenly stopped and were replaced by, *Ah! Looks like I just hit the jackpot.*

There was a ripple of female laughter as the door swung open and a group of women, who were obviously having a good time, entered. Even across the large restaurant, he could appreciate their assets. The first one was short, dark, a little on the round side and deliciously so. She appeared lush and soft and brought a smile to Sean's

10

lips. The second one was tall, thin, athletic looking, with straight, silky, unfussy blond hair. Obviously a gymnast or runner — a fine-looking woman. Next came a medium-sized redhead with a curvaceous figure, twinkling eyes and a bright smile. A feminine smorgasbord, he thought appreciatively. Sean did not discriminate — he was attracted to all kinds of women, not just one type. Next was —

Franci?

Nah, couldn't be, he told himself. He was just hallucinating again. He thought he'd seen her many times before but it was never her. Besides, Franci wore her hair long and straight and this woman's mahogany hair was in one of those hyper-short cuts that, on anyone else, might look butch, but on her? Oh, man, it just couldn't get any sexier. It made her dark eyes look huge. The woman shed her coat and she was thinner than Franci, but not by that much. But her eyebrows were exactly the same as Franci's — a nice, thin, provocative arch over those big, heavily lashed eyes. It got him missing Franci all over again.

She slid out of her coat and revealed a filmy dress. Maybe not filmy, but certainly silky. It was dark purple and fell loosely from her shoulders and was belted at the

11

waist, then flowed again to her knees. The dress accentuated her perfect breasts, narrow waist, slim hips and long legs. Franci had rarely worn dresses but Sean hadn't minded — her long legs and tight butt in a pair of fitted slacks used to blow his mind. But this dress was good. *Very good.*

The four women took a table near the front of the restaurant by the window. They were carrying boxes, shopping bags and party bags — a birthday dinner out? The one who looked like his old girlfriend crossed her legs and revealed a slit in the skirt of that dress that exposed a scrumptious thigh. Whoa. His eyes were glued to that shapely leg. His groin tightened.

Then she laughed. God, it *was* Franci. If that wasn't Franci, it was her twin. The way she tilted her head back and let go was a laugh with passion. Franci had always laughed from deep inside her. That was how she cried, too.

Sean was suddenly infused with mixed emotions — remembering the wonderful laughs they'd shared in bed after their typically great sex counterbalanced with how he remembered making her cry, and he was sorry he had ever made Franci cry.

Well, hell, he might have made her cry, but hadn't she infuriated him until he wanted to punch a hole in the wall? She could be maddening. Why was that again? He'd think of it, given a minute. That had been almost four years ago. What was she doing here in Arcata? After the breakup — which had been ugly — he'd looked for her. But he had let too much time slip by before doing so and she wasn't where he expected her to be. They'd met in Iraq when he was deployed in the F-16 and she was an air force flight nurse who regularly appeared to take the injured out of the theater. Later, when he'd been transferred to Luke Air Force Base in Phoenix as an instructor in the same jet, she was there, assigned as a nurse in the base hospital. They had dated exclusively for two years when a big shift occurred in their individual lives — her service commitment was up and she was planning to separate from the air force and return to civilian life. He was going to cross-train in the U-2 high-altitude reconnaissance aircraft — the spy plane. He didn't see how either of those events should effect any change. He told her he'd be relocating to Beale AFB in Northern California. He thought she could probably find work there if she was interested.

That had been the beginning of the end. After dating for two years, she, at twenty-six, was ready for a commitment. She wanted marriage and a family, and he didn't. Well, there was nothing new there — she'd been honest about that since the beginning of their relationship. Franci had always hoped to marry and have children. And that wasn't something he needed more time to consider — he really didn't see himself settling into that sweet little domestic trap. Ever. She'd been good about not pushing that too hard, but she'd never backed down, either. For Sean's part, he was monogamous. He told her he loved her because he did. If he occasionally glanced at and appreciated a pretty girl, it went no further. Even though they each maintained their own home, they spent every night together unless one of them was away from the base. But when it came to marriage and children, she was in, and he, at twenty-eight, was out.

She had said something like, "It's time to take this relationship to the next level or end it completely."

You don't want to be drawing a line in the sand in front of a young fighter pilot. Jet jockeys didn't take orders from girlfriends. Of course, it was no surprise that they fought and he made her cry with senseless, stupid comments like, "Not in this lifetime, babe. If I were interested in getting married, we'd *be* married," and, "Look, I'm just flat-ass not doing the rug-rats thing, all right? Even with you." Oh, yeah, he was brilliant.

She had said things, also in anger, probably things she didn't mean. Well, that wasn't exactly correct, as he recalled now, looking across a crowded room at her as she laughed and talked with her girlfriends. "Sean, if you let me go now I'll be so gone — you'll never see me again. I need a committed partner or I'm taking the walk."

And Sean, being the cocky genius he was, said, "Oh, yeah? Don't let the door hit you in the ass." He winced at the memory.

They had gone their separate ways, bitterly. He went to Beale because it looked as if getting a promotion and command position in the U-2 was more likely than in the highly competitive F-16. He was an Air Force Academy graduate; becoming a general was in his sights if he made the right moves. Franci had exited the air force.

Sean assumed, incorrectly, that he'd be able to find her at her mother's, or at least near her mother's, in Santa Rosa. A few months later, when his training in the new aircraft was complete and he was ready to talk about their situation, sanely and calmly, she was long gone. So was her mother. And there appeared to be no forwarding address.

So, flash-forward four years. Arcata, California? It really didn't make sense, but that woman across the room was definitely Franci Duncan. He could tell it was her by the way his heart pounded and he felt hot all over. And by the way he was fighting an erection just looking across the room at her.

She and her friends had all ordered frothy after-dinner drinks, and were joking with the young waitress. They leaned toward one another to whisper, sitting back to laugh — they were gossiping and having fun. One member of the group pulled a silky wrap out of a colorful bag and put it around her shoulders, admiringly. The birthday girl? There weren't any men around them and he could only pick out one wedding ring in the group, and it wasn't on Franci's hand. Not that it meant anything; people didn't necessarily wear wedding rings all the time these days.

"You still okay on that drink, pal?" the bartender asked to no avail.

As Sean watched the proceedings he missed her so bad he ached with it. Letting her get away was one of the great tactical errors of his adult life. He should have found a way to convince her they'd be fine

16

together without marriage, without a bunch of ankle-biters. But at twenty-eight, pumped up on his fighter-pilot prowess, he'd been overconfident. He had especially not been ready for some woman to be calling the shots. Now, at thirty-two, he realized how stupid he'd been at twenty-eight. In those four years there had been other women, and not one of them had come close to what he'd felt for Franci. For what he'd felt *with* Franci. And he was willing to bet she hadn't found anyone as good, either.

He was *hoping* that. He probably shouldn't bet on it. Franci was incredible; there had probably been a long line of able-bodied, good-looking, more-than-willing men lined up at her front door — wherever that was.

"You still on my planet, pal?" the bartender asked.

"Huh?"

"Seems like something besides my skill at pouring a drink has your attention."

"Yeah," he said, looking back at Franci. "I think maybe I know one of them," he said, tilting his head toward the table of women.

"How's your drink?"

"I'm good," Sean said, his eyes uncontrollably drawn to the woman across the room.

The women had a second order of frothy coffees. There was a lot more laughing, talking, rummaging through the gifts, and they were oblivious to anything else happening in that bar. They certainly weren't trolling for guys. They never even glanced toward the bar.

If she looked his way, even once, he'd have to think of something clever to say. He'd have to smile, walk confidently across the room to their table, say hello and get friendly. He'd have to make them laugh and like him, because he couldn't let her get out of here without finding out where she lived. She might be visiting one of those women, which meant that after she left, she'd be totally gone again. He couldn't let that happen. He needed to see her, talk to her. Touch her. *Hold her.*

"Why don't you go over there? Say hello?" the bartender asked.

He looked up at his new friend. "Yeah . . . well . . . The last time we talked, I wasn't her favorite person."

The bartender laughed. "Hard to imagine," he said.

Sean had been staring at that table of women for a long time and the bartender was probably watching that, in case he turned out to be some kind of pervert. Sean turned on the charm; he cheered up real fast so he didn't look so intense. "Hey, I

18

should settle up and get going, even if the scenery in here is incredible." He put some money on the bar, including a nice tip, and left without finishing his drink. He walked out with his head down, trying not to attract any attention.

It was colder than usual on the coast this October night. He wandered across the street, where he could keep an eye on the front door. He hoped they quit the bar before he froze to death. It made him sick to think she might get away from him.

He made up his mind and it took him less than fifteen seconds to decide — he really needed to see if he could get things straightened out with Franci. They should be together. He just hoped she would see it that way.

He actually said a prayer. There had to be a patron saint to ignorant, immature playboys, right? Saint Hugh? Saint Don Juan? Whomever . . . give me a break here and I'll change my ways. I swear. I won't be overconfident; I'll be sensitive. We'll negotiate and get back to what we had before . . . And then it happened. The four women came out the front door of the restaurant, one of them toting her presents. They lingered, laughed some more, hugged and then they went their separate ways. Two went left, two went right. At the end of the block, Franci and her friend went in opposite directions, and Sean, feeling as if this was the one chance in his lifetime, hotfooted it after her.

He had just about caught up to her when she was unlocking the door of a small silver sedan. "Franci?" he called out.

She jumped, turned and stared at him, wide-eyed.

"It *is* you," he said, taking a few steps nearer to her. "Your hair — wow. Threw me off for a minute."

She looked almost frightened at first. But then she seemed to compose herself, though she shivered from the cold and pulled her coat tighter around her. "Sean?"

"Yeah," he said, laughing. "I can't believe I'm running into you here, of all places."

"What are you doing here?" she asked, not looking thrilled to see him.

"Remember Luke? Remember, I told you we bought some old cabins together a long time ago? Long before I met you. Well, he got out of the army and came up here to work on 'em."

"Here?" she asked, aghast. She pulled her coat tighter. "Those cabins are *here?*"

"Back in the mountains, along the Virgin River," he said. "I was just burning some leave, visiting him. I came over here for dinner."

She looked around. "Where's Luke?" she asked. "Is he with you?"

"No." He laughed. "Married. Recently married. I try to get out of their hair in the evening because they . . ." He stopped and laughed silently, shaking his head. Then he looked at her face. "You look great. How long have you been here? In Arcata?"

"I, ah, I don't actually live in Arcata. I was just meeting some friends for dinner. Everything all right with you? With your family?"

"Everyone is good," he said. He took another step toward her. "Franci, let me buy you a cup of coffee. Let's catch up a little."

"Ah . . . No, I don't think so, Sean," she said, shaking her head. "I'd better get —"

"I looked for you," he said impulsively. "To say it was a mistake, the way we broke up. We should talk. There might be things we can work out that we were both too stubborn to —"

"Listen, don't even go there, Sean. It's all in the past. No hard feelings," she said. "So good luck and good —"

"Are you married or something?" he asked.

She was startled. "No. But I'm not looking to go back to the discussion that ended us. Maybe you were able to just blow it off, but I —"

"I didn't blow it off, Franci," he said. "I looked for you and couldn't find you anywhere. That's why I want to talk."

"Well, I don't," she said. She opened her car door. "I think you've probably said enough on that subject."

"Franci, what the fuck?" he asked, confused and a little angry by her immediate rebuff. "God, can't we have a conversation? We were together for two years! It was good, me and you. We never had anyone else, either one of us, and —"

"And you said it wasn't going any further." She stiffened her back. "In fact, that was one of the nicer things you said. I'm glad you're doing fine — you look just the same, happy as can be. Say hello to your mother and brothers. And really, don't push this. We decided. We're over."

"Come on. I don't believe you mean that," he said.

"Believe it," she shot back. "You made a decision — you didn't want a commitment to me. And here you are — you don't have one. Bye. Take care."

She got in her car and slammed the door. He took two giant steps forward and heard the door locks click into place. She backed out of her parking space quickly and drove away. He memorized the license number, but the most important thing he noticed was that it was a California plate. She might not live in Arcata, but she lived close enough to drive over for dinner.

Now that he'd seen her, he knew what he'd long suspected. He was far from over her.

Franci's hands trembled so much, she found it hard to drive. She always knew there was a chance she would bump into him someday, though she carefully avoided the most obvious places where that could happen. But she had never, *never* expected him to want to talk about it, to talk about *them!*

And when she thought of the months she had prayed for that talk to happen, it caused her vision to blur with gathering tears. *Angry* tears! She pursed her lips and thought, *No!* She'd cried enough over him; he wouldn't get the benefit of one more tear.

Franci left Phoenix after their breakup and went home to Santa Rosa to work as a civilian nurse in a hospital. She had lived with her mother. Almost a year later, she got a good job that fed her addiction to adrenaline

— a flight nurse position with a helicopter transport unit. Less demanding work hours, good benefits, more opportunities — but it meant a move. Because she had her bachelor of science in nursing, she was able to teach a couple of courses at Humboldt U in Arcata, perhaps building a future in academia.

Her mom, a family-medicine physician's assistant, had been ready for a change. Vivian found a position in a family-medicine clinic in Eureka. An *excellent* position. Vivian's hours were more demanding — full-time, in fact. So the two of them moved north together, closer to Vivian's job than Franci's, and twice a week, Franci drove over the mountains to Redding to pull a twenty-four-hour shift as a flight nurse. Most of her flights were routine patient transport via helicopter — getting a heart or C-section patient out of a small-town hospital to a larger facility where special surgery could be performed. But occasionally she was on board for an emergency — victims of a wildfire, car accidents in isolated parts of the mountain terrain, injuries requiring emergency surgery. She had loved in-flight nursing in the air force and had missed it. This new job fit the bill. She bought a cute little house on the outskirts of Eureka in the kind of quiet, lovely neigh-

borhood she most enjoyed and, until tonight, she thought her life was nearly perfect.

Looked for her, had he? Not very hard.
Once six months had passed, she thought
she'd come to terms with the fact that they
were not meant to be. They wanted different things from life; he wanted to play and
have fun till he was a grizzled old man and
she wanted to put down roots and grow a
family.

What wasn't fair about it was that she'd
been attracted to the very thing that seemed
to prevent him from wanting to settle down.
He was handsome and daring and reckless,
as good at snow and water skiing as he was
at snuggling up on the couch to watch a
movie. Of course, it was one chick flick to
every five action-adventures, but that was
okay with Franci — she liked action herself.
She thought their relationship could exist
within a marriage just as easily as it did
outside marriage. Half the couples they had
camped and traveled and played with were
married with kids. Kids didn't bother Sean;
he seemed to like them. But he was adamant; he didn't need any official contract to
show how he felt and he wasn't interested
in being tied down by the needs of children.

■ ■ ■ ■

The fifteen-minute drive south to Eureka from Arcata hadn't been enough to settle Franci's nerves, so she drove around town another fifteen minutes before heading to her little neighborhood. She wanted to be completely composed when she got home. She should have known she had only been kidding herself about being at peace with her decision to leave him. That myth was disproved the second she saw him. God, he still made her heart race. One look at his face and she felt the blood surge through her veins; she could feel the heat on her cheeks. She couldn't have a cup of coffee with him. She'd probably lunge across the table at Starbucks and tear his clothes off his body. She would have to be strong. Firm. Get herself bolstered and ready; she was weak. She might hate him, but she still loved him. And he still turned her on. All that meant he could hurt her again.

She finally parked in her little one-and-a-half-car garage, pulled down the door and walked into the house and through the kitchen. She could hear the TV in the living room and there she found her mother, sleeping while sitting up, and her daughter,

Rosie, curled up on the couch beside her. The only one who looked up when she walked into the room was Harry, their blond-and-white cocker spaniel.

"Hi, Harry," she said.

He wagged a couple of times and rolled over on his back, just in case anyone wanted to rub his belly.

"Mom?" she said, giving her mother a little jostle. "Mom? I'm home."

Vivian stirred and straightened. "Hm, hi. I must have dozed off." She stretched. "Did you have fun?"

"Sure. Those girls are always fun. I'll catch you up on the gossip tomorrow after you've had a good night's sleep."

Vivian stood. "Let me put Rosie —"

"I'll take her to bed, Mom," Franci said. "Tucking her in is the best part of the day. How long has she been asleep?"

"She probably stayed awake longer than I did," Vivian said with a laugh. She gave Franci a pat on one cheek and a kiss on the other. "Day off tomorrow. Call when you're up. We'll have coffee or something."

"Sure. Thanks, Mom." Franci grabbed Vivian's coat from the back of the chair and helped her slip it on. "I'll watch you walk home," Franci said.

"I'm sure I won't fall in the street. Or get

mugged."

"I'll watch you just the same."

Franci, Vivian and Rosie had lived together in this little two-bedroom house for a couple of years, Franci sharing her bed with Rosie. About a year ago Vivian had purchased a similar house at the end of the block. They'd always planned to have their own residences, both of them being independent, single women, but Rosie's arrival was the impetus for them to remain close enough so they could join forces to take care of her. When Franci worked those twenty-four-hour shifts, or went out on that rare late-night date, Rosie spent the night at Grandma's. If it wasn't going to be a late night or an overnight for Franci, Grandma came to Rosie's house so Rosie could fall asleep in her own bed. Now that Rosie was in pre-school and day care, both her mother and grandmother could easily juggle child care and manage their jobs.

Franci watched her mom walk down the street and up the flower-lined walk that led to her own door. Once Vivian was inside, she flashed her porch light a few times to signal that she was all right, then Franci went in and closed her own front door.

Franci hung up her coat, scooped her redheaded daughter off the couch and car-

28

ried her to bed. Her arms flopped; she was out cold. Her comforter was turned down and her bedside lamp glowed. Grandma had clearly been optimistic that Rosie would slip right into bed when it was time, rather than fall asleep on the couch, as she preferred. Franci tucked her daughter in, pressed the comforter around her and kissed her forehead. Rosie let out a sleepy snort.

"I saw your daddy tonight," Franci whispered. "There's a reason you're so beautiful."

Two

Sean hadn't slept real well after seeing his old flame, so he beat the morning rush in the bathroom before there was so much as a sound from the bridal suite. He was halfway through his Wheaties when Shelby came into the kitchen in her jeans and sweater, ready to head over to Arcata to school. She was studying nursing at Humboldt U.

"Well, well. It's rare to see you before I get home in the afternoon," she remarked, going for the coffee. "When you've been out prowling till the wee hours, you usually need your beauty sleep."

Sean grunted.

"I guess that was 'good morning,' " she said. "And same to you."

Luke came into the kitchen next. "Well, hey there, sunshine," he said to his brother. Sean lifted his eyes but not his head. Luke laughed at the grim expression. "Lumpy

30

mattress? Did we put out the scratchy toilet paper?"

"Bed's fine."

"You want to grab a couple of the general's horses and ride along the —"

"I'm going to be tied up. I have some errands," Sean said.

Shelby lifted a stack of thank-you notes from the table and gave her husband a glare. They'd been married a couple of weeks and he was supposed to be adding his gratitude and signature to the notes she'd all but completed. "Luke . . ." she began. "Before you think about riding or fishing —"

"I know, I know," he said, glancing at the notes. "It'll get done."

"You really think he's going to do that girlie shit, Shelby?" Sean asked.

Shelby sat down at the table, confusion knitting her brow. She'd known Sean for about a year; he was the playful brother — the flirt and the comedian. They used to joke that Sean would have fun at a train wreck; his mood was perpetually upbeat. Luke had been the grump, but she'd softened him up. This crankiness from Sean was so unexpected. "Are you all right?" she asked.

"Fine," he answered shortly.

Luke poured himself a coffee and sat

down. "Fender bender? Speeding ticket? Pretty girl reject you? Food poisoning?"

Sean sat back in his chair. "I ran into Franci last night," he grumbled. "Pure chance."

Luke merely frowned; he didn't remember her. Sean had dated prolifically.

"Franci *Duncan,*" he said in exasperation. "Who I practically lived with a few years ago. Remember? We broke up when she got out of the air force and I got assigned the U-2."

"Oh, I remember her now," Luke said. "Haven't you seen her since then?"

"No," Sean said impatiently, taking another spoonful of cereal. "I tried to see her, but she was gone. I tried to reach her mother to see where she was, and her mother had moved, which made no sense because she'd been in that house in Santa Rosa for at least ten years. Maybe twenty years, I don't know."

"You looked for her?" Luke asked. "This is the first I've heard about that."

"Because I didn't talk about it. And I didn't find her," Sean said. "Obviously."

"What about her friends?" Shelby asked.

Sean was silent. He grimaced and finally said, "I checked with a couple of them, but they didn't know anything."

"That's crazy," Shelby said. "Women don't give up women friends. Especially after they've broken up with a guy they've been with a while — that's traumatic, even when it's for the best. Who was her *best* friend? Her *other* best friend? I mean, it was kind of different with me — I was my mother's caretaker and, while I had good friends, I had very little time for them. But I was always in touch with them when I —"

Luke put a hand over Shelby's to stop her because Sean looked perfectly miserable.

"Oh," she said quietly. "Well, who'd you ask?"

Sean shrugged uncomfortably. "We used to do things all the time with some couples — guys from my squadron and their wives or girls. We went four-wheeling, skiing, boating, camping, hiking . . . Two of them were married and one couple lived together. I asked the women. They hadn't heard from her. I asked her former boss, the colonel in her old medical unit at the base hospital. I asked her neighbor."

"Oh," Shelby said again.

"Okay, she had a few girlfriends and I met them, but we didn't get together with them and I couldn't remember their last names. And it had been a while."

"Um. A while?" Shelby asked.

"Okay, what happened was this — we had a fight. I got orders and she was going to get out of the air force, all at the same time. And she wanted to know . . . Thing was, I was transferring. I told her there was nothing stopping her from relocating to be closer to my next assignment and that pissed her off — that I didn't exactly *invite* her to join me, that I didn't make plans with her. I probably said I was sorry for that — I bet I did."

"And you broke up over that?" Shelby asked.

"Sort of. Not exactly," Sean admitted.

Luke put his elbow on the kitchen table and lazily leaned his chin into his hand, watching. Amused. And *so* glad some other Riordan male was taking the heat.

Sean took a breath. "She wanted to get married," he said. "She said, either we at least get engaged and plan to get married, or I walk. Those were her words." He made a slash in the air with his finger. "Line in the sand. Ultimatum."

"Really," Shelby said with a questionable tone. "After only *two years* of practically living together?"

"Okay, now you're just making fun of me," Sean said in a pout. "I admit, I shouldn't have let her go. But I was younger.

34

I was cocky then."

"Oh, *were* you?" Luke asked.

Sean glowered.

"So, she said she was ready for marriage, you said you weren't, you split up — is that right?" Shelby asked.

"That's about it." He made a face. "We might've said a few unnecessary things during the discussion. You know — angry things."

"I'll bet," Luke said.

"And you tried to track her down? Later?" Shelby asked.

"After I transitioned into the new squadron. After training in the new jet. After I thought we both had time to simmer down a little bit. You know."

Shelby looked at Luke and shook her head dismally. "Does this run in the family?" she asked. She and Luke had had a similar standoff, but she hadn't let him get away with it and had pushed him hard. But Luke had been ready to be domesticated. All she knew about Sean was that he was considered a playboy by the brothers. This was the first time she'd heard about a steady girl.

"It's possible," Luke admitted with a shrug. "Except Aiden. He wants to get married, have a family, but if he didn't have bad luck with women, he'd have no luck at all.

He was married once. To a lunatic."

"Lord," Shelby said. "No wonder your mother is fed up with the lot of you. Sean, what happened when you ran into her?"

"She said I looked good and, no, she didn't want to have coffee or anything else with me. She won't talk to me. At all. And I even said I was wrong. Sort of."

"Hm," Shelby said. "Maybe she's moved on."

"Well, then, she has to tell me that. Explain that. Because —" He stopped. He couldn't think of a reason why she owed him that, but he was sure she did.

"Now what?" Luke asked.

"I'm going to have to find her."

"Why? You said you were done, she said okay, you caught up a few years later and it's still done . . . I don't see the issue."

"No, you wouldn't," Sean said in a very impatient huff. "Because you don't know Franci."

"Sure I do. We all knew Franci. Nice girl, Franci. Hottie." He grinned. "We kind of all thought you'd marry her. But then when you didn't and went to Beale alone, we all said, 'There goes another Riordan.' "

"Here's the thing — I shouldn't have broken up with her. What I should have done was explain why we should stay to-

36

gether and why we didn't need any kind of old-fashioned contract to be okay with that. We were young, only twenty-six and twenty-eight. There was lots of time to consider big leaps like marriage. There's *still* lots of time, for that matter." Luke, thirty-eight and barely through a similar crisis, lifted a brow toward his twenty-five-year-old wife. "We should have gone to Beale and worked it out. But I didn't do that because she made me so frickin' mad."

It was silent in the kitchen for a moment. "Well," Luke finally said with fake cheeriness, "I'd love to stay and chat about your pathetic love life, but I need to grab Art and get over to the hardware store before —"

Shelby was shaking her head dismally. "So you had a little hissy and said, 'Fine, just go, then.' Is that it? Kind of like, 'My way or the highway,' huh?"

"Aw, come on, Shelby," Sean said pleadingly. "You know I'm not a guy with a temper! I'm a sweetheart. I'm not a fighter, I'm a lover. And I don't have any problem seeing myself with one woman. You know? It's just the whole marriage thing — it was not for me. Marriage scared the hell out of me. A couple of my brothers tried it and it screwed them up bad. And kids?" He shook his head. "Maybe when I'm old and worn out like Luke I'll change my mind, but at the moment I don't feel like being tied down like that."

"Ah," she said. "I see. So you'd like to have a nice chat with Franci and explain all this to her?"

"Something like that," he said, making perfect sense to himself. "It's no crime to have a fight, but we never should've given up what we had. We were good together."

Shelby stood. "Not good enough, I guess. Too bad I have to get to class, Sean. You have such a deep hole to climb out of and I'd love to talk you through it. You know I've loved you since the moment I met you, and I'd be happy to help. But school calls . . ."

Sean stood from the table, as well. "What do you mean, such a climb?"

"Okay, the short version. You let her go because you didn't feel in charge. You didn't bother to look for her for such a long time that her trail went cold — and I imagine, to her, it seemed as if you didn't care. You didn't even know the names of her best friends. Or her mother's friends. You paid no attention to the woman, except where it was useful to you. You even socialized with *your* friends, from *your* squadron, and then you were surprised that they hadn't heard from her. And now I think you're a little hurt that she won't forget all that and give you another chance to treat her like someone you might get around to later, when it's convenient. While she, at least at one time a few years ago, wanted to be thought of as someone you couldn't live without."

"You don't understand," he said.

"But your real problem is, I do," Shelby said. "You didn't realize how much she meant to you until she was gone."

Luke drained his coffee cup. He put it on the table. "When you have time, Sean, you should take a little course from Shelby. She's seen every chick flick ever filmed. She knows things about this you and I have never thought of."

Sean swallowed. Looking down he said, "Real quick, from a girl's point of view, what do I do next?"

"Not what you think," Shelby replied. "You better not do what you did before. Whatever it was that made *you* arrogantly think she'd never be able to leave you? Not that. You better do whatever it was you did that worked for *her,* that made *her* think she wanted a life with you. If you can even remember that far back. Because, brother, I think maybe you're too late. And if you're too late, you're going to have to accept that and respect her space. If you turn crazy and give her trouble, I'm not on your side anymore."

When Sean was alone in the house, he began asking himself what it was that *had* worked on Franci. Once they'd become a couple, he'd had lots of tricks up his sleeve. He was remembering the many areas where they had been compatible. Suddenly, it was hard to remember that, on a few issues, they had rubbed each other the wrong way.

Getting her to go out with him in the first place had been a real challenge. She'd been in the air force a while and knew her way around the jet jockeys, and she had a firm policy against dating fighter pilots. They had a reputation for being arrogant, self-absorbed idiots with short attention spans where women were concerned. Sean and Franci never discussed it, but Sean assumed she must have dated at least a couple to come up with that assessment. Which, as Sean grudgingly recalled, wasn't far off the mark.

But there had been lots of positive things, too, and right now he was becoming uncomfortable imagining every little thing he had done to make her crazy with desire, to make her purr with satisfaction, because the chemistry they had in the sack was phenomenal. Those times she wasn't in the mood, he knew what to say to change her mind. There were places he touched that would not only convince her to give it some more thought, but could turn her into a wild woman. And could she ever turn those tricks back on him, making him gasp and groan, driving him right out of his mind. None of those little things had worked on any other woman the way they had on Franci. She had a way of taking him so far beyond pleasure, he went out of his mind. He'd never been to bed with a woman who could please him the way Franci had, and he'd been to bed with far too many women.

What had he been thinking, letting her walk away?

Sean searched his memory for how he'd convinced her to take a chance on him in the first place and his mind was a blur. He'd probably been relentless in his pursuit because he did remember how he had felt when he first saw her. He'd taken one look at her and thought, Oh, Mary, Jesus and Joseph! She just did something to him. He had a lot of experience with attraction, but this was animal attraction. Primal and raw. He'd wanted her immediately. And he still wanted her that bad.

Sean first saw Franci when she passed

through Iraq to pick up a planeload of medical evacuees. He'd tried to get her coordinates so he could get in touch when he was stateside again. He'd seen her a few times — she was in and out, arriving on a medical air transport, hanging around until they could gather up all their patients, taking off for the States again. She wouldn't give him anything — not even a name. Of course, he managed to find out her name pretty easily, but that was all.

Then when he saw her at Luke AFB in the officers' club, he decided it must be kismet; they were meant to be. But she hadn't been any easier to convince. He remembered hoping she was as beautiful on the inside as she was sexy on the outside, because anything less would break his heart.

And she was. She was smart, strong, independent, confident, sexy and loving.

Franci was the kind of woman men looked at, but her sexiness was understated, not blatant. Franci was not cheap or flashy; she was classy and cool. She was long legged and dark haired with large, deep, dark eyes and thin, arched, expressive brows. Her mouth was a little pouty — soft and full. He could remember every detail of her body. But he couldn't remember how he'd caught her. Sean's typical move was to charm a woman, make her laugh, smolder her with his half-closed eyes, suggest, without being crude, that he could deliver satisfaction. He'd never shown an ounce of humility; he'd always been confident.

But he wasn't confident anymore. Now he was frustrated, and he didn't have the first clue about how to fix it. For once in his life, he didn't know where to start.

He went to the second upstairs bedroom where Luke kept his computer. The desk was covered with so many wedding gifts that it was hard to see the computer. He moved a bunch of things out of the way and got the thing turned on. Franci had no phone or address listing when he'd called information, but after spending a couple of hours on Luke's computer, doing a real-estate property search, he found Francine Duncan had purchased a house. It wasn't unusual for women to have unlisted phone numbers, but property-title searches were public record. Still, he didn't think his best idea was turning up at her house uninvited. But what were the options?

Sean was in the kitchen having a sandwich when Luke and Art came back from the hardware store. Art was such a kick; every time he saw Sean he greeted him as if he hadn't seen him in months or even years.

Art was a thirty-year-old man with highly functional Down syndrome, a kindhearted soul who worked hard to help Luke around the property. And Luke, whom Sean had just barely realized would make a great father, worked hard to be sure Art felt appreciated.

"Sean!" Art said, beaming.

"Hi, Art. Go fishing this morning?" Sean asked.

"No, we had trash to haul to the dump and then we went to the hardware store for stuff. Later I might fish. Did you go fishing?"

"Sort of. I was looking up stuff on the computer."

Luke got out the bread and sandwich makings. "Any luck finding contact information on Franci?" he asked.

"Got an address, but no phone number," Sean said. "I did a computer search — and lucky for me, she bought a house."

"Do you have a new girlfriend, Sean?" Art asked.

For some reason, the question embarrassed Sean. The fact that Art, who didn't really know him at all and was about as worldly as a ten-year-old, would assume that he always had a girlfriend made Sean uncomfortable. Maybe Franci *was* right about him; she'd said he'd never settle down with one woman because he was all about the chase but not the commitment. It wasn't entirely true, as he was discovering. He'd settled down with Franci, just not all the way. "Not really," Sean answered. "I had a girlfriend a few years ago and we lost touch. I want to see her again, talk to her about that, see if we can . . . date again."

"Oh," Art said. "That's cool."

"And the problem is?" Luke asked.

"She took one look at me and fireworks shot out of her ears. I think she hates me. At least, she's still mad. But it could mean she still cares," he added hopefully. "If I knew where to run into her again, I could try my persuasive charm on her without crowding her. I might've tried something like that the first time around. Like being at the officers' club every time I thought she'd be there, till she got so sick of me shadowing her, she gave in."

Luke laughed. "Suave," he said.

"Think I should throw myself on her mercy? Nah," he answered for himself. "From what I saw, she doesn't have a lot of mercy in her right now. Besides, humility really isn't my strong suit."

Luke laughed at him. "And, God forbid,

we manly Riordans always play our best cards."

"You know what I mean. What woman wants a man who grovels? Did you grovel? When you and Shelby — ?"

"I hate to burst your bubble, pal, but I said I'd do anything that would make her happy. I know — it's hard for you to imagine your tough big brother caving like that, but when I got down to it, I was doomed without her. She's the breath in me." Then he grinned. "But she doesn't make me grovel anymore. She lets me pretend to be the big man."

"Swell," Sean said, a long way from understanding all the rules for this game. The part he did almost understand was *she's the breath in me.* "There you go — I'm just plain better at the whole short-term hookup."

"Well, if that floats your boat, have a good time."

There was the problem. Short-term hookups just didn't do it for him anymore. Truthfully, they hadn't in a long time. In fact, he'd been wondering why he'd been feeling so dissatisfied, so marginally happy rather than jazzed all the time, and the second he saw Franci, he understood why.

"Listen, mind if I ask you something?"

Luke asked, while he was shuffling lunch meat, cheese and bread. "You were with her a couple of years. Seemed like it was a good couple of years but it ran its course or something. You broke up, and for four years you were okay. You managed. Why can't you just walk away now?"

Hard to explain, Sean thought. "You ever get this idea in your head about how things should be, then you just stay the course, even if it doesn't feel exactly right?"

"Me?" Luke asked with a facetious laugh. "Did you think I was just faking being a dumb grunt who almost lost his own woman?"

"I wasn't ready to get married," Sean said. "I didn't like getting pushed up against a wall and we both walked away mad. Six months later I was thinking, I might not be ready to get married, but I'm not ready for this to be over, either. I thought I could compromise if she could. So I called her cell phone. I left a couple of messages and she never called back. A few more months and I thought, all right — if it takes marriage to make her happy, I could probably work with the idea, as long as she gives me plenty of time to adjust. Maybe we could have a long engagement, just to make sure we're doing the right thing. So I called again and the cell phone was shut off. Her e-mail bounced back — undeliverable. Her mother, who she's very tight with, had moved. And if you think I was teed off before, the idea she'd just ignore me like that when I'm fucking *trying* — that really pissed me off." *And ripped my heart out. Just like I'd ripped her heart out by saying no way. What a couple of fools.*

"That's a bad word," Art said very quietly. Art wasn't one to judge or harangue, but he also wasn't one to miss anything.

"Sorry, Art. I'm going to try harder," Sean said.

Luke said, "Well, you seemed to be doing just fine to me."

"Most days," Sean said with a shrug. "I got into the plane, man. I was all caught up in the missions. I was away a lot. I got by. But every time I met a girl, all I did was compare her to Franci." *And saw Franci everywhere I looked, till I thought I was losing my mind.*

"Did you keep looking for her?" Luke asked.

"No. I figured it would pass eventually. The second I saw her I realized it wasn't going to pass. I think, in a way, this is my fault. Well, I thought for a few years it was her fault — that she was bossy and impatient and that no woman was going to tell *me* how the hog eats the cabbage. Now, I think there's a good chance I was an idiot."

"Ya think?" Luke asked. When Sean glowered, he chuckled and said, "Listen, I'm not being a jerk — but I just walked this road, brother. I'm lucky Shelby is smarter than I am, that's all." Luke looked at Sean seriously. "The women are in charge, my brother. We don't have to like it, but it's the law. I just ask Shelby what I want and she never lets me down."

"I have to be careful here," Sean said. "She said she doesn't want to see me, talk to me. I can't show up at her house like some stalker — she might call the cops. I'd call her if I had a number, but —"

"Or . . . you can try to figure out where she'll be. She's a nurse, right? Working as a nurse, right? So call all the places she might be working as a nurse. Hospitals, doctors' offices, clinics, you know. Ask to speak to her. They'll either say they never heard of her, say it's her day off or put her on the phone."

Sean was stunned. "Wow," he said. "That's brilliant."

"And amazing, because I've never hunted for a woman before," Luke said. "Okay. Where do women go? Women like Franci?

Shopping?"

"We did everything together — camping, quadding, diving, skiing . . . We traveled anytime we could. Franci alone? Gyms," Sean said. "Franci likes to work out. She loves to read — she spent a lot of time in bookstores. She loves movies, but she wouldn't go alone — we used to rent 'em. Back then, between me, work, the gym and a little shopping, I can't remember what she did with her time." And Sean thought, there it is again. *I wasn't paying attention because it wasn't about* me. He almost wondered how she had endured him that long, but fought the thought that struggled to surface.

"There's always a list for groceries on the kitchen counter," Luke said, nodding in the direction of today's list. "Shelby usually calls to see what we need when she's on her way home from school, but knock yourself out. Shop for groceries in her neighborhood."

"Yeah. Yeah, I'll do that." *And drive around places I might bump into her,* Sean thought. Just in case.

50

THREE

Sean promised himself he'd just drive around Eureka, but his car was like a heat-seeking missile and he soon found himself in Franci's neighborhood and then on her street. He had no intention of bothering her, just a fierce need to see how she was living without him. What was the harm in driving by her house?

Franci's house looked like something that should belong to her. It was cute, small, tidy, at least forty years old and very homey. It seemed the kind of comfy place a woman who wanted a family would choose — a safe, friendly neighborhood, large trees and spacious yards. She had a curving driveway lined with some kind of fluffy green ground cover, flower beds that were just going fallow in the fall weather, and right outside the front door was a scarecrow and some gourds in a horn of plenty. It was pampered. Loved. A family home.

This was nothing like a house Sean would live in — he tended more toward flashy, modern, low-maintenance homes; he had a lot of toys and liked to spend his time at play, not mowing lawns and shoveling snow.

His first panicked thought upon seeing the house was: Oh God! She has a man in her life! A man to settle down with! That's why it looks so cozy and domesticated!

He didn't slow down too much as he passed by; he didn't want to raise any suspicions. Having satisfied his curiosity about where she lived, Sean decided to check out the local recreational facilities.

Finding a gym Franci might like was harder to peg. There were several in the general vicinity. One was the Y, which was small but inexpensive and functional. There was a relatively large fitness center on the edge of town near the freeway. There was a women's gym, which would be obvious for any woman but Franci; she was ex air force and therefore used to working out with men. Fairly close to her house was a community center that appeared to contain a fitness facility, judging by the people wearing sweats and carrying gym bags who came out of the building.

As he drove past the various gyms, Sean noticed there were a few used bookstores and one big bookstore in the Eureka Mall. God, how he hated malls. But this might be the price of finding his girl, so he checked out the bookstore *and* the mall. While he was there he bought a couple of pairs of jeans, two shirts and a down vest as the fall weather was getting very brisk in the evening. And he bought a bunch of books he knew he'd never read.

Sean located the grocery stores nearby — there were plenty of those. He had a list of hospitals, clinics, doctors' offices and such to call. So he got himself a coffee and used his cell phone to call from his car while he sat in a grocery-store parking lot. But after countless calls there was no Francine Duncan to be found.

Over the next few days Sean developed a new routine. He'd leave Virgin River in the morning, drive to Eureka and make the rounds. He began to think of it as driving his circuit — hitting her neighborhood followed by a trip past the gyms, mall, bookstores and grocery stores. As he'd done on that first day, he'd park somewhere to make his phone calls to clinics and such, checking them off one by one. At least it was turning him into a slightly better houseguest as he would bring home groceries for a change, saving Shelby the trouble.

He was only on his fourth day of hanging out in Eureka when he started wondering if the whole thing was a waste of time. He was beginning to think that even if he did get a number for her she would probably hang up on him, leaving him no option but to go over to her house, anyway. Would she call the cops if he did pay her a call? Was it a crime to knock on her door and ask if they could just talk? He wasn't going to beg or threaten — just *ask!* Avon ladies and Jehovah's Witnesses did it all the time, and Sean was far less annoying!

But that fourth day turned out to be magic. Near the end of the day he hit the grocery store to pick up a few things. As he was choosing a head of romaine, he recognized the hand in the bin next to him. She was squeezing tomatoes. Now didn't that say something? That he'd recognize her *hand!* He turned and looked at her. "Don't make 'em go squirt," he said.

Franci jumped a mile. She dropped her tomato and clutched her jacket tight at the throat. "God, you scared me! What are you doing here?"

He held up his produce bag. "I have a list of things to get for my sister-in-law. But I'm

54

really glad I ran into you, Franci, because we —"

Before he'd even finished talking she turned away from him, quickly selecting three tomatoes, then she tossed them in a plastic bag and tried to escape. He noticed she was wearing a navy-blue jumpsuit and matching jacket with some kind of unit patches sewn on the arms.

"Hey, are you in the coast guard or something? Why couldn't I find you after you left the air force?"

She stopped, looked over her shoulder and said, "I have absolutely no idea. I went to my mother's, where I lived and worked for almost a year before moving here."

"I left messages on your cell," he said, tossing the lettuce in his small handheld basket, following her.

She turned toward him. "How many messages? Because I never got any."

He was shaking his head. "I don't understand that . . ."

"How many?" she demanded.

"I don't know. A few. A couple. I don't know — but I did," he said. It was coming back to him now — the way she could poke him and get him all hot under the collar.

She could push him to be honest, and he hated it because he felt exposed. She smiled with mock patience. "Well, Sean, I guess we had a technological malfunction. If you had really wanted to talk to me, you'd have tried leaving more than a couple of messages a few years ago. Now, really, I have to get going. I'm running late."

He grabbed her upper arm. "I've been trying to think of the best way to get in touch with you. I found your address, but no phone number, and I —"

"You know where I *live?*"

He looked around a little nervously; she made it sound as if he was some ax murderer or something. "Let's not get loud here," he suggested. "I needed to find you. I looked you up on the computer. You bought a house."

"Oh, for God's sake," she said, rubbing her temples. She seemed to gather herself from within. "All right. What do you want?"

Now this was pissing him off all over again. "Gee, was I confusing you? I want us to have a conversation, maybe talk about what happened to us. I wanted to tell you that it didn't take me long to wish I'd been more . . . more . . . *cooperative* when we had the argument that broke us up."

"Well, Sean, it did actually take you too long," she said. "So there — consider your mission accomplished. You told me. Now, can you please go away and *leave me alone?*"

"No, I can't," he said. "So I get it — you're still mad. We can't really deal with that without talking."

"But I said I don't want to!" she stated, raising her voice again.

"Franci," he said quietly. "Could we try not to make a big scene here . . ."

"Look, I told you, I'm in a hurry. You still using the same cell number?" she asked. He nodded. "Great, I'll call you sometime. Now, excuse me, if you'd please just leave me alone, I'd appreciate it very much." Polite as that might've sounded, it was stated angrily, and people had stopped shopping and began watching them.

She turned away from him and he grabbed her arm again. "Franci, I am not going away. This is important."

Suddenly there was a very large shadow over both of them, and Sean, who was a little over six feet tall and in excellent shape, was looking up at Paul Bunyan. And Paul was not happy. He was scowling.

"Everything all right, ma'am?" he asked, looking at Franci.

"Fine," she said. "Old boyfriend. Nothing to worry about." Then she focused on Sean.

"Goodbye. Great seeing you again. Now scram."

In a moment of temporary insanity, Sean went after her again. "No you don't. We have to get together for that conversation," he said. "Since I can't call you, how about I go over to your house and wait for —"

He felt himself being plucked off his feet. His basket of produce went tumbling away as he was launched into a pile of melons. But Paul Bunyan didn't let go of him. "She said it's time for you to hit the road, bud."

"Listen, pal, you got it all wrong," Sean said. "I'd never do anything to —"

And suddenly Franci was there. Saving him. "Thank you, but it's all right. He's harmless."

Sean was being held down with his back against the cantaloupe and honeydew melons and he was suddenly incensed. That statement about him being harmless made him growl and snarl dangerously.

"You gonna leave the nice lady alone, bud?" the big man asked.

"You're gonna get your hands off me this second or you'll be sorry," Sean warned, his very masculinity threatened.

"I doubt that, my friend. So, when we understand each other, I'll let you up."

"Fine," Sean angrily shot back. "Let go of

me. Now."

The lumberjack backed away slowly as Sean eased himself off the melons, many of them rolling around on the floor as he did so. A couple of them split open as they fell, spilling their slimy, seedy guts in the aisle. Sean brushed off his jacket where he'd been grabbed, trying to appear both fearless and dignified. And then he took off after Franci, his hand on her shoulder to stop her from walking away again. "Now look," he said.

He felt the back collar of his shirt and jacket clutched in an iron grip and he whirled on the giant, hitting him square in the jaw with his fist. He suspected he'd broken his hand, but no way was he letting on. He did wince in pain, however, while the very large man merely turned his brick of a face to the side.

"You shouldn't'a done that, little man," the guy said. It took him roughly one second to draw back his fist and plaster Sean in the face hard enough to send him reeling into the melons. Then to the floor. Sean saw a lot of stars and was aware of the melons as they began to bounce around the produce section. And there was blood — he wasn't sure where from since his entire face felt as if it had been through a meat grinder.

"Hey!" Franci shouted. "What's the matter with you? I told you to leave it alone, he's *harmless!*"

"No good deed goes unpunished, I guess," the big man said. "It looked like you needed help. Maybe you like being grabbed like that in the grocery store, huh, babe?"

Sean muttered something about not being harmless and tried to get to his feet, without success. The big man said, "Just stay down where you are, buster." But Sean was intent on getting up and he'd just about made it to his feet when the man took two giant steps in his direction. That was all it took for Franci to launch herself on the lumberjack with a cry of outrage. She had her arms around his neck, her legs around his waist and screamed bloody murder while pummeling him on the back.

"I. Told. You. To. Leave. Him. *Alone!*" she shrieked.

Paul Bunyan whirled around and around, trying to shake her loose, but she was on him like a tick on a hound.

Then the scene got a lot more interesting. "No! No! No! No! No!" screamed a store manager, running up to them, followed closely by another man and a couple of young bag boys. A crowd gathered and the grocery employees peeled Franci off the lumberjack, but she was kicking her heart out the whole time. "The police are coming!" the store manager yelled. "Stop this at once! Stop!"

And Sean absently thought, This really isn't going how I planned.

Right about then, Sean attempted to stand and reclaim his manhood, only to slip on some slimy melon guts and crash into the floor again. He didn't exactly pass out, but he was on the nether edges, half listening to the conversation going on above him.

"He threw the first punch," a voice said.

"You threw him in the melons!" Franci yelled.

"He was grabbing your arm after you told him to go away and leave you alone! Shoot me for trying to lend a hand!"

"But then the little guy did hit the big guy," someone said. And Sean thought, I am not a little guy. I'm definitely six-one. I bench two-fifty with no problem.

"But the big guy *plastered* the little guy, knocked him out."

"I am not little," Sean mumbled through a swollen jaw, though no one was listening to him.

"I didn't ask you to protect me!" Franci shouted. "I told you to leave him alone!"

Yeah, Sean thought. Because I'm harmless. Just how I always wanted her to see me. Harmless. And that was Sean Riordan's last coherent thought.

The next time he was conscious, a paramedic was waving some disgusting-smelling ammonia under his nose and holding an ice pack to his cheek. The ammonia made him gag and the ice pack hurt like hell. And what was worse, they were all in handcuffs. "Damn," he groaned. "Damn, damn, damn."

Three hours later, Sean was being held in a windowless room with a locked door down at the Eureka police station. The paramedics had recommended that he go to the hospital to have his head examined, to which Sean replied, "Well, no kidding."

But while he was in the cell with his buddy the lumberjack, the big man apologized. Sean apologized right back. And what Sean learned was, Dennis Avery was not a lumberjack but a big rig driver who was on his way home, picking up some groceries for the little woman, when he got snared into that whole domestic between Franci and Sean.

So, as Sean was known to do, he told Dennis his life story. Or at least the part that had to do with breaking up with Franci.

"Man," Dennis said, running a hand over

his head. "Are you an idiot or what?"

"Watch it," Sean warned, though what he was going to do about it remained a mystery.

"Buddy, I'm six-five in my sockies. I been loading crates into a semitrailer for almost twenty years. And you swing at me?" He laughed. "You got this little gal who throws herself on Goliath to defend you, because you pitched her out without thinking about it twice? No wonder she's pissed."

"I told you," Sean said irritably. "She gave me an ultimatum. We get married or she's gone."

Dennis stood to his full height. "And you had to *think* about that?"

Then, mercifully, the police sergeant was at the door. "All righty, boys. You're out of here. Somebody loves you and you got cited with misdemeanor public disturbance — a pure gift. Be smart and make sure I don't see your faces again for a very long time. Like ever. In fact, a smart guy would get his groceries elsewhere, if you get my drift."

Sean didn't know why he should be so blessed, but he was taking the break without back talk. The last thing he wanted to do was call Luke and ask for bail money. After collecting his wallet, keys, cell phone, et cetera, he put on his jacket and made tracks, wondering how far it was back to the grocery-store parking lot to find his car. Meanwhile, Dennis Avery was calling his wife for a ride. Sean's head was pounding and his left eye was almost closed as he left the small cop shop, disappearing into the early evening night.

And there, leaning against her car, was Francine. She had a very disgusted look on her face. "Come on, get in," she said. "I'm taking you home. You can get Luke to bring you back for your car tomorrow, if you don't die in your sleep."

"You said that in a way that suggested you hoped I *would* die in my sleep," he said.

"Don't be silly. I'd like you to die much more violently than that. Now get in — I don't have all night."

"That's right," he said meanly. "You're in a *hurry*. How could I forget that?"

Once they were both in the car, she said, "You'll have to give me directions. I'm not sure where I'm going."

"Just take me to my car," he said. "It's at the grocery store."

"No, I'm taking you to Luke's," she said. "You can't drive after a possible head injury. You've been enough trouble without weighing on my conscience anymore. Where am I going?"

Sean sighed audibly. He really didn't feel

up to fighting with her. "South till you get to Highway 36, then east on 36 for about twenty minutes. I'll tell you where to turn off — Virgin River is about ten miles off 36, kind of hidden away in the mountains."

"I've been out on 36. Cute, how they call it a highway — it's only a two-lane," she said. "It's harrowing."

"Yeah, all these mountain roads take some getting used to. This is very nice of you, Francine. Or is it revenge? You're going to push me out on a sharp turn?"

She ignored him. "Here's what I'm going to do for you, Sean. I'm going to give you my cell-phone number and you can call me. When I can spare some time — like a half hour — I will meet you for coffee. We can have this conversation you're set on. Maybe we'll straighten a couple of things out. After that, you are going to stop hounding me. Got that? Because I'm in no mood for this bullshit. You've had plenty of time to make up your mind about me and you were *very* clear. No commitment. No family. Now, I've gotten on with my life, and if you haven't, it's time to do so. Understand?"

What Sean understood was he now had thirty more minutes than he'd had before. He'd have to figure out a way to make good use of the time. "It wasn't supposed to be like this, Franci," he said softly. He hoped he said it tenderly.

"And yet it is," she informed him.

After dropping Sean off at Luke's house, Franci headed back down 36, the darkest highway she'd ever driven. She had plenty of time to think and admit that she *had* received his voice mails — all two of them. The first one came while she was in labor, six months after they'd parted ways, and he had said, "Hey, Fran! How you doing, babe? Give me a call. We should stay in touch, huh?" The second one came when she was at home at her mother's with a ten-day-old baby, alternately nursing, walking the floor, sleeping and crying. That one was no better than the first. "So, Franci — you gonna call me back? Come on, babe — no reason we can't talk, is there? I wanna tell you all about the U-2. Gimme a call." That might explain her blind rage when the big guy in the grocery store casually referred to her as *babe.*

Back then Franci realized she was listening to those two calls over and over, alternately planning his death and praying he would come for her. She knew she was in trouble. After several weeks there hadn't been any more contact from him so, to save

66

herself, she had the cell shut off and got herself a new number. She changed her e-mail address. Then she started looking for a new job and a path out of Santa Rosa.

She had always known, from the time she'd said goodbye to Sean four years ago, that she would have to deal with him eventually. She wasn't sure exactly when or how, but she'd thought she would have a little more time.

Her daughter, Rosie, three and a half and as precocious as an only child can be, had just recently asked, "Where is our daddy?" Funny she would say *our* daddy, but then the whole concept was new to her as she had just noticed that they didn't have one. Preschool had its share of separated families, but almost all the other kids seemed to know where both their parents were. Most were being picked up alternately by their moms and their dads.

And Rosie hadn't asked *who* is our daddy, but *where.*

"He's flying a very fast, very high jet in the air force," Franci answered. "It goes all over the world and he's busy doing a very important job."

Rosie had said, "Oh." She probably didn't understand much beyond the important fact that Franci knew where Rosie's daddy was. But what Franci knew was that in a few months, maybe a year, maybe two, as her world became larger, Rosie would ask things like, "What's his name?" "Why doesn't he come to see us?" And eventually, "Why aren't you married?" These would be increasingly difficult questions to answer. And those questions formed the primary reason Franci had not wanted to face this — she couldn't imagine how she would tell Rosie that her daddy just didn't want anything to do with her because he absolutely, positively did not want to be a father.

Franci didn't tell her mom about Rosie's question because her mother had asked her so many times how she intended to handle her situation. From the beginning Vivian had disapproved of this approach. "Fine, don't marry him," she had said. "Don't have expectations of him. Don't be disappointed in his behavior. But he deserves to know he has a child."

Under any other circumstances, Franci would agree. "Mom, he was adamant! He did not want children. He didn't want marriage, either."

"All that has a way of changing when there's a child actually on the way," Vivian had said.

"Ex*act*ly," Franci argued. "That's why I

want to handle this on my own, at least for now. Because I'm only interested in marrying and having a child with a man who loves me as much as I love him, who wants our child as much as I do. Don't you *get* that?"

"Of course I get it. But, like it or not, when you accidentally get pregnant, you have a responsibility to tell the other parent and let the cards fall where they may. Deal with his response however you must, but you have to at least tell him."

"I will. Eventually," Franci had said. The problem wasn't that she found the concept of informing him so unreasonable. It had just been that when she found out she was pregnant, and then when Rosie was a new baby, she wasn't emotionally strong enough to have Sean in *her* life. She'd thought that, in time — time that so quickly stretched into four years — she would be ready to confront the reality without it completely disrupting her very existence. She knew what it could mean — Sean rejecting Rosie altogether, and that would hurt too much to contemplate. Or, best-case scenario, an arrangement of his visits and, too soon, of Rosie going to spend time with him. Ultimately it could be Rosie spending time with Sean's new family, because eventually he would find the woman he *could* commit to.

Being separated from Rosie was going to be so hard, and seeing Sean regularly? Seeing Sean happy with another woman would be sheer torture.

When she'd seen him in Arcata, she should have made a date for coffee; she shouldn't have shut him down like that. But she just wasn't ready to face it yet.

To her own embarrassment, she had fantasized a reconciliation. But Franci was, above all, practical and logical. And if there was going to be a reconciliation, it would have come long before now. As well, it was a horrible prospect to imagine that Sean would decide that, since they had a child, he would do the right thing and be with the child's mother. Franci didn't feel like being a consolation prize now any more than she had when she was two months pregnant.

When she ran into him again at the grocery store, her anger with him had erupted out of surprise. If she'd known she was going to see him, she would have been better prepared. Sane. Reasonable. But she hadn't been ready for him a second time.

Ever since Rosie was born, Franci had assumed that eventually she would have to go to Sean, explain as best she could why she chose to have the baby alone. For her it was such a simple decision, though not an easy one. If he didn't love her enough to make a commitment *before* he learned about a child, she didn't want him just *because* there was a child. And yet, knowing herself and how powerful her feelings were for him, she feared saying no would have been impossible. And living in a marriage that wasn't real and genuine would ultimately be too painful . . . for all of them.

Right now, the most important thing was Rosie — more important than Franci and Sean. Franci would have to take it slow, keep Sean from going off the deep end, make sure Rosie had a safe and normal life. They'd start with a couple of talks, she and Sean. She'd get him used to the idea that she'd moved on, that she'd accepted his decision to move on.

And then, when the groundwork was laid, Rosie would meet her dad.

Later that evening when Sean walked into his brother's house, Luke, Shelby and Art were just dishing up takeout from Jack's Bar. This was, of course, because Sean had failed to bring home the groceries. In he walked with a bruised cheek, black eye and swollen nose, which the paramedic said was probably not broken. None of it enhanced his killer good looks. Not to mention his hand, which he kept in his jacket pocket because he'd have so much trouble gripping a fork.

Everyone turned when he came through the door and they went completely still, staring at him with wide eyes and open mouths. Finally Art said, "Hey, Sean. Didn't that girl want to date with you?"

"Can we not talk about this, please?" Sean asked.

So the not talking about it hung over the dinner table like a shroud. While Shelby and Art did up the dishes, Sean took a beer out of the refrigerator, put on his jacket and stepped out onto the porch. About two minutes later Luke joined him, holding his own beer. There were five boys in the Riordan family. Luke was six years older than Sean and, when they weren't fighting, they were close.

Sean explained running into Franci in the grocery. After getting the story, Luke asked, "So, if I have this right, a great big hulk, who had about six inches and a hundred pounds on you, decided to protect Franci from you, and you attacked him?"

"That's about it," Sean said.

"And why would you jump someone who was obviously bigger and stronger than you?

You can usually talk your way out of anything."

"Because, Luke," Sean said. "He was trying to keep me away from her."

Luke thought about this for a second and then said, "Oh, boy. There's trouble, right there. What is it with this woman? Huh?"

"I don't know," Sean said miserably. "I thought I could just forget about her, but there's something about her. Maybe I was more into her than I realized."

"And why, just out of curiosity, didn't you know you felt this way about her four years ago?"

"How the hell do I know?" After some silence, Sean finally said, "I thought I had it all under control."

FOUR

A couple of days after the fight in the grocery store, Franci kept her word and made a coffee date with Sean. She needed to get this situation handled. When Sean showed up at the coffee shop, his face looked bad and his expression still worse. His cheek was bruised, his nose slightly mis-shapen, one eye blackened and closed more than the other — which unfortunately didn't mar his otherwise good looks quite enough. And he was scowling. His right hand was wrapped in an Ace bandage, which Franci consoled herself was better than a cast, but still not good. He walked up to the small round table she occupied and frowned down at her, his eyes glittering through mere slits. She recognized that look. She hadn't seen it often from the perpetually playful Sean, but she had seen it. He's had enough, she thought. He was done fooling around. Time to ratchet these emotions down to a manageable level if she hoped for him to actually listen to her when she found the right moment to own up to everything. She needed him reasonable. Understanding. Sympathetic to her concerns.

"Are you all right?" she asked him.

"I'll live. Can I get you anything?"

She lifted her cardboard coffee cup. "I'm fine, thanks." And then she took a deep breath while he went for his own coffee. When he sat down across from her, she asked, "How bad is it?"

"I have a headache," he said irritably. "It's probably just a minor skull fracture with brain damage."

She struggled not to smile. "Did you have that x-rayed?" she asked, indicating his hand with her eyes.

"Sprain. It's bruised and sore, that's all. You'll probably be very disappointed to know I'm going to completely recover."

"Hm. Good. Well . . . I think we should *both* concentrate on not letting things get out of control."

"You first," he said. He took a sip of his coffee and jerked his chin up, pinched his eyes closed and moaned deep in his throat. When eyes opened both were watering; he'd burned his mouth. Oh, Sean was having a rough couple of days. Franci's hand covered her mouth so there wouldn't be even the hint of a smile.

And she immediately thought, *Crap*. She didn't want to find him cute and funny! She wanted to be repulsed by him! Furious and bitter! Completely unaffected, except maybe with some hatred. She remembered what had hooked her in the first place — he was so good-looking and he made her laugh. Then later, when they were alone, he could make her *beg*. He could be darling and fun; he could be passionate and powerful. And she did *not* want to remember that!

She gave him a moment. He was probably blaming her for his burned mouth, too. "So, Franci," he finally said. "What's up with the uniform you were wearing?"

"I work for an emergency medical airlift unit, assigned to their helicopter transport." His eyebrows lifted. "I'm a flight nurse."

"I guess that's why I couldn't find you at any clinics or hospitals," he said, blowing on his coffee.

"You were looking for me at clinics and hospitals?" she asked. "Since when?"

"Since I ran into you in Arcata and you said you'd prefer to never speak to me again."

"I didn't exactly say that, did I?"

"Close enough. I found your address right away because you bought a house, but decided I'd better take it slow, since you're obviously still pissed off. I thought it might irritate you if I showed up at your front door. Back when I knew you, you had a gun — you were a military officer flying into a war zone. I was willing to brave that. That's how much I wanted to see you."

She sat back in her chair. "I no longer have the gun. But when did you decide you wanted to see me again?" she asked. "We bump into each other after years and everything changes for you?"

"Here's how it went," he said without even thinking about it. "We both walked away mad back then. I distracted myself by going to a new aircraft, a new training program, a new base and squadron, but after a few months of that, I couldn't leave it alone anymore — we ended badly and I couldn't believe it was what either one of us really wanted. So I called you. You didn't call back, so I tried again — the cell phone was shut off. Your e-mail bounced back — undeliverable. After another few months of licking my wounds I called your mother's house to see if she'd put us in touch with each other and she was gone. Phone disconnected. House sold. Moved away. None of your best girlfriends were around at Luke AFB anymore and I couldn't remember their last names, so I had no one to ask."

"You couldn't remember their *names?*" she asked.

He grimaced. "*Last* names. Shoot me. I didn't know there'd be a test. So, you didn't respond and had disappeared. I thought maybe you got married or something. I quit looking. But it never felt right — the way we broke up. It shouldn't have happened like that."

"Oh?" she asked, sipping her coffee.

"We were both too stubborn. Angry. I wanted to find you and tell you that we should talk about our situation some more. Sanely."

"Have you changed your mind about commitment? About family?" she asked.

"I was committed *before,*" he said, his voice low and gravelly, definitely annoyed. "I didn't need some document to prove that. That's why we should talk."

She sat back in her chair. "I can't see what there is to talk about," she said, exasperated. "That's why we went our separate ways. I want the document. I want a family — you don't."

"I wanted another chance," he ground out. "I wasn't happy with you forcing the idea of getting married before I felt ready, before I felt it was my idea, too. But I was a lot less happy once you were gone."

"Then why didn't you say that in your messages?" she asked.

He tilted his head, gave her a hint of a smile and lifted the eyebrow over the good eye. "The messages you never got?" he asked.

Oh, he was good. Great choice for a spy-plane pilot. He was quick and cagey. "Okay, I got them. They were so generic, there was nothing to respond to. Not, 'I'm sorry and I want to try again,' or 'I can't live without you,' but just, 'Shouldn't we keep in touch? *Babe?*' "

He leaned toward her. "Well, what do you want from someone who's talking into ether, not knowing what kind of mood you're in? Or wondering who *else* might listen to your messages? Like maybe a brand-new boyfriend or husband! I wanted to talk to you, not make life tough for you! You were pretty specific when you laid down the guidelines — it was marriage or you were out. For all I knew —" He stopped. He took a breath. "For all I knew you found someone who liked that idea. And settled down."

It was very tempting to just blurt everything out right then, right there, but Franci held her tongue. She did have to lower her eyes over her coffee cup to keep him from seeing the tears there. It all rushed back — how bad the breakup had felt, and remembering that he couldn't bear the idea of being stuck with her for life. Then came the fear that he'd like another chance, but they would probably only go back to the way they were. Or, he was ready for more now and would never forgive her for what she'd done. Franci's mind was churning.

"I'd given you a lot of opportunities, Sean. A lot of time. You didn't budge — you'd gotten as serious as you were going to get. I didn't want to find myself in a relationship as tenuous as that for a long time, for as long as it took you to say you'd had enough and didn't want me around anymore." She swallowed. "I didn't want to give my best years to a man who couldn't make a decision."

He leaned toward her and his look was earnest, though battered. "What did I ever do or say to make you think I was just playing around? Weren't we a couple? A serious couple? Didn't we practically live together? You thought I'd just do that for a few years and then dump you? You didn't trust me any more than that?" he asked.

She shrugged. "Why would I? We spent nights together, Sean — we kept our own places and you never suggested living together! You liked things loose and uncomplicated. You thought your buddies who got married 'bit the dust.' You thought the ones who had kids were trapped. I wanted something solid, and back then I wanted it to be you, but if it wasn't going to be you, I had to have the courage to move on. Right? Isn't that reasonable?"

Rather than answering the question, he said, "Maybe I'm not that guy anymore."

"Oh?" she asked with a cynical tone. "And what guy *are* you?"

"Things changed, Franci. Starting with not having you in my life. I thought I'd just keep having fun, but fun wasn't fun without you. I thought the Riordan men didn't settle down, until I watched the last one I ever expected bite the dust . . ."

"There it is again — he bit the dust."

"If you'd seen him fight it, you'd have been impressed. Bottom line, I was trying like hell to make it work without you because I thought I had no choice. And when I saw you at that restaurant in Arcata, I knew I wasn't going another day without trying to see if . . . I just want to see if we can work this out. If we can't, if you're in a

81

different place, I'm not a fool — I don't want a woman who doesn't want me. But . . ."

"Just like I didn't want a man who didn't want me," she reminded him, lifting her chin proudly. Then, as an afterthought, she added, "Enough. Didn't want me enough."

"Touché. You can have that one. I made a mistake. But so did you. I was an idiot. You were in a big goddamn hurry."

Well, he was right about that, she thought. She had been on the nest. She leaned toward him and shook her head. "I had no possible way of knowing if you would ever change. I couldn't wait around for that. My biological clock was ticking." Boy, had it been ticking!

Again, rather than responding, he asked, "Are you with someone now?"

She froze. In fact, she was. It had been a long time coming, too. But Sean's reappearance had caused her to barely give the guy a thought. It occurred to her to tell Sean she had a guy, just to back him off a bit. The temptation was equally strong to tell him there was no one, which might encourage him all the more. In the end, she said, "I've been dating . . . trying to be social rather than a recluse. You? Are you with someone now?"

He shook his head. "Let's try again," he said in a soft, pleading voice. As if it had all been a minor misunderstanding.

"Not so fast," Franci said. "I don't know if I want to try again. We have issues. Unless you've changed a lot, we don't want the same things out of a relationship, out of life. It's too late for couples' counseling. I'm willing to think about us being friends, but we have to take even something like that very slowly. The world didn't just stand still after we parted ways, Sean. I went on living."

"Of course you did, Franci," he said, reaching for her hand. He held it on the tabletop. "We both tried to get on with things, and both ended up back here."

"I'm sure we're not talking about the same things," she said. "I'm sure your dating was a lot different than mine," she said, meaning he'd slept with a lot of women. He'd been a real playboy when she met him and she had been a little surprised when he became exclusively hers. Sean going back to his old ways of making the rounds was more what she had expected of him.

"I dated," he admitted. "Not anything very . . . Nothing worked out."

She lifted her chin. "And I became very independent. I hadn't heard from you in

83

years. I didn't see this coming."

"It's coming," he said, in a low voice laced with meaning. "Let me take you out to dinner tonight."

"No," she said. "I'm busy."

"Tomorrow night, then."

"I'm going out — I have plans. I'll have coffee with you on Sunday afternoon, if you're free. I'll talk with you, Sean. Maybe we can put some of our conflict to rest and work out friendlier terms."

"I want to spend time with you —"

"You better let me think about that. There have been too many changes in my life to step back into a relationship like I had with you."

"Are you thinner?" he asked, changing the subject. "You seem thinner."

"I took up running after . . . Once I moved up here, I started running. I finished two marathons."

"No kidding?" he said, impressed. He grinned, then winced and touched his cheek. "Well, you look fantastic. I guess running is your thing. It works for you. And the hair — if you'd have said you wanted it cut to the scalp, I would have had a fit, but it's . . . it's hot, that's what it is."

She hated that she felt warm all over when he said that. "I'm completely different in a lot more ways than looks," she said as a warning. "I have baggage that I've accumulated in the past few years. I have commitments. For example, my mother and I moved up here together. She was widowed, I was single — it made sense."

"Sure. How is Viv?" he asked.

"Great. Working in a family practice as a physician's assistant. She's glad she made the change — she likes the area and has friends here. And I have two jobs, Sean. I pull a couple of twenty-four-hour shifts with the airlift unit in Redding every week and I teach a couple of courses at Humboldt University — nursing courses. It's a great schedule for me — gives me the time off I need so I can balance work life and home life. It works for me. I'm committed to both."

"You're teaching nursing?" he asked, surprised.

She nodded. "I've been doing that for the past year or so. Turns out I like it."

"My new sister-in-law, Shelby — she's a student there, in nursing. Cutest thing you'll ever see. Best thing that ever happened to Luke. Any chance you know her?"

"What year is she in?" Franci asked.

"First year. She got married in her first semester because Paddy and Colin were done with their deployments — she waited for all the Riordans to be available. She's way younger than Luke and is just starting college."

Franci tilted her head and smiled, thinking how sweet it was that cranky, womanizing old Luke ended up with a sweet young girl who was determined to get an education. "I'm pretty sure I haven't met Luke's wife. Most of the freshmen are stuck in liberal-arts courses the first year. I teach one medical-surgical course and one that boils down to charting ER patients. I'm just one of many instructors. Mostly, I teach juniors and seniors. I share an office on campus with another nursing instructor and I only teach a couple of days a week. Except for meetings, of which there are too many."

"You never did go for the meetings," he said with a smile. "I'll have to tell Shelby to introduce herself. You'll love her. You'll —"

"One thing at a time, all right?" Franci asked patiently. "How's your mom?"

"She's great. Greater since Luke got married and they're on the baby trail. She might finally get a grandchild out of one of us, after all."

Franci flushed. Oh, God, so many people were going to be pissed when they found out about Rosie. She had no idea how she'd have done it differently, however. Well, there was that one way — she could have told Sean about the baby. Good Catholic boy that he was, he'd have married her right off or his mother would have killed him. As she recalled, Maureen Riordan had powerful influence over her sons. "Good for her," was all she could say. "Sean, this is going to take time. Things have probably changed too much."

"Not as much as they've stayed the same," he said.

"There's only one way I can even think about this, and that's if we get to know each other all over again," she said. "We can't go back four years and try to untangle that mess — we have to accept ourselves as the people we are today, and go from here. You said you're not that guy anymore. And you know what, Sean? I'm not that woman anymore — the one who cried every day after we split up. I'm a lot stronger. We're both different."

"Maybe so," he agreed. "Maybe better," he suggested. "But, Franci, like it or not, we have history."

She felt her heart take a fearful jump. "Yeah. You have no idea."

As it happened, there had been a man in

Franci's life for the past few months. Meeting Dr. T. J. Brookner had been one of the great perks to that little part-time teaching job she'd taken at the college. He was a terrific guy — a marine biologist and professor of oceanography. The forty-year-old was a divorced father of two preteen girls. Franci was one of the few certified divers in the nursing department and was the instructor with the most "open time" in her schedule, so she had been recruited to teach a short first-aid course to freshman dive students. Since she loved diving she jumped at the chance, which is how she met T.J. They ended up going on a couple of dive dates, which led to a few phone calls, which led to a few getting-to-know-you dinners, and what she found was an entertaining man who enjoyed many of the same things she did.

She liked the fact that he was ten years older than she; he seemed settled and he was definitely sure of himself. He had a stable career and was happy with where he was in life. She respected his parameters for a relationship: if they were intimate, they had to be exclusive, and while he was open to the idea of a long-term relationship, it had to be understood up front — he wasn't having more children. After his second daughter was born, he'd had a vasectomy and he steered clear of women with ticking clocks and the expectations that went along with it. As far as what he was looking for, Franci knew he wanted to meet a fun, attractive, intelligent and mature woman to spend time with.

Franci had no trouble signing on to that deal. It was nice to have someone to dive with, to go on long runs with, even to have sex with. Up to that point, Franci hadn't done any serious dating — just the occasional evening out with a work colleague, or one of the guys from her running club. For the first time in a long time, she'd been feeling content — she had her little girl, her mom, a job she loved and a guy. What a relief it was to feel settled and on track!

Since Franci hadn't been associated with the college for long, the gossip about T.J. didn't reach her right away. She'd already been going out with T.J. for a couple of months when she learned he was known as Professor Hottie by the coeds. She was completely amused by the nickname and teased him about it, but learned fast that he didn't think it was so funny. He said the girls flirted with him shamelessly and it was the sort of thing that could lead to irresponsible talk — something that could cause a lot of trouble for a man. T.J. allowed that this kind of talk might have even contributed to his bitter divorce from a jealous wife years ago.

"Good grief, I hope your ex-wife didn't cave into jealousy just because freshman girls have crushes on handsome professors! We all did. I had mine and I bet you even had yours," she added with a laugh.

"Trust me — I never had an older woman professor who looked like you!" T.J. informed her enthusiastically.

"Aw. That's sweet. You should just be flattered by the attention. Professor Hottie."

"I am, as long as no harm is done," he admitted.

In all seriousness, he came by the nickname honestly enough; T.J. was divinely handsome and had a very sexy smile. Franci had no trouble admitting that his smile was the first thing to catch her attention. She immediately dismissed the giggles and rumors as predictable and didn't give them a second thought.

But then, just as Franci thought her life had begun to resemble something close to normal, who should show up but Sean? Now that she thought about it, Sean's timing had always sucked, and she had a little three-year-old redhead to prove it.

Now, out of the blue, Franci was conscious of a little problem: When she thought of T.J., she wondered what they'd find to do next weekend — movie or dinner out or maybe a dive? But when she thought of Sean, all she wanted to do was take her clothes off.

When Franci told Sean she couldn't meet him on Saturday she didn't explain fully — she had a date that night with T.J. But after Sean threw her world into a spin, she really wasn't in the mood for a date with anyone. And there was no way the date with T.J. could culminate in the usual way. She was much too distracted for that and considered canceling altogether. She complained to her mother of a headache.

"Take something," Vivian said. "Rosie and I have a big slumber party planned at my house. Go out. Try having fun. Either stay out very late or have a slumber party of your own." Then she had winked.

"Oh, Mother," Franci said with humor.

"Take a couple of aspirin and enjoy yourself!"

Franci hadn't mentioned Sean's sudden reappearance in her life because she knew Vivian would work it like a hangnail. She'd start all that business about Franci's responsibility to level with him; she'd want to force the paternity thing. Franci was struggling enough by herself without Vivian nagging about it. So, more to keep her mother out of her business than to spend a nice evening out, she kept her date.

T.J. came for her at six and, when she opened the door to him, she was immediately reminded why she'd agreed to that first date — damn, but he was a good-looking man. It wasn't hard to understand why there was always a long list of females waiting to go on dive trips, or on research missions, with him. It hadn't been *that* long since Franci had been a college coed. She'd had a crush of her own on her biology professor. It hadn't gone anywhere beyond a few delicious fantasies, but if he'd been game, she would've crossed the line in a second.

"I'm taking you to a fantastic new restaurant up near the campus," T.J. told her, once they were in the car. "They specialize in salmon for obvious reasons — it's our local catch. They have a salmon fettuccini that will knock you out."

"You know I don't like salmon," she reminded him.

"You're the only diver and fisherman I know who won't eat salmon," he said. "Will you try it? We're bound to find a salmon dish you love eventually."

"Will you order something I like so we can trade if it doesn't work out that way?" she countered.

He sighed. "Don't I always order the best for both of us?"

"No." She laughed. "You order two meals you like. There's no point in even showing me a menu."

"Do you get enough to eat?" he asked, a little irritation in his voice slipping through.

"Oh, always. You're never stingy about it — and I love the appetizers and salads you pick. By the time we get to your main courses, I'm usually full, anyway."

"That sounds slightly ungrateful, if you ask me," he grumbled.

"Absolutely not!" And she laughed. "You order enough for four people and I'm always happy to let the doggie bag go home with you so you can enjoy it all over again! Really, T.J., you should review restaurants! Now let's stop arguing over the menu before we even get to the restaurant. Tell me about the trip to Cabo."

T.J. was more than happy to do that. As they made the quick drive north to Arcata, he talked about his recent diving trip to Cabo San Lucas. He'd gone with a group of instructors and students. It wasn't clear from his conversation whether they'd gotten all their research done, but they'd had some great dives and had eaten at some fantastic Mexican restaurants. Altogether they had taken only sixteen students, twelve of them were women, he said.

And suddenly Franci asked, "Aren't you *ever* tempted to sleep with them? The female students who worship you?"

He gave her a surprised look, which was followed by a huff of laughter and a shake of his head. "Franci? What the hell? I thought we went over that." He grabbed her hand and gave it a squeeze. "Are you serious?"

"Curious," she said. "I'm sorry, was that offensive?"

"Depends on the reason for your question. Did you hear something? Some gossip about me?"

"Nothing like that," she said with a laugh. "But it must be difficult sometimes," she said. "To be a single man thrown into so many situations with young women — like trips out of the country and on boats where you spend days at sea or anchored offshore. Probably surrounded by beautiful, nubile, irresistible young women who are sure you just walk on water and wouldn't even have to think twice about —" She stopped before

94

she really became offensive.

He frowned and gave her hand another squeeze. "It might be, if I were interested in any of them. I'm much more comfortable with women I can have a conversation with. I'm not interested in being with a college freshman or sophomore who'd be more than willing to help me lose my tenure." He glanced at her. "Just in case you're thinking of dipping into that well, it's how you get fired. Messing with the student body — so to speak."

"Oh, please," she said with a laugh. "Not in a million years. But men are different."

"Not that different. This is so strange, coming from you. You've never even brought it up before . . ."

"Sure I have," she said. "It's apparently well-known around the campus that the girls are hot for you. And you are a bachelor . . ."

"Be careful you don't start to sound like Glynnis, the ex. She was obsessed by my female students, especially after she'd had children and didn't feel as comfortable in a bikini." He grinned at her. "For a woman who's had a child, you sure didn't lose your bikini body!"

"Well, that's exactly what brought it to mind," Franci said. "That you're out of the country with a dozen beautiful, barely dressed eighteen-year-old women who think you're nothing less than a god, and . . ." She cleared her throat. "I would imagine it has its distracting moments . . ."

He chuckled. "You've never once asked me a serious question about how I handle that situation. Just so you know, I have to go to a lot of trouble to keep things on the up-and-up. I have an assistant or associate professor on hand at all times. I can't visit with female students in my office behind closed doors. If the door is closed for a meeting, a teaching assistant is right outside. On trips, everyone is assigned a buddy or two — I only travel in groups. Seriously, the first time I touch one of them, she'll be the one to scream foul and get me fired."

"But *aren't* you tempted?"

"I'm actually made of flesh and bone, Franci — of course I've been tempted. Not in the past several months, however," he added with a smile. "Now what brought this on? You aren't jealous, are you? Are you worried about being completely safe with me? Because not only are we careful, I told you I've been screened and I —"

She laughed uncomfortably. "Not at all, T.J. It just occurred to me. You're back from a week in Cabo, had a great, fun time away

96

from all the prying eyes, and I wondered."

"I'm aware there's gossip from time to time and there doesn't seem to be anything I can do but ignore it. Believe me, if there was any truth to the rumors about my behavior with the young women on campus, someone would have caught me with my pants down by now." He laughed again. "You give me credibility. Having a steady woman with your looks and brains has slowed a lot of that idle bullshit down to nothing."

"My pleasure," she said.

"Paranoia about all my potential affairs kept my ex-wife up nights, but it's pretty new coming from you. I'm only human. But I'm smart enough to know better."

"Bronson married his student — she was nineteen to his forty," she pointed out, speaking of another one of the professors.

"Yeah, well, that doesn't show so well on him. I'd rather not be that kind of legend." He grinned at her. "Besides, that's not what I'm after. If you came with us on a dive trip, the only kind of talk you'd hear would be about the two professors rocking the boat."

"That could be fun, T.J.," she said. "One of these days you'll throw out an invitation for me to go with you on a specific trip and I'll shock you by saying yes."

97

"It's a deal!" he returned enthusiastically. "The next good one, you're coming with me. With us," he amended. "Me and the students."

"Where are you going next?"

"I'm putting together a trip to Kino Bay, Mexico — a nice little shrimp town. I'm saving you for a more exotic trip, so be patient. But before Kino Bay can be accomplished, there's a coral study to finish — that's about five days offshore . . ."

Having effectively kept the subject on him, Franci was able to listen more than she talked. They got to the restaurant, were seated right away and he ordered wine for them. He was the expert at that, as well, she thought, but she didn't mind. It seemed only moments before the salads arrived and T.J. was still second-guessing whether they'd made the right choice for their appetizers. She hoped he wouldn't change his mind — she didn't care if he ordered for her, but she hated it when he caused a lot of trouble for the waitstaff. Plus, she was looking forward to the crab-stuffed mushrooms; that and the salad might be all she enjoyed of this dinner. She really didn't like salmon, and tonight T.J. had insisted upon it. But dinner out, for T.J., was a constant negotiation, a complicated ordering process. She got a kick out of it, but he took it way too seriously.

As they ate, she listened to more details of his work, his plans for doing a coastal coral study with one of his classes that would take an intense five days off campus, and then in winter there would be a couple of dive trips out of the country to warmer climes. And —

"Francine?" he said, drawing her attention. "Ms. Duncan?"

"Huh?" she said, looking up. "I'm sorry, was I somewhere else for a moment?"

"I was just saying, I think I'd really like you with long hair," he said dreamily, gazing at her.

"Well, ordering for me is one thing, T.J., but I'm going to be in charge of my own hair. This cut is so easy!"

"You won't even consider growing it out? Even if I said I think I'd love it?"

She was gazing off again. "Huh?" she said, when she realized he'd been talking to her again. "I'm sorry."

He put down his fork. "You've been a little weird all evening. Different."

"Really? Sorry." She sighed. "Well, I was this close to calling you to cancel. I have a nagging headache. I know I'm probably not the best company."

"You're not only distracted, you've brought up a couple of things you've never even mentioned before. Like the girls — the students. This isn't a symptom of a headache."

She looked into his beautiful brown eyes for a second. He had a slight smile and it made her laugh. T.J. was too intuitive for her mood to slip by him. "I do have a headache. His name is Sean Riordan."

"Oh?" T.J. asked. "Dare I hope he sells insurance?"

She shook her head. "He's an air force pilot. I knew him when I was an air force nurse. I ran into him the other night while I was out with some girlfriends."

"Ah," T.J. said, sitting back. "And can't get him off your mind?"

"You can say that again," she said, putting down her fork. Not only did she feel like getting this whole thing off her chest, she felt she owed T.J. an explanation. After all, they were a couple . . . "I haven't told anyone this, T.J. Not my mom, not girlfriends, certainly not Rosie . . ."

"Should I be honored?" he asked, lifting his wineglass to his lips, taking a sip. "Or should I panic?"

"He is Rosie's father," she said, staring

him straight in the eye. But then she glanced away.

He put down his wineglass. "You don't say."

She looked back. "I always knew the day would come when I'd have to face this, but I thought I'd get to choose when and where. Just by chance he saw me a couple of weeks ago, chased me down and asked to buy me a cup of coffee. He said our breakup was a big mistake that happened to a couple of stubborn people, and that we should talk about things."

"Well, direct, isn't he? Obviously you didn't agree."

"I told him to get lost, but that was just my anger talking. I have no right to keep him away from Rosie. I'm going to have to tell him about her, T.J. And I don't look forward to it."

"Uh-oh. This doesn't sound good. When you said Rosie's father didn't know her, I always assumed it had been his choice to take off, ignore his responsibilities."

"Not exactly," she said, shaking her head. "It wasn't like that. But it wasn't a mistake, like he says. The mistake was us getting together in the first place. He always said he'd never get married or have a family. I always said that's what I ultimately wanted

101

for my life."

"Well, hell — why were you with him, then?"

"I don't know. Because I couldn't resist him? Sounds like the pining of a teenager, doesn't it? I wasn't a teenager. And I had a wonderful time with him — it was just the whole marriage and children thing he couldn't do." She shook her head. "I knew either one of us would have to change our minds or we'd part ways. My date of separation from the air force was coming up, Sean had accepted a change of assignment and we'd been together almost two years. And guess what? I got pregnant. And being a nurse, I knew immediately. So I made him talk about what was next for us. Where were we going, as a couple. He said things like, 'You're getting out of the air force. You can go anywhere you want. You can move to where I'll be, or not.' It went downhill from there. I said I wanted to be married, have children, and he said, 'Me? Not in this lifetime.' "

T.J. swallowed. He looked down for a moment. He picked up his fork and poked at his food but didn't eat, a clear indication he was unhappy. When he finally did look up, he said, "And you didn't tell him." It wasn't a question.

She shook her head. "The parting standoff was I needed to take the relationship to a committed level and he wasn't interested. I said that if it was possible he'd never be ready, I should move on, and he said if I needed guarantees right then, I'd better start planning my move."

"Well, the man clearly knows what he doesn't want," T.J. said with an unmistakable sneer.

"We were both angry," she said with a shrug. "I told him if he wasn't serious about a commitment with me, I was going to take the walk. He told me not to let the door hit me in the ass. We both said unforgivable things. I could have told him about the baby, T.J. I could have shouted it at his back as he was leaving. He probably would have done the responsible thing." Her eyes glistened and she swallowed hard. "And I would never have known if . . ." Her voice trailed off. She inhaled deeply, straightened proudly. "I didn't want it that way."

"Good God, Francine," he said. "You lied to him."

"I always intended to tell him," she said. "Really, I thought I'd tell him when I found out she was a girl, then I couldn't. I thought I'd tell him before she was born, but I was still so angry, so lonely. I planned to tell him right afterward, but he left me a couple of messages — a couple of those arrogant, cheerful, we-should-keep-in-touch-*babe* messages, and I couldn't do it then, either. Next thing I knew, four years had passed."

He shook his head and frowned at her. "You should have told me this before — you owed *me* that much if we were going to be involved. And you should have told *him*."

"You know what, T.J.? I owe a lot of people a lot of stuff, but at the top of the list is Rosie. I owe her my absolute protection. Not just physical but emotional and psychological protection. I know Sean's going to be angry — his mother's going to be *very* angry and, trust me, she's a force of nature. But, in the end, you know how much I meant to Sean? He let me go at the mere *idea* of a child!"

"Listen, there are men who don't want children. But we still need to know the truth," T.J. said.

"When Rosie was a new baby, just a couple of months old, I realized that I cried every single day. On and off for hours. I cried through the second half of my pregnancy and every day after she was born. And I made a decision — I couldn't do that to her. If the only way Rosie could be raised by a happy, positive mother was to forget

Sean Riordan, then that's what I would have to do. Yeah, Sean might've been willing to do the right thing, but it wasn't what he wanted. Rosie and I — we deserve to be loved and wanted. We deserve to never doubt it."

They sat quietly for a moment before T.J. replied. "This explains a lot. You've always kept a part of yourself back. Tell me, Franci, just where did you think we were headed? You and me? Because your ex and I have a few things in common . . ."

"You and I aren't headed for any kind of standoff, T.J. We seem to agree on everything. Everything except salmon," she added with a smile. "I thought it was only fair to tell you why I'm a little distracted."

"How's that headache?" he asked.

"Actually, not a lot better."

"I think I caught it," he said. "I was very optimistic about where Rosie's sleepover at Grandma's was going to leave us."

"I should have canceled," she said, shaking her head. "I can't invite you in tonight, T.J. I'm just not in the right frame of mind."

He laughed a bit loudly. He leaned toward her. "Believe me, Franci — tempting as you are, I'm not getting in the middle of this situation. You work this out with the man, draw your single-parent lines in the sand, refine the details and, when you're all set there, we'll pick up where we left off. There is one more thing you might tell this guy, if you're going to be completely honest."

"Hm?" she asked, frowning.

"Tell him you're not over him."

She let a burst of laughter fly. "After all he's put me through?"

T.J. wasn't smiling. "Tell him you've had exactly one man in your life since you took that walk. One guy, in that intimate way."

Shock was etched into her features for a moment. Then she attempted a recovery. "You don't know that."

"Yeah, I know it. You were damned hard to warm up. I couldn't figure out what was holding us up. I had myself almost convinced it was Rosie, so young and all. But there was always a part of me that wondered what the hell was missing because I knew there was more passion in you. If you've made up your mind that he's not going to screw up your life anymore, tell him and get this behind you," he said. "Then when we're together, maybe we can turn up the heat a little bit. Because I like what we have together, you and me, but I don't want to be some platonic bed buddy."

"Excuse me?" she said, pure shock keeping her from laughing out loud. "Platonic bed buddy?"

"I want more than a Friday-night girl who, when she's with me, isn't really with me. I knew something was missing when we crawled into bed."

"No," she said, shaking her head. "No, we've had a very nice —"

When she got to *very nice,* he did smile. She didn't go any further. Really, what man was looking for *very nice* sex? For that matter, what woman? And now the truth was out — he blamed her. And she realized with a guilty flush that he might be right. T.J. barely stirred a spark in her, much less a flame. She felt as if she'd cheated him.

Franci looked down at her half-eaten dinner. She couldn't meet his eyes with what she was thinking — Sean had barely to caress her skin with his breath and she was on fire. He knew where to touch, how to tease, what to do, and nothing brought him greater satisfaction than to torture her with orgasm after orgasm. It had been like that with them since the first touch, the first night. They had never grown tired of each other — never bored, never disinterested. And absolutely never just *very nice.* Their sexual relationship had never been anything less than magnificent.

She was conscious of T.J. lifting his hand

toward the waiter, asking for the check, instructing him to box up their leftovers. She almost smiled — there wouldn't be any coffee and dessert tonight.

With his hand on her elbow, T.J. escorted her toward his car rather quickly. As they walked down the sidewalk, Franci looked up to see a familiar figure walking toward them. His hands were plunged into his pockets and his head was down. Just as they were about to pass, he lifted his eyes briefly. Franci said nothing, gave no reaction, but managed to keep walking. She listened for his footfalls behind them, but there was no sound. She knew then that Sean had stopped dead in his tracks and was probably staring after them.

Afraid to turn around Franci sighed deeply. Ah, well. Now they knew about each other. And yet they didn't know anything at all.

The drive back to her house was twenty minutes of uncomfortable silence. T.J. sulked and Franci realized she might have risked losing the best shot at a stable relationship she'd had in years. But maybe not — according to what he'd implied, she'd risked it the first time she'd crawled into bed with him and had proven to be a barely adequate lover. What she hadn't quite admitted until tonight was that it wasn't all it could be for her, either.

Finally, T.J. pulled into Franci's driveway. When he walked Franci the short distance to her door, he said, "Remember our agreement, Francine. We're exclusive. I have a feeling you're forgetting that."

"I remember our agreement . . ."

"I want you to give me your word that you're going to take care of this matter. Get this guy together with his kid, if that's what he wants. And then tell him you're involved with someone."

"I'm planning to take care of this situation the best I can," she said. "I guess it's best if you just give me a little time to work out the details."

"Don't take too long. I'm not that patient."

"Thank you for the dinner, T.J. Sorry it ended on such a negative note."

"Let me know when you get this worked out with Rosie's father. And try to be smart, Francine. You may have run into him here, but he's not hanging around. Not for you, not for Rosie. Get rid of him. When that's done, let me know. Don't make me wait too long. When he's gone, we'll have a second chance." Then he leaned toward her, gave her a platonic kiss on the cheek. "You'll be fine. Just do it."

And after looking deeply into her eyes for a long moment, he got into his car and backed away.

FIVE

Tonight was the third time the completely impossible happened — Sean ran into Franci on a random street in a small town. At loose ends, he'd decided to go back to that bar where he'd seen her the first time, just on the off chance he'd meet her again, even though he knew the odds were slim. Before he even got inside the bar, he saw her walking down the sidewalk, a man guiding her along with a hand on her elbow. And he carried a take-out sack; they'd already had their dinner.

He considered this sighting some kind of miracle. It was meant to be.

He watched them walk down the sidewalk and turn the corner. He stood there like an idiot for a few moments and then, knowing it was wrong on every level, he headed back to his own car to follow them.

He had no way of knowing what was next on the agenda for Franci's evening, but if that had been him walking her away from a restaurant, the night would just be getting started. He had an overpowering urge to know if Franci had moved on, if she had found love in her life . . . if it was time for him to disappear for good.

By the time he reached his vehicle he was too late to spot the make and model of the man's car. He couldn't follow them now, which was probably a blessing. But because he was unsuccessful in talking himself out of it, he drove to Eureka — to Franci's street. When he got there he parked across the street, a couple of houses down, and killed the lights. He sat there for a moment. Well, this was just what he deserved — the joke was on him. Her house was dark but for the front door light, and there was no car in the driveway, nor on the street in front of her house. If there was more to Franci's evening, it wasn't happening here.

Just then a car slowly pulled up the street and into her driveway. Sean watched as the man got out of the car and went around to her side to open her car door. He guided her up to the door and Sean thought, *If they go inside, I have to find it in me to drive away. Like she said, neither one of us stopped living. She deserves the same option to move on that I took for myself.*

He told himself that, but it didn't feel right.

Then he watched as the man spoke to her, then gave her a brotherly kiss on the cheek and left. Sean's mouth hung open as Franci stood in the glow of her front door light, watching her date leave. And finally Sean's head fell forward onto the steering wheel.

Now he *really* had to make himself drive away! He shouldn't be here in the first place, and he definitely didn't have the right to push himself on her now! This could ruin any efforts he made at reconciling and he damn sure wasn't going to —

Tap-tap-tap at the window completely interrupted his attempt at sanity. He looked up and there was Franci, smacking his car window with a key. He brought down the window.

"Now you're *following* me?" she asked, outraged.

"Not exactly," he said. "I'm sorry. You know I'd never scare you on purpose."

"You don't *scare* me, Sean! I think you're an *idiot!*" she said, turning to walk back across the street to her house. She stopped in the middle of the road and, over her shoulder, she said, "You are a truly clumsy spy! I saw you in Arcata! I saw your car when we turned onto my block! I know your car, you dope, from when we met for coffee!"

Sean jumped out and went after her. When he was right behind her, he asked, "Is that why you sent your date away?"

"No!" she said. She kept walking. "I said good-night, just as I'd planned! And what were you going to do if I'd invited him inside? Pound on the door? TP the yard?" She got to her door, stuck her key in the lock and turned it.

"I was going to leave," he said in his quiet voice. "It wasn't going to be easy, either. But I knew it was wrong to come here, to watch your house, to spy on you. It was bad and wrong and I'm sorry — and I couldn't help it. I've never been like this before."

She turned and faced him. "Like what? Nuts?"

He nodded. Then he grinned that Sean grin that melted her, even though he had a black eye and a weird-looking nose.

"I know good doctors," she said. "We can get you medicated for that."

His hand came up to cradle her jaw, his fingers reaching into her short hair. "Before we do that, let's just talk about it."

"What do you want from me, Sean?"

He moved still closer, leaning down, his mouth just barely above hers. "I want you,

114

Franci. I shouldn't have let you get away."

Tears gathered in her eyes. There was a time she'd have given anything to hear that! Oh, who was she kidding — she still wanted to hear that! And tonight was one of those very vulnerable nights! She had just been informed by Professor Hottie that she wasn't very exciting in the sack. She had tried to be with someone who was right for her, and it obviously hadn't been working all that well. "What if it's too late?" she asked in a whisper.

"Don't we have to know?" he asked. "Don't we *both* have to know?"

"Most of the time I think I'd be happier not knowing . . ."

But instead of speaking, he lowered his lips to hers. He slipped an arm around her waist, pulling her against him, and kissed her. And there it was — the feelings that rose up in her instantly! With a defeated moan, she melted to him and opened her lips under his.

Franci had what can only be described as a flashback, an out-of-body experience, while Sean's lips hovered close to hers. As he held her there, their mouths slightly open, breathing each other's warm breath, images from another time and place filled her mind. It usually came to her in the form

115

of dreams that left her moody for half a day. She felt herself wrapped in his old red sweater, the one she kept at her apartment for cold nights, the thing steaming with his scent, his musk. She heard their laughter as she chased him down a ski slope and he made away; laughter as they played in the lake, splashing each other; in bed after satisfying lovemaking, still wrapped around each other. Scenes popped into her mind — standing in his kitchen, fluffing up a big salad while he turned steak or fish on the grill; washing their cars in his driveway; working together to put fresh sheets on the bed; sitting by a fire in the vast Arizona desert, talking softly under a million stars in an endless black sky. She imagined herself in his arms, just like now.

Once, when they'd been skiing in Colorado, her lips were so chapped and cracked, she didn't dare smile. She told him that if they made love, she couldn't use her lips in any way. He told her to lie down on the bed and close her eyes. He began to smooth healing bag balm salve across her lips in long, slow, careful strokes. Not just enough to coat her poor lips once, but over and over and over for long minutes, a lip massage, until they had become as soft and plump as a baby's butt. He didn't stop, but kept stroking the salve on her lips, putting her in a trance. Gently, sweetly, perfectly, healing her, taking care of her. Sometimes when she dreamed or remembered that, she felt hypnotized; sometimes it caused her to wake up crying out for him. Remembering all of this and more, and feeling it now, she was in a deep state of longing.

And she was utterly lost.

"I am so screwed," she whispered.

"Not quite yet, you're not," he whispered back.

"Sean, don't do this . . ."

"I want you," he whispered against her opened lips. "So. Bad."

She tried to pull herself out of the dream because she knew they should be talking, but it wasn't working. This happened to her sometimes in an actual dream, her refusal to wake up because it felt so good to feel her skin against his skin. But she managed to shake her head weakly and whisper, "Not a good idea."

But he just lingered there, lips to lips, bodies held comfortably close, and the irresistible memory that came was how much Sean loved pleasing her in bed, how committed he was to her pleasure. It was as if his own satisfaction was secondary. How he would tease her, tell her she took advantage of him;

that just because he was accommodating didn't mean she had to be such a glutton about it. In the aftermath, in laughter, he would say things like, *Oh, that's right, if I make you come twice, you'll let me have one.*

She couldn't remember him ever once suggesting she was holding back, that she needed more warming up.

She felt herself growing soft and moist. And weaker by the moment.

Then he went in for the kill, covering her lips in a powerful and familiar kiss that left absolutely no doubt that he meant business. And she yielded completely. She didn't know he was going to do that, though she should have. She certainly wasn't prepared for it, for which she had no excuse, and suddenly all she had in her was acquiescence. She had needed him so much, for so long. His breath came in and out through his nose roughly and she could barely breathe at all. His big hands ran up her back while her arms slowly, cautiously, rose to circle him, join the embrace.

The kiss was long, deep, delicious, hard. Her lips opened; his opened. It was his best demanding kiss, as she remembered it; he was pushing her back against the front door and she pulled him against her harder, making small noises that did not sound like protests. She was pressed to him tightly and one of her hands crept up his neck to the back of his head, holding him against her mouth. She was actually counting the seconds, then lost count and started again. It felt like a ten minute kiss. She couldn't stop. And she couldn't take this back, couldn't pretend she wasn't in the mood or had decided it was a bad idea. This was it — her statement. The truth was out. She wanted him every bit as much. Then he reluctantly pulled back.

"Let me come in," he whispered.

She shook her head. "That guy who just left. That's the guy I've been seeing."

"I don't care. I'm going to take you away from him."

"We have issues to sort out . . ."

"Yeah, and about a lifetime to do it in. Franci, Franci, for just a little while, let's think about all the things that are right with us, and not the few things we couldn't agree on."

"It wasn't just a good-natured little debate," she reminded him. "It was so major it caused us to —"

He came down on her mouth hard, pushing her back, taking her mouth with power. She counted the seconds till she couldn't resist him and then opened her lips, letting him inside. He slipped his hands inside her coat and ran them slowly up her ribs. Her coat open, he pushed her against her own front door with the length of his body, and the press of his arousal right at the V of her legs caused her some serious amnesia. Maybe it *was* a disagreement, one that wouldn't be so debilitating now. Whatever it was — she *needed* him. *Needed.*

And as had happened only with Sean, acquiescence turned to throbbing hunger. He could make her crazy with desperate desire.

He turned with her in his arms, never releasing her lips, and opened the front door, allowing both of them to move right into her house. He closed the door behind them with a bang and pressed her against it on the inside.

Oh, boy, she remembered this trick. If there was anything as likely to weaken her as taking her to bed, it was pushing her up against the wall. Something most men didn't have a clue about, Sean had perfected. And she clung to him. He ground against her and she gyrated her hips against him, knowing there would be no turning back now. Sean had an unfair advantage; their sex life had been *incredible.*

In the distance, she heard Harry whine,

then growl. It wasn't like Harry to growl . . .

"Franci?" he whispered against her lips. "Do you have a dog?"

"Uh-huh. Harry. Little guy. It's okay."

"Hm," Sean answered, going after her lips again. His hands ran smoothly over her bottom to her thighs and he lifted her up. Her legs wrapped around his waist, and he held her there, moaning his approval, slipping his hands under her purple dress to hold her perfect ass. He loved that dress; it felt as silky under his hands as it looked on her body . . . and he was going to get rid of it as soon as possible.

The growling intensified. Then there was an angry bark and snap just as Harry sunk his teeth into the back of Sean's leg.

"Arrrggghhh!" Sean rumbled, pulling back sharply, jumping in surprise and shaking one leg, interrupting and disturbing some totally perfect foreplay. "Jesus!"

"What?" she whispered, breathless.

He looked over his shoulder at the dog. "Don't do that!" he yelled at Harry, causing him to back up and whimper a little. Then he turned back to Franci. "Where's the bedroom?"

She tilted her head. "Down the hall, first door on the left," she said weakly. He carried her like that, his big hands under her butt, her legs wrapped around him, down the short hall to her bedroom. He limped slightly. Just inside the bedroom, he kicked the door closed, locking the dog out. He peeled off her coat, dropping it to the floor, then he fell with her on the bed, still crushing her to him, still possessing her mouth. Without releasing her lips, his jacket joined her coat on the floor. In the back of her mind she knew she wasn't supposed to be doing this. But in the front of her mind, this was *perfect*. He felt absolutely *perfect*. And she was so hot that if anyone tried to stop her now, she might tear them limb from limb.

It had been a long time since she'd been this person. Of course, the last time had been with Sean, which partially explained *this* time. As she ran her hands over his chest, shoulders, arms, back, she couldn't get enough of him, couldn't get him close enough, and she began pulling at his shirt. She tugged it out of his pants and pushed her hands underneath to caress his naked chest. His pecs were hard, his belly flat; there was a soft mat of hair. Her fingers teased his nipples and brought them into hard little bullets. She was panting, gasping, biting and tugging gently at his lips. She had become completely wild with absolutely no concept of how this was possible just minutes after she had suggested this was a bad idea. But it didn't matter — she grabbed the front of his shirt and tore it open, sending the buttons flying, pinging off various surfaces around the room.

"Whoa," Sean said against her lips. He let the shirt fall off his shoulders, then tugged her dress up. He sat back on his heels between her spread legs, pulled her to an upright position and worked that purple dress up and up, over her head and away. His hands went to her panties . . .

Her hands were on his belt buckle while his fingers tested the elastic of her very tiny panties. They came off faster than his belt buckle opened; she found herself kicking out of them crazily, frantically. Then she went after that belt again and it wasn't moving. She whimpered her need to get past that belt, that zipper.

"Easy," he whispered. "Easy."

"If it was easy, you'd be naked," she returned, her breath coming unevenly.

Sean chuckled. "Hang on," he said, giving her a hand and getting out of his jeans. All their clothes were suddenly flung around the room and they were pressed together, naked, hot and panting. His lips went to her breast, his tongue teasing a nipple into life, while her hand immediately coiled around him and he shuddered, groaning. Mouths together again, bodies pressed tight, he slipped a hand lower. His fingers glided smoothly into her and she ground against his hand. "Yeah," he groaned appreciatively. "Okay. Okay. I just need a second, honey. Hang on."

He rolled away from her and grabbed his jeans off the floor, shaking out his wallet, sifting through it quickly, locating a condom.

In that moment that he wasn't touching her, Franci froze. Her dark eyes were wide, her body suddenly growing cool in his absence. Temporary sanity. She noticed a picture of herself and her daughter on the bureau across the room and pinched her eyes closed, pulled her legs back together. She couldn't go through with this, no matter how much . . . He never forgot the condom; he didn't want children. Well, he forgot it that once . . . How can I let this happen?

But then he was back, against her, covering her with his large, warm, hard body. He grabbed her wrists, pulled her hands over her head to hold them there, gently parted her legs with a strategically placed knee and claimed her lips. Ah . . . she thought. That's what she remembered — that mouth, those lips, all that feeling. Sean. Passion. Hunger. She let him kiss her, let his tongue enter. But her response had cooled; she was worried about what she was doing!

Sean left her lips and rose above her, looking into her eyes. "Uh-oh," he said. "You're thinking. All of a sudden, you're thinking."

"This shouldn't be happening now," she whispered weakly.

"Oh, it's happening," he said. "Believe me, it's happening."

"This will make sorting everything out even harder," she said.

"Fuck the problems for a little while. Stop *thinking*. Go back to that other place, where you were just *wanting*."

"I'm not sure I can," she said, giving her head a little shake.

He touched her lips softly, then harder. He traced them with his tongue. "Sure you can," he whispered. "Nobody wants like you do, Franci. Work with me here." He possessed her mouth, then his fingers found her most vulnerable spot between her legs and a delicious moan escaped her as she lunged her hips toward him. Amazing, she thought, how Sean's skillful mouth, his talented hand, could completely numb her mind and quiet the chatter. He let go of her wrists; his lips found her breast and, with precision, he entered her in one long, deep thrust that made her gasp and push back against him to bring him home.

"God," she said in a breath. "Oh, God, oh, God." Her hands were on his back, holding him tightly against her, running up and down in slow, rough caresses. She grabbed the hard muscles of his butt and pulled him against her, into her, hearing him groan. Every nerve ending was on fire; there was a longing inside her that needed to be taken care of right away. She did exactly what she thought she couldn't — she stopped thinking and let her body take over, bucking beneath him, moaning, whimpering, clinging to him, riding with him in a powerful, stormy, wild pumping that teased the deepest part of her into a hunger so strong, it robbed her of breath. She gasped, wanting and craving and needing. She wrapped her legs around him, scraped her nails down his back and felt the tension shatter inside her, bathing her in a blinding, pulsing heat that flowed from her core to every extremity.

"Ahhhh," he sighed. "Oh, honey," he whispered so softly she barely heard. "Oh, baby, that's the way . . ." And then he took his — thrusting into her hard, letting it go, throbbing with his own pleasure.

Then she fell limp, satisfied, a pile of stress and yearning that had gone all soft and weak beneath him. A small laugh escaped her. Something about a fabulous orgasm always made her laugh a little.

Really, she hadn't had one like that in a good four years.

"Funny?" he asked.

"Not even," she said. Then she laughed again, softly, lightly. "I suddenly feel so *good.*"

"No kidding," he said, and he rolled off her carefully, lying beside her, spent.

He dashed off to the bathroom to dispose of the condom, then was back, holding her again. They were quiet for a few moments. Then Franci turned onto her side, raised up on an elbow, looked down into his handsome green eyes and said, "Now, we can't do that again. We have to sort out our issues."

"Oh, Jesus," he said. "Why me?"

"Why you, what?"

"This isn't the best time to become completely irrational," Sean said.

"Well, I don't think I'm irrational at all, but why do you say that?" she asked.

"We're naked," he answered. "We're naked after the best sex either one of us has had in a long time, and we should be cuddly. You used to want to be cuddly. What's wrong with you?"

She frowned at him. "How do you know that's the best sex I've had in a long time?"

"You tore my clothes off. You left scars on my back." He smiled at her. "Just an observation, hardly a complaint."

"Well . . . actually . . . Oh, never mind, it's really not your business."

"Your dog bit me," he said. "I think he severed my Achilles tendon."

"I told you," she went on, "I didn't stop living when you told me to hit the road," she said, ignoring his accusation about her cocker spaniel.

"Franci, Franci, that isn't what I did. You said you were leaving — I said fine, if that's the way you feel. Come on, not now. Not tonight. And it doesn't matter if you had sex with someone. Or with a hundred — Forget I said that. I don't want to think about this."

"I don't sleep around like you do," she said, curling against him. "We can't do this again," she said, but she made no attempt to cover herself and neither did he. They lay there, snuggled, nude, in post-coital rapture.

"I think we can do it again before morning," he said.

"No, this isn't going to work. We're not lovers, Sean. We're *ex*-lovers. That's why that went so well. That's all it is."

"I doubt that's all," he replied.

"Oh, that's all. You and I had pretty much perfected it by the time we split up."

"Wanna bet?" he asked, covering her body with his. "We had it perfected the first time. I remember, and so do you."

Damned if he wasn't right. She couldn't see her way out of this mess.

"We do have one little problem. I had that one condom, just for safekeeping. I don't have another one."

She sighed in resignation that came too easily. "I might have a couple."

"That's my girl."

"Don't get your hopes up."

"Baby, everything is up."

Great sex not only made Franci feel good, it made her very sleepy. They made love twice more. Softer and sweeter and slower, but just as mind-bending. They spent *hours* making love. Then she pushed herself up against Sean in a way that was at once brand-new and very familiar. She used to sleep with him this way — her back up against his front, her head on his arm while his lips bothered her neck. He used to pull her long hair aside to kiss, lick and suck on her neck, but there was no hair to get in his way now. His arm was draped over her waist, his hand capturing her breast. She felt, for the first time in such a long time, like she was in the right place at the right time. But probably with the wrong man.

Morning would be soon enough to feel guilty and stupid. So, she slept.

"Were you ever lonely, Franci?" he asked in a whisper against her neck. "Without me?"

Her eyes popped open, but she kept her breathing even, pretending to be sleeping.

"I never thought about it, about being lonely without you," he whispered. "But I kept wondering why I was so *empty.*" He kissed her neck. "I looked for you in so many women and never understood why it didn't work. Never understood it was because I loved *you.*"

She pinched her eyes closed against a tear.

He sighed deeply, pulling her close against him. "I want to take you to the Alps to ski — we used to talk about doing that. Remember? And I want to go with you to Aruba, to dive and lay on the beach. We'll get one of those huts on stilts — we'll make love outside."

She heard him yawn deeply; he kissed her

neck again.

"I thought eventually I'd get over you. I didn't know I'd never get over you because I loved you."

And then the talking stopped and she heard his light snore. Very softly she whispered, "Yes, I was lonely. You have no idea . . ."

At six-thirty in the morning, amazed to have slept so well, Franci slipped out of bed. She showered, toweled her short hair, pulled on jeans and a T-shirt. She stepped out of the bathroom to see Sean lying on his stomach, one arm dangling off the bed, the sheet pulled over his head and shoulders, but one long, muscular leg and his naked butt peeking out. The shower hadn't even disturbed him; he was out cold. She shuddered. She'd completely worn him out. She hadn't had sex like that in more than four years. That wasn't exactly their typical lovemaking, but then there was no typical with Sean. It could be wild. Or sweet. Daring. Luxurious. It was never the same old thing. And it had always been whatever Franci needed at the time.

He had probably the nicest butt she'd ever seen, and some unattractive scratches on his back. There was also the perfect imprint of a small canine mouth right on his Achilles tendon. She shivered again. *Oh, boy,* she thought. *I have really screwed this up. Now everything is about ten times more complicated.*

She remembered a time she'd been so grateful to meet a man with whom she shared that kind of powerful chemistry. Now she was pretty sure she was cursed.

She turned the picture of her with Rosie facedown on the bureau before leaving the room.

She'd have to get him up, have a little talk with him before she went to fetch Rosie. Franci's nerves were getting the best of her so she tried to keep busy, first feeding Harry on the patio, then coming back indoors to brew coffee in the kitchen. When it was ready she sat with her coffee and thought, *I should probably get checked for STDs.* Then she thought about the talk she was about to have with Sean — it would be quick and to the point. It was obvious a child lived here. If he hadn't noticed Rosie's picture in her bedroom, he would never miss the lavender bedroom right next to her own. There were toys in the dining room and right outside the French doors on the patio.

As these thoughts raced around her brain she had to admit she was afraid of his reaction. If anything happened to hurt Rosie, she'd never forgive herself, and yet she dreaded the thought of never having another night like last night again in her life. Because when he found out what she'd done, he'd be furious first, then he'd be gone.

In Franci's bed, Sean rolled over with a moan, opening his eyes. He smelled coffee. She was up ahead of him. His very next thought was that maybe he could get her back in here. Soon. If he had the strength. He couldn't remember the last time he'd experienced a night like that. At least four years ago, he thought with a smile. He sat up slowly. He found his jeans on the floor along with a lot of clothes. Stumbling to the bathroom, he took a look in the mirror; yep, it was him. Good — he was afraid he'd just been hallucinating again. He rinsed his mouth, peed, then pulled on his jeans.

Sean found Franci sitting at the breakfast bar behind a steaming cup of coffee, and the first thing that came to mind was that she looked like a mere girl — her cheeks rosy, lips pink and swollen from hours of kissing, her face a mixture of innocence and something that seemed almost shy, but she was a demon lover. A phenomenon. There were times during the night he felt as if he'd rubbed up against both death and eternity at the same time. He took a step; he intended to kiss that mouth before there was any talking.

"We have to talk," she said.

Oh, Jesus, she was *thinking* again. If there was one area in which they were complete opposites — Franci took everything so *seriously.* He, on the other hand, had trouble getting serious about much of anything and it drove her crazy. He stopped where he was and just stood there, trying to get his bearings. "Can I have a cup of coffee, please? Before you get started?"

"Help yourself," she said, tilting her head toward the pot.

He leaned against the counter and took a few sips, trying to clear his head. She took a few sips, remaining blessedly quiet. He could tell by the expression on her face, there was going to be some drama about last night. He mentally prepared himself; she was going to warn him it didn't mean they were getting back together. She could say that all day; he wouldn't argue with her. But he wasn't leaving; he wasn't letting her walk away from him again.

Franci was thinking, too. She thought maybe the best thing would be to just blurt it out — Sean, I left you because I was pregnant. I have a daughter, your daughter.

I have twenty reasons why I didn't feel I could tell you before now and I —

Just then there was a sound at the front door and Franci gasped. She knew instantly what had happened. Franci and Vivian had an understanding. Vivian would go out to get the newspaper from the end of her sidewalk, look down the block at Franci's house and, if there was a car in the driveway, Rosie would not be allowed to go rushing home to her mother until after a long, leisurely breakfast at Grandma's house. And a quick phone call to clear the way.

There was no car in the driveway! Sean's car was parked across the street along the curb.

Rosie pushed the door open, all grins and bouncing red curls. "Mama, we watched a scary moobie and ate pizza on Grandma's good couch!" She ran to Franci, her coat not even buttoned, and Franci reached for her. Rosie threw her arms around Franci's neck and Franci lifted her up, hugging her fiercely, rocking her back and forth. Once she had her daughter in her arms, she wasn't afraid anymore. It was that way with Rosie and Franci — little else in the world really mattered.

"Morning, cupcake," Franci said. "You didn't let Grandma sleep in, did you?"

She shook her head, giggling. Then she spied Sean, leaning against the stove in the small kitchen. He held a coffee cup in one hand; his green eyes were wide and fixed, his mouth open in shock and disbelief.

"Where's his shirt?" Rosie asked.

Franci pulled Rosie onto her lap more firmly, one leg on each side of her. "I think he forgot something," she said. "Rosie, this is Sean. Sean, this is my daughter, Rose."

"Wide Iwish Rose," Rosie corrected her mother.

"That's right," Franci said with a smile. "My wild Irish Rose."

"Mama, what's Iwish again?"

"A country. A beautiful country that's green like your eyes." She glanced at Sean. He was in a state of shock. She hoped she wouldn't have to resuscitate him in front of Rosie.

Franci heard footsteps. The door squeaked open farther and the doorknob rattled. "Good Lord, Franci, you left your keys in the lock! Not exactly safe! And presumably not locked, either, since Rosie —"

Vivian stopped dead in her tracks as she spotted Sean. She gulped.

"Mom, you remember Sean, don't you?"

Sean recovered himself. His eyes were no longer wide, but narrowed, and his mouth was fixed in an unhappy smile. "Vivian," he said with a nod. Then he sipped from his mug.

"Sean," Vivian said, her hand rising to her cheek as she looked at the purple bruise on Sean's.

"It's healing up nicely," Sean said. "How've you been, Viv?"

"Good," she said a bit weakly. "Very well. Thank you."

"Mama, did he fall down?"

"Yes, poor thing. But he'll be just fine. Will you do something for me, peanut? I'd like to have a cup of coffee with Sean before he has to leave. Would you mind having breakfast at Grandma's? Then I'll come get you, and later, after we clean our rooms, I think we should take Harry to the dog park, then maybe we'll bake something and put on one of your best movies."

"Aww," she whined.

"Come on, Rosie," Vivian said authoritatively, a hint of panic in her voice. "I'll let you scramble the eggs. Come on, right now." She plucked Rosie off Franci's lap and had her out the door so quickly it was almost a magic trick.

That left Franci and Sean standing in a very small kitchen in deafening silence. No one moved as the seconds ticked by. Then

Sean lifted the coffeepot and filled both their cups. He pulled out a bar stool and sat down. He focused on her eyes and waited. When she didn't speak, he said, "Tell me you didn't — ?"

She gave a brave nod. "I was just about to tell you when she came bounding in the front door. Rosie doesn't walk anywhere."

"You were just about to tell me? A few years after the fact?"

"I told you I needed a commitment, that I wanted a child . . . children. You were adamant — you were not interested in the same things I was."

"You might've left out a couple of things — like you were pregnant. That red hair and those green eyes — they've been in my family for generations."

"Did you really think I would tell you? After the way you acted about the whole idea?"

"I didn't have the facts," he said, anger seeping into his tone.

"Do you even remember how it was? Do you remember that I cried and said it was the most important thing to me and you said I'd have to come up with other important things because you weren't getting into all that? Do you remember telling me not to let the door hit me in the ass? Do you remember saying, 'Fat chance! Not in this lifetime'?"

"And do you remember telling me I was a child, an irresponsible fuck-around who would never grow up? That if I couldn't settle down and have a wife and children, you weren't interested in wasting any more time on me? Remember, Franci? But you *didn't* tell me you were pregnant!"

"I couldn't! I was afraid to!"

"Aw, Jesus, Mary and Joseph — *afraid?* You've never had any reason to be afraid of me!"

"I was afraid you'd marry me!"

"That was what you *wanted!*"

"I didn't want you to marry me because I was pregnant! I wanted you to marry me because you *loved* me!"

"I did love you! I just didn't want to be married!"

"Or have children!" she shouted back. She pinched her eyes closed and took a steadying breath. She spoke quietly. "I didn't want you to be stuck with us. More to the point, I didn't want us to be stuck with you, regretting our accident every day of our marriage. I *wanted* my child. I wanted to raise her *knowing* she was wanted. Loved. You will never understand this, Sean, and I don't expect you to — but when my period was five minutes late, I started to love her. Passionately. And it grew by the day. If I couldn't be a hundred percent sure that you'd love her just as much, I wasn't willing to take a chance on you."

"Were you never going to tell me?" he asked. "If I hadn't bumped into you, were you —"

"Yes, I was going to tell you. I was going to have to — Rosie has just started asking questions. I was dreading it, but I was going to tell you."

"Dreading it? Because you knew how pissed I'd be?"

She gave a huff of laughter. Sometimes he was so dense. "No, Sean," she said patiently. "I don't care if you get mad at me. I was afraid you'd hurt Rosie. Reject her. Ignore her. Break her heart."

Sean got that stunned look on his face again because he hadn't even gotten that far yet with processing all that had happened. In his mind he'd just found out Franci was pregnant, and it really ticked him off that he hadn't been told. But life had hit fast-forward; she was almost four years old and asking questions about her father. He had absolutely no idea what a father did with a four-year-old. He had even *less* idea what a single father did!

"I won't," he said, though he was afraid, through ignorance, he just might. "I wouldn't do that."

"Thank you," Franci said. "If you don't want to see much of her, I can find ways to get around that so she isn't hurt, and if you —"

"Franci," he nearly barked at her, stopping her. "Gimme a minute, huh?" He took a breath. "I just found out you were pregnant!" He shook his head, trying to clear it. "You haven't told her yet?"

Franci shook her head. "Not yet."

"Okay, first you have to let me digest this — I think I'm in shock. Then we'll talk about how we'll manage things. When we've had a little time to work things out, then we'll tell her. But first —" He took another deep breath. "You've had a few years to get used to this idea. I've had a few minutes." He lifted one brow and peered at her. "And I haven't had much sleep."

In spite of herself, she flushed.

"Now, I'm going to get dressed. I'm going to leave. I need a little time to think. I need some fresh air and you made promises to your 'wide Iwish rose.' I'm going to call you tonight." He tilted his head. "Are you going to give me a phone number now?"

"Sure," she said.

"Don't tell her until I'm ready, Franci."

"Do you want to help tell her?" she asked, frankly surprised.

"I don't know," he said honestly. "I just don't want you to tell her until I have some time to think. I want to work things out in my head, then we'll get to . . ." He gave a half smile. "Rose? Why'd you name her Rose."

"That hair," she said, smiling. "She came with a head full of that hair. I thought I was going to name her Taylor, till I saw the hair."

He couldn't quite smile back. Then he pushed back from the breakfast bar and went into the bedroom to gather up his clothes. As he limped out of the kitchen, she saw the scratch marks she'd left on his back and winced. "Oh, God," she whispered, mortified. When he came back into the kitchen he was fully dressed, though he couldn't button his shirt. She said, "Please, whatever you decide, let Rosie be your first consideration. Her feelings, her little heart."

"Whatever I decide?" Sean asked. "You mean there's some kind of choice? She's mine, right? Nothing I decide will change that, right?"

"She's yours. I wouldn't be able to hide that."

"Then you don't have to worry about her

142

heart," he said. He buttoned his leather jacket over his destroyed shirt. "Write down your number for me. When does she go to bed?"

Franci scribbled down the number on a notepad. "Eight or so."

"I'll call you after that so we can talk," he said, grabbing the paper. And without touching, hugging, kissing or the smallest display of affection, he left her house.

SIX

It wasn't even eight on Sunday morning when Sean left Franci's, so he drove around Eureka and Arcata for a couple of hours, hoping to spy an open bar. Of course the kind of classy bar where Sean preferred to spend his time wasn't open on Sunday morning, or any early morning for that matter, but he was willing to settle for a dive if he could only find one.

Pregnant, he kept thinking. Then he would remind himself, not pregnant anymore. There was a child, a little girl. How could Franci do something like that to him? Man, he could use a stiff drink.

Right away the many things he'd have to do assaulted him. He'd have to step up, offer to marry Franci and somehow become a father. He'd have to act like a father to a little girl who hadn't had one since birth. Even though he had plenty of friends with young children, he hadn't been paying attention; he wasn't sure how that was done. Nor was it something he *felt* like doing! Next he'd have to tell his family and they were all going to go crazy, his mother, Maureen, at the head of the pack.

He'd have to get over being angry long enough to convince Francine to move to Beale AFB as his wife, living with him full-time, and he had only five weeks of leave to do it in. Joint checking account, sharing a dirty clothes hamper, knowing each other's whereabouts at all times, working out child-care issues. Maybe he could convince her to be a housewife and take care of everything.

Sean began to feel claustrophobic.

His cell phone vibrated in his pocket and then let out a little *ping.* He pulled it out and looked at it — a text message from Cindy. A *long* text message; he didn't try to read it while he drove. In fact, he might not read it at all. Ever.

Cindy had been a very brief girlfriend. He should have broken off their relationship, which wasn't much of one to start with, when he took leave to go to Luke's. Instead, Sean, being Sean, had kept the thread alive just enough to think about it a while longer because Cindy liked him a *lot,* and that meant regular sex. She was a civilian who worked on base, twenty-five years old, kind of cute. They had met at the officers' club one Friday night. The girl went from zero to naked in twenty seconds — they were in her bed that very night. Though he knew better, he took her out a couple of times after that. He knew it wasn't going anywhere, but she didn't. She started calling him, having expectations, getting serious. He tried to slow her down, but she was very hot to trot and not easily discouraged. Sean was a gentleman most of the time and returned her calls or texts when she asked him to, and that was probably another mistake. So he told her he was going to his brother's place, would be gone a couple of months, and this would be a good time to cool it. He wasn't interested in having a steady girl.

She *was* interested. She left voice-mail and text messages on his phone at least once a day, sometimes the cheery *how are you* variety and sometimes the desperate *why don't you call me I miss you so much* type.

What he wanted was a message from Franci that said, "Come back here, I can explain." But he wasn't likely to get that. She didn't want him if he was merely taking responsibility. She wanted him in all the way, wanting her and a baby. Was it some kind of felony to be a guy who didn't feel like having kids? He knew a lot of guys who didn't feel like breeding up big families! It didn't make him a bad guy.

Sean found himself driving back toward Luke's in Virgin River. And he was thinking that he really liked the guy he'd been with Franci, before all this. And he liked the plan he'd had. He wanted to travel, do fantastically adventurous things with her: see the world, ski the Alps, snorkel in coral reefs, dive in clear, warm waters, parasail, balloon, four-wheel, do a motorcycle cross country, go mountain climbing. He hadn't ruled anything out. And Franci seemed to be having a great time; they were good together. An air force pilot and a nurse pulled together a decent enough income to indulge in all the fun entertainment life had to offer.

She had no right to do what she'd done. Without even telling him. She was *wrong* to do that. Franci was the one who was wrong, not him. He'd been *honest!*

He pulled up to Jack's Bar, the only game in town. The open sign was lit. Sean wandered in and found the place deserted. He went up to the bar and said hello to a smiling Jack.

"Morning," Jack said. "Breakfast?"

"Shot of Chivas, if that's okay."

Jack lifted his eyebrows. "Fine by me," he said, getting a glass and the bottle. "Rough night?"

Beautiful night, Sean thought. Maybe that's what pissed him off the most, that he'd had that old, familiar, phenomenal, mind-blowing sex with Franci and had started thinking, *I'm home, I'm home, I'm home with my woman!* He'd begun formulating how they'd work things out; he'd convince her their life was good; he'd assure her she was secure with him. He loved her; he looked forward to a life with her. It was the trappings of marriage and children that made him nervous, made him feel like the confinement would suck all the fun out of him. But if that was the price of having her in his life he would compromise. He could do the marriage thing, but that whole family thing — he was maybe years away from that.

Think again, idiot, his conscience chided him. It's here. Your Wide Iwish Rose.

"Sean?" Jack asked, putting the drink in front of him.

"Oh. Thanks. Just a lot on my mind."

"Oh," Jack replied. "Well, can't say I haven't resorted to Scotch before 10:00 a.m. Sunday morning to clear my head. A time or two." Then he turned away like a good bartender and busied himself behind the bar.

Sean kept his jacket closed because there were no buttons on his shirt and he didn't want his bare chest hanging out. He spent thirty minutes with a Scotch, convincing himself that all of this was the fault of Franci and he would do what he had to do, but she would have to beg his forgiveness for the deception. And that was just the beginning! She would have to explain why, after doing that, she hadn't contacted him and told him about Rosie before she was three and a half and old enough to know he hadn't been around! That was unforgivable!

He shook his head dismally and thought, Wait a minute — you don't want children, and you're angry that you didn't know you had one? He was confused. So confused.

"Ah, Sean?" Jack asked. Sean looked up. "Can I freshen that for you?"

"Yeah," he said, pushing the glass forward.

Jack poured a shot and said, "Listen, Preacher's in the kitchen if you need anything. I'm going to wander next door for about an hour, then I'll be back."

"Next door?" Sean asked.

"Yeah. You met the new minister, right? The guy who married Luke and Shelby? Well, we're not real churchy, but Noah's good people and he gives a passable sermon. Preacher and me — we trade off Sundays. The wives like to go. We're doing our best to support the church — I think we need to keep it going. Besides, he makes me laugh a lot more often than he makes me feel guilty. I'll be back in about an hour."

"Sure," Sean said. "Enjoy yourself."

"If you're still here when I get back, maybe we can lay a little breakfast on top of that Chivas."

"Yeah, maybe," Sean said.

Sean sat there a good bit longer, focused on how much this was not his fault, and finally he had bored himself to death. He figured he'd settle up with Jack later and decided to just slip out. He was inexplicably drawn to the church out of curiosity. He wondered, when Jack said they were doing the best they could to keep it going, what that meant. So he walked in the front doors of the church, which opened to the back of the sanctuary.

It was not nearly full. Maybe half. Most of the people were seated toward the front, but in the back pew on the left were a few grizzled old mountain boys with graying beards past their sternums and ponytails down their backs. Sean took the back pew on the opposite side of the aisle. He got a whiff of mountain living from their side.

He recognized a good many people he knew well — Luke, Shelby and Art for starters. Mel, Jack and the kids; Preacher's wife, Paige, with theirs. Walt Booth sat up front beside Vanessa, Paul and the little ones. No sign of Walt's lady friend, Muriel. She was probably out of town, which was often the case. There were others — people who'd been at Luke's wedding. But Sean had entered quietly and no one turned to look his way.

And there was Noah up front. He wore jeans, boots, a plaid work shirt open at the collar and rolled up at the sleeves, a powder-blue T-shirt underneath. No suit or vestments like he'd worn at Luke's wedding. Beside him, patiently listening, was his border collie, Lucy. Noah was animated, talking about Simon the fisherman, the most stubborn man alive, who couldn't make a commitment to Jesus even after he'd witnessed countless miracles! He clung so powerfully to his pigheadedness that he almost missed out on the most amazing, life-altering commitment of the millennium! He was a real holdout, that Simon. Noah started talking a little bit about his own years fishing the Pacific out of Seattle and he spoke about his own obstinacy, which he claimed was legendary.

And Sean's mind wandered. I could have been softer, he thought. More sensitive to her need to have a family. I could have tried to talk it out; instead, I said mean things. I said, "Go, then — have a blast! You'll never have it this good with anyone else!" Oh man! Small surprise she didn't return his calls!

A small voice said, Try to imagine finding your father for the first time when you're only four years old!

While Sean was daydreaming, Noah completed his sermon and then there were a few announcements before the benediction, a perfect time to scoot out before Luke saw Sean and wondered what he was doing in church.

"The Presbyterian Women's Group will have their first meeting here on Tuesday night at seven — please come and bring a dessert to share. Someone suggested the need for a nursery during services so the parents of little ones can concentrate on my profound and memorable sermons." There was a chuckle. "That means volunteers — anyone interested, give me a call. It's time to start thinking about Thanksgiving baskets for the needy, and Jack Sheridan has offered to head up the committee. He'll round up the volunteers and will work with them to get a list of people we'd like to share with. He will need a group of men and women to help out. And, finally, one last announcement. I have bent the church secretary to my will and Ellie Baldwin has agreed to marry me."

Laughter and applause filled the church.

"She is a generous woman," he added. "She might make something out of me yet. We haven't set a date, except to say it will be as soon as possible, small, simple and —"

Ellie, who had been seated at the piano in front of the church, stood. "But we will invite anyone who wants to come, right, Noah? Everything else can be small and simple, as far as I'm concerned. Except the guests."

"Absolutely, Ellie. Whatever makes you happy," he said. "But the reason I'm making this announcement today . . ." Noah said, turning back to his congregation. "We're looking for a house. No way we can fit two adults, Ellie's two kids and a dog in my RV. So any suggestions would be appreciated! And with that final announcement, let's bow our heads and —"

Sean left the church quietly before anyone could spot him. He went around the back side of the church and immediately thought how silly it was to even try to be scarce; Luke would spot his SUV and, within moments, Jack would tell Luke just what Sean drank for breakfast — it was that kind of town. Still, he waited around the back of the church until it had emptied of congregants and then went around to the front doors again.

Noah had the back of his old truck loaded up with the mountain boys and stood at the open door, ready to get in, but he still had an arm around his girl's slim waist. Sean was used to priests; it threw him for a moment to see a preacher so openly affectionate with a sexy young woman. He thought it would be best if he just disappeared before he made a giant fool of himself.

"Sean?" Noah called. He'd not only spotted him but, of course, remembered his name. "Looking for someone?"

"Never mind," Sean said. "I can see you're tied up."

"After I drop these boys back home, I have plenty of time. If you're in no hurry."

"Noah, I'll take 'em," Ellie said. "Go ahead, talk to Sean. I'll see you at Jo and Nick's a little later."

"You sure?" Noah asked Ellie. "Because I'm sure Sean could just —"

"Come back," Sean interrupted, finishing the sentence for him, because it had suddenly seemed like a really bad idea to talk to a preacher about his situation. "I could just come back."

Ellie laughed lightly, gave Noah a kiss on the cheek, pulled the truck keys out of his hand and said, "Go on, Noah. I'm perfectly happy to drive the boys home."

Noah grinned and gave her a squeeze. "You're a flawless female."

"Yes, I know." She laughed. He gave her a boost into the old truck and, while Noah watched, away they went.

Noah walked over to Sean, hand extended. "How are you?" he asked.

"Got a few things on my mind," Sean admitted.

"Can I help?" Noah asked.

Sean shook his head. "I have no idea. First off — I'd never take this one to a priest."

"Well, now, I'm not sure if that's a compliment or not." Noah put a strong hand on Sean's shoulder. "Tell me where you'd be most comfortable. There's the church office, the RV, Jack's. We could have coffee, breakfast or maybe even more of what you've been having. Your call."

Sean grinned a lopsided grin. "I had a little Chivas to handle the news. I just found out I'm a father."

Noah's eyebrows lifted and he smiled. "Depending on where you are in life, I can understand the need for a Scotch. Let's head for the RV. We're less likely to be interrupted there."

"Good idea. Sorry I didn't make an appointment."

Noah laughed. "Did the news make an appointment?" he asked. "We have to be flexible in this business. Come on."

Sean soon found himself settled in a slightly messy but comfortable RV behind the church. Noah closed an open laptop, cleared away some papers and poured Sean a cup of coffee. "Want to take your coat off and stay a while?" Noah asked him.

"I'm fine like this," Sean said, though he was getting real warm. They sat at what served as Noah's table and Sean dove right in, telling the story. He started with the ending first — how he'd found Franci four years after their breakup and realized how foolish he'd been to let her get away. Then he went back to the beginning to explain the one and only issue — as far as he knew — in which they weren't compatible. And finally he talked about the fight that caused them to part company.

"We both said things we shouldn't have

said. It got ugly — I don't know if we were mad about not changing the other one's mind, or if we were each standing by our own convictions. Honest, Noah, I don't know anymore." And while looking into his coffee cup, he went through some of the things they'd said to each other before parting ways. The he-said-she-said of it all.

"I can't help but notice, you got yourself a bruised hand and a shiner," Noah said.

"Oh," Sean said with a laugh. "Oh, man, did you think — ? No way, Noah — it wasn't a physical fight between us. I'd never strike at a woman or child. And I'd only hit another man in a fair fight. I got these 'souvenirs' when I ran into Franci in the grocery and got a little insistent that we get together to talk. I did grab her arm, at which point a man about the size of a Mack truck threw me into the melons and pummeled me. He was protecting Franci, though he didn't know her. And then Franci jumped him to defend me. And then we all got arrested."

There was silence for a moment. "Gee, Sean, you've had an interesting few days."

"Tell me about it. Then I spent the night with her." He boldly connected eyes with Noah, waiting to be told how many Hail Marys that would cost him, but Noah didn't even flinch. "It was like coming home, I swear. I was never so happy in my life — I found my girl again. I told her how much I'd missed her, how much I loved her, and when the morning coffee was perking, her daughter came bouncing in the house after spending the night at Grandma's. Franci hadn't told me yet, but there was no mistaking those bright red curls and powerful green eyes."

"You don't have red hair," Noah supplied.

"It's on both sides of the family — my mother, my dad's sister, a few cousins. Believe me — it's Riordan hair. Besides, Franci would never —" Sean took a sip of his coffee and cleared his throat. He didn't want to even consider the idea that someone else was Rosie's dad. Noah listened and, at a point, got the coffeepot and refilled both their cups.

"Mind if I ask why you were so adamant about not marrying or having children?" Noah asked.

"I didn't think it was right for me," Sean said with a shrug. "At the time, four years ago, I was twenty-eight. I had a whole plan for traveling the world with Franci, for having the freedom to do the things we both loved. Guys in my squadron who married their college sweethearts could only afford to go on camping vacations, and they couldn't afford regular babysitters so they had to take turns caring for the kids if they wanted to go out on Friday or Saturday nights. If they stayed too late at the bar, their clothes might be burning on the lawn when they got home, and they needed a kitchen pass for poker night. I didn't want that life," he said. "I just flat-ass wasn't ready for that. I was young, flying fast jets, living large, had a beautiful woman — there wasn't anything else I wanted. Plus," he said, taking a breath and glancing away, "it would've helped if I'd had a chance to come up with the idea on my own. You know? She gave me an ultimatum! Now or never. I called her bluff."

"Um, Sean?" Noah said gently. "Apparently she wasn't bluffing."

"I'm better at poker," he said.

"Hopefully," Noah said.

"This is a mess. I'm furious with her for not telling me sooner, but at the same time I'm not sure I want to be a father."

Noah coughed into his hand. "Uh-huh, but it sounds like that ship has sailed."

"Yeah, ask me how much that pisses me off! Plus, I can't let her get away again. She asked me to please not break Rosie's heart — it tears me up that she's afraid I'd hurt the kid. I'm sure this is my fault, but it must be hers even more. It would help a *lot* if it was more her fault than mine."

"You about ready for some input?" Noah asked. "It's free advice, and you're under no obligation."

"Go for it," Sean said.

"Forget all that — it's in the past. You'll work through it, hopefully without hurting each other. Right now? Get to know your daughter. It's the most important part of this whole drama. Get to know Rosie. Whether you want to be a father or not, you are one, so press on — start a relationship with her right away. Both of you have been missing out."

"How'm I gonna do that?!"

"Show up. Talk to her. Play with her. I let Ellie's daughter put ribbons and clips and stuff in my hair. It's a bonding experience for us both — I get to look stupid and she gets control."

"What if she asks . . . ?"

"Tell her before she asks," Noah advised. "If you know for sure you're her father, you better tell her the second you meet her. There's a period of adjustment for both of you. Get started on it. All that stuff that went before? That separated you from Franci? You don't have to work on that with

Rosie. You and Franci will work that out. I'm available if you need me. I can help with that."

Sean just stared at him for a long moment, silent. Finally he asked, "Do you really know what you're doing here?"

"I do," Noah said. "I actually studied and practiced counseling before the seminary. I have a degree and everything."

"What am I going to tell Luke?"

"Everything or nothing," Noah said. "The most important thing right now is not what you tell other people, it's what you tell Rosie. She's a little girl. Whether she knows it or not, she wants a father. She needs a father. You're that person. Good luck — you're going to have to learn fast to fully understand what that means."

"The next person who needs to know about this has to be my mother. In case you haven't noticed, my mother is a very strong woman with very firm ideas."

"I'm not as good with mothers," Noah admitted. "You'll be fine. I bet she loves you."

Sean shook his head. "It never kept her from whacking me in the back of the head if I didn't do what she liked. Strict. My mother was strict. All five of us were altar boys. She's wanted grandchildren for a long,

long time. The fact that she's had one for this long without knowing? Oh, man, I'm never going to hear the end of that."

Noah chuckled. "Just duck," he advised.

On Sunday mornings after church, it wasn't unusual for Paul Haggerty to set up a work station at Jack's Bar. He had an on-site construction trailer and a small office in his home, but he liked getting a little work done here. He'd set up his laptop at the end of the bar, jump on Preacher's satellite for the Internet connection, kibbitz with Jack a little. It wasn't quite as dreary as the trailer and there weren't a couple of toddlers running around calling Daddy this, Daddy that. At home, he'd have one, if not two, kids on his lap.

So after church, Vanni promised to take the kids home, give them lunch and put them down for naps. Then she winked at him and said, "Naps," again. Paul intended to get a few things done at the bar and then hurry home.

Jack brought him a cup of coffee. "Big project?" he asked.

"Small project made big. Remember Ian Buchanan's old cabin? His sister-in-law, Erin, wants to spend some time there next summer, but she is definitely not the outhouse kind of chick. She wants it completely renovated, enlarged and furnished. She sends me pictures of her ideas and I send her pictures back of what I have available." Paul shook his head a little, looking off at nothing. "She doesn't plan to be on site even once before she arrives for the summer. Busy lawyer type." He grinned. "One tough taskmaster. Not much gets by her."

"You have to buy her furniture?" Jack asked.

"No." Paul laughed. "It'll be shipped from Robb & Stucky when the interior is done."

"Robb and who?" Jack asked.

"Top-end furnishings, pal. Ms. Foley will be living in style out on that mountain. We're moving real fast right now to get an add-on bedroom and bath, the roofing and wiring done and a hole dug for a septic system before the first snowfall up there. I'd say we have another month and then we'll be close to having the big stuff done. We've been at it since September. And there's always spring if we get pushed. We'll do some interior work during the winter."

"I remember her," Jack said. "Kinda uppity."

"Never met her," Paul said. "Her e-mails, which are pretty frequent, are real business-like, but I figured her being a lawyer, they'd

163

be that way. She definitely knows what she wants," he said, clicking on a picture and turning the laptop toward Jack. There on the screen was a beautifully furnished rustic living room with rich leather furniture, shining wood floors, rough wood paneling, classy window treatments and a big, stone hearth. Included were accessories from rugs to throws, from artwork to bric-a-brac.

Jack whistled. "I thought Ian had himself an old wood-burning stove."

"Uh-huh. Stonemason's been out there for a week building the fireplace. That old place is not the same, if I do say so myself."

"I hope she's paying well."

"She put the work out for bid," Paul said with a laugh. "The girl knows what she's doing. But this is the first time I've ever completely rebuilt a house via e-mail." He pushed Send on something and said, "That ought to do it for today." He closed the laptop. "I have to get home before I miss nap time."

"Pretty soon you'll have cartoons. Well, they used to call 'em cartoons," Jack said. "Now it's something else, but they still look like cartoons. Mel says they were invented so the parents could have sex."

Paul lifted one eyebrow with interest.

"The downside is, every time I hear the

cartoon music I get a woody."

After chatting with Noah, Sean went home to Luke's and found three expectant faces in the house, looking at him oddly. They were all seated in the small living room as if waiting just for him. Luke, Shelby and Art. "What?" he asked. As if he didn't know.

"Your Jeep was at Jack's, but you weren't anywhere to be seen. You didn't come home last night. What's going on?"

"I'm going to catch a shower, then I'm going to be out of town for a couple of days. Just a couple of days. I'll be back. I'll explain everything then."

He was answered with complete silence. "All right, fine," Luke finally said. "Or you could tell us now, before you leave town for whatever reason. What's going on?"

Sean sighed heavily. "If I tell you, can you keep your big mouths shut till I square things away with Mom?"

"If that's what you need," Luke said with a shrug.

"Shelby?" Sean asked, and she nodded. "Art?" That man just stared at him, not quite getting the gist of this. "Okay, here's the deal. It turns out Franci had a reason for drawing her line in the sand — marriage and family or she's gone. She was pregnant.

She didn't tell me. I found out by accident this morning. She has a —" He cleared his throat. "*We* have a daughter. Rosie. Age three and a half."

"Whoa," Luke said with a groan, lowering his head to his hands.

"How wonderful!" Shelby said, jumping to her feet. "Oh, how wonderful!"

"Rosie doesn't know about me yet. I have to take care of that. And I have to tell Mom. I'm going to have to go to Phoenix to tell her in person, because I have no idea what she's going to do. She's . . . you know . . . dramatic about some things. I think I'd rather auger in than tell Mom."

"What do you mean Rosie doesn't know about you? Weren't you with Franci last night? You weren't out all night trying to drink this away, were you?" Shelby wanted to know.

"Yes, I was with Franci, but Rosie was spending the night at her grandma's down the street. I think Franci was just about to tell me when Rosie came through the door and jumped into Franci's arms." He put his hands in his pockets and smiled contritely. "Red hair, green eyes. She calls herself the Wide Iwish Rose." His shoulders shook in a soundless chuckle. "Ah, no question about the DNA."

"Well," Luke said. "Talk about a revelation."

"Yeah. So I'm going to get a shower, pack some things, go back to Franci's to talk to my Wide Iwish Rose, then fly to Phoenix to tell Mom, who is going to beat me to a bloody pulp for every bad thing I've ever done."

"She'll be thrilled," Shelby said.

"No, she will not," Luke and Sean said in unison.

"She will be happy to have a grandchild," Sean added, "but unhappy that she is three and a half and doesn't know her Riordan grandma. And she's going to want to kill me for not being married to Franci. If I don't take a little time to talk her off the ledge, she'll take over. She's going to be a giant pain in the ass." He looked at Art pointedly. "*Ass* is a swear word. I won't say it again and don't you."

"I know which ones are the swear ones," Art said indignantly. "Sometimes when we're fixing the roof, we don't say fuck piss shit, right, Luke?"

"That's right, Art. We don't say that. Good — you remembered." Luke rolled his eyes. Then he swiveled his head toward Sean again. "Now what?"

"Now I'm going to have to get this

167

straightened out. Franci will have to marry me. Or something."

Shelby laughed and immediately covered her mouth. Sean was glaring at her so she said, "I was just thinking — you're going to work on the proposal a little, right? Because, as proposals go, that one sucked."

Sean ground his teeth. This whole thing was way bigger than he was. "I'm going to get that shower." And then he took the stairs two at a time, hoping he could spend some time with his daughter and get to Phoenix before Luke told on him.

SEVEN

Dan Brady lumbered into Jack's and headed up to the bar. He took his Shady Brady off his head and sat it on the stool next to him. It was early Sunday afternoon and he was the only person in the place. It took a minute before Preacher came from the back.

"Yo, Brady," Preacher said, whipping a napkin onto the bar. "Don't usually see you around town on Sundays. Your day off, isn't it?"

Dan nodded. He worked for Paul Haggerty and had been promoted to the foreman's position, which not only brought more responsibility, but more hours. He was on the job five and a half days a week, and that half day, Saturday, usually stretched into a full day. "How about some coffee?"

"You got it," Preacher said, pouring. "Don't you usually have a date with your girl on Sundays? Or did Cheryl finally get smart and dump you?"

The normally serious Dan grinned. "She's meeting me here." He looked at his watch. "In about twenty minutes. Where's Sheridan? Taking a day off?"

"We switch off on light days like Sunday afternoons. Mel has a long list of honey-do's for him." Preacher leaned on the bar. "It'll be nice to see Cheryl. Don't see enough of her around here."

Dan looked up at the big man somewhat apologetically. "I doubt she'll come in and visit, Preach. Since she found sobriety, she likes to stay away from the memories of her hard-drinking days."

"Yeah, I get that. Our loss, though."

"She's planning to face a big memory today," Dan said. "If she doesn't change her mind. She's coming to town to look at her old house. She's only been inside a couple of times since she left for treatment a long time ago. She's going to have a look today and, if she likes the shape it's in, she'll be talking to a real estate agent about selling it."

"Then what'll you do for a place to hang that Shady Brady of yours?"

"I'll find another place nearby. I work around here — you're not getting rid of me that easy."

They were silent a moment. Preacher was

thinking. You could always tell when he was concentrating; his heavy black brows knit together, his eyes narrowed, his jaw ground a little. Then he came out with it. "Maybe sometime you can tell Cheryl from me that it stands to reason she'd think about those hard days a lot, but she probably thinks about it way more than anyone else does. Folks around here, we mostly think about how amazing she is, whether she comes around to visit or not. We're all real proud of her, real happy for her. She's good people. You tell her that, if you ever get the chance."

"I'll do that, Preach," he said. And he thought, Preacher's one sweet dude.

Preacher put a thermos coffeepot on the bar. "I'll be in the back. I'm making pies."

Dan pulled out his wallet.

"Pah, forget about it," Preacher said. "It's just a cup of coffee between friends, man." And then he was gone.

A few minutes later the door to the bar swung open and Cheryl said, "I'm here, Dan. I'm ready."

He turned to look at her and smiled. She just got prettier all the time. He walked out of the bar with her, holding her hand. "I walked over — let's jump in your truck," he said. "Want me to drive?"

She handed him her keys and got in the passenger side.

"Still want to do this?" he asked her, when they were both in her truck.

Cheryl nodded. Cheryl had grown up in the house and it was one of many things she left behind when she moved away from Virgin River. She also left her morbid childhood, her alcoholism, her bad reputation and her perpetual failure. Her sense of hopelessness fled when she met Dan Brady. "Turns out I can do a lot of things when I'm with you."

For a break on the rent, Dan had been renovating and upgrading her house. She'd seen it exactly one time since Dan had moved in, and that had been a mere month after she'd handed him the key. It had been greatly improved from the miserable dump it was in that short month, but she hadn't been able to force herself to look at it again. Just walking through the door, even if it was changed and improved, was a fearful prospect for her. It brought back so many horrible memories. Cheryl had spent close to fifteen years mostly in a drunken stupor. And she wasn't an ordinary drunk; she had been the town drunk.

As for Dan, he had his own ghosts. They were just different ones. He'd been a grower; he'd done prison time.

"You don't have to do this," Dan told her, holding her hand. "You can slap a for-sale sign on it without even going inside. The Realtor can give you a good idea what it should sell for with all the improvements."

"I can do it," she said. "I want to see it."

"Are you sure, Cheryl? Because I want us to go forward. There's no reason we ever have to be stuck in the past. Our pasts — we beat 'em. We just have to keep a green memory so we don't walk back that way."

She turned and smiled tenderly at him. She squeezed his hand. "I've been sober a year and change," she said. "I feel good. My worst day sober is so much better than my best day drunk. I want to see the house, sell it, make a life with you. You're the best thing that ever happened to me."

"Then let's do it," he said.

They'd been together for more than six months. They were taking it real slow, one baby step at a time. They'd spent their first whole night together just a few weeks ago and now the long-term plan was to sell her house, begin building a new one on the edge of Virgin River. Since the lot they'd picked out wasn't in town, Cheryl wouldn't have to go in unless she wanted to. The decision to build there had more to do with Dan's work needs than her preferences. Since going to work for Paul, his life had turned around completely. His income and benefits were excellent, but his days started early and ended late. There was also lots of overtime, which meant money in the bank. Living close to work would be an advantage for him.

They pulled up in front of the house and Dan got out and walked around the truck and opened the door for her. She put her hand in his as they walked up to the solid porch of a pretty little house. He opened the new front door and let her enter first. He had spent more than six months completely rebuilding her house so she could sell it and move on, and he was proud of his work. He couldn't wait for Cheryl to see it.

She immediately remembered what that house was like when she had lived in it. She was thirty years old before she found her way out, but the memory flooded back to her. It had smelled so bad, for one thing. She couldn't remember when it had ever been properly cleaned and her now-deceased mother had woofed down two packs a day so there had been a perpetual smoky cloud in the air. There had been so many gaps in the doors and windows that it was always cold through the winter no matter how high they turned the heat. She'd gotten used to things like ripped linoleum, missing bathroom tiles, cupboards without doors, nicotine stains on the windows and walls.

But today she looked at a pristine little house. The wood floors shone, the walls were textured and painted bright colors, the lighting fixtures were new. She walked into the kitchen — it was very small, but it was a masterpiece of wood, glass, granite and stainless-steel appliances.

The only furniture Dan had in the house were some bar stools pushed up to the newly constructed breakfast bar, bedroom furniture and one La-Z-Boy recliner in the bedroom — his reading chair. Sometimes his sleeping chair.

"Incredible," she whispered. "Just amazing. You are so gifted. I can't wait to see what you do on *our* house."

He shrugged. "I had some help, you know. And I like to build. I was born into the trade."

She pushed open the bathroom door — it was unrecognizable. Gone was the big sloppy shower and old pedestal sink and chain-flush toilet. In their place was a Whirlpool tub, separate glass shower, marble interior tile, sink and countertop. Dan had had to borrow one of Luke Riordan's cabins for ten days while he gutted the bathroom and rebuilt it. Paul helped him wire it, Jack helped him plumb it, Preacher helped him cart in the tub, sink and toilet and install them. The four of them together installed and finished the cabinetry in one day.

That was the best part of the whole project — Dan now had friends, when a year or two ago he'd had no one.

And Cheryl's support system through AA had grown and spread beyond that tight circle. After six months as a waitress she was now working at the community college in the cafeteria. She was taking two courses with the hope of one day getting her degree. Cheryl had moved out of her group home a couple of months ago and was renting a small apartment in a big old Victorian house that had been divided into three apartments. Her newfound independence was giving her confidence she didn't know she had.

She turned full circle, looking around at the impressive remodel. While she'd lived here with her parents, her bedroom was little more than a shed pushed up against the house. Dan had poured a foundation, framed and rebuilt the room, complete with large windows. The washer and dryer had occupied a spot on the back porch; now that porch was framed, enclosed and had become a sunroom with a small, separate laundry closet at the far end. The nasty, dirty, falling-down heap of a house Cheryl remembered was a charming, beautiful little home.

"I can't ever possibly repay you for this," she said.

Dan pulled her into his arms and kissed her. It started out as an affectionate kiss that, as usual for them, deepened and became more passionate. "Aren't you lucky? You don't have to."

She looped her arms around his neck. "Now what?"

"We get the Realtor to put up a sign. Chances are pretty good it won't sell right away, especially this time of year. When it does, I'll find something small to rent. When you're ready — if you're ready — we'll start building something we can get old in."

"Together," she said. "When it's time, I'll be ready."

Dan sometimes spent the night with Cheryl if he was invited, but they had no plans to move in together anytime soon. Long-range plans included getting engaged, finishing a small but perfect house on a nice lot, eventually getting married. Slow moves worked best for Cheryl, and Dan constantly reassured her that he wasn't going any-where.

"Want to have lunch at Jack's?" he asked her.

"Maybe eventually," she said. "One thing at a time, okay?"

"No rush, baby," he said. "You have friends here whenever you're ready."

"I know. I don't deserve any of them, but I sure appreciate them."

"Lucky for you," he said again. "You don't have to deserve them. Let's go find food. Seeing you happy makes me want to celebrate."

This Sunday afternoon for Vivian Duncan turned out to be a lot less relaxing than she'd counted on. She had planned to give herself a home-spa day — manicure, pedi-cure, facial, several hours lost in a good novel while she fluffed and buffed — fol-lowed by a nap! But the events of Sunday morning had been wildly illuminating and relaxation went right out the window. She recalled walking into Franci's house that morning, with Rosie in tow, to come face-to-face with Rosie's father. He was as handsome as she remembered, despite the bruise on his face. He'd been standing in the kitchen, shirtless, in only jeans and bare feet, looking for all the world like a Calvin Klein ad. Clearly he'd spent the night.

She had rushed Rosie out of there fast, giving the kids a chance to talk, but the second the coast was clear, she went back. She and Franci had had to speak cryptically and quietly in the kitchen; Rosie was in her bedroom with Harry, putting on her play princess gown and dressing Harry in a tutu.

"He's *back?*" Vivian asked in a whisper.

"He sure is," Franci said. "And he asked me not to tell Rosie about him till he gets his bearings. He'll call tonight."

"When did he turn up?" Viv asked.

"Actually, over a week ago, and I didn't say anything because I wanted time to think about how I was going to handle telling him about Rosie. The past couple of days have been an emotional roller coaster."

"Was there more than one way to handle it?" Vivian asked.

"Okay, Mom, let me be blunt — and I'm sorry if it hurts. I wanted to decide how I was going to handle it without any pressure."

Vivian was quiet for a moment. Then she gave a sharp nod. "Nicely done. Blunt but not painful. You get that from me." Franci grinned at her mother. Then she laughed.

"Oh, good," Viv said. "No crying. This is all going to work out, then?"

"Did you hear me?" Franci said. "I have no idea what's ahead."

"I just assumed your date last night was with T.J.," Viv said with a chuckle. "But —"

"It was," Franci whispered. "At dinner I told him that I'd run into Sean and explained the situation. He dropped me off early and told me to handle things and let him know when we'd worked out our single-parent issues. All the time he was saying good-night, I knew Sean's car was parked across the street, the engine running. He was waiting for me to get home. I have a feeling T.J. isn't going to approve of the way I worked things out. I let Sean stay the night . . . *before* I told him about Rosie . . ." She swallowed. "I don't know who's more upset with me — T.J. or Sean. T.J., because there's another man in his territory, a man he didn't know existed. Or Sean, because he thought he got his girl back, and he got a lot more than he bargained for."

"Well, I'm sure you had your reasons . . ." Viv said.

"That's just it — I had no sense of reason at all! I swear, all that man has to do is . . ."

"I'm okay with not knowing those details," Vivian said. Then she fanned her face with her hand.

"I don't know how it's going to shake out," Franci said. "I'll work with Sean the best I can. I'll give him time to think first. He made a point — he just found out I was pregnant while staring into the green Riordan eyes of a three-and-a-half-year-old."

Once Vivian was caught up on all the news, she went back to her little house, leaving Franci and Rosie to their afternoon of chores and promised playtime. And when home alone, she placed a call to Carl's cell phone and left a message. Carl, her significant other, was having a home day himself, catching up on chores and fixing a nice dinner for his kids, a boy aged seventeen and girl aged nineteen.

Carl and Viv were both ensnared in rather complicated family obligations that they balanced with a work relationship and romantic relationship, all with great care. Vivian had been widowed since Franci was seven, so it wasn't considered weird or unusual for her to have dates; there'd been a couple of men in the past twenty-three years she thought might find a permanent place in her life, but they had not. Since

Rosie's birth, Vivian had been Franci's partner in helping to care for and raise Rosie.

Carl, on the other hand, had been widowed for two years, and his children were still essentially teenagers, still grieving the passing of a beautiful, brilliant mother who had died too young from breast cancer.

Carl was fifty; Vivian was fifty-five. Both of them were fit and attractive and there was no reason they wouldn't notice each other if the chemistry was right. He was a family practitioner in the practice that employed her; she was a family-practice physician's assistant who worked for Carl and his two partners. She'd been with them for almost three years. First, Carl had been her boss and colleague, then friend, and for the past year, the man in her life.

They were a gorgeous couple, she thought. She was small and trim and blonde; he was large, solidly built and biracial. When she'd moved to the small town of Eureka, finding a man like Carl was the last thing she'd ever expected.

But because of Carl's teenagers and Vivian's commitment to a single daughter and granddaughter, they could only look forward to a time when they could concentrate on each other. Carl called it a rebirth; Vivian called it the blessed empty nest.

Of course, neither of them kept the other secret, but their kids being kids — even kids of thirty! — they didn't think about their parents' love lives. At all.

Her cell phone finally chimed at about three in the afternoon. It was Carl. When she picked it up, before saying hello, she said, "Carl! It's happening!"

"What?" he asked, his voice quiet and maybe nervous about just what was happening.

"Rosie's father is back in their lives! Half of me is overjoyed — they could make a family if they try, I just know it. I could end up with a grown-up life of my own one day. The other half of me is already grieving. He's an air force pilot, Carl. He's going to take them away from me."

"I think you need someone to hold you."

"Possibly," she said. "But not just anyone."

"After I shovel pot roast into the mouths of my kids — should they show up for dinner — I'll step out for a while."

"You are so lovely," she said.

When they hung up, Vivian made a beeline for the manicure, pedicure and facial stuff that had been set aside earlier in the day. If he was going to hold her for a while, she was going to be soft and perfect. And there would be a car in the driveway and the dead bolt would be thrown into place.

Sunday afternoon found Sean packing a duffel at Luke's house. Then he grabbed himself some fast food that didn't exactly go down well, and headed back to Franci's house in Eureka. Not only did he have a nervous stomach, he'd had Scotch for breakfast. When she opened the door, she was completely surprised to see him. "You're back." She was wearing an old sweatshirt and pair of jeans, big fluffy slippers and had some kind of feathery dusting thing on a long handle in her hand.

And she looked delicious. He wanted to tackle her on the spot. But . . .

"Did I screw up your plans for the day?" he asked.

"That depends on what you want. We're cleaning our bedrooms," she said. "Well, I'm cleaning mine and Rosie gets a little sidetracked. But she tries."

"Can I come in, please?" he asked.

"Sean, why are you here?" she asked, but she stepped away from the door to allow him to enter. "You were going to call later tonight."

"I have to talk to Rosie," he said. "I have to tell her."

184

"Shouldn't we talk about it first? As in, how it should be done?"

He shook his head. "I'll just try to get to know her a little, tell her who I am — and I have to do this because next I have to tell my mother."

Franci put a hand on her hip and let out a breath. "This is moving a little fast," she said.

"Tell me about it. But that's what we have, Franci, so let's just go with it."

"What do you plan to say to her? Want me to help you? Tell her with you?"

"I don't know what I'm going to say," he said first. "No, I want to do it alone. But could you stay kind of close in case I get in trouble?"

She grabbed his upper arm. "Sean, are you going to tell her and then disappear on her? Because if that's your plan, I need to know so I can do some damage control. I don't want her devastated."

He looked into her large dark eyes. God, she was beautiful. He was an animal; he was preparing to tell his daughter he was her father and at that moment all he could think about was getting Franci alone. Alone and naked. "My plan is to begin a relationship with her that will last a very long time. Cut me a little slack — I don't have a frickin' clue how that's done. I'm going to wing it. How much does she know?"

"Nothing. Basically, nothing."

"You said she started asking questions," he reminded her.

"Just little-girl questions. She noticed even the divorced kids had dads around from time to time. She asked where our daddy was. I told her you were in the air force. You have to learn to tell children only what they want to know — she didn't even ask who you were, just where. But that's when I knew I couldn't waste much more time and would have to track you down." She shrugged. "That was pretty recent."

"Why'd you wait so long in the first place?" he asked.

"I don't know," she said, shaking her head. "I didn't want to face it. I knew you'd be angry . . . she'd be confused — things could get real complicated. And I was afraid you might not acknowledge . . . her . . ."

He frowned. "Not acknowledge her?" he asked in confusion.

She took a deep breath and stiffened her spine. "I knew you didn't want a child — you were very clear. And really, I didn't want anything from you. So I thought you might say she wasn't yours and you didn't want —"

He grabbed her around the waist and pulled her close to him, his nose nearly touching hers. "*Listen* to me. It was only you and me. There were never any others — not for either one of us. We were more married than half the married people we hung out with. If you had a baby, she was *mine.* You think I wouldn't own that?"

She let her eyes fall closed. Not purposely, but it was a natural response. What she wanted to do was push him away and take control of the situation. Instead, she inhaled, drinking in his breath, his scent. And she whispered, "I could only hope, Sean. There was a lot of anger between us."

He relaxed his hold on her waist, giving her a little space. "Franci, the stuff we have to work out about all that — that doesn't have anything to do with what I have to work out with Rosie. Let's try to keep those two things in separate corners. I don't want to hurt her because of our anger with each other. That wouldn't be fair."

She tilted her head to one side and looked at him quizzically. "Wow. It almost seems like you got some counseling or something."

"Can I just talk to her now? And will you stay around in case I need you?"

"What if she wonders why you're telling her instead of me telling her?" Franci asked.

187

"How do we handle that?"

He shrugged. "Tell her you were surprised to see me. And I'll tell her that from now on, she'll always know where I am. We can do this."

She was totally shocked. "It sounds like we can. She's in her room and I'll be right next door in my room. Good luck."

He inhaled and it was a quivering breath. "Thanks." And he turned and walked into his little girl's room.

Sean stood in the doorway of the lavender bedroom for a moment, watching. Rosie had a very large play-kitchen wall unit and she was busy there. She was wearing a yellow princess dress that had seen better days — must be a costume she made supergood use of because she looked like a little princess vagrant. On her bare feet were some oversize plastic sparkly pumps and, stuck lopsided into her red curls, a tiara. She was talking softly to herself while she stirred nothing in a pan on one of the play stove burners.

"Hi, Rosie," he said quietly.

She glanced over her shoulder at him, but went immediately back to work on her cooking.

"Okay if I come in your room?" he asked,

and she answered with a shrug. He cleared a space filled with toys, dolls, picture books and unrecognizable kiddie paraphernalia and sat on the edge of her bed. "Watcha doin'?"

"Making stuff . . ."

"Do you like to cook?"

She nodded and turned toward him. "I like to cook on the real stobe, but only wif Mommy or Grandma."

"Sounds like a good policy," he agreed.

She walked toward him, holding the pan in one hand and a spoon in the other. She stretched the spoon toward his mouth.

"What is it?" he asked.

"Chicken," she said, pushing the spoon at his lips.

He wondered where that spoon had been and made a slight face at the possibilities.

"It's bery good!" she insisted.

He opened his mouth a bit and let her spoon in some imaginary chicken. "Mmm. That is good. Are you supposed to be cleaning your room right now?"

She turned back to her stove before saying, "No. I'm making stuff."

And he thought, Yeah, right. "Want some help in here? Putting away toys and your things?"

"No." She turned back to him again, pan

and spoon in hand, and lifted the spoon to his lips.

"More chicken?"

"Brocc'li. It's bery good for you."

"Hm. And not too filling, either," he observed. "Listen, I was wanting to ask you a couple of things. Like about your daddy. What do you know about your daddy?"

She turned back to the stove again, very busy, very intent on her imaginary project. "He has a big plane," she said without looking at him. "He's bery important with a big plane."

"Is that so?" She nodded. "I have news for you, Rose. It turns out I'm your daddy. How about that?"

She looked over her shoulder at him. She didn't look terribly impressed. "Where's the plane?"

Sean's hearing was exceptional, despite the roar of jet engines for the past ten years and the blasting of rock bands in the O Club on top of that. He heard a muffled giggle he recognized as Rosie's mother. The sneak. He leaned over to peek out the bedroom door, but he didn't see her.

"At Beale Air Force Base. That's where the plane is kept when it's not flying. Would you like to see it sometime?"

Rosie nodded so vigorously her curls

bounced and her tiara slid farther to one side. "Can I go for a wide in it?"

"That's not allowed, I'm afraid. You can go inside with me while it's parked on the ground."

"My mommy goes in the helifropter."

"You mean helicopter?" he asked.

Again she bobbed enthusiastically. "Uh-huh. Helifropter."

"She mentioned that." And he braced himself for the difficult questions — such as, *Where have you been? Why are you here now? Are you moving in with us?*

But she asked, "Do you have a dog?"

He shook his head. "But you do, don't you?"

"Harry," she said. "Do you have a grandma?"

"I used to," he said. "When I was little like you, I had two grandmas. My mommy's mother and my daddy's mother." Now would surely come the tough questions.

"Do you have a bike?"

He grinned. "As a matter of fact, I do. Do you?"

She shook her head. "But I have a all-trebain-beekle."

"Huh?" he asked.

"I'll show you it," she said, taking his hand and leading him out of the bedroom and through the house to the garage. She opened the door and there, beside Franci's car, sat a pink and purple miniature plastic quad. An all-trebain-beekle.

"Wow. Does it run?"

She made a face at him as if he was a total idiot. Then she hopped down the step into the garage, climbed into the vehicle, flipped a switch and applied her foot to the little pedal. It moved about one mile per hour forward until it hit the wall.

"That's awesome," he said. "Come on, Rosie. Your room is a disaster. I'll help you pick up toys while we talk about stuff."

"Noooo," she whined.

"Didn't Mommy ask you to? I don't know about you, but when my mommy asked me to do something, I didn't dare say no." He took her hand. "Let's clean up a little, then you can make me some more chicken and broccoli. And I'll tell you all about my plane."

"Can I have a wide in it?"

Sean rolled his eyes. Her attention span was either extraordinary or terrible, he wasn't sure which. "You can go inside when it's parked on the ground if I'm with you. We can do that sometime, if you want to. Come on."

So they went back to the bedroom. Sean

did more picking up of toys than Rosie did, but none of the traumatic questions he worried about came. He asked the names of stuffed animals and dolls, they read a couple of books together, made up the bed, did a little pretend cooking, got things generally shaped up and talked. He told her that his mother would be her grandma, too, and that she also had red hair and green eyes like Rosie, except she was much older. He said he had brothers who would be her uncles. She seemed to accept this news without getting excited. So he asked her about school, which was of course preschool, and the names of her friends. He found that in her closet she had several princess dresses, all of them pretty much the worse for wear, and a bunch of play high-heeled shoes.

"I taked them to school for my friends to wear — Marisa and Jason."

"No kidding?" He laughed. "Jason takes to those shoes?"

"Huh?"

"You know what, Rose? You're a kick."

"Don't kick," she said, shaking her head. "Don't neber be mean."

"Yes, ma'am," he said.

Sean lost all track of time. The room was sort of tidied: they had a remarkable conversation about everything and nothing, and

Sean began to feel the high tension roll out of him. This wasn't that bad. He hadn't wanted to do it without Franci in the next room, but he thought he was getting along pretty well, for a guy who knew nothing.

He asked her if she took a nap and she informed him she didn't *want* a nap. So he suggested reading a couple of books while lying on her small, child-size bed. She went for that reluctantly, but he was thrilled. He was *exhausted*. He hadn't slept much the night before and the morning had been filled with internal stress. So he got a couple of good-size picture books, propped himself against the headboard of the little bed so he could fit, invited her to sit beside him and began to read.

He didn't last long.

Franci was scrubbing out the shower in the master bath when she heard her cell phone twittering. She wiped off her hands, dug the cell out of her purse and looked at the number. T.J.

"Hi, there," she said.

"What's up?"

"Not much. Just some housecleaning. You?"

"Wondering if that whole drama with Rosie's father has been tackled yet."

"Gee," she said, sitting on her bed. "I have a start on it. I told him this morning. He's not happy with me — he needs time to adjust to the idea, and he's with her now, playing with her, talking to her."

"And you?" he asked.

"Me? I'm cleaning my bathroom while they play and talk."

He chuckled, but there wasn't a cheerful note to it. "Francine, did you tell him he has to clarify his visiting terms with you and then hit the road? Like we agreed?"

She frowned, not answering at once. "Is that what we agreed to? He just found out, T.J. I don't think he even knows what he wants."

"Did you tell him that —"

"Frankly, I haven't talked to him since he arrived a couple of hours ago and asked if he could spend some time with Rosie, which he has done since he got here. They're on their own for now."

"Is that wise? Leaving him alone with her? You don't really know him that well."

Sudden anger rose up in her, which she put a lid on for the moment. "Yes, I know him very well, T.J. In fact, I know him better than I know you. Now —"

"Did you tell him you're committed elsewhere and he has no chance of resuming the old relationship?"

She sighed into the phone. "I told him I'd been seeing someone. That isn't one of the issues we have to work out."

"It doesn't sound like you're making much progress on this."

"Oh, but I am," she said. And she thought, *When did I allow this man to think he had such control over my actions?* "I'm working things out just fine, but apparently not quickly enough to suit you. So, I suggest you let me have a little time to work through it all and I'll let you know how it goes. Hm? How's that?"

"Do I have a choice?"

"Absolutely!" she said. "You can refuse to be patient and look for someone who enjoys having her dinner ordered for her! Maybe someone with long hair!"

"You're being childish," he accused.

"You're being controlling," she countered.

"Try to be intelligent in this matter," he said. "Just use your head."

If there was something Franci found even more repellant than being told she was a dud in bed, it was the inference that she wasn't smart. "I will absolutely try to be intelligent, T.J.," she said. "It could be a struggle for me, but I will definitely try. I'm sure I'll talk to you soon."

And she clicked off.

And she thought, Wow! She hadn't had quite this much attention from T.J. since they'd started dating. He must feel completely threatened.

She wasn't sure if that amused her or worried her. But she turned off her phone just in case T.J. decided he had something more to say.

EIGHT

Sean awoke in a darkened little girl's room. He could hear Rosie and Franci talking somewhere in the house. He sat up from his scrunched position in the short bed and thought, *Dang. I passed right out in a toddler bed.* He pulled a couple of big picture books out from under him.

The door had been closed, but there was life in the house. He stood and stretched, then walked into the kitchen. Memories flooded him as he saw Franci making a big green salad. He loved her salads; she put absolutely everything in them. Franci stood on one side of the small island in the center of the kitchen while Rosie, now wearing jeans, a sweater and heavy socks, knelt on a bar stool on the other side. Something simmered on the stove and Rosie held a couple of wooden spoons, stirring and tossing the salad as Franci added ingredients. Then Franci had to pick up all the leaves that bounced out onto the counter.

They both turned to look at him. Franci chuckled, but tried to cover it with her hand while Rosie beamed at him. "Did you hab a good nap?" she asked very happily.

"I did," he said. "Sorry I fell asleep. Guess I was tired."

"We maked cookies and watched a moobie," Rosie said.

"Jeez, how long was I asleep?" Sean asked.

"Couple of hours, I think," Franci said. "I have some spaghetti going. You're invited to dinner. Then of course you have to go because I have work in the morning and Rosie has school."

"I was going to drive to Sacramento and catch a flight to Phoenix. My mother, you know."

Franci winced slightly at the mention of Maureen. She actually liked Maureen, even if her sons tended to both idolize her and cut her a wide berth. But she wasn't looking forward to Maureen's reaction to Rosie. "You can use my computer to check flights, but my bet is you're not going to catch anything tonight. You'll probably have to try again tomorrow."

"Might have to," he said. "Will you ladies excuse me? I have to use the bathroom."

"Sure," Franci said with a grin.

Well, he thought, my being here certainly isn't stressing Franci anymore. She thinks it's all very funny. He went into the hall bathroom that separated the two bedrooms and lifted the lid. He yawned. He scratched his head and felt foreign objects in his hair. While he continued to aim the stream into the commode, he leaned to the left to look in the small mirror over the sink and almost had heart failure. He actually might have jumped and briefly missed the pot.

Sean had little-girl "things" in his short hair — clips, bows, ponytail bands, jeweled bobby pins. And there was something else — he scraped off some Scotch Tape. His hair was too short so some of that stuff was taped on! But that was the least of it — he had a bright red Angelina Jolie mouth that went way out of the lines. Blue eyelids and pink cheeks. He looked like a clown. He zipped his pants. Then he wet a finger under the faucet and rubbed it over his eyelid. Nothing changed, except that he saw his fingernails were bright green. He washed his hands vigorously. Oh, God — he'd been tattooed in his sleep! He took the bar of soap to his lips; no amount of scrubbing helped.

"Frannnnn-ciiiii!" he yelled.

A moment later she tapped at the door

and he jerked it open. She was casually drying her hands on a dish towel while he was scowling. "Magic marker, I think," she said, before he could ask the question.

"Why?" he asked desperately, totally stunned.

Franci shrugged. "She's not allowed to touch my makeup. And she thinks you look wonderful." Then she grinned.

He stiffened and pursed his lips. "I'm pretty sure I'm out of uniform."

She chuckled. "We'll think of something. Are you staying for dinner?"

"I can't go out like this!"

"Okay, let's try some fingernail polish remover on your green nails, have some dinner, and then I'll see what I can do about your, ah, makeup. Really, Sean, rule number one — never close your eyes on a three-year-old."

Franci managed to get the green marker off Sean's fingernails and made progress on the "lipstick" and "eye shadow," but he was still a shade or two off. It went well with the bluish-green of his fading black eye. She fixed him up with some cover stick from her makeup bag. "Why'd you take it off?" Rosie wanted to know.

"I can't wear it to work," he explained.

"But are you going to work?" she wanted to know. "You said you're on bacation!"

"The air force has rules about boys and makeup," he said.

"And about girls and makeup?"

"No, girls are allowed to wear makeup."

"But why?" she asked, shaking her head. Then she turned to Franci. "Why, Mommy?"

"Because makeup is a girl thing and shaving is a boy thing. And you should never color on someone's face without asking first."

"Oh," she said, apparently satisfied. " 'Kay."

And Sean said to Franci, "How do you do that?"

"Practice." And then she smiled at him.

After a dinner of spaghetti and salad, Franci supervised Rosie's nighttime rituals — bath, reading time, bed. Sean cleaned up the kitchen and went to her small living room to wait patiently for Franci to join him. He heard a low, faint growl and looked toward the end of the couch to see that little blond-and-white dog baring his teeth. The little bastard was wearing a tutu. "You bite me again, we're going to have cocker spaniel soup," he said by way of warning. Harry pranced away. "By the way, you look ridiculous," Sean called after him.

"Who are you talking to?" Franci asked as she came into the room.

"Harry. He hates me. Animals usually like me — what's his problem?"

"Maybe he just doesn't trust you," she offered. "If you want to say good-night to Rosie before you go, now's the time. Her light is going off in . . ." She looked at her watch. "Fifteen minutes."

"Fine," he said, standing. "Did I do all right today? I mean, she didn't run screaming from the room or anything."

"You did very well, Sean. I'm impressed."

He smiled a small smile, asking himself why that felt so good coming from her. And why, he wondered, did she seem so much older now. She didn't look older, but she was completely mature. Grounded. Stabilized. If he didn't have recent proof that under that veneer of serenity there was a sexual bobcat of a woman, he'd think Franci had a double, and he'd got the calm one tonight.

Just thinking about that other Franci got him a little riled, and he thought it was completely reasonable that since he'd played good daddy all day, he might score tonight. Since he couldn't head for the airport before morning at the earliest, the plan made sense to him.

Rosie gave him a hug good-night, but was busy with her toy laptop computer, making words and pictures. She didn't look the least bit tired. He said, "Thank you for a fun day."

And she just said, " 'Kay."

Back in the living room, Franci sat in the corner of the sofa with her feet curled under her. He sat down close to her and reached for her hand. "Let me stay over," he said.

"No. I have things to get ready for tomorrow. I teach a couple of classes on Monday and Thursday mornings and keep office hours for students in the afternoons. Then I work my twenty-four-hour shifts in Redding on Tuesday and Friday mornings. Tomorrow starts a real busy week and I —"

"Okay," he said. "I'll watch TV while you get your stuff together."

"No. You'll seduce me and I have a child in the house."

"Gee, how do you suppose all the families with more than one child managed to do that?"

"Those first children were used to their mothers and fathers sleeping in the same bed, but Rosie's not. Sometimes she crawls in with me in the night."

"I have sweatpants in my duffel. I'll sleep in those," he tried.

"No."

"Can I have the couch?"

"No. Because I know you and you'll seduce me. I think the only thing more important to you than sex is air. Now be on your good behavior. She isn't even asleep yet."

"We should get a few things settled," he said. He thought, *And then I will spend the night!* "We should make some plans."

"Like what?"

"We should get married, I suppose."

She smiled at him. "Oh? And why is that?"

"Because we're parents?" he answered as a question.

She was shaking her head. "We'll be parents either way. That's not enough of a reason. Besides, how exactly would you handle that? The details?"

"I don't know. Does it matter?"

"It matters, Sean," she said. "For one thing, I live in Eureka — you live at Beale Air Force Base, a few hours away."

"Well," he said, "the air force owns me. I was hoping you'd consider coming to Beale. You and Rosie. That would sure make things simple."

She just did that frowning-smile thing at him. "That isn't what you want. You don't want to be married or have a family."

"To quote a famous minister I know — that ship has sailed."

She was quiet for a moment, looking down at her crossed legs. When she lifted her eyes they were very large, but surprisingly soft. "I really need you to try to hear what I'm going to tell you, Sean. You've been back in my life a week or so — you've known about Rosie less than twenty-four hours. There was a time I would have sold my mother for a commitment from you, but just like four years ago I don't want that offer simply because we made a child together."

"She needs a mother and a father," he stressed.

"She has them," she answered. "There's no way we can beat the stork — there's no point in making a big mistake. Besides, you just want to make some plans so you can spend the night, and you can't. Not tonight."

He lifted one light brown brow. "You gonna tell me that wasn't a real good night, last night? Because if I'm any judge, it worked for you."

"Totally rocked my world," she admitted. "I need some time for the rest. I just don't take something like marriage lightly. If I do it, I'll mean it, and I won't change my mind.

But I think you'd do it right now for all the wrong reasons."

"Does this have anything to do with the guy you didn't let stay last night?" he asked.

"My boyfriend?" she asked, smiling. She knew it was naughty to taunt him like that; she wasn't thinking of T.J. as a boyfriend at the moment. "It would be nice of me to tell him if things change in my personal life. But until I have matters settled . . ."

"No, Franci, tell him matters *are* settled. You *won't* be dating him!"

"And the woman who keeps calling you?"

"What woman?" he asked.

"Your phone keeps picking up text messages and voice mails. That has to be a woman."

He took a deep breath. This didn't seem like a good time to lie, just as he was trying to close a deal. "I dated this girl a few times back at Beale and I told her I wasn't getting into a steady thing. When I went on leave, I told her we had to cool it because it wasn't working for me, but she's deaf. I thought when I left town for a couple of months she'd let it go, but she's hounding me. I'm going to call her, Franci, and tell her I'm off the market. That I'm getting married. She won't call anymore. Now, come on."

"Poor thing," Franci said. "She might be

as sick in love with you as I was."

"As you were?" he asked, a little frightened of the answer.

"And I said I'm not marrying you."

"Okay, let me get this right — I suggested marriage and you said no?"

"How about that? What a shocker, huh?"

"Well, what the hell am I supposed to do? I thought that's what I should do!"

"Okay, you still don't get it. We don't want to because you're doing what you *should*. Listen carefully, Sean. I want you to be absolutely sure you want to commit to a life with me and Rosie, because you don't have to marry me to have time with your daughter. She's your daughter — I won't get in the way of that. Though I have to admit, the way you suggested marriage really just knocked me off my feet."

He would never admit it to anyone, but her refusal gave him an instant feeling of relief. He wasn't ready to take it all on. But it would sure make things tidier if they could just do it the way it probably should be done.

He slid close to her and, before she could protest, pulled her right up against him. "You wanna get knocked off your feet, sweetheart? Because we both know we do that to each other." He put a big hand around the back of her neck and ran his thumb from her earlobe to the hollow of her throat. Then he kissed that spot. "I want you with me, Franci. Tonight, and from now on."

"Sean," she said gravely, "when you rejected me four years ago, there were times I wondered if I'd lost my mind *and* my heart. The things we said to each other — I don't want to risk a marriage like that. After we split and I moved to Santa Rosa, sometimes I grieved so badly I worried that I was hurting the baby with endless crying, sleepless nights, loss of appetite. I just can't face something like that again."

He ran a knuckle across her soft cheek. "Baby, I didn't reject you. I wanted to be with you — I just had a hang-up with marriage."

"Well, now the shoe's on the other foot. Suck it up."

Life would be made a lot simpler, Sean thought, if he could deliver the news to his mother along with a plan for a quick wedding. He made a lot of blunders, but he wasn't quite stupid enough to admit that to Franci. Instead, he covered her mouth with his and moved over it with passion. He tongued open her lips, pulled her close against him, got hard. It was hell, but he broke away just long enough to say, "I'm gonna show you we need to be together tonight, Franci. When I'm done with you, there won't be a doubt in your mind." Then he went after her mouth again.

"Mooommmm-eeeee! What are you dooooo-ing?"

Sean broke away abruptly and turned scarlet. There, at the end of the couch, stood Rosie, her pajama bottoms and panties missing, Harry standing beside her, his tail wagging out of his tutu. Sean grabbed a throw pillow and held it over the bulge in his jeans, although there was no way Rosie would know what was going on with him.

"Kissing Sean," Franci said very naturally. "Where are your pants?"

"I pooped! I called you to check if I wiped good, but you dint come!" And with that she turned her back on them, bent over at the waist to touch her toes and exposed her butt.

"Arrrggghhh," Sean groaned, covering his eyes and sliding lower on the couch.

Franci chuckled and stood. "Okey-dokey, looks like you did a good job. I like it when you save the inspection for the bathroom, though," Franci said. "Let's get your bottoms on and back to bed."

Sean collapsed against the couch and

thought, I am not ready for this! How does a person get ready for this?

When Franci came back, she was laughing at him.

"Come on, stop it! The learning curve is really high here!" he complained.

"When we get right down to it, marriage would be the least of your adjustments."

By the time Sean left Franci's, it was getting late enough that he didn't want to go back to Luke's. He decided to head toward Sacramento and stop for the night at a clean, friendly looking motel along the way. He had just pulled into one such motel when his cell phone chimed.

Now, he thought, is as good a time as any to deal with Cindy, and he took the call, saying hello.

"Congratulations, man," his brother Aiden said. "How about that, huh?"

"Uh, how about *what*, Aiden?" he asked cautiously.

"A little girl, I hear. Three and a half? Almost four?"

"Who told you?! How do you know that?"

"Who do you think? Luke. He said you caught up with Franci. He told me about the reason she bolted a few years ago. Bet you were surprised, huh?"

"I told that son of a bitch not to say anything yet!"

"I haven't talked to Mom, so relax. You in Phoenix yet?"

"No, Aiden, I'm not even to the Sacramento airport! I just left Franci's a few hours ago and stopped for the night. I'll head there first thing in the morning. She doesn't know I'm coming."

"You're not going to warn her?"

"Nope. Mom never leaves town without checking in with at least three of us, so worst case I wait around while she finishes a bridge game or round of golf. Thing is, I couldn't head for Mom's before I squared things with Rosie. I had to tell her who her father is."

Aiden whistled. "How'd she take it."

Sean thought for a second. "Truthfully? She wasn't that impressed. She knew her daddy had a plane and she wants a ride. She took it right in stride, like she'd been expecting me to show up any second."

"And you?" Aiden asked. "You take it in stride?"

"Aw, hell, it wore me out so bad I fell asleep on her little bed. Slept until the sun was down. After spending about three hours with her — eating her imaginary chicken and broccoli, reading books, picking up toys, talking about bikes and dogs and playmates at school — I was shot. She has these high heels she wears. She took some to school so her friend Jason could wear them, too." He grumbled. "While I was asleep, she painted my face with magic markers . . ."

Aiden whooped with laughter.

"Yeah, you laugh. I'll turn her loose on you."

"I'd love that," Aiden said. "When can I meet her?"

"Gimme some time, Aiden. I'm way behind the power curve here. I don't know anything about kids, and there is so much to know. You have no idea."

"She's just a kid, Sean. Don't overthink it. Enjoy her."

"Did you know that when a little kid poops, you have to check their little butt to make sure they wiped it clean? Did you know that?"

Aiden chuckled. "Yes, Sean, I knew that."

"Where the hell do you learn something like that?"

"I dated a woman with a couple of little kids. Haven't you? Ever dated a single young mother?"

Sean was quiet for a moment. "Not really."

"How can you *not really* date a young

mother?"

"I've gone out with women with kids before, yeah. But I've never been around the kids. I have friends with kids, but I never paid attention to that stuff. I'm in way over my head."

"Franci will help you with all that. How *is* Franci?"

"Cautious. I told her I thought we should get married and she told me to slow down — she wants to be sure it's the right move."

"Bullshit. She wants to be sure you're in love with her. That you can be a lover *and* a family man. Don't you know anything about women?"

"Not as much as I thought I did," Sean admitted.

"My little brother the playboy," Aiden said. "Time to take life a little more seriously, huh? I want to meet her. Rosie. Let me know the minute I can. And I'd love to see Franci again."

"You know, just because Rosie took me in stride doesn't mean the entire Riordan clan won't be a little overwhelming for her," Sean said. "Let's not throw her in the deep end of the pool, huh?"

"Red hair and green eyes, I hear," Aiden said. "Like Mom and Paddy and half our cousins. That must have been a shock."

"The second I saw her, I knew. Plus, it couldn't be anyone else's kid — Franci and I were tight." He paused. "Till we weren't."

"Well, lucky you — you get another chance. Call me after you talk to Mom. I can't wait to hear how she likes this news."

"About Mom . . . I'm going to tell her in person because she's going to kill me and then she's going to rush to California and throw herself on Rosie. I can't let her do that, Aiden. What am I gonna do about Mom?"

"Reason with her," Aiden said easily. "Just tell her she'll meet Rosie very soon, but you have to introduce your very large, very excited, extended family one at a time *after* you work things out with Rosie's mom. Be firm — she'll be fine. Call me if you need me."

"I'll give you two thousand dollars to meet me in Phoenix and tell her for me."

Aiden laughed. "Talk to you tomorrow, little brother. Good luck!"

Sean arrived in Phoenix before noon the next day. He rented a car and headed for his mother's condo complex.

He remembered when she'd bought the place, almost ten years ago. They'd been born and raised in the Chicago suburbs, but after their father died twelve years ago, Maureen Riordan had had enough of harsh winters, especially when she had to face them alone. The boys were all devoted to her, but they were also all military and it wasn't easy for them to be on call to help out their mom. The oldest was Luke, who back then had been in the army flying Blackhawks, and the baby of the family, Patrick, or Paddy as they called him, had just entered the naval academy. All of them had left home and visited their mother at the pleasure of Uncle Sam.

Maureen, as she was known to do, took matters into her own hands and found a condo in Phoenix. It was in a complex much like a resort — more the kind of place Sean might choose, and that had surprised him about his mom. There was a golf course, tennis courts, a community center, swimming pools and a hefty association fee. More importantly, there was no grass to cut or snow to shovel, and there were guaranteed friends. All she had to do was sign up for certain activities and she met people. Thus, Maureen had learned to play golf and tennis and had put her bridge-playing skills to the test.

On the outside, it probably seemed like the perfect life. A deeper look gave Sean the impression his mother was filling the days just to stay busy. He wondered if she had a true passion about any of the things she spent her time on.

The place had never seemed to fit her, in Sean's mind. Their da, an electrician, had been a hard worker who'd earned a decent living, but they'd had five sons to raise. They had lived in a smallish three-bedroom house — three boys in one bedroom, two in another — on a tree-lined street on the outskirts of Chicago. The house had been forty years old the year Sean was born, and his parents had been mortgaged to their chins. When his father died, between insurance, retirement plans, Social Security and the sale of their home, Maureen was finally able to do whatever she pleased. So she moved her furniture into the small two-bedroom condo that had a Whirlpool tub in the master bath and, for the first time, a dishwasher, though she only had to run it once a week.

"I don't know," Sean had said. "It doesn't *feel* like you."

"It feels very low maintenance," she had replied.

"You won't have a vegetable garden."

"I'll buy my peas and tomatoes. Besides, I don't necessarily have to stay here for life. I might find something I like better."

"You might find a second husband."

"Pah," she scoffed. "It's more likely one of you boys will find a wife and settle somewhere. And I might want to be nearby."

"We're all in the military! If we do find wives, we'll be moving them around for twenty years!"

"Sean, if there's one thing I've learned, you can count on things changing more than on them staying the same."

In ten years, however, nothing had changed. And his mother's traditional, homey furniture still looked awkward in the modern digs. Maureen had gone back to work a couple of times since moving here — twice for three years each — but at present she was retired. She had been a crackerjack administrative assistant and worked once for the police department and once for a brokerage firm. The boys all assumed boredom drove her to work and a need to relax drove her back home. If their dad hadn't left her well-enough fixed, they'd been prepared to take care of her. Aiden, a navy doctor, was the one to watch over her most closely and he kept his brothers up to speed, when he wasn't out to sea.

On the rare occasions that all five boys could visit at the same time, there were a couple of guest apartments at the complex that they could reserve — his mom's place wasn't large enough for big family gatherings. The kitchen seemed too small for a woman who loved to cook but, as she quickly pointed out, her cooking skills were not exactly in demand these days.

Sean parked in the guest parking space nearest her condo and called her from the car. When she answered, he said, "Hi, I caught you at home. I'm in your parking lot. Do you have time for some company?"

"Sean? What in the world . . . ?"

"I grabbed a break from the honeymooners' cottage. I'll be right over." He signed off, grabbed his duffel and headed for a building on the far side of the complex's largest pool. He had to admit, his mother had found one of the best locations available. But then she'd bought it when the development was new and she had been one of the first tenants.

Maureen met him outside her patio door. She looked as if she was ready to go out. "Sweetheart," she said, opening her arms.

"Oh, nuts, I interrupted your plans," he said.

"Nothing important. I played tennis this morning with the women's group and this afternoon I was supposed to go to a bridal shower of all things! For a woman in her sixties! Who has a bridal shower in their sixties? I'll take my gift over there and we'll go out to lunch — how's that? I had no interest in going, anyway. They're going to play *games.*" She made a face. "That's the best reason to be a man, Sean. No shower games."

The shower games that came instantly to Sean's mind had nothing whatever to do with hen parties and everything to do with Franci. He was going to be fired as a father within thirty days, he was sure. What he felt every time he thought of Franci was not paternal and had nothing to do with little Rose. He flushed in spite of himself.

"Are you all right, Sean?" his mother asked.

"Is it hot here?"

She laughed. "It's cooling down, finally. Come on, come in."

He threw his duffel just inside the door and she asked him if he'd like something to drink. Coke? Tea? "Any chance you have a cold beer on hand?" He was feeling a little weak, nervous and anxious to get the worst of this over with.

When they were seated in her living room, her with an iced tea and he with a cold beer, he asked her about tennis, about her bridge club, about her volunteer work.

She smiled at him. "I think you've just about exceeded your limit for small talk, Sean. And you're fidgeting. Either you have to go to the bathroom or you have something to tell me." She squinted at him. "Are you wearing makeup?"

He frowned, then thought back to the day before. "Oh. Sort of. Some kind of cover thing for my . . . rash. I guess I'm allergic to . . . must be pizza . . ."

"Pizza?" she asked, confused. "With your lifestyle? That would be tragic."

"I don't know what it was, but I broke out in a rash and it's almost gone." She had that pleased look on her face. She was expecting him to tell her something that would make her happy. He could only hope. "You remember Franci?" he asked. "That steady girl of mine a few years ago? Long, pretty hair?"

"Of course, though I think I saw her four whole times while you dated her. Five at the most. I liked Franci. And I thought you did, too."

"I did, absolutely. I ran into her recently. I was out one night and, of all places, not far from Luke's, she was out to dinner with friends. We've kind of resumed contact, you could say."

"How nice for you. I never met many of your girlfriends, but of the few I think I liked her best. Nice young woman. Beautiful, too, if I remember."

"Uh-huh. She cut off all that long hair," he said, getting momentarily distracted. "She looks fantastic." Maureen looked at him expectantly, and at that moment he really felt as if he was back in catechism, half expecting Sister Thekela to sneak up behind him and twist his ear for not paying attention.

He shook himself. "Listen, Mom, I never told you the whole reason we split up, me and Franci. I loved her and she loved me, but we weren't in the same canoe. She wanted a commitment, a family, and I was running from marriage. I —"

"Good Lord," Maureen interrupted him. "What did your father and I do to turn you boys off marriage?" she asked, half pleading, half annoyed. "I thought we had a good marriage, your da and me. He was so wonderful to me. I tried to take good care of him and you boys! It makes me wonder where we failed that the lot of you are terrified of marriage."

"It wasn't you and Da, Mom. It was the two marriages in the family and the Pope, if you get my drift. I mean, Aiden and Luke had a couple of short, train-wreck marriages that just about killed both of them, and then there was this whole Catholic thing of not recognizing their next marriages, if they were crazy enough to have them. I mean come on — Luke's wife had another man's baby and Aiden's crazy Annalee was ballistic, totally certifiable. And they stuck by both those women as long as they could but, bottom line, the women left them. And still, no future marriage in the church? Come on! You know what kind of —" He realized he was on a rant and stopped himself. He hung his head. You didn't knock the Catholic church in front of Saint Maureen. Without looking up, he said, "If I could have been guaranteed a marriage as sweet as you had with Da, I'd have jumped in. Those other things — they worried me."

"You've always overreacted, Sean. Luke and Shelby were married by a priest! His marriage most certainly counts in the church!"

Sean flushed and hoped Maureen wouldn't see it. Only the boys knew that Luke never even tried to get an annulment from his former wife. He told the priest his marriage to Shelby was his first. Luke was fine with that, but that knowledge would have had Maureen praying for his soul night and day for the rest of her life.

"It's all right, Sean. Even I can admit Papa is sometimes a little behind the times," she said. Papa was an affectionate nickname for the Pontiff. "He's sometimes a little antiquated. I pray for change. My parish priest is very with it, you'd like him. He'd probably give you peace of mind."

"Yeah, right. Well, back to Francine. She had an agenda I didn't know about. She kept it from me. She had her reasons, I get that. But see . . . Okay, here's the deal — we had an ugly fight. She wanted marriage and family, and I said I thought we were good just like we were. We said mean things. We split with hard feelings. I tried to catch up with her later, but the air force kind of scattered us — she got out and I got transferred. So when I saw her, it was so —" He stopped. He took a gulp of beer and swallowed hard.

"Mom," he went on. "Franci was pregnant and I didn't know it. She left because I didn't want to marry her. Of course I would have if I'd known, which is why she kept it from me. She didn't want it that way so she chose to do it alone."

He watched the slow transformation of his mother's face. *When she was pregnant* made her stiffen. *Because I didn't want to*

224

marry her made her glare angrily. Now she was maintaining that scary silence he remembered from his youth.

He brazened on. "Mom, I have a daughter. She's three and a half. I've only known about this for a day. I don't even know her birthday, but I made sure she knew I was her dad and that, from now on, she will always know how to find me, and I'll be nearby whenever it's possible. And yes, I asked Franci to marry me, make us a family, but she's pretty leery of me. I'm going to have to convince both of them I'm worth the risk, I guess." He swallowed. "You have a granddaughter, Mom. Red hair. Green eyes. Scary smart. Her name is Rosie. She calls herself the Wide Iwish Rose."

Maureen wilted before his eyes. She got teary and, as redheads are wont to do, her nose got pink and the edges of her lips blurred as she pursed them. She sniffed back emotion to keep control. "How did you let this happen?" she asked, her voice catching.

"I didn't let it, Mom. It took me completely by surprise!"

"How did you have an intimate relationship with her for . . . for presumably a long time, then refuse to marry her? Is that how you were raised?"

225

He sat forward. "No. I was raised a whole other way, which might have a lot to do with — Listen, it's a different world than when you and Dad were young."

"Not that different," she said. "Tell me everything. And don't hold back because I'm going to find out eventually."

"Mom! I didn't skip school or go to a kegger! Of course I'll tell you everything. Thing is, I just found out. I spent a day with them — Franci and Rosie — and knew the first thing to do was tell you. Mom," he said, scooting forward in his chair, "I have so much catching up to do. I don't know anything about kids. I spent one afternoon with her and it brought me to my knees. Do you have any idea how exhausting a three-year-old is? Yeah," he said, nodding at her, "you might know that, huh? Well, it's going to take me a while to get a handle on this. Thank God I'm burning leave at Luke's for another . . . God, less than six weeks now! It's going to take me at least that long just to know how to —"

"Tell me about *her.* Did you bring a picture?"

He shook his head. "I didn't even think that far ahead. But here's what I'll do — I'll take a picture and send it to your cell phone the second I get back. You remember how I showed you to send the cell-phone picture to the computer? And I'll take more digital pictures right away. But the first thing I had to do was get to know Rosie, and I have to keep getting to know her. And the second thing was tell you about her."

"And Franci?"

He locked eyes with his mother. "I have to find a way to get us back together. I know she's not like Annalee or Luke's Felicia. Never a question about that, but I was still gun-shy back then. I'm not now — I'm going to court Franci and Rosie and hope for the best. There's a lot to do. First thing — I need to set up a college account and find out what Franci needs for expenses. I have to take Rosie to Beale — she wants to see my plane. I have to learn how to play with her, talk to her, teach her things. I have to . . ."

But Maureen got up and left the room, walking down the short hall to her bedroom. Sean was stunned for a moment, confused as to why she'd walk out on the conversation. Was she driven to tears? Really pissed at him? He followed her, feeling panic rise inside. The door to her room was open. "Mom?" he said.

She came out of her walk-in closet, dragging her largest suitcase. She stopped in her tracks and turned to look at him. "Sean, how did you let this happen?"

"I didn't *let* it — I told you, I didn't *know!*"

"Obviously you know what happens when you —"

"Stop!" he said, holding up a hand. "Stop right there. We both know the biology of it. I'm not talking about things that Franci would consider very personal, so back away from that, Mom. You know how children are conceived. We have one, Franci and me. I'm doing the best I can." He stopped. "What are you doing?"

"I'm packing. I want to meet my granddaughter."

"Mom, she's a little girl. Aiden wants to meet her, too. So does Luke. I imagine Shelby is . . . Okay, wait. I was afraid of this — you can't just rush in on her. We have to take this slow."

"I've already missed her first three years!" Maureen said.

"Me, too! Now slow down!"

"I'm not in the mood to slow down! I want to meet her as soon as possible!"

"Listen, if you want things to work out for all of us, you have to let me . . . Okay, hold on a second." Sean pulled his cell phone out of his pocket and dialed up Aiden.

Aiden picked up. "I have a woman at eight

centimeters, this better be good."

"I'm with Mom," Sean said. "She's packing. She wants to meet Rosie right this second. I'm passing the phone to her. Talk her down."

Maureen took the phone.

"Put it on speaker," Aiden said to his mother. Then, "Sean, can you hear me?"

"I'm here."

"Good. Let's keep as much of this out in the open as possible. Secrets breed trouble, as you're only too aware. Now, are you two fighting?"

"Not yet," Maureen said. "I want to meet my only grandchild."

"Are you in poor health?" Aiden asked.

"She played tennis this morning. She has a few more days in her, at least," Sean answered, irritation in every word.

"Mother, I want you to wait until you're invited. This small family has issues to sort through and a little girl who might be confused and upset by too much change."

"But I have rights, too, Aiden! As a grandparent!"

"Indeed you do, and your grandparent's rights will be respected. But the first thing to remember is that Sean and Francine are the parents and you are a *relative*. They are neither unfit nor negligent — you are in perfect health and can be patient. This isn't a deathbed request."

"But, Aiden, I —"

"You're smarter than this. Do you want your granddaughter's mother to love you? Don't alienate her. She's in charge. Let her know you accept that or, believe me, there will be trouble."

Maureen sat wearily on the edge of her bed. "Of course, you're right."

"You can go as far as Luke's house in Virgin River, Mom," Aiden said more gently. "But if you're very smart, you'll ask Luke if one of those nice little cabins is available, or it's going to be that much longer until you get the *next* grandchild. Do you remember what it was like when a mother-in-law visited?"

Maureen made a derisive sound. She remembered. It put quite a crimp in all the conjugal privacy. "Well, with five sons maybe your father's mum didn't visit often enough," she said quietly.

Aiden and Sean both laughed at that. "Space and patience, Mother," Aiden said sternly. "Or you're going to muck up the whole business."

"I just don't understand how all this could have —"

"Enough of that," Aiden said. "You know

as much about that end of it as you need to know. Sean, get her a glass of wine and check in with Luke. Mother, you throw too much of your mom around and I'm not going to be able to save you." Just then there was a loud sound in the background.

"Did someone just scream?" Maureen asked.

"More of an enthusiastic grunt," Aiden replied. "I'm signing off. Behave yourself!"

The line went dead and Sean and Maureen just looked at each other. Finally Maureen spoke. "Well, I think calling in the reinforcements is a bit over the top."

"For some reason, Aiden can get through to you like no one else can," Sean said. "I think because he's a doctor. The big show-off."

"He's always been the peacekeeper in the family," she said. "Now, let's go out to lunch, then we'll call Luke. I bet we can get a flight out today."

"You're going to wait until the timing is right to meet Rosie?" Sean asked.

"I give you my word, but don't test me by making it too long a wait. I'm a weak old woman," she said, walking back to the living room and grabbing her purse off the table by the front door.

"Yeah, right," Sean replied to her back.

"Let's eat something Italian," she said. "That'll hold us till we get to the outback."

He chuckled and walked out the patio doors as she followed. They'd only gone a few steps when she whacked him in the back of the head. "Ma!" he yelled, a hand going to his head as he whirled on her.

"Holy Mother Mary, you ought to be ashamed of yourself! Were you raised by *wolves?*"

NINE

Forty-eight hours after receiving a phone call from Sean and his mother, Luke rode his motorcycle up to Walt Booth's stable and parked it outside, right next to Shelby's Jeep. He walked in, pulling off his gloves as he went. When he found his wife in one of the stalls with a rake, he slapped his gloves into the palm of one hand to get her attention. When she turned to look at him, she smiled and shook her head.

"Where's your uncle Walt?" he asked.

"I think he has plans with Muriel. He called my cell phone around noon today and asked me if I could tend and feed the horses on my way home from school. His truck is gone."

Luke stuffed his gloves in his jacket pockets and pulled the rake out of her hand, leaning it up against the stall. "His truck better stay gone or he's going to see us naked."

She laughed at him. "Can't you wait for bed?"

"I could, but the house is full of people. Why'd you insist my mother had to stay with us in the house? She was perfectly willing to take a cabin."

"First of all, there's only one cabin empty and it's hunting season, and second, I'm not going to have your mother stay under a different roof when we have two perfectly good upstairs bedrooms. That would be rude. Besides, we're married — we're allowed to have sex in our own house, in our own bed."

He grabbed her perfect behind in two large hands and pulled her against him. "You're noisy when you come." Then he swooped down on her mouth and kissed her like a starving man. When his lips were somewhat satisfied he broke away slightly and said, "And before and after."

"No, I'm not," she argued.

"Uh-huh. Then you snore and talk in your sleep."

"Do not."

"And you missed a period."

"You noticed that? It's just a little late."

"Did you pee on a stick yet?" he asked her.

Shelby shook her head. "I think it's too

soon and I don't want to be disappointed. Besides, it might be coming — I feel weepy and my breasts are a little sore."

"You're pregnant," he said. "And I want to do you in the hay. You can scream until the horses stampede." He grinned at her. "Maybe I can get you more pregnant."

"Luke . . . I don't want to go home with hay in my hair . . ."

"I can take care of that problem," he said. He picked her up and carried her out of the stall, closing the door behind him, and into the tack room. He tugged her shirt out of her jeans, deftly opened her belt and popped the snap. Before sliding them down he lifted one of her legs and grabbed a boot heel, pulling it off. Then the other. And then the jeans and panties were in a heap on the tack room floor and Shelby was left mostly naked in her shirttails and socks.

"We should do this kind of thing more often," he said. "Adventure sex." He drew off his belt because of the large buckle and let it fall. Then he pulled her against him once more, kissing her deeply while his hand wandered to the V of her legs and gently, slowly, sweetly and deeply caressed her. He smiled against her lips. "Shelby, you're not very good at this hard-to-get game. You're ready for me."

"I know," she said in an exasperated tone. "And you're bursting," she added, her hands going to the snap on his jeans. In a second she had his jeans around his hips and him in her hand.

He laughed low in his throat. "My innocent little wife. Prepare to start screaming." He lifted her up; her legs went around his hips and he sat down on the bench with her straddling his lap. A little maneuvering was required to seat her on him just right, but the sensation took his breath away and caused her to gasp. She held him tightly and rocked on him, with him. "God," she said. "Luke, Luke, Luke." All he could do was groan and pump his hips, hanging on for her. And she talked and moaned and whimpered until it happened, and it happened quickly — she shattered and spasms tightened her around him. She bit his lip, then sucked it.

He enjoyed every second of her orgasm before he cashed in. It shook him, like it always did, leaving him with a loud groan, clasping her tightly to him. In a few minutes, he realized it was actually cold in the stable. He hadn't noticed that before, and neither had she.

She shivered and he tightened his embrace. "Feel better?" she asked him.

"You are so good to me," he said. "Do you feel better?"

"I was faking," she teased.

"You know what, baby? As long as you keep faking that good, I'm okay with it. And see? No straw in your hair." He grinned at her. "You are sooo loud."

All of a sudden her chin quivered and her eyes welled with tears. "Oh, Luke," she said softly. "What if I'm not a good mother?"

"Shelby, don't be ridiculous. You're the most loving person I've ever known. How could you *not* be a good mother?"

"I'm very selfish in some ways. And I like my sleep." She sniffed and hiccuped.

"Um, we're still attached here and you're crying about being a mother," he said. "I suggest we get dressed, finish up with the horses and go home. And while I build a nice warm fire, you better pee on a stick. Seriously."

Having his mother at Luke's, waiting so impatiently for her chance to meet Rosie, didn't exactly make for a relaxing atmosphere for Sean. Before springing a new grandma on the little tyke, Sean had some business with the first grandma. He phoned Vivian Duncan at the family practice clinic in which she worked and asked her if he could buy her lunch. She was completely surprised by the invitation. "Sure," she answered with some hesitation.

"Let me pick you up," he offered. "Just give me a time and some coordinates."

He found she was waiting outside the clinic for him at exactly twelve-thirty. He popped out of the car and held her door for her. "Thanks for doing this for me, Viv," he said. "I haven't said anything to Franci about us having lunch together, but I thought you and I should talk."

"I kind of thought your mother might be with you," she said. "Franci told me she's at Luke's, standing by."

"Standing by very impatiently," he admitted. "I wanted some time alone with you first. There's a little Italian place right around the corner. Will that work for you?"

"Fine. That's fine. Should I be dreading this conversation?" she asked with some trepidation.

"I hope not." He tried to sound reassuring, but wasn't sure he pulled it off. Then he laughed. "I should probably be the one dreading it." He reached across the front seat for her hand. "I have a few things to say, that's all."

To his great relief, she let it go during their short drive, not asking any more questions.

Sean settled her in the restaurant, at as quiet a table as he could find, and cajoled her into ordering something before they talked.

"All right, Sean, the suspense is killing me," Vivian said impatiently. "What's this about?"

"This is about me apologizing to you," he said quickly. "Franci told me that you weren't at all pleased with the way she handled the situation with her pregnancy. Now, I have to tell you — she did the only thing she could do. Cards on the table, Vivian — I didn't give her an opening to trust me with that kind of news. If she had insisted on having a baby, I would have insisted on marriage. And it would have been a terrible marriage. In short, she was right about me."

Vivian lifted a blond brow. "Was?" she queried.

He laughed, but his cheeks took on a pink stain. "I might've come a long way since then, but I didn't come fast and I'm not all the way there. The truth is, I had to suffer without Franci for a long time before I realized I needed her in my life. And this whole business of suddenly being a father . . . It's going to take me some time, but I'm working on it. I want you to know, I'm doing my best." He took a breath. "You should have gotten in touch with me and told me. Then I could do my learning without a three-and-a-half-year-old watching."

Vivian was shocked and her expression reflected it. Was he taking her to task? She let out the breath she was holding. "I thought about it," she admitted. "At the end of the day, I couldn't betray my daughter's wishes."

"Since we can't go back, let's let each other off the hook for any imperfections. How about that?" he suggested.

Vivian was quiet for a long moment, during which time the waitress brought iced tea for both of them. She measured her words carefully before she spoke. "Listen to me, Sean — I want my daughter to be happy, but Rosie is the beat of my heart. When Franci told me she was having a baby and having her alone, the first thing I felt was resentment — I was barely fifty! I still feel I have a lot of life left to live! And I'd already raised a child alone, so I knew firsthand how hard it would be for her. Franci was going to need a lot from me, and I didn't really have a lot to give. But I held that baby and, within seconds, I felt she was as much mine as my daughter's. If you think for one second I'm going to be patient with you while you try to figure out if you have what it takes to be a good father, you're wrong. Dead wrong."

Sean briefly wondered if in an earlier life he had pissed off a bunch of tough old goddesses; he was surrounded by strong, opinionated women. "I completely understand. I have a lot to learn about her. About Rosie."

"I don't care what happens between you and Francine — she's all grown up and can shoulder disappointment. But you'd better not let down my granddaughter, Sean."

"I know," he said. "You're going to have a lot of backup in that department. My mother's on the job, beating me with the guilt stick every chance she gets, and no one does guilt like an Irish Catholic mother. Are you going to give me a chance?"

"Yes," she said, relaxing back in her chair. "Every chance. Don't screw it up."

"I'm doing everything I can, for both of them. I'm trying."

"Well," she said, taking a calming breath. "At least you're honest."

He sipped from his glass of iced tea. "Hm. Well, honesty didn't buy me as much sympathy as I thought it would."

"And you're surprised about that? Listen, when the heart of a small child is at stake,

241

there's not a lot of wiggle room. I suggest you get this right the first time."

He smiled in spite of himself. He shook his head and laughed. "I think you're going to like my mother," he said.

Aiden had jarred Maureen into remembering what it was like when one's mother visited, and it didn't matter if it was the maternal or paternal mother. There was a definite lack of privacy for the newly married couple, but the upside could be domestic assistance, and Shelby needed some of that. Although Shelby and Luke had been together quite a while, they hadn't been married a whole month yet — and the bedroom Maureen was using was filled with wedding gifts that had yet to be put away. Shelby was a new college student and Luke worked hard on his property, his cabins and house, all day, seven days a week. And there was Art, who was very attached to Maureen and often spent his time with her.

So Maureen busied herself by making sure she spent quality time with Art, often fishing with him, and trying to tidy the house and put away the wedding gifts. She made sure that Shelby and Luke ended their busy days to find dinner prepared, clean and folded laundry on their bed and the house polished and smelling good. That much she had learned from her own mother and mother-in-law.

As for daughters-in-law, Maureen didn't have much experience with them. Sean had been painfully accurate in describing Aiden's and Luke's attempts at marriage as train wrecks. She'd go a step further and label their wives difficult, high maintenance and selfish. Shelby was none of that, and although she hadn't seen Franci in years, Maureen remembered her as good-natured and sweet. However, Shelby had been extremely moody just lately and Maureen wondered if her mere presence had become an irritant. Also, she had not yet been invited to meet Rosie; she wasn't sure if that was Sean's doing or Franci's. She suspected Sean; he'd grown very protective of his new-found daughter. And Sean was unusually quiet. Something weighed on the mind of her most entertaining son. She suspected it had a lot to do with his being down to four weeks and a few days of leave left with which to get his entire future settled.

As for Maureen, she hadn't been this lonely since her husband's death twelve years ago, when she found herself so isolated in a dark Illinois winter. That's what had motivated her to move to Phoenix where she could work, make friends, be outdoors year-round and live somewhere her boys might enjoy visiting her.

But playing the waiting game at Luke's while everyone around her was busy with work, school or chores was wearing on her last nerve. Four days had passed with no reprieve. Sean helped Luke until mid-afternoon when he was allowed to fetch Rosie from day care and take her home. Then he had dinner with Franci and Rosie, and then he was back at Luke's before ten. Home, without much to say, although he had kept his word and taken pictures every day.

On her fifth day in Virgin River, Maureen finally got her break. The next day was Saturday and she was invited to accompany Rosie and Sean to Beale Air Force Base. Sean would introduce Rosie to both her grandmother and his plane, at least one of which Rosie had expressed great interest in.

"Will Franci come along?" Maureen asked.

"Franci is pulling a twenty-four-hour shift in Redding with a medical airlift group and Rosie stays with Franci's mother. Since Franci leaves at about 5:00 a.m. to make the drive over the mountains, I'll be picking Rosie up at Vivian's first thing tomorrow morning and returning her tomorrow night. So, we have her all to ourselves."

"What will I say to her?" Maureen wondered out loud.

"Tell her you're happy to meet her. Then ask a question or two — like what color her bedroom is, what she likes to wear for dress up or what she likes to cook in her play kitchen. That'll get you two talking in no time. And rest up — she's exhausting!"

Sean could see that the hardest thing for Maureen was trying to keep her enthusiasm in check enough so she didn't completely overwhelm Rosie. He shouldn't have worried — Rosie took the edge off things right away. "You have wed hair like me!" she exclaimed. From that point on, the two redheads chattered like a couple of magpies all the way to Beale — more than a three-hour drive. They took along books and a couple of Rosie's favorite toys — her toy computer helped her practice letters, numbers and writing. Maureen sat in the backseat with Rosie and they played and read the whole drive while Sean chauffeured. Franci called his cell twice to check on them before he even made it to Beale.

An air force squadron is a little like a small town. The men who work and fly together get real tight, and Sean had a close working relationship with their squadron commander, Lieutenant Colonel Jacob Sorrell. That came in real handy, since Sean had to phone and tell Jake the circumstances that would bring him to Beale during his leave — he wanted to give his mother and *daughter* a tour of the base and the airplane, the U-2. Given the high security, he had to have special permission and an escort, even though it was basically Sean's ride.

"Daughter?" Jake had asked during their phone conversation. "Our most notorious bachelor has a daughter?"

"That's right," he said, and for the first time it struck him how lucky he was that little accident had happened with a woman he happened to have had a serious relationship with. Then he thought of something that struck him damn hard. What if that accident had happened with someone he hardly knew — like Cindy? "I'll explain more about that later, but obviously I just learned about her and the one thing she's asked of me is to see my plane. And my mother happens to be in town also."

"Good," Jake had said. "Your mother can keep an eye on your daughter while you and I steal a half hour for a conversation."

"On Saturday?" Sean asked.

"I'll be in the office when you're done with your tour."

Sean drove his mom and Rosie around the base and showed them the hangar and an airplane that happened to be in for maintenance. He laughed when Rosie put both her little hands over her cheeks and gasped at the size of the U-2. He took a picture of her in the cockpit without getting any of the instrument panel in the photo. In fact, he'd have Jake download the pictures, delete them from his camera and send them to Franci's e-mail address when he was satisfied there wasn't the slightest security breach. It wasn't as though the U-2 was a secret — the plane sat on static display during air shows. But this was a working plane.

He also showed her the KC-135 tankers that refueled the jets in the air, a batch of C-130s and a staggeringly huge C-5. By three o'clock, Rosie was completely exhausted and Maureen was looking a little worn, as well. He took them to the squadron's waiting area — not very fancy — and asked them to read for twenty or thirty minutes. "I won't be long. We can have dinner on the way home. I'm sure Rosie will nap in the car after I fill her belly."

Jake Sorrell stood from his desk and came

around to shake Sean's hand. "I'm glad you had an excuse to come in from leave, Sean. I thought about calling you . . ."

"What's up?" Sean asked, before sitting down.

"What's up is four years. You only got on the waiting list for an open slot at Air Command and Staff College when you pinned on major and you've been flying under the radar. You know you're maxed out here. It's time for you to be reassigned. Have you thought about that?"

Sean looked down and shook his head. "Think there's any way I can get this put off a few months? I just found my daughter, man. She and her mother live close to Beale."

"I'd sure like to hear about that, if it's something you can talk about."

"I can guess what people might think, but it's not sleazy at all. Franci and I were a couple." Then he proceeded to explain how he'd given the woman plenty of good reasons to think she was better off going it alone. He didn't even realize how differently he was seeing the situation now. In less than a week he'd gone from *it's all her fault* to *I made her do it*. "I need some time to get this straightened out a little bit, Jake. Franci's not jumping into anything with me

248

and I can't just run out on Rosie the minute I find her. It could screw the kid up for life."

"Any chance you can put things together with the mother?"

Sean gave him a contrite expression. "The woman I told I'd never get married or have children with four years ago? She might be slightly wary."

Jake, father of four, sat back in his chair. "Smooth."

"I need time, Jake."

"You have to look at your options," he said. "You're overdue."

"I did look at my options, but they were all different before I knew I had a child. I figured if I didn't get Air Command and Staff the first try, I'd go to Iraq or Saudi in the U-2 and earn my slot to ACSC. I'm not real anxious to do it that way now."

Sean was an Air Force Academy grad, a former fighter pilot, a distinguished graduate of several training programs — and all of that added up to not only a command position in the not-too-distant future but, if he hung in there, the rank of general. From the age of eighteen, that had been his plan — to end his career running the world from the Pentagon. Of course, there were steps — assignments, career-building training programs like Air Command and Staff College, remote tours, et cetera.

"Well, I suggest you take another look at the options," Jake said. "Your leave is approved through November, but if you don't put in for an assignment somewhere, orders are going to be cut without any input from you. You know what's out there — U-2 overseas accompanied or remote, change of mission to U-2 in weather, a staff job somewhere, or you might get lucky and slip into an open slot at Air Command and Staff . . ." Jake leaned forward, folding his hands on top of his desk. "The hard part about being a family man in the military — we serve where we're needed. The air force gives you a chance to put together an assignment if you can, but you know what's expected of you, and the air force will take its pound of flesh."

Sean was quiet for a long moment. Finally he said, "They've been right here all along and I didn't know it until last week."

"I'm sorry about that but, Jesus, Sean, you do your next assignment right and you've got stars in your pockets. But you can't sit here any longer. Get in touch with the flesh peddlers who make assignments at the Military Personnel Center and find out what they're trying to fill. Get the jump on 'em before they send you remote. All I can do is give you a heads-up, Sean."

"Yeah," he said.

Jake stood. "Listen, be honest with the woman. Tell her the situation, ask for her input. Maybe if she feels involved in the decision . . ."

"Yeah, right," Sean said. But he was thinking, She barely got her life together the way she wants it and here I come, showing up unannounced, and before I can even get checked out on spending the night, the air force is ready to ship me out. "She'll probably think I did this on purpose."

"You knew this was coming, Major. No one sits in the same assignment for this long. You should have come up with a better plan."

Sean stood. "Until a week ago, I thought I had a plan. I was going to do a couple of years of hard time in the sandbox and ACSC, and then take your job right out from under you. I just wanted to fly, then take command of a flying squadron. Until now, there wasn't anything to keep me in one place."

Under any other circumstances, Sean would be really grateful for that kind of a heads-up from his boss. It was real tough to get into Air Command and Staff in a residence program; making the waiting list alone was a good showing. He had an itch to get on the phone to MPC, but no one would be at the office on a Saturday night, so instead he took his mom and Rosie to Denny's for dinner, and afterward they headed back to Eureka.

Once again the girls settled in the backseat and, while there was still light, they looked at books together. When the sun lowered in the sky and Rosie had fallen asleep, Sean called Franci's cell. "Reporting in," he said, when she answered. "She had mac and cheese and fish sticks for dinner and a little bit of salad. A glass of milk, too. And she loved the planes."

"Did she have a good time?" Franci asked. "Did she mind her manners?"

"She was perfect and she had a blast. She's asleep in the backseat, and yes, she has her belt on. I'm not supposed to talk and drive in this state, so I'm going to sign off. Want me to check in when she's home?"

"Yes. And Sean? Is Maureen very angry with me?"

"Near as I can tell, she's not even mad at me anymore," he said with a laugh. "Am I invited to dinner tomorrow?"

"Yes. I'm going to need a nap to sleep off my twenty-four-hour shift. Why don't you entertain Rosie and . . . and why don't you cook."

"Be happy to," he said. "Any special requests?"

"Anything, but remember the food groups — Rosie's growing."

"How about Stroganoff, fat noodles, peas and salad? I'm good at Stroganoff. I'll make it with chicken instead of beef — for Rose. She's partial to chicken."

"That would be awesome," she said.

"You got it. And some nice snacks and a good white wine."

When they were back at Vivian's, he parked and lifted Rosie out of the backseat. He asked his mother to carry Rosie's books and toys to the house while he helped get his daughter in her pajamas.

Rosie had her own room at Viv's house, as well. This room was all little girl, too, but was yellow in color. She had her arms locked around his neck so tight, he'd have to peel her off. "We're home, shortcake. Let's find your jammies." She squirmed and murmured, not letting go of his neck. He laughed at her and said, "I can't help you change clothes if you don't let go."

With her face buried in his neck, she asked, "Are you still my daddy?"

Sean felt his heart catch. All at once he

was filled up with so much emotion he was sure he wouldn't be able to swallow if he tried. And he suddenly couldn't focus his vision. He turned his head and kissed her cheek. "I'll always be your daddy, pumpkin."

"You're a silly daddy," she said.

"You're a silly Wide Iwish Rose. I'm so glad I found you."

TEN

While Sean was helping Rosie into her pajamas, Maureen was handing toys over to Viv. The two women had never met before today and had spent a whole ten minutes together in the entirety of their acquaintance, and that was when Maureen and Sean had picked up Rosie earlier in the day. "I want to thank you," Maureen said. "Rosie is an incredible, brilliant, wonderful child and I bet some of that had to do with what a fantastic grandmother you are."

Viv put a hand on Maureen's forearm. "I have things to tell you," she said quietly. "Important things about Rosie — what she likes, what she hates, momentous moments in her little life . . . about her temper, her giggles, her ear infections and her love for animals. And also, I want you to know that I argued hard for Franci to find Sean and let him know about his daughter. Maureen, there is only so much we, as mothers, can do when our adult children have relationship issues. In fact, in most cases, the more we do, the worse it's bound to get."

Maureen laughed ruefully and nodded in agreement. "Oh, I know. I have five sons. Do you think they talk to me about the women in their lives? Even though I might be able to answer the hard questions? It's true what they say about sons and daughters — your daughter is your daughter all her life, but your son . . ."

". . . is your son till he takes a wife." Viv gave a short nod. "We've both been wives. We'd probably both agree it's all right that way."

Again Maureen laughed. "I want to stay on and dominate Rosie's time. Not just to get to know her, but for her to get to know me. But I've been with Luke and Shelby for almost a week now and they need their house back. In fact, Sean needs the freedom to work things out with Franci and Rosie! I don't want to be in the way of that! No matter what's to come with them, I want my granddaughter to have a father and I want to be part of her life."

"You will be — please don't worry about that. I have an idea. I'm sure the three of them will want to spend tomorrow afternoon and evening together as they have the past week, but Sean can drop you here, with me. We can look through photo albums, go to an afternoon movie, have a nice dinner out, and I'll be happy to drive you to Virgin River tomorrow evening so Sean and Franci don't have to work their schedule around either one of us."

"Really?" Maureen asked. "Really?"

"I'd enjoy it so much. Your position right now must be tough."

"You have *no* idea." Maureen laughed. Then she dropped her voice to a whisper. "My new daughter-in-law is certainly pregnant and I'm not sure she even realizes it herself yet! She is moody, nauseous, cries at the drop of a hat, and they want a baby. Vivian, I have to get out of there so they can be alone together for this news. I remember when I was barely pregnant with Aiden and my mother-in-law just wouldn't leave. I thought about killing her in her sleep!"

Viv laughed. "I have a spare room if you think your life's in danger."

"I can't stay much longer or it will be, though I do try to be helpful . . ."

"I know — and sometimes the more helpful you are, the worse it gets."

"You *do* know!"

"I didn't have five, but I've been there for

257

Franci for thirty years. Come over tomorrow and spend the day. Maybe we can get a game plan, you and me. For example, you can always come for a visit and stay here. That way you'd have lots of time to spend with Rosie and you'd be able to give both those boys their space with their women. As for me? I'd get a companion!"

"You don't even *know* me! Are you so sure I wouldn't be a burden? I could be a slovenly houseguest!"

Viv tilted her head and smiled. "I work full-time as a physician's assistant for a small family practice in town. More than full-time, some days. I'm betting you cook like a dream."

"Ohhh, what are you getting yourself into?" Maureen asked.

"I lived with my pregnant daughter and then Franci and a baby! Do you intend to be more trouble than that?"

The two of them were laughing and holding on to each other when Sean came out of Rosie's bedroom. He stopped in his tracks, looked at them and said, "Uh-oh."

After hearing from Sean, Francine was kicked back in a recliner at the station on Saturday night. Also in the same room were two flight crews — another nurse, a couple of paramedics, two pilots and two copilots. They shared the station with other emergency first responders — two fire-engine crews, two paramedic ground crews and a staffed ambulance crew. She'd been on a couple of runs during the day, routine hospital transports that were serious but not critical — one cardiac patient in need of bypass surgery and one expectant mother of twins in early labor.

She was just thinking about grabbing some sleep in case the night proved busy when her cell phone chimed and she recognized the number. T.J. on a Saturday night. She jumped out of her recliner and left the rec room to take the call so as not to bother the people watching TV. "Hello," she said as she stepped into the next room, which was the kitchen. "How are you?"

"A little disappointed," he said. "It's been a week, Francine. I thought by now you'd have something to say to me."

She shook her head. "Say to you? I'm completely confused. I've given you almost daily updates. Sean is trying to get to know Rosie. His mother is in town and met Rosie for the first time today. I heard from him fifteen minutes ago that Rosie had a fun day, seemed to get along fine with the new grandma, and —"

"What about him?" T.J. asked.

She laughed a little. "What about him?" she countered. "I don't know what you mean."

"Yes, you do. Think, Francine. Give the guy visiting privileges that don't interfere with your personal and professional life. Tell him you're committed, that he can't be hanging around."

"I've pretty much done that," she said. "He's asked if he can pick Rosie up in the afternoon from day care, bring her home for me, have dinner with her. He's doing all this because he's on leave right now, but he's not on leave forever, and it's not only good for Rosie, it helps me out."

"And I haven't seen you at all," T.J. said.

"I only see you about once a week, anyway, and that's if you're not in Cabo or Alaska or out on the research boat. We're busy people with demanding work schedules and kids. In fact, I've never had so many calls from you during the week! Does this whole situation *threaten* you?"

"It *concerns* me," he said. "I thought a week would be enough to get things lined up with this guy so we could have our lives back as they were."

"Well, that makes you a lot more optimistic than I was," she said. "Getting to know a small child you didn't even realize you had takes time and patience, and I'm certainly not going to toss Rosie at him and expect him to sink or swim! She's my baby, for God's sake!"

"Are you purposely — ?"

God bless that siren! It went off, followed by the official and somewhat mechanical voice giving the coordinates of a motor vehicle accident on Highway 5 with critical injuries, dispatching a helicopter, one paramedic ground unit and two ambulances — one of which came from a different service. Must be a bad one.

T.J. would have heard the blast. "Gotta run!" she said, signing off.

She ran for her helicopter with the rest of the crew and didn't think about him again before morning.

Sunday morning in Virgin River found Ellie Baldwin, the Presbyterian church secretary, getting herself and her kids ready for the church service.

Ellie's life had changed so much in just a few months that she barely recognized herself. To start with, she'd grown up poor. Not kind of poor, dirt poor. She'd lived with her grandmother in two rooms and they'd shared a pull-out sofa bed her entire life.

They had managed on Social Security checks and food stamps. Then she had two children without the benefit of marriage or support of any kind. Her grandmother kept them while Ellie worked day and night to keep body and soul together. She took any kind of work. After her grandmother died Ellie even held a job as a stripper for a short time. It paid the bills and put food on the table.

Now at the ripe old age of twenty-five she lived more comfortably than she ever had, and so did her kids, four-year-old Trevor and eight-year-old Danielle. Ellie rented a lovely, but tiny, room over the Fitches' garage. For the time being, her kids stayed downstairs in the big house with Jo Ellen Fitch and her husband, Nick. Ellie got the kids up in the morning and put them to bed at night. She had a wonderful friendship with Jo and Nick, and if life went on like this forever, she wouldn't dare complain. But just when she thought it couldn't get any better, she fell in love with Noah Kincaid, the local minister, an amazing and wonderful man.

Noah, now her fiancé, had been in search of a house where they could live like a real family. It was only right, she knew. As it was, he was creeping into her rented room more nights than not, and this really wasn't the best behavior for the town pastor. Noah didn't fret over that and, this being Virgin River, Ellie assumed everyone knew everything; they probably just didn't say anything in front of them.

Right before the church service this Sunday morning, Noah whispered that he had a house for her to look at. "It's not much," he said, "but it's in our budget and it might be redeemable. I just want us married and all under one roof."

Bless his little heart, Ellie thought with a flood of warmth. When a girl is looking for a passionate man, common sense would say that she doesn't go looking for him in a church. But what she had learned from Noah was that men with passion and commitment don't limit themselves to one single agenda — their passion, commitment, honor and courage will permeate all the facets of their lives.

Noah loved her passionately and he made her whole; he made her life full.

Their service that morning showcased the Virgin River Presbyterian church choir's very first performance, accompanied by Ellie and her rusty piano skills, and it was just short of horrid. But in this town people were so supportive of one another, they actually stood and clapped. It made her flush, but she was just happy to be through it. Then after some coffee and cookies in the church basement, Noah spirited her away. He said it was best to send the kids home with Jo and Nick so they could view this potential house alone.

It wasn't far from the church — just on the edge of town, past the established neighborhood. They were in Noah's old truck and he pulled off to the side of the road where the weeds had gotten tall and the shrubbery overgrown. He turned toward her. "Ellie, if this isn't right, we'll just keep looking. Be warned, it needs a *lot* of work. Here's what's good about it — it's large, even if it is in disrepair. It has a big piece of land under it, not a small yard. It's not in the middle of town, but it's only a half mile away. It has a huge kitchen . . ." He paused and cleared his throat. "A big kitchen without a single working appliance, but that's just fix up. And —"

"Noah, how did you come across this house?" she asked.

"Oh, Buck Anderson knew someone who knew someone who'd been renting the place out for years but only because he couldn't get rid of it. He said if I was clever, it could go cheap. I don't know if I'm clever with negotiating a price, but I'm okay with a hammer. And we might not be as settled as we should be, but we get by thanks to Jo and Nick. I saw some promise in it and thought I'd show you before I write it off."

"Good idea, Noah. Because I *am* clever with money, you lucky dog. I've had to be."

He grinned his handsome grin. "I haven't once complained about your assets, have I?"

She leaned over and kissed his cheek. "In the beginning, you did nothing but complain." She patted the other cheek. "You're coming along very well, though. Now, come on — the suspense is killing me."

"I just hope seeing it doesn't do any permanent damage to your opinion of me." He put the truck in gear and took them down a short overgrown driveway to a house that had the washed-out, gray appearance of worn paint. It was surrounded by a totally neglected yard that was dominated by weeds, out of control bushes, rotted-out flower beds, untrimmed trees, cracked sidewalk and copious litter. There was no telling the age; it could be older or younger than it looked. It was a wreck.

It was a two story and it had a porch that stretched the length of the front of the house and a front door that was probably worth as much as the whole structure. Ellie was surprised it hadn't been ripped off and stolen — it was a stained and polished dark wood with a beveled-glass window. It was a breathtaking door on a nightmare of a house.

Wordlessly, Ellie got out of the truck and went to the house. She got the heel of her shoe stuck in a rotting board on the porch, but she gamely pulled it out and kept going.

The inside opened up into a very large living room that was adjoined by an equally large dining room. Both rooms had filthy fireplaces, suggesting the house was old and had been constructed before central heating. Also, it was built before the days of family rooms and foyers. She walked right into the middle of everything. It was very large and the ceilings were high. The two rooms were divided by an ornate wooden arch that had been sloppily covered with many layers of white paint. In fact, the whole house had been painted in a cheap coat of renter's white that hadn't held up well.

The staircase to the second floor was right between the two rooms inside the front door and, again, cheap paint had been used to cover a banister that was undoubtedly real wood. The staircase led up to the second floor and an open balcony that ran along a hall leading to the bedrooms. This old style had gone out of fashion many years ago — it reminded Ellie of the saloon in the *Gunsmoke* series. She could almost see Miss Kitty poised at the top of the staircase.

She walked through the trash-strewn rooms toward the back of the house. Behind the living room and dining room she found a large kitchen and a small bedroom. "There are three bedrooms upstairs," Noah said. "One's pretty big and two are average. There aren't any big closets and only one bathroom in the house — it must have been built in the days of one-bathroom homes. But there's a back porch that's wide and deep and can be closed in. And it might even be possible to put a half bath downstairs. And the bonus is an unfinished basement. Well . . . a cellar. But there are so many possibilities for that."

Ellie ignored him, heading into the kitchen. It was the largest kitchen she'd ever been in, and Jo Fitch had a very big kitchen. The appliances looked not only useless but maybe dangerous. However, there were many cupboards and a big bay window. She could envision a large oval table sitting right in that nook; she could imagine friends coming for dinner and children doing homework there while she cooked. Ellie had never dared have such visions before.

Through the bay window Ellie could see the side yard, deep and surrounded by trees and overgrown brush; outside the window over the kitchen sink was the porch, which, as Noah said, could be enclosed to make another room. Beyond that a long, wide backyard went right up to the forest. She spotted blackberry bushes, all gnarled and thorny. She could almost taste the jam . . .

She put the fingers of both hands over her mouth and her eyes welled with tears, which quickly spilled down her cheeks.

"Aw, baby, don't cry," Noah begged, pulling her into his arms. "It was just an idea, but we'll look at lots of houses. I just got hooked on the size of the house and lot, and my imagination might've gotten a little —"

She turned in his arms. "It's the most beautiful thing I've ever seen," she whispered. "Noah, it's wonderful. I mean, it needs love, but isn't it perfect? Is it stable? Will we fall through the floor if we go upstairs?"

He was shocked silent for a moment. "Are you *serious?*"

"About the second floor?" she asked with a hiccup of emotion.

"I've been upstairs," he said, shaking the confusion out of his head. "You actually *like* it?"

"It would be so wonderful to fix it up and make it ours, wouldn't it? Did you see all the terrible paint in this place? I bet if I stripped the paint off the arch that divides the rooms and off the staircase and banister we'd find beautiful wood. And the yard? I can make that yard look like Jo Ellen's yard! Give me a year and I can turn it around." She sniffed, took a breath and said, "Thank God it's almost winter — I don't think I could face both house and yard at once, but by spring . . ."

"Ellie?" he asked, stunned. "You *like* it?"

"Noah, whoever owns this house lost interest in it years ago. You can't think of renting it and fixing it at the same time — that's where the owner lost control of it. My gramma and I did more with our two rooms than was done here, and we had nothing. Either we make a commitment to it or forget it. But first we have to have the plumbing and wiring and structure checked. Does it cost the moon to do that? Because we should check that before we even think of putting down good money."

Noah grabbed her suddenly and pulled her against him. "Ellie," he whispered, burying his face in her neck. "I didn't realize how much I hoped you'd see the potential in this old thing. It's a horrible mess — no woman in her right mind would —"

She laughed and sniffed at the same time. "Lucky for you, you got a woman with no right mind. Noah, be honest now, are there things you like about this old house besides the price?"

"The same things you like," he said. "The big rooms, the big yard, the wide porches, the real wood. I can get Paul Haggerty to check it out for structural competence and the other stuff before we get emotionally moved in. We can try to sell the RV — that'll give us some fix-up money."

"Noah, I want to work on it. Really — I'm good at this stuff. It might take a while if I'm needed at the church and helping the kids with all their school stuff, but I know how to make something good out of a falling down piece of —" She stopped herself and smiled. She'd been trying to stop cursing in deference to her fiancé the preacher. So she whispered, "Really is a piece of shit, isn't she?"

He laughed loudly. "Totally," he agreed. "But she has so much promise."

"All kinds of promise."

"Ellie, I've been wanting to ask a question. It's not a real big issue with me, but I still should ask. You can say no and it won't make a difference, but just in case —"

"For God's sake, Noah! Spit it out."

He took a breath. "How do you feel about more children?"

"Why?" she asked.

He struggled for a moment. "Well . . . because if you wanted more . . . I could be talked into it . . ."

She punched him in the stomach. "Never lie to me like that. Do you want a baby of your own, Noah?"

"I'm nuts about Trevor and Danielle and I want to adopt them if we can work that out, and I think we can, but, yeah — if I could have one with my receding hairline and bowed legs —"

She laughed and ran her fingers into his overlong, curly dark hair. There was a strand or two of silver; Noah was thirty-five. "Oh, what I'd give to have a little girl with your dark curls," she said. "And your legs are better than mine."

"No one's legs are better than yours," he said. "Did you ever think about another one?"

"I'll think about that. Not right away, Noah. I have house problems and adoption problems to deal with first."

"Not to mention a wedding. Ellie, we need to get married. I just can't keep sneaking into your room . . ."

"Afraid God disapproves?" she teased.

"I'm pretty sure God masterminded it, frankly. But I'm uncomfortable with the whole subterfuge. I want us settled in, no matter where we spend our nights. We gotta get this done, baby. Let's get a move on."

"Sure. Fine. But maybe I should be the one to negotiate with the seller here, huh? You lean toward the nice side."

"Isn't that a good thing?" he asked.

"In church and school and bowling," she said. She gave him a peck on the lips. "Not in politics or real estate."

He smiled at her. "Sometimes you really turn me on."

The only thing that surprised Sean more than how easily it had been to fall into a routine with Rosie was how readily she had seemed to take to him. The other thing that shocked him was how much he looked forward to spending time with her.

On Sunday at noon he dropped Maureen at Viv's house only to find Rosie had already gone down the block to her own house. Once there, he found Franci lying on her couch. She wore a loose and comfy sweat suit and looked fresh from the shower.

"Long night?" he asked her.

"I thought we were going to get off easy," she said. "It was real quiet. Then we had one run after another until eight this morning. I'm really going to need a nap."

"You got it. I'll take Rosie to the park and on some errands, and when we get back here we'll be real quiet. You want me to wake you at any special time?"

"I'll get myself up. Sure you don't mind making dinner?"

"Not at all — it's gotta be my turn." He smiled at her. "Where's the tyke?"

"Cooking," she said, inclining her head toward Rosie's bedroom. "Maybe she'll help with dinner."

"Oh, I'm sure she will," he said with a laugh.

Just then, they heard a brief shuffle down the hall, the clicking of plastic high heels, the rustle of a princess dress, a soft gasp and then Rosie ran toward him, her little feet clapping along the floor. She yelled, "Daddy!" and threw herself into Sean's arms.

Franci and Sean both looked at each other, shock evident on their faces. Seven days and it was done — he was *Daddy*. He was too stunned to even allow himself the pleasure that title could bring, and he could see from Franci's face the chasm had been crossed and there was no going back. Everyone was assigned their roles and dare not shirk from them.

It was at once the most complicated yet simplest transition imaginable. The problem was that Sean and Franci had not yet negotiated their unified lifestyle or defined their positions. They were still nibbling around the edges of what kind of relationship they were going to have. Oh, Sean had suggested marriage right away, the moment he realized they had a child together, but that really wouldn't win him any points. He'd done so only because of Rosie; if not for Rosie, he would have suggested he and Franci resume their old relationship, with marriage possible down the line, whereas four years ago he hadn't been willing to consider it. As progress went, it was slight.

They were right where they started, with one additional player, and he held her in his arms. He turned his gaze from Franci and buried his face in Rosie's sweet-smelling neck. "What are you cooking, short stuff?"

"Chicken," she said, and giggled from his tickle.

"And broccoli?" he asked with a laugh. She nodded vigorously and he looked at

Franci. "Don't you feed this kid anything but chicken and broccoli?"

"Lots of things," she said, getting up from the couch. "Are you good to go? Because I should get that nap or I'll be useless tonight."

"Go," he said. "We're going to do stuff."

"Now remember, always —"

"Wear seat belts, make frequent bathroom stops, never let her out of my sight," he finished for her.

"And never —"

"Send her into the ladies' room. I will take her into the men's room with me, if necessary, make sure it's clean and private and, when possible, use the handicapped facility for privacy. And plenty of vegetables and nothing that tastes *fun*."

"You don't have to be a wise a—"

He grinned.

But inside he wasn't grinning. He was thinking of all the things he really had to discuss with Franci. It had been his plan to talk to her over the next several weeks about what kind of future the three of them might have, a little piece of it at a time. The meeting with his boss, Jake, upped the urgency.

His cell phone chimed with a text and he lifted it out of his pocket, glanced at it and put it back. When he looked up, Franci was staring him down. "Haven't you taken care of that yet?" she asked.

"I meant to, but I've been busy," he said. "By the way, have you taken care of *him* yet?"

"We should talk about this later," she said.

"We should," he agreed. He shifted Rose onto a hip and walked toward Franci. He leaned down and kissed her forehead. "Get some rest, Franci. Being tired makes you cranky."

"I'd slug you if that weren't true." Then she went to her room. Harry ran after her, scratched at the door and was let in to nap with her.

"Well, what do you say, sport. Wanna get some warm outside clothes on so we can go play and shop?"

"I'll wear dis," she said, touching her worn-out taffeta.

"You can't wear that to the park and the store — it's getting cold out."

"I'll wear *dis!*"

Sean furrowed his brow, narrowed his eyes and pursed his lips just the way his father had done and was surprised to find this all came quite naturally. He lowered his voice a notch. "Fine, then we'll stay home and read and nap." He lifted one brow.

She stared him down for a long moment.

Then she said, "Oh-*kay!*" But she didn't say it happily.

Sean had never spent much time alone with children. When he socialized with friends who had kids, he fit in just fine — he could toss the ball, throw a little one up in the air, make goo-goo faces, tickle and tease. But he'd never had any actual responsibility for a child before he met Rosie.

This was their first full-day outing alone and Sean learned something he had never before known. Women paid even more attention to him with a child in tow than they had before! He wasn't bad looking, had an adorable daughter and no wedding band. Women approached him in the mall, in Target, at the playground, remarking on his beautiful child, making small talk. They smiled hugely while they said, "Well, having a daddy-daughter day?" Or, "If you live around here, we could get the kids together for a play-date sometime." He was shocked and astounded.

When he was checking out of the grocery with his dinner makings, the checker said, "I'm about to go on a coffee break, if you feel like a cup of coffee. Maybe your daughter would like some ice cream?"

Sean immediately said, "Thanks, but I

have to get going. My wife is waiting."

And Rosie said, "Who's your wife, Daddy?"

The checkout girl nearly threw the groceries into the bag as she shot daggers at him with her eyes. He felt fortunate she didn't bean him in the head with the produce. On the way to the car he said to Rosie, "We're going to have to get our story straight, kiddo. I don't know if you're helping or hurting the situation."

"Daddy? Daddy, I know the baby is in the mommy's tummy and the baby comes out of the mommy's tummy, but, Daddy? How do that baby get in the mommy's tummy?"

He stopped dead in his tracks in the parking lot, his daughter in the rider seat of the shopping cart, his bagged groceries in the cart, and stared at her dumbly. Time stopped. He tried to channel Franci, who seemed to do all this parent stuff with such ease, but nothing came.

"Daddy?" she asked.

He smiled with what he hoped was confidence, pinched her little chin and said, "After you have Stroganoff and peas tonight, would you like chocolate or vanilla ice cream?"

"Chocolate!" she yelled.

"Whipped cream and a cherry?"

"Whip cream and a cherry!" she yelled.

"That's what I thought. No chicken and broccoli for you tonight. No, sir. You're having fun food! Daddy's Stroganoff and ice cream!"

"Yay!" she yelled.

Later that evening, while Rosie was singing in the tub, Sean and Franci did dishes together and talked about Sean's day. "Here's a shocker, Franci — Rosie is a babe magnet." He grinned at her. "I'm a catch. You can't believe the number of women who almost propositioned me today."

"While you're with my *daughter*?" she asked, appalled.

"Well, nothing racy. Just a cup of coffee or a kid's playdate. Who'd guess, huh?"

"What a comfort that is," she grumbled.

"Should Rosie be alone in the tub?" he asked.

She smiled at him, happy that he was over-protective. "The bathroom is ten steps away and as long as you can hear her singing, she's not underwater."

So Sean told her about the question Rosie had posed while they were in the parking lot of the grocery. Franci had to lean against the counter, laughing so hard she was doubled over, yet trying to keep quiet lest Rosie come running soaking wet to the kitchen to see who would dare have fun without her.

"Yeah, funny," Sean said. "What would you have said?"

She wiped her eyes. "Well, I have a special book about all that. It's right about time to look at it together, but I didn't know how to explain you to Rosie, so I've been putting it off. I guess I can go ahead with it now."

"A book? Come on!"

"No, really. It talks about all the differences in the mommy's and daddy's bodies — it's very cute. Sweet. Non-threatening." She smiled at him. "If you're very good, I'll read it to you later."

"If you're very good, I'll show you how it's done." He leered at her. "By the way," he said. "How was it done in this case? We were always very careful. Do you remember?"

"Every detail," she said, turning away from him to put away dishes.

He turned her back. "Could I have a couple of details, please?"

She took a breath. "Remember I used to go off the pill for a couple of months a year and your job was to be very good about the condoms? Well, there were a couple of times you got real worked up and just let it slide." She shrugged. "It was as much my doing as yours. I was also a little worked up."

Silence enveloped them for a moment. He leaned forward and kissed her brow. "We were like that," he whispered. "I'm not sorry about that. Big accident. Huge reward. She's awesome."

Franci hugged him. For once he managed to say the right thing. "You've had a nice week with Rosie, haven't you?"

"She's pretty amazing. Listen, there's no good way to do this, Franci. I've been thinking all day about how to sneak up on our issues, but I'm kind of up against the wall. The air force wall. After we get Rose settled in bed, can we please have a glass of wine and talk about things? Practical things."

She looked terrified. "Like what?"

"Everything from insurance to . . ." He took a breath. "Franci, I've been at Beale four years. I'm going to have to call MPC tomorrow, first thing in the morning, and see if I can get the boys down there to work with me on an assignment or I'm going remote. Maybe to the Middle East."

Iraq. Afghanistan. She went visibly pale. "In the U-2?"

He shrugged. "If there's a need for manned surveillance. But the U-2 travels to a lot of places. I don't want to go since I have you and Rosie here. That aside, they're not above changing my weapon system back to a fighter or finding me a staff job in the desert. I pinned on major — I owe 'em three more years at least."

"Sean," she said weakly.

"I know you'd like to just roll with this awhile — see where we are in getting to know each other — but we're gonna have to face it. I'm only on leave another four weeks and two days. I'm sorry, Fran."

"You've been at Beale four years, and you know that's a long time for an air force assignment," she said. "This can't have come as a total surprise."

"No, it didn't. You and Rose came as a surprise. I tried to get into Air Command and Staff College and I'm on the waiting list as an alternate. My plan was just what you'd expect out of me — do whatever I have to do, go wherever I have to go, to head toward a command position. I wanted this job for life — so it didn't matter where they sent me, as long as it all added up to a real good command slot down the road. I figured I'd take a remote for a year and come home to a year in Air Command and Staff College, a lieutenant colonel promotion and a squadron of my own." He swallowed. "Now I don't want to get too far away. I don't want Rosie to think I can't keep my word.

And time's short."

Franci was quiet. "She's still singing in there," Sean said, tilting his head toward the bathroom.

"But I bet she's pruny by now."

Vivian and Maureen had a very nice day together, too. They'd gone out to lunch and then did a little shopping at the local mall — Maureen felt woefully behind in adding her special grandma gifts to Rosie's coffers. They went back to Viv's for the rest of the afternoon, looking through pictures of Rosie from her birth to the present.

There were, of course, many pictures of Franci. "Sometimes when you catch her looking at the baby, her eyes are glowing, but other times . . ." Maureen's voice trailed off.

"I know. It was a very hard time — she wasn't at peace with her decision to be away from Sean. She was already three months pregnant when she came home to Santa Rosa, but she got right to work in the local hospital. She took six weeks of maternity leave and went back. It was not only a long year, but heartbreaking to watch my daughter's sadness. I kept thinking that any second he'd realize what he'd let slip away and come looking for her. But he didn't."

Maureen pursed her lips so tightly they nearly disappeared. "I'd like to box his ears," she muttered.

"Remember, he didn't know. Franci was the one to leave him. I was twenty-five when Franci was born," Vivian said. "And thirty-two when my husband, a trucker, was killed in an accident. I went back to college almost immediately, in search of an education that would guarantee me a good income so I could raise my daughter alone. Franci at least had that much going for her — she wasn't going to have any trouble supporting Rose. But, except for that, I knew how hard life was going to be for her without a partner."

"I had a good husband while I raised my sons," Maureen said. "He was devoted, worked hard, stayed involved. But he worked long hours and, with five kids to support, he took as much overtime as he could get. I had to be able to do it alone — I had to be strong and keep control of that brood. It wasn't easy, even with a good husband. It's hard to imagine how you and Franci —"

"We had each other," Viv said. "Franci came alive when we moved up here. Actually, I said I'd come north only if I could find a good job. I only agreed to take an unpaid leave from my Santa Rosa job to give it a try. Franci flies out of Redding, so we initially went there, rented a small apartment and, on Franci's days off, I scoured the area for work. When I had a good offer in Eureka, the decision was made — we bought a little house together here. Franci works a couple of twenty-four-hour shifts three weeks a month, then only one on the fourth week. It's a long commute — but it's only seven or eight days a month, and my job never requires an overnight or on-call status. After two years in one little house, another just like it down the street came on the market and I bought it. We joined forces to make sure Rosie always had one of us plus the babysitter. It's been all right. It's been good. She was even starting to date again. But . . ."

"But . . . ?" Maureen asked.

"You didn't know her after she broke up with Sean, so you wouldn't see the difference — but since Sean's been in the picture, she's a different person. She loves him so much. And I believe he loves her just as much. I don't know how this is going to work out, Maureen, but those three need to be together."

"Sean told me he suggested marriage to Franci . . ." Maureen said.

"Really? That's the first I've heard of it," Vivian said with some astonishment. "I'm surprised Franci didn't jump on that offer. There must be something not quite settled between them. Frankly, I don't care whether they get married or not as long as they follow the strength of their obvious feelings! Well, I'm staying out of it. Except for one thing — I'm going to be sure Franci knows she doesn't have to consider me in her decision."

"You?" Maureen asked.

Vivian nodded. "I don't want her to think I need her to take care of me — not emotionally or in any other way. I have a full life and look forward to the next stage. I have a wonderful man in my life — I expect he'll be around a very long time. We've been seeing each other the past year and both of us have had commitments that have kept us from moving forward — he's a fairly new widower with two teenagers, and I've had my responsibilities to Francie and Rosie. But Carl and I have both known for quite a while that when our kids don't need us quite as much, we'll have more of each other."

"Really?" Maureen said, intrigued. "A man?"

Vivian laughed. "A wonderful man. He

was one of my bosses. A year after his wife's death he invited me out to dinner, and that was all it took."

Maureen leaned toward Vivian. "An office romance? I heard that was taboo!"

"Pah! We work together very well! I imagine we will for many years!"

"How amazing."

"You'll meet him sometime. In the meantime, my offer stands. If you want to stay close to Rosie, but give your boys some space, Rosie's overnight room makes a perfectly useful guest room. You're welcome to it."

"But you obviously have a private life!"

Vivian just laughed. "Don't let that get in your way! Especially in your wild imagination! Once you meet Carl, you'll be completely at ease around him. He's a physician — a wonderful, warm, loving man. Besides, we don't have many pajama parties, Carl and I. As I said, he has teenagers at home!"

Maureen was thoughtful for a moment. "You're very liberal in your thinking, aren't you, Vivian?"

"I suppose I am," Viv said. "And you're quite the prude, aren't you?"

"So I'm told," Maureen said, somewhat grumpily.

Vivian laughed. "We should make an interesting and strange pair!"

ELEVEN

Once Rosie was tucked in, the lights were out and it was quiet, Sean and Franci sat on the living room sofa, a couple of glasses of wine on the coffee table. They talked quietly and the side of Sean she rarely saw was illuminated. Franci had wanted him to grow up, act like a family man, show responsibility. Then when he did, she wanted the old Sean back, fanciful and full of spontaneity. Seeing Sean act like an adult was a little scary.

She had to admit, when he got down to business, he was up to the job. His list of things that had to be done immediately was impressive. First he intended to visit the air force JAG and get a new will drafted so his daughter would be taken care of. He was going to transfer money out of his investments into a college trust for Rosie, a large enough stake so that even if Franci never contributed another dime, it would probably grow into enough. He had a hundred-thousand-dollar life-insurance policy in which his mother was beneficiary — all the Riordan boys did. They had not begun to help support their mother yet, but it looked as though the time was growing near. As often as these boys were involved in risky jobs, they had all agreed on individual policies so that each one would be holding up his end.

But Sean was going to immediately apply for an additional two hundred and fifty thousand, plus sign over his military death benefit to Rosie, with Franci as the executor, so that if the worst happened she and Rosie would be cared for.

"I'll get those things taken care of right away," he told her. "And I'll spend the morning on the phone with MPC about assignments but, as you probably remember, that can take weeks. Now I have to ask you this — will you even consider going with me on assignment?"

"I don't know," she said wearily, uncertainly. She sipped her wine. "Sean, I'm so enmeshed in this place. I own a house and Rosie is settled. I don't need that job at the college, but it's good for me — it not only keeps me sharp, but I use their track for some running, and work out in the college weight room. And there's my mom . . ."

"I know," he said softly.

"She's my best friend. And she moved up here with me to help take care of Rosie. They're real close."

"I know." He leaned toward her. "Is there anyplace you'd be willing to go with me?"

"Huh?" she returned. "I don't under—"

"There are U-2 assignments around the world, Fran. Accompanied tours. Alaska, England, Okinawa, the Philippines, the high desert in Southern California. I could probably sell my soul for a non-flying staff job in San Antonio at the Military Personnel Center or the Pentagon until Air Command and Staff materializes. It's always hard to get back in the cockpit once you do that, but I'm willing to take that chance." Then he shrugged. "I could skip any assignments that come with a time commitment, just get the three years I owe them out of the way, then do my best to get an airline job."

She gave a huff of laughter. "Sean, the airlines are in the tank. They have such a deep pilot furlough list, none of them are hiring."

"I could go in the cabin business with Luke," he said. He reached toward her and ran a finger through that super-short hair at her temple. "You need time to think."

She felt her eyes glisten with tears. "I wanted time for us to get to know each other again. So far so good," she said. "But it's only been a little over a week."

He grabbed her hand and pulled her toward him and across his lap, holding her against him. "And it's been good. Very good. Think as fast as you can, Franci."

"Maybe the best thing for us to concentrate on is how we can be the best co-parents. We seem to do that pretty well. We both love Rosie."

He put his lips against her neck. He licked his way up to her ear. "We'll always be more than co-parents, and you know it."

Sean and Franci made out on the couch until clothing got in the way, then by mutual consent they went to her bed. Sean was the one to close the door so Rosie wouldn't find them and be traumatized; Franci was the one to supply condoms.

"I missed a condom once," he murmured against her lips. "What a lucky break that was."

"You wouldn't have thought so at the time," she pointed out.

"You were right about one thing, Franci — we've both changed a lot in the past few years and I'm for not going back."

And then he went to work on her body in his own expert way. He kissed her ankles, sucked her toes, licked her inner thighs, worked her clitoris with his tongue. He pushed his thumb into her velvety softness while he licked at her core. He snaked the other hand up to her mouth to cover it so that her moans of ecstasy were muffled. When she claimed she couldn't bear another orgasm, he was inside her, rocking her slowly and gently — excruciatingly slowly and gently. He pressed rhythmically against the deepest part of her and the build came upon her gradually, but when she tried to hurry him, to push him to move deeper, faster, he kept up that easy pace until she whimpered. Begged. "Please, Sean . . . Finish . . ." She dug her heels into the mattress and pushed back *hard.*

His chuckle was soft and low; his thrusts grew deep and powerful, and that was all it took. She broke apart from the inside, clenching against him, grabbing him to her, bathing him in hot liquid. And he said, "Ahhhh, baby. I love that sweet spot." And he slammed into her, letting himself go in a low moan of pleasure.

He held her in the aftermath for a long time, the blanket drawn over them. She finally whispered, "You should go. You have a lot to do in the morning."

"I'm staying tonight. Put on my T-shirt and I'll sleep in my jeans in case someone's wandering in the night. But I'm staying."

"Your mother will know you spent the night with me . . ."

"I dare her to say one word to me," he said. "I want to be with you."

Franci wanted to argue, but not really. She pulled on his shirt as he told her to and enjoyed the scent of him. She was vaguely aware of Sean slipping into his jeans and she smiled to herself. She knew he liked to sleep in the nude and would be uncomfortable, but she appreciated his protection of Rosie's innocence.

And when she woke hours later in the predawn, she found Rosie curled against his chest, sleeping between them, safe and content.

Francine cut out of school a little on the early side on Monday. Her classes were finished and she didn't have any appointments, and she knew that Sean would be at the house with Rosie. Maureen would probably be there, too. She found herself anxious to hear about their day. Rosie was having a circus with a new daddy and grandma.

Franci had to hand it to Maureen; she was

coming off very relaxed and accepting. If memory served, Franci knew her to be rather stiff in her morals — she did not, for example, approve of unmarried people having sex. For Sean and Franci, that ship had sailed long ago. And Maureen would notice that Sean had not gone back to Luke's last night.

Franci had called Sean between her classes and asked, "Did your mother say anything about you spending the night?"

"Of course," he said with a laugh. "She can't keep her mouth shut about anything!"

"What did she say?"

"She asked me if I wasn't complicating an already complicated situation. And I told her I wasn't discussing it with her, so if she wanted to enjoy her time with Rosie she'd better drop it. And to my amazement, she did. Grandchildren, I discovered, provide amazing leverage."

When Franci walked in the house a few hours later, she encountered one of the biggest messes she'd ever seen. Newspapers were spread over the island in the kitchen, covered with pumpkin guts. She could see the spills on the floor — seeds that had gotten away — and three pumpkins were in the middle of the carving process on the dining room table. One huge, one large and one small. The pumpkin family.

"Nuts," Sean said. "You're home early. We were going to surprise you. We've gotta have jack-o'-lanterns for Halloween!"

"Mama!" Rosie shouted excitedly. Then pointing, she said, "Daddy, Mommy, Rosie!"

"Were you going to surprise me with the cleanup?" she asked hopefully.

"Of course," he said. "Maybe you should just go to your room and read or something until I have a chance to get things under control."

"I'll go change and then come and help," she said. Briefcase in hand, she went to her bedroom and within five seconds she was immediately back in the dining room. "There appears to be a large duffel bag in my bedroom."

"I'm moving in for a while, unless you throw me out. My mom is at Luke's for the evening. She and I will spend tomorrow afternoon with Rosie while you're in Redding at work. I thought I'd take babysitting duty while you do your twenty-four-hour shift. If that's okay with you. Wednesday morning, while Rosie's at preschool and day care, I'm driving my mom to the airport. She's going home to get some things done around her condo so she can come right back. I guess the plants are dying, and the bills need to be paid. On the way over here this afternoon, after picking up my things at Luke's, I scoped out the pumpkin patch and bought new pajamas." He grinned at her. "I thought you might be annoyed we didn't invite you along, so I took lots of pictures."

"Weren't you going to ask?" she said.

"About the pumpkin patch?" he returned.

"About the *pajamas,*" she stressed.

He straightened and his expression was serious. "I was going to beg. I have four weeks of leave, if they don't call me in early. Can you put up with me? If I'm neat?"

Her heart swelled, but she was afraid to let it show. He'd always been neat. In fact, he was a little on the fussy side. Things he valued had to be perfectly maintained — his home, his car, his man toys. Put up with him?

"We've never actually done this before, you know," she pointed out to him. "We've never really lived together."

The look in his eyes was tender. "We should have."

Rosie was a princess for Halloween, big surprise. There was a battle about wearing the plastic high heels without socks, and Sean was relieved when Franci handled that war without getting him involved. She let Sean take Rosie around the neighborhood for candy while she stayed home to hand it out to the goblins who came to her door. And then the tussle over how much candy Rosie could eat was handled again by Franci.

Franci thought she'd won the battle. Rosie was allowed two and a half pieces of candy, followed by bath and bed. The combination of the cold weather, the trek around the neighborhood and the excitement of the whole thing wore her out and Rosie crashed by seven-thirty. However, she sprang awake and was ready to party at 2:00 a.m. She was suddenly standing right beside Sean, wearing her princess dress. "Daddy?" she asked. "Are you still on bacation?"

"What are you doing up? And in your fancy dress?"

"I dunno," she answered with a shrug. "Can we twick or tweet again?"

"It's two in the morning, Rose. Everyone is in bed. Everyone but *you.*"

"The candy," Franci moaned. "A sugar charge, then a sugar drop-off, and then a recharge." She lifted up on an elbow and looked down at Sean. "Your turn, Daddy. You're on bacation."

■ ■ ■ ■

Franci was a little surprised by how much relief she felt when Maureen left town; she hadn't realized that Sean's mother made her tense. Once it was back to just the three of them, life seemed calmer. Simpler and easier. When Franci worked, Sean was in charge; when Franci was home, Vivian didn't interfere, but left them to what passed for family life. It wasn't as though she and Sean had made concrete plans, though they couldn't until Sean had some idea what was next for him with the air force. They were still rolling along, one day at a time. They did a lot of talking about the possibilities, but so much was up in the air until Sean had some idea what his next assignment would be.

They hadn't said the *I love you's* yet, at least not in the clear light of day. She'd heard him whisper it in the dark of night when he thought she was asleep. But everything they talked about had them moving forward as a team as best they could under such uncertain circumstances.

Franci decided that when Maureen came back to town, which she was planning to do fairly soon, she would make the time to have a private conversation with her, make sure they were on the same page, so their relationship could be as smooth and tension free as possible — for all their sakes.

One thing that she had to deal with immediately, however, was T.J. She hadn't spoken to him in more than a week — ever since that last call he'd made to her cell phone while she was working in Redding. She could almost feel the trouble brewing like a storm cloud — he had stopped calling and she had made no effort to get in touch with him. It was a standoff. She had to put it to rest. Even if she and Sean didn't go one step further in their relationship, she'd never again spend time with T.J.

She knew he kept office hours on Thursdays when he was in town, so after teaching her two classes she went to his office. She found he was in conference with a student when she arrived, so she jotted a note on the clipboard hanging outside the closed door. *Went to get a soda,* she wrote. *Be back in ten minutes to see you.* When she returned, his door was ajar and he was seated at his desk in the small campus office. She tapped on the open door and he looked up. Then he sat back in the chair, pulled off his reading glasses and swiveled in her direction. "Come in, Francine. Close the door.

300

I've been wondering when you'd show up."

"I should have stopped by sooner, but life got real hectic," she said, entering and pulling the door closed. There was one chair beside his desk and she sat there.

"I can imagine," he said. "How's the new guy working out?"

She laughed uncomfortably. "That was direct," she said. "He's not new, as you already know. And he came with a mother and four brothers and lots of other complications. But we're getting along just fine, thank you."

"I can see that," he said.

She tilted her head and frowned a little bit. "You can?"

He leaned toward her. "I used to be the one to put that shine in your eyes." Then he laughed when she took on a slight blush. "So . . . I guess it's all settled. You're taking the leap. You've moved on."

She didn't know what to say for a moment. She was frankly surprised to find he was as pleasant as that. "I guess you're letting me off without any explanation."

"Don't waste your breath. No matter what you say, Francine, we both know you're making a big mistake here. And we both know you're going to do it, anyway."

"Mistake? Do you have any idea what it *is*

I'm doing? Because I don't recall explaining my plans to you."

"As if that's necessary," he said with a harsh laugh. "You're going to give up everything you've established here — the stability of your job, your friends, the option of a normal relationship with a man you can count on who will make sure your happiness comes first. And you're going to do that for some flyboy *kid* who wouldn't commit to you in the first place. You'll end up sorry. Unhappy and full of regrets. He let you down before and he'll let you down again."

Ah. Now that was what she expected. She almost smiled — she'd never seen this side of T.J. when he was ordering her meals and asking her to grow out her hair, and she wondered now how she could have been so naive. Undoubtedly he thought he had been doing her a great service. But the second Sean turned up, he'd let his true colors come out. He must have thought she would defer to him forever. He thought he owned her. She leaned toward him. "When did you turn into this person?" she asked, her voice rather soft under the circumstances. "Were you always like this and I just didn't realize it? When you were telling me what to eat and how to wear my hair — was that just the tip of the iceberg and I was too accommodating to understand what a mistake it was to allow that behavior?"

He actually sneered at her. "How like you to see the worst in a good situation. I should have known better than to get mixed up with someone like you. You're a *child.*"

"Oh, T.J., when did you become this kind of man? What did I miss? We dated for a few months, and in fact no more often than once a week, but I don't recall that we had the kind of relationship that would invite this kind of anger from you. We didn't have future plans, you and I."

"Our relationship was *stable.* This thing you're trading it for, it'll be a disaster because he isn't moving to Humboldt County. Even if he could, you and I both know he isn't the kind of man who will give up anything for you. Or for his daughter. You'll have to give up everything you value and go chasing him around the world if you want to be with him. Trust me, you'll be right back where you started. Abandoned."

"Whoa," she said, affronted. "I'm not even going to ask you how you came to all these conclusions. I'm not going to defend Sean to you, but have you ever *met* him?"

"I know that any man who cared about you would have made it his business to find you a long time ago. I would have. If I thought you had any feelings for me whatsoever, I'd tear up the country looking for you. And he never even tried."

Well, she thought, she *had* told him the whole, sad story. "There are things to resolve about that, but —"

"Before you pull up stakes, you'd better try to think clearly, Franci. There's still time for you to be smart, use that little tiny brain of yours. You know how I feel about you. And you know I can keep the blush on your cheeks, too. He might seem a little dangerous and daring and have that sex appeal that goes with jets and secret missions, but that will wear thin. He's a young idiot who likes living on the edge, and that isn't father material. You're going to be very disappointed."

A huff of laughter escaped her in spite of herself. "Sean? Dangerous?" Then she laughed outright. "My *tiny* brain?" She stood. "I guess I'm a little confused, T.J. I thought you liked me, but I had no idea you took our relationship as seriously as that, nor did I realize you didn't think I was smart. I'm sorry you're angry. But I can't possibly describe how positively relieved I am that I won't be spending time with you *ever again.*"

He stood as well. "If I'm angry at all, it's because you led me on. I'm not a kid anymore, Francine, and I know what works and what doesn't. A lot of that I learned the hard way, through my own mistakes. Just the way you will."

"Best of luck, T.J.," she said, turning to leave his office.

"If you come to your senses soon, get in touch. But I won't wait around long."

Well, that's a good thing, she thought. She turned back to look at him. "Don't wait for me. In fact, go ahead and delete my phone number." And then she left the building.

It hit her that something about that little confrontation was all wrong! What was this talk about being the one to put the shine in her eyes? Hadn't he complained that they needed to "turn up the heat"? And how in the world had she led him on? By not complaining when he wanted to order for both of them? When going along with his plans for a date, though he never once asked her what she'd like to do? She hadn't questioned the relationship because it had worked for her. And it had worked for her because she hadn't been emotionally invested. But neither had he!

She left the campus. All the way home she was asking herself how she had missed who

he really was. And why hadn't the relationship grated on her more? *You're a child,* rang
in her ears.

And then something occurred to her —
she'd lost her father when she was only
seven. She'd always longed for her father,
for *any* father. The loss had devastated her!
It was one of the many reasons she was so
protective of Rosie — she didn't want her
hurt by a loss like that! In some convoluted
way it seemed safer to raise Rosie alone
rather than watch her little heart break with
longing for a father she couldn't have!

And maybe it was that same sense of loss
that allowed her to be so cooperative with a
man like Professor Hottie! He took charge;
he made as many decisions for her as she
would allow! And if Sean hadn't come back
into her life, who knows how far she would
have let him go with his controlling, ma-
nipulative behavior.

He was right; she had been a child. She
had allowed the whole thing to happen; she
had no one to blame but herself. She hadn't
realized what was happening.

But she had never behaved that way with
Sean; she had been strong, independent and
convicted. And to his credit, Sean had never
tried to control or manipulate her. He didn't
always bend to her desires, but neither did

he act as if he owned her. It was with great relief that she realized that, even in the worst of times, they didn't have that kind of relationship.

Oh, if they could ever get everything straight, she thought they had a chance of having the *right* kind of relationship. She almost laughed! As hard as things had been for them, they were healthy, well-adjusted people — unlike T.J.

When she got home, she found Sean in the kitchen. He was turning thick pork chops over in a marinade and Franci could hear Rosie in the bedroom playing.

Sean grinned at her. "How was your day, dear?" he asked, tilting his head in the direction of Rosie's room.

"Surreal," she said in a whisper. "Did you by any chance deal with that girl who's been texting you night and day?"

"Didn't I tell you? I finally got around to that a few days ago."

"How'd it go?"

"As expected. I asked her not to text or call anymore because I was back with my old girlfriend and she told me to go to hell."

"That's all?"

"No. She said if she saw me again she'd kill me, and if she had a chance to loosen a few bolts on my airplane she'd do it. She called me some choice names and hung up. Why?"

"Nothing," she said, shaking her head, looking away.

"You had a meeting with *him,*" he said. "Let me guess, he listed my shortcomings even though he doesn't know me."

"How'd you know?"

Sean pulled her close and, on his way to whisper in her ear, he gently sucked on her lobe. "He doesn't want to give you up, because you're you. Now, let's not talk about why. It makes me want to kill him."

"I saw a side of him that's always been there, but I completely overlooked it. It was very disturbing," she said. "Guess what I just realized? You're the devil I know . . ."

"Good," he said. "Let's stick with that."

Maureen had gone home to Phoenix as planned. She only stayed in her condo for a week, during which time she gave away her houseplants, stopped the paper, forwarded her mail, closed up her condo and headed back, her trunk and backseat full of her essentials.

Maureen and Vivian had worked things out; Maureen was going back to Humboldt County for a rather long visit. She would stay through Thanksgiving — a good three weeks. Although she would make use of Vivian's second bedroom, usually reserved for Rosie's overnights, and having her own car would allow her to spend quality time with Rosie, and everyone else. This arrangement would also allow her to give them all their space. In fact, not being dependent on her sons or her new friend Vivian for transportation would enable her to come and go as she pleased. After all, Vivian had a man in her life and would surely appreciate time alone with him now and then.

Other than telling Luke and Sean that she'd be back for a visit and that she planned to stay through Thanksgiving, they didn't know her plans. They would no doubt be secretly thrilled to learn she wouldn't be staying with them! Vivian was a remarkable woman who wanted to assist Maureen in getting better acquainted with their mutual granddaughter, a gesture generous beyond belief. But as it turned out, different as they were, the women enjoyed each other's company.

While she was headed north, driving through the Arizona desert, she decided to check in with all her sons. Of course, she only had to call one to do so. "You're doing *what?*" Aiden demanded.

"Driving to Virgin River. So I'll have a car

while I'm there. And I'm staying with Rosie's other grandma so I don't become an annoying mother-in-law. I like Vivian. She's too liberal, but very sincere."

"Oh, God," Aiden moaned into the phone. "How many hours is the drive?"

"Well, that all depends on how fast I go," she said. "It's very long. I plan on stopping off for the night."

"Stopping off *where?*" he asked in frustration.

"Okay, I might be all done talking to you now, since you insist on treating me like I just got my learner's permit."

"All right," he said, deliberately calming his voice. "Where do you suppose you'll stay the night?"

"I don't know. I left early, so I might make it all the way to Carson City. I've been there — nice little town. And Gardnerville is nearby. So is Reno and Lake Tahoe and —"

"How many hours of driving is that?" he asked.

"Many," she said. "I wish you'd stop this. I'm a very good, confident driver. And I've lived alone for twelve years. I know how to be safe."

"Why didn't you call me? I would have come to Phoenix and driven you," he said tiredly.

"Oh, doesn't that sound like fun," she said with a short laugh. "It would probably turn into elder abuse. Besides, it's not practical. Someone — probably me — would have had to drive you back to Sacramento or at least Redding to catch a flight home."

He sighed into the phone. "Do Luke and Sean know your plans yet?"

"I told them I'd be back for a long visit, but they might be in denial," she said. She heard Aiden laugh. "It makes sense for me to stay with Vivian. I'll be very busy, running between Rosie, and Luke and Shelby, and also hanging around with Vivian when neither of us has plans. I only want to be nearby to get to know Rosie better and I don't want to be a burden to my sons."

"You're not a burden, Mom," he said.

"Oh? Then why does my doing as I please make you yell?"

Aiden took a breath. "I want you to check in every few hours as long as you have a signal. I want to hear from you when you stop for the night — I want to know exactly where you are. Can we please agree to that?"

"I hope I live to see you at sixty-two. I'd like to hear firsthand just how you handle people pushing you around as though you're some doddering old —"

"I didn't do that! I'm just being cautious.

It's not your age, it's your . . . your . . . You're a woman out on the road alone, Mom! And if I remember my geography, from Las Vegas to Reno is a pretty lonely stretch of road."

"I'll lock my car doors so the wild mules don't get me."

"What do you mean, she's too liberal? Rosie's other grandmother?" Aiden asked.

"Oh, you know. A lovely woman, really. Very likable and with a wonderful sense of humor. Just . . . Her values are more on the relaxed side, if you know what I mean."

"I wouldn't dare guess," Aiden muttered into the phone.

"For example, she's not too worried about Sean and Francine making this whole event right and proper. She'd be happy as a clam if they'd at least get together romantically, as if that will solve their problems. Wasn't that what got them into this mess? Not that I'm the least sorry about Rosie — she's the most *brilliant* child! I'm so crazy about her! She reminds me a lot of Patrick when he was little — except for the princess dresses and high-heeled slippers."

Aiden chuckled into the phone. "I take back everything I said, Mom. Maybe this is a good idea."

Maureen got the impression Aiden hoped

staying with liberal Viv would loosen her up. "Don't get your hopes up, Aiden. I'm pretty firm in my convictions."

"Yes, Mom. Understood." He laughed a little more. "Call in a few hours. Please?"

"I'll try. Now relax, Aiden. I'm listening to a book on tape and enjoying the ride."

"I hope it's not the Bible," he said.

"It's James Patterson — death and sex and everything." And without another word, she hung up on him.

It was less than thirty minutes before her cell phone chimed. She glanced at the phone and saw it was Luke. She let him go to voice mail. Next was Sean, then Patrick and finally Colin. She smiled to herself; it was nice having all five boys in the United States. She let them all leave messages. She would entertain herself later by listening to them.

Really, she thought with amusement, how did they think she got to be this old without knowing anything? Pups. They were just pups.

As Maureen had fully expected, her sons welcomed her a little more warmly given the fact that she was staying with Vivian and not with them. But she was very surprised when Franci walked down the block to her mother's house a couple of days after Maureen's return. It was the afternoon, before Rosie was due home from day care. "Hi," she said almost sheepishly, when Maureen opened the door.

"Franci! I thought you were working!"

"I was. I got off at eight this morning, had a nap and I thought I'd catch you before Sean brings Rosie home. I think maybe we should have a chat. Alone."

"Of course," Maureen said, and she braced herself to be lectured not to interfere, to be seen and not heard, to not get in the way of things. "Please," she said, holding open the door. "Can I make you a cup of coffee or something?"

"No. I just wanted to say I'm sorry you missed so much time with Rosie. I wish it hadn't been necessary."

"Oh, Franci," Maureen said before she could stop herself. "*Was* it necessary?"

Franci came inside the house. "I thought so, yes," she said gently. "The Sean I knew four years ago and this Sean — really, they're very different men. But that aside, most of it had to do with me. I loved him so much, I just couldn't bear to have him know everything and still walk away. Even worse was the thought that he'd grudgingly man up and marry me, but hate his life."

She shook her head. "I didn't know which way it would go, Maureen. I had to do the best I could with the facts at hand. I'm terribly sorry for what that cost you."

Maureen took one of Franci's hands. She smiled softly. "I wish it hadn't gone the way it did, but I don't blame you, Franci. And I'm so glad that's in the past and we can all move forward now. You've done an amazing job with Rosie. She's the most wonderful child."

"Then you won't hold it against me?" Franci asked.

"Of course not, darling," she said, pulling her into an embrace. Maureen held her tightly. "Of course not! That boy of mine, however . . ." She pulled back and looked into Franci's eyes. Maureen's were dancing, laughter making little crinkle lines at the corners. "Is it too late to ground him?"

Franci laughed with her. "I think so," she said.

"I'm glad he's different. I guess he had some growing up to do. Maybe it was his fault, maybe it was mine. Maybe I let him get by with too much when he was a kid. Whatever, it's too late for all that blaming. Right now there's a family to mend. You and Sean are doing a very good job of that. I'm very proud of both of you."

Luke and Shelby had met Rosie, but only briefly — over the past few weeks everyone had been very focused on letting her get used to the large Riordan clan slowly. And there was more to come — Shelby's whole family was in Virgin River. Luke wanted to have a big party and invited not only his family but also Walt Booth, Muriel St. Claire, Paul and Vanessa Haggerty and their two little ones. And of course there was Art, who was as much a member of his family as anyone. It was the first Riordan gathering since Luke and Shelby's wedding, and this time it would include Franci, Rosie and Vivian.

On a Saturday when Franci wasn't working, they all gathered at Luke's house, and royalty could not have been welcomed with any more enthusiasm than Franci and Rosie. It was just enough family to stuff Luke's relatively small house. All the women brought dishes to accompany a very large ham and prime rib. Furniture had to be moved around, and with the November weather growing so cold, the fire blazed in the hearth and the house throbbed with the noise of good times and the laughter of children.

The cold didn't affect Rosie — she wanted to fish . . . and fish and fish. First, Sean took her along with Art, then Luke took her, then Franci took her and finally Maureen had a turn. She wanted to fish rather than eat; she wanted to fish rather than have a nap. She was told she could *only* fish with Mommy's or Daddy's permission and *never* without an adult along. She squealed and pitched a little fit about staying in, even though her fingers, toes and nose were bright pink. As soon as her fit ended, however, she passed out cold, exhausted.

In the late afternoon, as everyone allowed their big meal to settle before they tackled dessert, the children napped peacefully on the sofas. The women gathered around the dining room table, Art wandered off to fish some more and the Riordan brothers, plus Walt and Paul, stood on the porch with beers and cigars.

Luke was the one to broach the subject that was on everyone's mind. "What happens now, Sean?"

"Anyone's guess. What should happen — I should go remote without a family or to a foreign base until a slot at Air Command and Staff opens up. But I've been all over the flesh peddlers at MPC looking for a job that carries me over a year or two and has a squadron in my future. The possibilities have been interesting — everything from an attaché position in Belgium to a test-pilot job in the high desert in Southern California." He coughed. "They've suggested plenty of open time in the sandbox."

"What does Franci say?"

"She says to let her know when I have an actual question and she'll try to come up with an answer." They all laughed. "Listen, isn't it obvious? I don't want to be away from them, but asking her to leave her mom, her home and her job right now is asking a lot, and I don't even know that I'll go someplace I can take a family. I'm trying to keep so many balls in the air, I don't know which end is up. And on the first of December I have to go back to work. To Beale. Any second now, my orders will be cut."

"What's your dream job?" Luke asked.

"Air Command and Staff on my way back to Beale as squadron commander," he said. "I'd probably have to do some time at the Pentagon or MPC en route to pay my dues for my upgrade. I had it in my head I was going all the way — retire as a full bull at least." He glanced at Walt, who had retired from the army with three stars. "To tell the truth, I had my eye on a star or two. Sir. Now, I'm not so sure I'll make it to retirement."

"It's going okay with Franci?" Aiden asked.

"With my mother living four doors away with Franci's mother? I'd say we're doing pretty well in spite of that. One more person gets in our business and we're probably doomed." He laughed and shook his head. There was silence for a few moments and Sean finally said, "I regret that I didn't know about Rosie four years ago, but it terrifies me to think how I might have reacted. I thought I was a man of the world at twenty-eight, but —"

Walt Booth put an arm around his shoulders. "Son, I bet there's not a man on this porch who doesn't feel like looking back and changing a few things. Just do right by your family now. And if there's anything I can do to help, just say the word."

"Got any favors to call in, sir?" Sean asked.

"I'll give it some thought, son, but the problem there . . . they'd be army favors."

Sean shook his head. "That's kind of the way my luck's been going lately."

When the men walked back in the house, Rosie popped up from her sleeping position on the couch and said, "Daddy? Go fishing now?"

TWELVE

Ellie Baldwin was very proud of herself. Although she and Noah met with the seller's Realtor together, he hardly opened his mouth. She had researched the property and hired Paul Haggerty to check the house for its structural competence. Paul took care of things immediately and provided them with a folder filled with notes that brought the price down by a quarter. The money would be spent on the extensive repairs the owner should have made on the house, she told the Realtor.

Of course their offer was accepted; the seller was anxious to unload the money pit. The closing on the property was scheduled right away, which thrilled Ellie to no end. She asked Noah why he didn't get more involved in the negotiations. "You had the situation well under control, and you're absolutely right about me — I might've backed down. Ellie, pretty soon you're going to have to accept how smart you really are."

She stayed tense about the sale until the closing on the property. It had been less than a week but, to Ellie, it had felt like a month. The seller owned the place outright and Noah had some kind of retirement trust as collateral. The mortgage approval was a banker's dream and the closing followed quickly.

When they left the title company after signing the final papers that Friday morning, and the old house was completely theirs, she flew into Noah's arms and almost knocked him down in her excitement. He laughed as he grabbed her. "Whoa! You're the only woman I know who would be so grateful for that trash heap of a house!"

"Noah, one day that's going to be the most beautiful house in Virgin River. It's going to take a while and some hard work, but it will be. You wait and see!"

"Let's get married now. We have the license. We have to get married before we can send legal paperwork to Trevor's biological father to release him for adoption, so let's get it done. We'll put up a notice for Friday night, a week from today." He grinned. "In England they call it posting the banns. We can call Harry Shipton from

Grace Valley, ask him to officiate —"

"Noah! What about George? Don't you think George would want to marry us?"

"I just hope he can get away on short notice so he can be my best man. Let's do it, Ellie."

"So fast?" she asked. "Is that what you want to do? It won't be much of a wedding," she said, concerned. "You're the town pastor. You should probably put more effort into it."

"We'll have a nice little ceremony and a potluck in the basement —"

"The basement? But we don't have tables and chairs yet. The kitchen might be ready for a potluck, but I don't feel right about rounding up volunteers to clean up for our wedding. We've only known these people a few months. I don't want to take advantage of them. If we only have ten guests, we don't want them working for their supper."

"Then let's ask Jack. I hear that's where most town parties happen."

"I guess we could do that," she said. "Do we pay Jack for that?"

"I'll talk to him about it. It works for me if it works for Jack," he said. "But how about you, Ellie? Do you want more time to plan? To make it fancier? I know you've never had a real wedding."

Nor had she ever expected one. Oh, every young girl dreams of that special event when she's gowned in splendor and is queen for a day, but Ellie knew that in her case it was *only* a dream. She was a poor girl, marrying a simple minister; she had no family but her children. Her life right now was better than it had ever been; she wasn't going to get greedy. "Marrying you is the best thing that could ever happen to me. I'm very happy, Noah. Will you wear your wedding-funeral suit?"

He nodded. "Are you going to wear a huge white dress?" he asked with a grin.

"No. I'm about the most unlikely virgin in Virgin River. Vanessa is way ahead of us — she said she has a dress that's perfect for me, with just enough cleavage to make it look like I bought it for myself."

He dug in his pocket and pulled out a ring. "Will you wear this?"

The diamond wasn't large as diamonds go, but from Ellie's perspective it was enormous. She never in her wildest dreams expected jewelry. "Is it real?" she asked in a breath. When he nodded, she asked, "Can we afford this?"

"Ellie, we can't afford *anything!*" He laughed.

"Noah, have you lost your mind? I don't

need something like this! I'd rather have a washing machine!"

He took her chin in his big hand, tilted her face up and said, "Ellie, I love you. I want you to have something special. I wish it was more special — you're a nine-carat woman." He shrugged. "It's a speck. You can hardly see it with the naked eye."

"It's incredible."

He gave her a kiss. "I don't know how you manage to be so grateful for such simple things, but I want you to know I'll never take that for granted. It's priceless. *You're* the jewel!"

She put her arms around his neck and held him close, kissing him back. "You're one crazy preacher," she said. And then she smiled. "Okay, then. If Harry's available, I'll do it. But until we can get that lean-to in shape, we're going to be spending the night over the Fitches' garage."

"I don't care where I sleep as long as it's next to you," he said.

Virgin River was especially good at things like last-minute weddings and impromptu parties at the bar. Harry Shipton didn't have enough of a social life to prevent him from performing a wedding on Friday night and was glad to do it. When Ellie asked Preacher if he could come up with some kind of a small wedding cake for them, his grin was so big she was afraid his face would crack.

Noah announced it at Sunday service, which had grown by a few people each week so that now it wasn't unusual to have as many as fifty people in church. Jack put a notice on the front door of the bar saying they'd be closed Friday night to celebrate the marriage of Ellie Baldwin and Pastor Noah Kincaid, and the price of admission was a covered dish. Right next to that, Noah put up a for-sale notice for the RV.

"And where are you two lovebirds going on your honeymoon?" Jack asked.

"Down the street with a hammer and bucket of nails," Noah said. "First of all, Ellie won't even consider a honeymoon that doesn't include the kids . . ."

"Doesn't that kind of defeat the purpose?" Jack asked.

"That was my question," Noah said.

Jack clapped a strong hand on Noah's shoulder. "After you're married, I'll explain about the reason for cartoons. There are side effects, but it's worth it." Noah's brow crinkled in confusion. "You said, 'first of all' . . . Was there a second thing?" Jack asked.

"Ellie is so excited about that old house,

she can't wait to get in there and start cleaning and fixing. To tell the truth, I'm a little excited about it, too."

"Haven't you had enough fixing for a while?" Jack asked. "You threw yourself into that old church."

"I had a lot of help," he said, "but I'm proud of it now. Doesn't she just shine? You don't have to be embarrassed to walk in *that* church. Not that I couldn't be every bit as profound in a dump, but that church *shines!*"

"Noah, one of the things I like best about you is your humility." Jack put a complimentary beer on the bar. "Loosen up, why don't you. So, you're letting the RV go?"

"Can only support so many households, Jack," he said, lifting the beer.

"You expect to sell it, with gas prices like they are? With this economy in the toilet?"

"Nah," Noah said. "Not as a travel vehicle, anyway. But the price is right for an apartment."

"What is the price?"

"I don't have any idea," Noah said. "But I'll know it when I hear it."

George Davenport hadn't been in favor of Noah's ardent pursuit of the old church in Virgin River; he was afraid the boy would waste away there. But he had to admit, that was hardly the case now. Noah was thriving. It was a three-tiered success for the young minister. First, the church had needed his attention, and once it was a functional building, the people came. Noah did what he did best — he inspired them. Second, the town had embraced him, and George didn't know when he'd seen a more special, nurturing small town. But third, and probably most important, Noah had found himself a good woman.

It made George very happy to see Noah settling down with Ellie and her children. They were good together; they had great balance. Noah seemed to have the stability and commitment Ellie needed in her life, and Ellie had the spark Noah needed in his. Together they were going to parent Ellie's children well. And they'd already established a fine extended family in Jo and Nick Fitch, and solid friendships at the core of the community.

In addition to all that, George found he loved visiting Virgin River. At seventy, he was putting in fewer teaching hours, traveling more, socializing often. He'd retired as a Presbyterian minister at the age of fifty and had been held captive at the university ever since. He worked to stay busy, to keep from getting old, but he was beginning to think more play would keep him younger longer.

The moment Noah had called him, George turned his two classes over to his teaching assistant and packed his bags. He liked the drive to Virgin River from Washington; it was long and beautiful. He'd always enjoyed solitude as much as he enjoyed people.

It was the dinner hour of a cold November day when he hit town; the sun was down and a welcoming light shone from the window of Jack's. He went there first, thinking he might run into Noah.

"Well, look what the cat dragged in," Jack called from behind the bar. "I heard you were coming for the wedding. Didn't waste any time, did you?"

George grinned and hung his coat on the peg by the door. He glanced around quickly to see if he could spot Noah, but what he saw instead knocked the wind out of him. That stunning redhead from the wedding he'd attended here about a month ago was having dinner with her family. He recognized her immediately as Luke Riordan's mother, Maureen. Before he could shake himself, he realized he was staring at her. She sat at a table by the fire with Luke,

Shelby and Art.

George had to force his eyes away and go up to the bar. He stuck out his hand and greeted Jack. "I thought maybe I'd find Noah here, getting dinner."

"Haven't seen him since this morning," Jack said. "If he doesn't turn up soon, I bet you'll find him down at the Fitch house. You just drive in?"

"This is my first stop after a very long day."

"Let me get you something to drink," Jack offered. "What's your pleasure?"

"My driving is done for the day. How about a nice Scotch? Ice and water, please."

"You got it, George. And if you're interested, Preacher whipped up some pork tenderloin in sauerkraut that is *not* sour. He simmers it in beer all day and it's out of this world. It's one of his best dishes." Jack turned away to fix a drink for George, but as it was with Jack, he just kept talking. "So, we're having a wedding. Party here afterward. Everyone's pretty excited about it. I never would've guessed when Ellie hit town that she'd snag herself our minister."

"You sure Noah didn't do the snagging?" George asked.

"Now that you mention it, I'm not sure."

George managed some small talk, but his

330

mind was elsewhere. He remembered meeting Maureen at Luke and Shelby's wedding reception out at the general's house. His first thought was that she was a damn fine-looking fifty-year-old woman, but when he was informed she was Luke's mother, making her over sixty, he was speechless. He did his best to charm her right on the spot, but she was preoccupied with the wedding. And having all her military sons present distracted her; she'd not seen them in quite a while.

George had had an immediate hope of seeing her again, but he doubted he'd be so lucky. She lived in Phoenix, her sons were scattered everywhere with only Luke in Virgin River, and what were the chances he'd visit Virgin River at the same time she did? With disappointment, he'd given up on the idea of getting to know her better.

"George?" Jack asked.

"Hm?" he said, jerking to attention. "Sorry, Jack. My mind must have been wandering."

"I said, why don't you go say hello to them. The Riordans."

"I think you read my mind."

"No, George. I followed your eyes." Jack tilted his head toward the Riordans' table.

George just laughed; he didn't embarrass

easily. "Good idea. If Noah comes in, see if you can keep him busy for a while."

As George approached their table, Luke immediately stood. "Sir," he said, stretching out a hand. And George remembered that these Riordan boys gave the impression of being scamps but their manners toward women and their elders were impeccable. The lot of them were a long way from being boys — George suspected Luke was nearly forty — but clearly they'd been raised with a firm hand. Probably by their parents, their priests and their military bosses.

"Luke, Shelby," George said with a nod, taking Luke's hand. "How's married life?"

"Excellent, sir. Thanks."

"Art, how are you? And, Mrs. Riordan, wonderful to see you again."

Maureen looked at him with a slight frown. "Forgive me, I know we met, but I just can't remember —"

"George Davenport," he said with a slight nod of his head. "A friend of Pastor Kincaid's. I was in town for Shelby and Luke's wedding as it was Noah's debut at the church. Splendid affair."

"George, please sit down," Luke said. "Visit a while."

"Thanks, don't mind if I do." George pulled a chair over from an empty table and sat right beside Maureen so that she was sandwiched between himself and Art. "What brings you back to town so soon?" he asked her.

"I'm, ah, visiting."

"Fantastic," he said. "A long visit, I hope."

Luke took his seat, chuckling as he did so. "I have a brother here right now — Sean. You might remember him as my best man. He just discovered he has a young daughter in the area. Mom is visiting us and getting to know her first granddaughter, Rosie, three and a half and smart as a whip."

"How wonderful!" George said enthusiastically. "You must be having the time of your life!"

Maureen lifted a thin brow, wary of his reaction. "I am enjoying her, yes."

"First one? I suppose before too much longer the other boys will be adding to the flock."

"Only the married ones, I hope," Maureen said. "Do you have grandchildren, Mr. Davenport?"

"Oh, let's not be so formal — I'm George. Only step-grandchildren. I had no children of my own, in fact. Noah's the closest thing to a son I've ever had, but I started out as his teacher. I'm a professor at Seattle Pacific University. I've known him quite a few years now. I'm here to be his best man on Friday night. I hope you're all coming to the wedding."

"Wouldn't miss it," Luke said, grabbing Shelby's hand.

"And . . . Maureen?" George asked pointedly.

"I'm not sure," she said evasively.

"Well, try to come," he said. "These Virgin River people know how to have a good time. In fact, I have an idea. Once I have my best-man duties out of the way, I suggest we go to dinner. I'll take you someplace nice in one of the coast towns, though it'll be hard to improve on Preacher's cooking. But we deserve some time away from all these young people, don't you think?"

"Excuse me, George?" she asked. "I assume you were married?"

"Twice, as a matter of fact. Divorced a long time ago and, more recently, widowed. My wife died a few years ago. Maybe we should pick an evening and exchange phone numbers," he suggested.

"That's very nice of you, but no. I don't go out with men."

"Really?" he asked, surprised by her immediate refusal. "And why is that?"

"I'm a widow," she said. "A single woman."

"What a coincidence. And I'm a single man. I'm all for free thinking, but I wouldn't ask you to dinner were I married. Are you *recently* widowed?" Out of the corner of his eye, George saw Luke snicker and look away.

"Yes," Maureen said.

"Oh, I'm sorry," he said. "I was under the impression it had been years. When did you lose your husband, Maureen?"

She looked a bit shocked to be put on the spot like that. It was apparent she was trying to gather her wits. She put out her hand. "It was so nice to see you again, Mr. . . . George. I'm glad you sat and visited a while. Maybe I'll see you at the wedding this weekend if I'm not needed for anything else. I should probably get on the road — I have to drive to Eureka."

She stood and George did, as well. "Eureka? You're not staying here in Virgin River with your son?"

"I'm staying with a friend just down the street from my granddaughter so I'm free to pick her up after preschool. We spend most afternoons together. Really, nice seeing you." She turned to Luke. "I'm going to head back to Viv's, Luke. Good-night, Shelby. 'Night Art. Thanks for dinner, it was great as usual."

"Wonderful seeing you, too," George said. "Try to come to Noah's wedding. I guarantee you'll enjoy yourself."

Luke gestured to Shelby to visit with George while he walked his mother to her car, but he had to move pretty quick to do that. Maureen was shrugging into her jacket as she exited the bar, apparently in a very big hurry to leave.

"Hey, hey, hey," Luke called after her with laughter in his voice. "Mom!" Maureen stopped and turned to him. "What was *that?*"

She just tilted her head in a questioning way. "Excuse me?"

"That! You aren't recently widowed! You brushed him off. Totally."

"Oh *that,*" she said. "I'm not interested in dating anyone."

"Why, for heaven's sake? George seems like a very nice guy. And he's not exactly Stranger Danger — Noah's known him for years. He was at our wedding. Maybe the two of you would enjoy yourselves."

She put a hand on his cheek. "That's very sweet, Luke," she said. "I'm just not interested."

"But why? Is there something about George you don't like?"

"Not really," she said, shaking her head as

if disinterested. "I don't want to go out with a man." She shivered. "Now, I need to get going. It's a long drive and I'm cold."

He just stared at her for a second. He leaned toward her and kissed her cheek. "Thanks for coming out, Mom. Drive carefully."

He watched as she got in her car to drive away from him and he thought, *I'd better get to the bottom of that!* As far as Luke knew, as far as he could tell, his parents had had a good relationship. They weren't overtly physical or affectionate in front of their boys but — it was a well-known fact — his mother was way uptight. He assumed, since they had five sons in ten years, they were very physical in private. At his father's insistence, his mother was always treated with the utmost deference and respect; the man worshiped her. If there was anything she needed, she had only to snap her fingers and he was there for her. She called him her knight, but she called him that softly, quietly.

What the hell was wrong? If she'd had a positive marriage, shouldn't she be at least amenable to the idea of dinner with a nice man? And now that he gave it some thought, his mother was a knockout for a woman in her early sixties; she looked at least a decade younger than she was. She had a good figure, a quick wit, excellent health and a positive attitude. Logically, she should have been dating, possibly remarried, years ago.

Aiden, Luke thought. Aiden knew women inside and out. *Literally.* He would figure this out.

Maureen *absolutely* remembered George, but it just wouldn't do to let on that she had noticed him. She'd be mortified if he even suspected that the very *moment* she met him a month ago she'd found him handsome, charming and amusing. Because she was *not,* definitely *not,* interested in ever having a man in her life again. Romance was for young girls, not women her age.

She was finally where she wanted to be in life. Comfortable in her skin. Confident in her independence. She was busy all the time, felt good and didn't mind looking at herself in the mirror . . . provided she was fully clothed. Her sons were, if not completely settled, at least not as frivolous and immature as they'd once been.

She had wanted grandchildren and now she had one, and a little girl at that. She had always wanted a little girl of her own, but just hadn't been up to a sixth child. If Shelby and Luke would ever own up, she'd be informed that a second grandchild was on the way. They must be keeping the news tight until they got past the shaky first trimester; lots of couples did that.

And Vivian had literally come to her rescue so she could be near Rosie without interfering in Sean's attempts to gather up and secure his family.

Viv had turned out to be more than just a port in a storm — she was becoming a good friend. Maureen got a kick out of her, though they didn't have much in common. While Maureen had kept busy with things like golf and bridge and her church, Vivian had been working full-time, helping out with her daughter and granddaughter and seeing a man. Maureen was so much more old-fashioned than Vivian — she'd never have done such a great job of helping and supporting a daughter who had chosen to be a single mother. But then Maureen was about ten years older and Vivian had herself been a single mother, widowed as a young woman.

When Maureen got back to Viv's house, she found her roommate was just tucking Rosie into bed.

"Well, hello," Viv said. "I thought you'd be out a bit later. I hope you had a good time."

"Of course. I didn't know we were babysitting tonight," Maureen said. "I'd have stayed home."

"It was last minute. Sean and Franci decided on a nice dinner out and I didn't have plans, so I said I'd keep Rosie here. If they decide to let her stay the night, she can snuggle in with me. But I'm pretty sure they'll come for her."

"Gramma Mo-ween, you do me a story?" Rosie asked.

"You've had a story already," Vivian reminded her granddaughter.

"But another won't hurt," Maureen said. "Just a short one, then get some sleep. Okay?"

Fifteen minutes later Maureen was back in Viv's tidy, comfy little living room. Vivian had a fire going and the TV off; she was curled into the corner of the sofa that had her imprint in it, her book in her lap. "It's getting so cold," Maureen said. "The fire is nice."

"How are Shelby and Luke?"

Maureen smiled. "They still haven't unleashed their news. To me, anyway."

"Sometimes the mothers are the last to know. Sometimes they tell us things we wish they'd keep to themselves."

"Hm," Maureen agreed. She picked up a

magazine from Viv's coffee table.

"Turn on the TV if you like," Vivian said. "It won't bother my reading."

"I'm fine. The quiet is nice," she said.

Another ten minutes passed when Vivian put aside her book and said, "What's wrong, Maureen?"

"Huh? Nothing! Nothing at all. Why would you think that?"

"You're not doing your needlepoint. You're not looking at that magazine, which is a medicine monthly and probably of no interest to you, anyway. And you're no magpie, but you're usually lots more talkative than this." She smiled. "Even when I'm reading."

Maureen tossed the magazine back on the coffee table. She smiled and asked, "Have I been rude?"

"There's not an unappreciative bone in your body, rude or otherwise. So, what's wrong? Are you upset with your boys?"

Maureen sighed. "Not any more than usual. I did do a rude thing tonight, Viv. I told a lie and I think I got away with it, but it didn't make me feel any better. I just didn't like the spot I thought I was in."

Vivian sat forward a little bit, crossing her legs under her on the sofa. "I can't imagine — I thought a lie would turn to acid in your mouth!" She grinned almost happily. "Do tell!"

"It's pretty silly. A gentleman I met while I was here for Luke's wedding happens to be visiting again and we ran into each other at that little Virgin River bar. I pretended I couldn't remember meeting him. I don't know why I did that. Probably because he was coming on a little strong."

"Strong?" Viv asked. "Did he make a pass?"

"God, no, I'd have had a coronary! He hadn't even started flirting, thank goodness. But I could tell he was happy to run into me again and I thought it best to just discourage him right away rather than have to reject him later. Turned out he wasn't nearly discouraged enough and asked me out to dinner."

Viv was silent for a long moment. Her brows drew together and her eyes narrowed suspiciously. "And the problem is?" she finally asked.

"I don't want to go out to dinner with him."

"Ah," she said, sitting back on the couch. "He's not your type?"

"Vivian," Maureen said with surprise. "I don't *have* a type!"

Again Viv was silent. "I don't think I

understand, Maureen. We all have pretty basic likes and dislikes. Are you put off by his looks?"

"That's not it — he's actually handsome. Probably a little older than me, but still handsome."

"Bad manners?" Viv asked. "Bad breath? Slippery dentures? What puts you off?"

"Nothing, he's nice. Attractive and charming. But I don't go out to dinner with men."

"Why ever not?" she asked, completely baffled.

"I'm a single woman. A widow of a certain age. An *older* woman!"

"Maureen, you must draw the interest of men regularly. You're a very attractive woman!"

"No, never," she said. "Not at all. But then, I'm never in places where something like that might happen. I pretty much keep to church things or pastimes with women who live in the condos. Golf, tennis, bridge, the occasional potluck. If I do run into men, they're with their wives."

"But don't you have friends your age who date? Friends who are divorced or widowed who have men friends or boyfriends?"

Maureen made a sound of annoyance. "Yes, and some of them act downright ridiculous! I've seen some of these women I play golf and tennis with, chasing men as if they're . . . they're . . ."

"Horny?" Viv asked with a smile.

Maureen was shocked. "Really, that's an *awful* word!"

"Oh, brother," Viv said with a laugh. "Be right back."

Maureen was left to wonder what Vivian was doing in the kitchen until she returned and handed Maureen a glass of wine. "I've already had a glass of wine. Earlier. Before dinner."

"You have some special medical condition I should know about?" Vivian asked with a raised eyebrow.

"No, it's just that I —"

"Two glasses of wine in one day won't kill you. In fact, if you decide on a third, I won't tell a soul. You and I need to have a talk."

"A talk?" Maureen asked.

Vivian went back to the couch with her own glass and nodded. "Since your mother is no longer available, God rest her soul. You know, when you told me your sons considered you a prude, that you considered *yourself* a prude, I didn't take you that seriously. I should have. Maureen," she said gravely. "It's one thing to be strait-laced, but another entirely to stop living!"

"You can't say that of me, that I've

stopped living! I'm very active! True, I'm a little . . . Well, my son Aiden calls me 'starched.' But I like to think of it as moral fiber."

"Uh-huh. Maybe we should put it all out on the table here, girlfriend. Let's talk about the difference between moral fiber and uptight fears. Because —"

Maureen got a little red in the face. "Is it an uptight fear to wish your son would marry the woman before he has a child with her?"

"Oh, I wish that, too. Or rather, I wish my daughter had told Sean about Rosie before bolting like she did. I do understand — she was terrified and her heart was breaking. Still . . . But that's beside the point. What we wish other people would do has nothing to do with us. That's not moral fiber, that's being judgmental and unforgiving."

"I've never been judgmental or unforgiving a day in my life," Maureen protested.

"Know what? I absolutely believe you. You couldn't embrace my daughter and granddaughter if you were. So, it must be that what you call moral fiber for yourself is closer to heavy starch or moral constipation! Otherwise you'd have dinner with that nice, handsome, charming man and see if you could become friends. And leave it open to the possibility you could become better friends. And even *better* friends."

Maureen shook her head dismally. "You and I come from such completely different backgrounds, Viv. I was planning to be a nun!"

Viv's eyes widened in shock, but very briefly. "Well, you'd have been some kick-ass nun, that's for sure. I've seen you with your boys — they don't even sass. But something obviously changed your mind about the convent . . ."

"Patrick Riordan, Sr., my husband. He hounded me until I gave in and dated him, then married him. And he's been the only man in my life. The *only* one. I can't imagine another man . . ."

"You must have loved him very much."

"Well, of course I did, but that's got nothing to do with it. I'm just far too mature to be thinking about a relationship with a man. Those days are gone. It was hard enough for me when I was young and my body was —" She stopped, unable to finish.

"What? Maureen, you're beautiful! Your figure is amazing! You play sports and your mind is quick and you seem so confident."

Maureen snorted. "Of course I'm confident. With my *clothes* on!" She took a drink of her wine. "Patrick was and will be the only husband of my lifetime."

Vivian laughed softly, respectfully. "Maureen, I wouldn't even suggest you should marry again. My interfering does have *some* limits." She scooted forward on the sofa, closer to her friend. "I guess your dating girlfriends aren't keeping you in the loop, giving you the inside skinny —"

"They know I don't want to hear about their love lives," she said, a hint of sadness in her voice. "I'm from the old school, Vivian. The one where we don't talk about personal things."

"We're going to do that now, Maureen," she said. "I want to tell you some things about grown-up love. It's easier, Maureen. And better. There's more time, more tenderness, more patience. Our bodies aren't what they were and things don't always perform on schedule like they did when we were mere kids in our twenties. Sometimes a little help is called for — something to help with the erection, or maybe with the lubrication — but it's all part of intimacy that can be wonderfully fulfilling. Maureen, no one's body is what it was forty years ago — but I'm here to tell you, it's probably in perfect working order."

Maureen seemed to think about this for a moment, and it did bring a flush to her cheeks. "You must have a very nice gentle-man friend," was all she said.

"Carl is a lovely man and I'll save you the trouble of asking, because you won't be able to work up the courage — we're intimate. He's actually a bit younger than I am — I'm fifty-five and he's fifty. Fifty-year-old men without medical problems are usually still quite virile. For we ladies, the symptoms of menopause hound our sex lives — we get so dry. But that's completely normal and easily remedied. Carl and I don't manage a lot of alone time with our work and family obligations, but the nice thing about being this age . . . there's no pressure. Simple unhurried affection is so rewarding. And I wonder, do you know what the hottest erogenous area of a man's body is?"

Maureen fanned her face with her hand. "I imagine it's his, you know, penis . . ."

"Nope," she said, shaking her head. "Just like with women — it's the mind. When people like each other, Maureen, the rest follows as naturally for a woman in her fif-ties and sixties as for a woman in her twen-ties."

"You're lucky with Carl."

"I can't wait for you to meet him," Vivian said. "But, Maureen, I wasn't in the market for a man — I had my hands full with

Franci and Rosie. Besides, I was working for him during his wife's final days, God bless her. I was supporting him through his grief along with the rest of the office. It surprised me completely when he asked me out on a date a year or so after his wife died."

"But you knew him — you must have been comfortable with him."

"When a good man comes along, you owe it to yourself to at least have a look."

But Maureen just shook her head. "I have to admit, only to you, this is the only area of life in which I feel completely vulnerable. Thankfully it hardly ever happens. But I wouldn't know where to begin . . ."

"Then let me tell you," Vivian said. "When you go out to dinner, if he has good manners, is pleasant to both you and the wait-staff, is enjoyable company, you've begun. That's all it is. Friendship, companionship, affection — one day at a time. Women our age with our life experience don't have time for nonsense — we need substance and sincerity. The minute the relationship isn't one hundred percent positive, we can always find a good book." She smiled and glanced at Maureen's needlework on the accent table beside the chair. "Or sewing."

Maureen sipped her wine and saw that it

was nearly gone. "I think maybe you know what you're talking about."

"I'm a physician's assistant. I see patients our age in all manner of menopausal dilemma. Some have come into a sexual rebirth and are wearing their husbands out, others miss their former libido and want help to find it again. Still others wish their husbands would just leave them alone. Because I'm a female PA, they talk to me more often than the male PAs or doctors, and I've made a lot of referrals to female gynecologists who can relate to these patients. I'm not speaking from just my own dating experience, which has been relatively slim over the years." Vivian glanced at Maureen's glass. "Let me give you just a half glass more since we're in for the night."

"Good idea," Maureen said, extending the glass. "Because I have a few questions. And some of my good friends from way back call me Mo."

"Really? You don't look like a Mo at all. I can't wait to hear the questions."

"Why don't we start with, how can a man of any age be attracted to a woman whose naked breasts hang down to her lap? Good God, that's a reasonable question!"

"He's probably wondering how a woman of any age can overlook that flat butt or potbelly. But do you know what men are most self-conscious about? Their hair! They get all freaked out by thinning hair!"

By the time Sean and Franci dropped by to pick up their sleeping daughter, Vivian and Maureen were sitting on the floor in front of the fire with steaming cups of hot chocolate, whipped cream piled high on top, laughing like a couple of high-school girls, looking guilty as hell.

THIRTEEN

Sean had been spending every night at Franci's house and Franci was comfortable with it, having been convinced Rosie wasn't going to be traumatized by the two of them sleeping in the same bed. In fact, Rosie seemed to like sleeping between the two of them.

While Franci and Rosie were at their respective schools, Sean usually spent some time helping Luke out at the cabins, or he ran errands, or he did chores around Franci's little house. It was his mission to make sure her house was in complete repair before he went back to Beale right after Thanksgiving. If he ended up going remote, Luke would look after her.

"I managed fine as a single woman," Franci told him. "I know how to call a repairman if I need one."

"It's just as easy to call my brother," Sean said. "Not only is Luke cheaper, he'd be offended if you didn't."

On this particular Sunday night Franci had work to do; she had a couple of demanding classes on Monday because it was nearing end of term. So Sean took over bath and bedtime duties with Rosie while Franci sat on her bed with her laptop balanced on her knees, perfecting her lesson plan.

Once Sean had Rosie in the tub, they sang what Rosie called the soap song: "If I were a little bar of soap, I'd go slippy slippy slidey over everybody's hidey . . ." It had many verses and Sean now knew them all. Then it was off to bed to read Rosie's favorite book: *Everyone Poops.* When Rosie was all settled, Sean gave Luke a call.

"I'm not interrupting anything, am I?" Sean asked.

"Are you kidding?" Luke said. "Shelby's already asleep. She feels like shit."

"Again?" Sean asked. "Jeez, what's the deal?"

"You haven't guessed? She doesn't want to tell anyone yet, but she's pregnant."

"Luke!" came Shelby's loud, strident voice out of the background.

"It's just Sean!" Luke yelled back. "I thought you were asleep!"

Sean chuckled into the phone. "Well, kind of seems like you two don't have to try real hard to reproduce. You might want to keep an eye on that."

"No kidding. Don't tell Mom yet. Shelby wants to get past a couple of months. Even though she hurls every morning and falls asleep by seven every night, she wants to be *sure*."

"Perfectly understandable," Sean said. "I'll see you tomorrow after I drop Rosie at preschool."

Then he puttered around the house for a while, quietly, not even turning on the TV in the living room because Franci was working. He took out the trash, leafed through the newspaper again, brushed Harry's hair off the sofa, enjoyed domestic balance and tranquility. He checked on Rosie; she was sound asleep with her little bird mouth open. When he watched her sleep, he always thought, *She's mine!* And while a few weeks ago that idea had terrified him, now it filled him with wonder. With awe. She was a miracle he just didn't deserve.

He left Franci alone until about nine o'clock, then he dished up a bowl of vanilla ice cream and took it to her. "Can you take a break?" he asked.

"I can be all done," she said, closing the laptop. "This for me?" she asked, reaching for the ice cream.

"Yes, ma'am."

"You're working out very well. I like having a good-looking manservant around the house."

He got a pained look on his face. "I'm not going to be around the house much longer, baby. But I'll call every day, and anytime I'm not flying or have more than one day off in a row, I'll be here."

She touched his cheek. "Don't worry about us, Sean. We'll be okay. I think of this as temporary. Once you know what the air force has in store for you next, we'll come up with some more permanent plans."

"As permanent as possible, given the fact Uncle Sam owns me."

"Don't grouse. It's a good life. And I'm proud of you. You have *general* plastered all over your personnel file, Sean. You can go all the way, and you should."

"I want to make sure I say a few things before I have to go back to Beale. I've done everything I can do for now, Fran. Got the college trust set up, made a new will, have a new life-insurance policy, worked my charm on the boys at the Military Personnel Center in assignments." He took a deep breath. "I have to say something to Rosie about not being around all the time. Think she'll understand if I say I have to work?"

Franci smiled and nodded. "She under-stands that I work, that grandma works. She knows you've been on 'bacation.' " Her eyes glistened. "She's going to miss you a lot. So will I."

"I think Jake will work with me on time off, especially since I'm short." That was the term for someone who could be reas-signed without warning. The short guy doesn't get any long-term or real important projects; he might not get to finish them. "Franci, it's likely I'm going to go away for a while. You know how hard it is to stay in touch. Think she'll be able to understand something like that?"

"I can help her get through it," she said. "You know, you being in the air force was never a problem for me, right?" she asked. "I liked the military — I loved my job. I just didn't want to do that kind of job with a family, and family got real important to me." She shrugged. "All of a sudden."

He laughed and rubbed her knee. "Yeah, I got excited, forgot the rubber and family got real important to you. Listen, I was go-ing to rehearse this and say it right, but here's the thing. I'm ashamed of the kind of guy I was, Franci. Cards on the table — I was a selfish, egotistical asshole who ex-pected you to stay with me forever, but I wasn't willing to make it worth your while. I thought I was a man of the world, but I was a stupid kid. I was mad as hell I didn't know you were pregnant, but it scares me to death to think how I might've reacted if I had known. Franci, the truth is, I probably would have asked you to end the pregnancy, and when I think about what that would have cost us, it almost brings me to my knees. My world is so huge right now — when a Wide Iwish Rose puts her arms around my neck and calls me a silly daddy, my heart almost doesn't fit in my chest. That Rosie — she isn't just an idea. She's more than I could have imagined if my imagination had gone into overdrive."

Franci was quiet for a moment. Then she put a spoonful of ice cream to his lips. "I know," she said. "You've turned yourself into a wonderful silly daddy."

He swallowed the ice cream. "I need you to forgive me for the man I was . . . If you can."

"I forgave you when I saw you with our daughter. It's all different now."

"I know I suggested marriage before, but you were on to me. I was just trying to check off the items on my to-do list. It isn't like that now. I want to marry you because you're the most important thing in my life.

You're the beat of my heart, Franci — the mother of my child, my best friend and my future. I love you more than anything. I love Rosie as much. I'd lay down my life for either one of you."

"Sean . . ." she said in a whisper, tears coming to her eyes.

"I'm so sorry I had my head up my ass when we were together before — if I could do that whole time over, I'd prove to you that I'm not completely brainless. I love you, baby. You and Rose."

"I know," she whispered. "We love you, too."

"Will you marry me?" he asked. He grinned. "Bite the dust with me? Spend our lives as husband and wife?"

"I will, of course. You're obviously useless on your own."

"We can plan a wedding or do it quick or wait to decide when I get orders — it's up to you. Anything you want. But let's get a license right away so we're ready, because I need the official contract. I want to be your legal partner as well as your lover and best friend. And let's get you a ring. Will you consider taking my name, baby? And let me give it to Rosie?"

"Uh-huh," she said, a fat tear rolling down her cheek.

"It's just details, honey — but the important part is right this minute, when we make the decision that we're a family now."

"We're a family now," she said.

"Whew," he said. "I thought you'd probably say yes, but there was a little worry in the back of my mind that maybe I had more to prove. Thank you." He leaned toward her and covered her lips with his. "Thank you," he said again. "I love you so much. So let's get the license and ring this week — what do you think?"

She put her bowl on the bedside table. "I think my ice cream is soup, so you should close the door and take my clothes off. What do *you* think?"

He grinned hugely. "I think I'm going to love being married to you."

Ellie Baldwin asked Jo Fitch, her landlady and friend, to be her matron of honor, and Jo said, "I'm thrilled to be asked, but I'd rather be the mother of the bride. Ask Vanessa or Brie and let me do some special mother-of-the-bride things for your important day."

"Like what?" Ellie asked.

"Well, I'd like to get some of your friends and mine together to put some flowers in the church, dress up myself and the kids,

359

maybe decorate the bar for the reception . . ."

"Jo, I don't want you to go to a lot of trouble and expense," Elly said. "You've already done so much for me. You saved my life and got me my kids back."

"But see, that's why! That's what a mother does! And you're like a daughter to me." She grabbed her hands. "Let me."

So Ellie said, "Sure, fine, just don't go crazy."

And Jo said, "You are the bride — you stay out of my business and I'll make it nice without going crazy. Just let me — it's my one and only chance."

On Friday afternoon Vanessa dressed Ellie in a cream-colored cocktail dress with a swoop neck for the big day. Vanni wore the pale green chiffon that she'd married Paul in. They dressed at Jo's house; ordinarily Ellie walked to the church every day, but this day she and Vanni would drive down to keep their dresses and hairdos fresh and their shoes clean. Ellie followed instructions and went in the side door leading to the church basement, waiting until they were called upstairs, to the sanctuary foyer, when it was time. That was when she first saw what her kids were wearing.

Jo Ellen had shopped for special dress clothes for Danielle and Trevor to wear; Jo insisted they weren't expensive, but they cost more and were more beautiful than anything Ellie had ever purchased for them. In their lives! Danielle was beaming in her ruffles and Trevor stood proud in his very first suit. "Where will they wear them after the wedding?" the ever-practical Ellie asked Jo.

"They can wear them to church as often as they want until they grow out of them," Jo answered. And then Jo handed Ellie and Vanni beautiful bouquets, a surprise to Ellie.

"Oh, Jo!" Ellie gasped. Tears came to her eyes; she had checked the cost of flowers and asked Jo to just get her a long-stemmed rose. "Oh, how beautiful!" In her hands she held a bouquet made of pale yellow roses, lacy ferns, baby's breath and white chrysanthemums.

"I knew you'd approve, once you saw the flowers."

"But you weren't supposed to do too much!"

Jo shook her head. "I didn't do too much. I did everything just right." She smiled warmly. "This is a happy day. No tears."

"They go with the flowers in the church,

Mama!" Danielle said.

"The flowers in the church?"

"It's beautiful," Vanni said. "Wait till you see."

"Some of your friends helped us," Jo said. "Brie, Shelby, Muriel . . ."

"Me, too!" Danielle said. "I helped a lot!"

Vanni smoothed Ellie's blush with a soft finger. "Nervous?" she asked.

"About marrying Noah? Oh, shoot, I won the lottery! About the kids wrecking those fancy clothes? You bet!"

Jo Ellen looked absolutely stunning in a blue chiffon dress, and she was beaming — so proud of the kids, so proud of her new family. "I don't think I've ever seen a more beautiful bride," she said to Ellie. "Nick, are you ready? Because I think it's time."

"Let's go upstairs, everyone," he said, presenting his arm to Ellie.

Once they were upstairs standing behind the closed double doors to the sanctuary, Jo said to the kids, "It's time for us to take our seats. Then right after that Vanni will go down the aisle and then Nick and your mom will follow her. Ready to go inside?"

And with that, Jo and the kids slipped through the doors and into the church.

Vanni leaned toward Ellie and kissed her cheek. "Have a wonderful day, sweetheart.

And many happy years of married life. This couldn't be happening to two nicer people."

"Thank you, Vanni. I've never had a friend like you."

"You have lots of friends here, Ellie. This town? We're quick to notice when people are kind and generous and loving. It was our lucky day when you came to live with us." At exactly that moment the tempo of the recorded music picked up a bit and Nick reached for Ellie's hand, tucking it in the crook of his arm. "I'll see you up front," Vanni said, as the double doors were opened and she began her walk down the aisle.

Ellie looked at Nick. "This was supposed to be just a little thing. I didn't expect to do the whole walking down the aisle bit. We never even practiced."

"I think it'll come natural," Nick said with a laugh.

"The best part is, I'm not attempting to play the piano for this gig," Ellie said. And at that point the sanctuary doors were opened again by handsomely suited-up Jack and Preacher. Ellie stood there, getting her first look into the church. She gasped and clutched Nick's arm tighter. Not only was the church full of people, far more than they had for Sunday services, but it was *filled* with flowers and candles. November's early dusk had darkened the church, but candle-light glittered everywhere. "Who did this?" she whispered in shock.

"Me and Jo Ellen, the kids, your husband to be, your friends," Nick said proudly.

She glanced to the right and in the very back pew sat some of the boys from the vagrants' camp, men Noah not only visited regularly but also brought to church. She smiled and felt a huff of laughter escape as she noted they weren't one bit cleaner or dressed up than usual, but she was so touched to see them there. And in addition to the Sunday regulars, she saw people she knew from town, people who didn't come to Sunday services — Dr. Cameron Michaels, his wife and twin babies; Luke Riordan's brother Sean with his girlfriend, his daughter and mother; some neighbors she'd met at Jack's Bar; a young man named Rick and his fiancée, Liz; and Dan Brady with a woman she'd never seen before. Hope McCrea was there — that old crone had previously owned the church but had never before officially set foot in it. And right up in front was Dr. Nate Jensen, who had saved Noah's adopted dog's life, and his fiancée, Annie.

"Wow," she whispered.

"Ellie, don't stare," Nick said. "Just smile

at Noah. He's waiting for you. He looks like he's been waiting forever."

"Well, he hasn't," she whispered through gathering tears.

The flowers and candles in the church had been a big surprise for Ellie, but the number of people at the wedding, and at Jack's afterward, had surprised Noah, as well. It felt as if half the town was there and, unlike typical weddings, there were people Noah and Ellie had never met before. These people brought gifts and potluck dishes, and they offered congratulations and partied as if they'd known Ellie and Noah forever. The happy couple hadn't expected the large number of guests, nor the many, many wedding gifts. What Noah realized was that he might not be everyone's pastor — they had individual preferences of faith and denomination — but they were everyone's neighbors. That realization brought a satisfaction that was indescribable.

The bar was decorated with colorful streamers, flowers from the church, napkins embossed with Ellie's and Noah's names and the date. The centerpiece of the event was Preacher's cake — a two-tiered white masterpiece that he beamed over. "I'm going to start doing more of this," he said proudly. "I think I have a knack."

It was only a casual gathering with covered dishes and well wishes, but Preacher had rigged up his speakers from his house stereo and there was some dancing, even though there was hardly room to move. There was no garter to throw and Ellie wouldn't part with her bouquet but no one seemed to mind.

Typical of Virgin River parties, people began to leave early. Those who had a drive ahead were the first to depart, followed by the farmers, ranchers and vintners, who didn't get days off. Sean Riordan left early, taking his family back to Eureka. Noah smiled to see his friend George bow over Maureen Riordan's hand as he said good-bye, brushing his lips against it like a courtier. Nick and Jo took Ellie's kids home to bed, but a hard-core group remained at the bar — the diehards who were willing to endure a lack of sleep for a good party. As the evening grew late, the men were found on the porch with brandy and cigars, Jack's space heaters lit to warm them against the chill November night. The women sat by the fire indoors and laughed together. And, finally, around eleven, everyone wended their way home.

And at three in the morning in the little

apartment above the Fitches' garage —
tonight, the honeymoon suite — no sleep
had taken place at all. Noah rolled onto his
back and groaned, "Oh my God, I love
you!"

"You're a maniac," Ellie said. "I've never
met a man who liked sex so much."

Noah laughed. "That's nice, Ellie. I'll take
comfort in that."

"Really," she insisted. "Have you finally
had enough?"

"For now," he said. His eyes were closed,
but there was a smile on his lips.

She rolled over on her belly, propped up
on an elbow and looked into his beautiful
eyes. "So, is married sex better than sneaky
sex?"

He ran his fingers through the hair at her
temples. "Yeah. For me, it is." Then he
pulled her head down and kissed her deeply,
his heart completely hers. He couldn't
remember ever being more content.

"It is for me, too," she whispered. "Can
we sleep now?"

He pulled her against him, her head rest-
ing on his arm, and holding her tight they
drifted off to sleep. But not for long. Ellie
was up, showered and pulling on jeans and
a sweatshirt first thing in the morning. The
smell of fresh coffee filled the small room

and she jostled Noah awake. "Come on, don't be a bum — I promised the kids we'd start poking around the new house as soon as everyone woke up."

He rolled over with a loud moan and put the back of his hand over his eyes. "What's the matter with you?" he asked.

"I'm so excited." She laughed. "That house has been ours for a whole week and we haven't had time to do anything to it yet! You said we'd get down there right away, as soon as we got married."

He moaned again and rolled over. "My right away and your right away are at least a couple of hours apart . . . Aren't you in the afterglow from a wedding night of magnificence?"

She giggled. "Not anymore. Come on, Noah. Don't be lazy."

"Lazy, she says," he muttered, dragging himself out of bed. "There should be a warning attached to marrying an energetic younger woman . . ."

They went downstairs to Jo and Nick's kitchen; the kids were just rising, so they were talked into more coffee and breakfast. By the time everyone was moving at a normal pace, Ellie was jittery with anticipation. She loaded a few things in the back of Noah's truck — broom, mop, rags, detergent, scrub brushes, trash bags. Jo promised she and Nick would follow behind with the kids. So, on their first official day of married life, Ellie and Noah took off down the road to their new old house.

Ellie and Noah could hear the sound of heavy equipment well before they could see it, but neither said a word because they couldn't imagine that it would have anything to do with them. The next thing they noticed was that the road to their house was difficult to navigate because it was lined with parked cars and trucks.

"What in the world . . . ?" Ellie said. Noah edged his old truck closer, and the moment they broke through the trees they were both momentarily stunned. Their property was a beehive of activity. Someone was driving a large farm-size mower around the property. There were men on ladders propped up against the house; more men pounded hammers on the roof, and at ground level people were raking up the cuttings, hauling trash, scraping off old paint, replacing boards and sanding porch rails.

George was standing on the porch wearing a carpenter's apron, looking very much at home. Noah walked up the porch steps. "What's going on here?"

"Looks like your friends have decided to give you a hand to get you started. Don't worry, Noah — there's going to be plenty of work for you to do." Then he grinned.

Paul Haggerty walked up behind Noah and Ellie, balancing a dozen or so long baseboards over one shoulder. "Morning, Noah, Ellie," he said as he passed.

Inside the house they found Muriel up on a ladder, using a liquid chemical mixture to slowly remove years of white paint from a solid oak archway that separated the living room from the dining room. She had about two feet of the arch's natural wood exposed. Walt was at work doing the same thing on the banister. "Hi, Ellie," Muriel called from her place on the ladder. "I had to take paint off the most beautiful wood at my old house and, let me tell you, it looks awesome when it's done! You're going to love this when it's stained and varnished. It won't be quick, but it's worth it. And there's nothing we can do about the beveled stairs. Each step will have to be replaced from the wear, but it's not a hard job. I can do it."

Ellie's mouth fell open. This was the woman who had been in movies and nominated for Oscars, and was most commonly seen on TV in strapless evening gowns and glittering jewels. And she was talking about replacing the wood on her steps for her? It was unreal.

Luke Riordan came out of the kitchen with his arms full of crinkling, old, rotting wallpaper he'd torn off. He dumped it in the empty dining room. "Morning," he said. "Art," he yelled back into the kitchen. "Can you get this pile of trash in the back of my truck? I'll run by the dump on the way home."

"Wow," Ellie said. "Whose idea was this?"

"I don't know," Walt said. "Paul, whose idea was this?"

"Not sure. Jack's maybe?"

Preacher walked out of the kitchen. "Mine," he said indignantly. "I think it was my idea. We pitch in around here when it's practical. We need to get you up and running before it gets any colder. Gotta replace all the window glass that's cracked or broken, and the fireplaces need to be cleaned. You're gonna need a new furnace I think — you're on your own there. I don't know anyone who does that, but I did get a friend from Clear River who said he'd come out this afternoon and get fifty years of soot out of those chimneys in the living and dining rooms. He's gonna do it as a donation, just to help out. He's probably got something he's gonna ask you for, Noah. Like a wedding or funeral or baptism or something — as a rule he's usually not that generous."

Noah just laughed. "Hope he's not planning a funeral. That doesn't sound good."

"Ellie, you should get some measurements," Muriel said. "See what size appliances will work in that kitchen and maybe measure the windows for blinds and the floors for area rugs. It's not going to take much to get this place habitable. But to get it pretty? That's going to be a six-month project. But I can help. I love doing this stuff."

Ellie walked toward Muriel's ladder and looked up at her. Muriel wore work coveralls, boots, a ratty long-sleeved sweatshirt, gloves and a ball cap. "Muriel," she said in awe. "You're a *movie star*."

"She's also a crackerjack carpenter, painter and renovator. You should see what she did to her place, almost entirely alone," Walt said.

"You were a wonderful help, Walt," Muriel said. "Of course, you had ulterior motives, but that wasn't a problem for me. Come see my restored house sometime, Ellie. I love showing it off."

"Vanni wanted to be here to help, but she's tied up with the kids, and they'd just be in the way," Walt said. "Most of these guys have to work all week, but a few of us have time on our hands and will get back here after the weekend. Me. Muriel. George."

"Someone call me?" George asked, sticking his head in the door.

"No, George. Get back to work," Walt said.

Ellie turned around and leaned her face into Noah's chest. He put his arms around her and felt her shoulders shake, heard her sniff. He leaned down and kissed her cheek. "Don't cry," he whispered.

She lifted her head. "They're so wonderful. How can they be this wonderful?"

He smiled. "I think they practice."

Fourteen

Maureen Riordan heard from her son Luke about the rally of neighbors who surprised the Kincaids with a work party over the weekend. She was completely charmed by the notion. It sounded like the way things had been in her parents' day — barn raisings and such. So on Monday morning she drove out to Virgin River. She had a cup of coffee with Luke, then, following his directions, she made her way out to the old house to see what progress had been made.

There was only one beat-up old truck outside the house. Then she heard the sound of a saw inside. For a moment she thought maybe it wasn't such a great idea to poke around. Obviously a man was working the saw and she was a woman alone. But in a place where the community had pulled together to help one of their own, could there be danger? It must be just another good neighbor inside the house.

The door stood open, even though it was cold outside.

Right inside the front door in what must be the living room, who should be standing at a circular saw cutting planks but George Davenport. She let out a breath. Well, avoiding him wasn't going to work. She'd tried to give him a wide berth at the wedding party on Friday night, but he'd singled her out, complimented her, made small talk and even kissed the back of her hand! There seemed to be only two options to deal with the man. Face him head-on or leave town.

And there he stood, his white hair, which was not terribly thick, askew and spiking, wearing jeans and a sweatshirt, covered with sawdust. His face was tan — but hadn't he said he'd come from Seattle? Cloudy, dreary Seattle? Despite herself, she noticed his shoulders were broad, his butt was solid and his legs were long. What was a man his age doing with broad shoulders and a solid butt? She wondered what he'd look like without a shirt and was immediately *appalled* that she would even think that!

The thought must have caused her to make a noise because he turned toward her. The smile that split his handsome face was bright. No slippery dentures there; his teeth were white and strong. He must have been good about brushing and flossing all through the years, probably the *only* thing they had in common.

"Mrs. Riordan," he said. "What brings you here?"

"Curiosity," she said. "My son Luke told me about all the activity here over the weekend and I thought it was such a wonderful thing that I just wanted to see it for myself." She entered the house farther. "What is it you're doing?"

"I'm cutting the boards for the new stairs. Noah will be along when he can clear some of his morning appointments. We'll install the stairs and, later today and tomorrow, Muriel will help with the sanding, staining and varnishing."

"Muriel?" Maureen asked.

"You've met Muriel St. Claire, haven't you? She's an ace woodworker and she completely restored an old farmhouse on the outskirts of town. She moved in right next to Walt Booth's place, which is how they met. They've been a hot item for the past year."

"Hot item?" she said. "For a year?" She frowned. "I guess I thought they'd been a couple for a long time." Even though many of her female acquaintances found romance later in life, Maureen never really got used to the idea. Viv told her it was high time she dispelled the notion that romance was strictly for the very young. Still, when she thought about couples the age of Muriel and Walt getting together, she couldn't help but think of it as more practical than passionate.

"Fairly recent, as I understand it," George went on. "Walt was widowed several years ago. And while Muriel has never taken me into her confidence, the movie rags say she's been married and divorced a number of times." He grinned. "She must think the day she ran into Walt Booth — stable old war dog that he is — was one of the luckiest days of her life."

"George, I probably owe you an apology," Maureen said. "I don't think I was as friendly as I could have been when we ran into each other at Jack's a week or so ago. The fact is, I do remember meeting you at Luke's wedding. I don't know why I was acting as if I couldn't remember you. It isn't like me to play coy like that."

"I knew that, Mrs. Riordan," he said.

She was stunned. "You knew?"

He smiled gently. Kindly. "I saw it in your eyes," he explained, then shifted his own back and forth, breaking eye contact, demonstrating what he saw. "And the moment I met you I knew you were more straight-forward than that. I'm sorry if I made you uncomfortable."

She was a little uncomfortable *now,* in fact. She felt vulnerable, being found out before she even had a chance to confess. "And I was widowed quite a while ago."

"Yes, I know that, too. Twelve years or so?" he asked.

She put her hands on her hips. "And you know this how?" she asked, not trying too hard to keep the indignant tone from her voice.

"Well, I asked," he said with a shrug. "That's what a man does when he has an interest in a woman. He asks about her."

"Is that so? Well, what else did you find out?"

"Nothing embarrassing, I swear. Just that you've been widowed quite a while now, all five sons are in the military, you live in Phoenix and, as far as anyone knows, you're not currently seeing anyone special."

Special? she thought. Not seeing anyone period with absolutely no intention of doing so. "Interesting," she said. "Well, I don't know a thing about you."

"Of course you do. I'm a friend of Noah's. A teacher." He chuckled. "And obviously I have time on my hands."

378

"That's not very much information," she said.

He took a rag out of his back pocket and wiped some of the sawdust and sweat off his brow. "You're welcome to ask me anything you like. I'm an open book."

"How long have you been a teacher?" she asked, starting with a safe subject.

"Twenty years now, and I'm thinking of making some changes. I'm seventy and I always thought retirement would turn me into an old fuddy-duddy, but I'm rethinking that. I'd like to have more time to do the things I enjoy most and, fortunately, I have a small pension and some savings. Besides, I'm tired of keeping a rigid schedule."

"You would retire?"

"Again." He laughed. "I retired the first time at the age of fifty and, after twenty years at the university, I could retire again. There are so many young professors who'd love to see a tenured old goat like me leave an opening for them."

"And before you were a teacher?"

"A Presbyterian minister," he said.

"Oh! You're joking!" she said.

"I'm afraid it's the truth."

"I'm Catholic!"

He laughed. "How nice for you."

"You're making fun of me," she accused.

"I'm making fun of your shock," he said. "Don't you have any non-Catholic friends?"

"Of course. Many. But —"

"Because I have quite a few Catholic friends. And Jewish and Mormon and other faiths. I used to play golf with a priest friend every Thursday afternoon for years. I had to quit. He was a cheat."

"He was not!"

"You're right, he wasn't. I just threw that in there to see if I could rile you up. No one riles quite as beautifully as a redhead. Actually, he was transferred to a new parish. I hear from him once in a while. We used to have the best time with those minister-rabbi-priest jokes. We were in search of a golfing rabbi for a long time. We never did find one."

"You don't take things very seriously, do you?" she asked.

"Not as much now as I did when I was younger. I'm proud of that, by the way. So, what do you say we pick a night for dinner?"

"Have you ever been married?" she asked.

"You asked that before. Twice," he said. "Does that disqualify me as a dinner companion?"

Truthfully, she'd been too rattled to pay

attention to his answer. "Are you a widower?"

"Yes. My second wife died of cancer a few years ago. You'd have liked her — she was such a lovely, funny woman. My first wife is alive and well. She left me over thirty-five years ago. You wouldn't have liked her at all. Hardly anyone did. Does." He frowned and shook his head. "Really, she was one of the most difficult women I've ever known. Beautiful, however. Very beautiful. But very . . . Oh, never mind. I thought I was long past complaining about her."

"Divorced?" she said. "A divorced minister?"

"You'd be amazed at how many real-life issues priests, ministers and rabbis deal with in their own lives. Now . . ."

"You know, you're a peculiar man," she said. "Why would you want to have dinner with me?"

"I thought it was obvious," he said. "You're a striking woman with a strong and entertaining personality. In fact, you're even more entertaining today. What a lot of funny questions and concerns you seem to have. Does the Catholic church have some sort of punishment for parishioners who date out of the faith?"

"Don't be glib," she said. "I'm old school.

When I was growing up, one didn't even contemplate a date outside the faith. Of course, attending an all girls' Catholic school pretty much ensured that. Besides, I wasn't an ordinary Catholic. I was, for a short time, a novitiate."

"Well, now." He grinned.

"Well, now, what?" she asked.

He shrugged. "Very devout, are you? Then it turns out we have more in common than we have at odds." He grinned. "I, for one, am glad that didn't work out, but it certainly explains how you can seem so sophisticated on one hand and so old-fashioned on the other. Want to think about that invitation a while longer?"

She sighed deeply. "I like to spend whatever afternoons and evenings I can with my newly found granddaughter. Obviously I can't spend every evening with her. That gets in the way of my son having quality time with Rosie and her mother. But —"

"Ah. But you like to keep evenings open for her. Understandable. How about a nice, leisurely lunch? How does that sound?"

"Lunch shouldn't be out of the question," she said, surprising herself.

"Bravo! Tomorrow?"

"What about your work on this house?"

"I imagine I'll be spending plenty of time

on this old house," George said. "I'm planning to stay through Thanksgiving. And, besides, a man has to be well-rounded. All work and no play is no good, you know."

"You're very persistent, aren't you?"

"Absolutely," he agreed. "Now, may I at least call you Maureen? Or do I have to continue with this Mrs. Riordan business forever? It makes it seem like I'm trying to get a date with a married woman!"

She laughed in spite of herself. "My sons are going to be flabbergasted."

"Why?"

"You might as well know the truth. I haven't been out with a man since my husband died. And, in fact, I hadn't been out with many before I met him."

"Somehow that doesn't surprise me at all, Maureen. I haven't run into a woman as difficult to get a date with as you. We're going to have a good time, you and me." And then he smiled at her.

Maureen had no idea how many people George Davenport told that they were having lunch together, but she saw no need to mention it to anyone. She told herself she wasn't keeping a secret, just not making an issue. The real truth was that she couldn't bear to answer any questions — before or after the lunch. She was nervous, excited, a little frightened, afraid of disappointment . . . and even more afraid of *not* being disappointed. All morning while she tidied up Vivian's small house and got ready for George to pick her up, her stomach was in flutters and she went over possible scenarios in her mind. What if he came on too strong? Or made a pass? Or tried to kiss her? Or worse — what if it turned out he was a terrible bore and she never wanted to see him again, for lunch or anything else?

All those flutters and possibilities were gone minutes after he picked her up. "Have you been to Ferndale, Maureen?" he asked her.

"I haven't been much of anywhere around here."

"Good!" George boomed. "Actually, I didn't mean it was good you haven't seen the sights, just good that I get to show you some of them. It's a beautiful little town. The restored and renovated Victorian houses and buildings are wonderful. There are plenty of shops, and just outside of town there's an amazing cemetery built straight up a hill. It's old and interesting. One of the big old churches in town has been remodeled into a large bed-and-breakfast. I thought we'd walk the town and poke into the shops. I put a picnic basket and cooler in the trunk — if the weather holds and the sun stays out, we can sit at the top of the hill, above the river, and have crackers, wine, cheese and fruit. There's a blanket in the back. It'll be brisk, but not too cold."

"That sounds so nice," she said. Perfect, she thought — not too fancy.

"Will that hold you? Not much of a lunch, but I'll take you to get dessert afterward if you like. There's a wonderful old Victorian hotel with a restaurant in town."

"I think you've given this a lot of thought," she said. "Do you date a lot?"

"I suppose you could say I do," he answered. "There are women I'm friendly with and we share certain interests. There's a neighbor woman I've known for years who is a food critic for the newspaper, and sometimes she invites me along to restaurants she's reviewing — what an opportunity! She doesn't listen to a word I say about the food, but I love the whole experience. I have a colleague I can invite to those college parties I'm forced to attend — she's single and doesn't usually have a date, either. Mainly I have a number of friends who happen to be women, and if I'm looking for something to do, I might give one of them a call." He turned and looked toward

her. "Maureen, I don't have anything romantic going on with anyone. Ridiculous as
it might be to think a man my age could be
a playboy, I promise you, I am *not.*"

"I didn't mean —"

He grinned and grabbed her hand. "Of
course you did, and not only am I encour-
aged, I'm *flattered!*"

"Well, don't be," she said. "I didn't mean
that."

And then he laughed at her.

George drove toward Ferndale, but went
past the exit and took a back road that
wound up a hill. He pulled off the road
across from a corral that held four nice-
looking horses. "The first time I passed by
this spot, what came to mind was that it
was a perfect picnic site. I know it's a little
brisk for a picnic. Will you be comfortable?
I have an extra jacket in the backseat."

"I think it's a great idea," she said. "I love
being outside."

"Good, come with me. You take the basket
and blanket and I'll take the cooler. Let's
go up this path a little bit, just until we can
get a view."

Maureen followed him for a while, then
when he stopped she turned around and
sighed. The hill sloped down sharply and
the river and valley spread out beneath

them. "That's beautiful," she said.

"Isn't it?" he agreed. He put down the cooler, spread the blanket, got down on his knees and began to unpack the things he'd brought along. He had an aged Gouda, some soft Brie, cheddar and Muenster. He put out two small boxes of crackers and, using the cooler lid as a table, spread out grapes, apples, some sliced kiwi from a Baggie and a small plastic container of melon balls.

"George, you went to some trouble," she said. "You very nearly cooked!"

"I'm not a bad cook, either. Will you have a glass of merlot? Or a soda or a bottled water?"

She chose the wine and toasted him. "I'm glad you're persistent," she said. "This is wonderful."

During the course of their leisurely picnic, they learned about each other. How it was he had never had children. "I wanted them, but my first wife and I didn't have children, and my second wife had a couple from a first marriage and, given her age, wasn't keen on more. My first wife remarried and had a son, so I suspect it was my physiological problem that prevented pregnancy. God has always saved my butt in the clinches. It was a terrible relationship."

George wanted to know what it was like raising five sons. "Like war," she answered. "My husband was a good father, but he worked long hours and plenty of overtime. I learned early that I'd better make sure they understood my word was law, or I was doomed. I know they called me the Enforcer behind my back. God knows what they call me now!"

They talked about their friends, their hobbies, their favorite foods and books, trips they'd like to take, their homes and what they liked about them. They talked about their community service — he liked the soup kitchen and food drives, she moderated a grief group at church and was drafted for every fundraiser they had. Eventually they talked about their spouses and their deaths. Maureen's husband had developed congestive heart failure and, although he was being treated, he didn't live long after the diagnosis. "I guess he tried to ignore his symptoms too long and, though I hounded him, he wouldn't see the doctor. Men don't, you know. And *good wives* don't want to aggravate them by nagging. If I had to do it over, I'd have had him abducted and taken off to the doctor for a full exam."

"No doubt," George said. "I know what you mean."

She asked about his wife. "Well, a similar situation. Her doctor harped about a colonoscopy to be safe, to make sure there was nothing wrong. Something a person should really have done around the age of fifty. But Mary was obstinate — it sounded dreadful to her and she put it off. She had no symptoms of any kind, after all. What neither of us realized, once you have symptoms, you might have waited too long. She went through surgery and chemo, which bought her a year." He gave her a small smile.

She surprised herself by covering his hand. "Time eases a lot. I did the best I could back then, and so did you."

In the early afternoon they packed up their picnic and proceeded to Ferndale to stroll the neighborhoods to see the houses, dawdling and talking and laughing. They had an ice cream and looked in the shop windows and finally climbed the steep cemetery hill on the outskirts of town. Maureen was fascinated by the headstones and read many of them. Suddenly she looked at her watch and realized she hadn't been paying attention to the time. "Oh, my God!" she said, plucking the cell phone out of her purse. "Rosie!"

"It's only three," George said.

"But I promised to pick her up today at three!"

"I can have you there by three-thirty. They're not going to leave her on the curb, are they?"

"No, they're open till six for working parents, but . . ."

He grabbed her wrist firmly to get her attention. "Maureen, call the day-care center and tell them you're on your way. No harm done."

"Sean. I should call Sean. He might be at Franci's and waiting for me to bring Rosie home."

"Then call him," George said softly. "She's safe, Maureen. And you haven't been a bad grandmother by going on an outing with me."

She stilled immediately. Then she looked at her cell phone and called Sean. "Hi, Sean, it's me. I've been out to lunch and lost track of time. I can be there to pick up Rosie by three-thirty if you — All right, I'll see you at Franci's in a half hour or so. No, I'm on my way." She ended the call and slipped the phone back into her purse. "He said he'd run over and pick her up and I should take my time. But I'd better get going."

"Of course," George said. They stood on

an incline in the middle of the cemetery and he stepped closer. He lifted her chin to look into her green eyes. "You lost all track of time because we were enjoying ourselves. That means the date was a success." He leaned toward her and gave her a peck on the lips. "Now relax and I'll take you home."

And out of nowhere, completely un-planned and unprepared, Maureen threw her arms around George's neck and planted her lips on his. He stumbled backward a couple of steps before he came up against a large tombstone that balanced him. He was finally able to get his arms around her and hang on to her. He kissed her back, but as kisses go it wasn't much. It was the gesture that was startling.

She let him go.

"Well," he said. "You should warn me when you're going to do that. We could have gone down the hill, then we'd have to explain a couple of broken hips. That's more complicated than being a little late to day care."

"I don't know what came over me," she said.

"It doesn't matter. Just make sure it comes over you again before long. I like it." He held out his hand. "Come on. I'll walk you down. Slowly."

■ ■ ■

As the end of November approached, Franci and Sean talked to Rosie about the fact that Daddy had to go back to his flying job after Thanksgiving. It would mean that he could only visit when he had a few days off. They explained that he hoped they could spend Christmas together, but he wasn't sure he'd be able to. "But I will call you and talk to you on the phone whenever I can. Sometimes every day."

To which Rosie replied, " 'Kay."

They avoided telling her about the larger problem — that Sean would be transferred somewhere, probably soon after the new year. Perhaps someplace where he wouldn't be allowed to take a family.

They did get their marriage license and a very nice ring was being made for Franci, but their plans would have to wait until they knew more about the future.

Franci was past all the fear and anger she'd felt when Sean had first reappeared in her life — she no longer worried that her heart would be broken again, nor was she still angry about the way they'd parted four years ago. Those thoughts were now all forgotten and she wondered how she had managed to live without him. As well, she didn't know how he'd accomplished it, but he'd turned into a wonderful father — affectionate and devoted and completely comfortable in his role.

"Didn't we used to fight all the time?" she asked him.

"It seemed like a lot of arguing, but once we broke up all I could think about were the things we had going for us," he said. "Here's what I know, babe. I think now we got it down. We might have some hurdles with the air force assignments, but from here on we're making it."

"I'm sorry I didn't tell you about Rosie," she said to him.

"I'm sorry I was so impossible to tell," he replied.

Every day Maureen found herself in very unfamiliar territory. Without saying a word to anyone besides Viv, she'd spent several lunch hours with George Davenport over the couple of weeks before Thanksgiving. Like herself, he was heading back to Seattle after the holiday weekend. "End of term," he said. "I really need to be there. But what say we meet right back here for Christmas?"

"I'd like that," she said.

"How attached are you to that condo in

Phoenix?" he asked.

"It's perfect for me," she said with a shrug. "I don't have to cut grass or shovel snow."

"But do you *like* it?"

"Sure. Do you like where you're living?"

"It's been a good home for over twenty years, but I'm thinking ahead. Mary's grown kids have moved away and they're really my only family besides Noah. I don't believe I'm going to stay in that house in Seattle much longer. Or at the university, either. I'm ready for the next step. A more portable lifestyle — more freedom and travel."

She smiled and said, "Maybe you'll visit Phoenix."

"Maybe I will. You'll let me have your guest room, won't you?"

She grinned and shook her head. "The complex has some guest apartments we can reserve for out-of-town company."

He lifted a brow and said, "You're not afraid to be alone with me, Maureen."

"Not at all, but I won't have the gossip."

"You would have made a *fantastic* nun," he told her. And then he laughed.

But she let him kiss her. Small, affectionate kisses — that was enough. But something she was completely unprepared for was beginning to happen for her. Bringing

George into her life was not simply about practicality or companionship at all, but more about the little tremors that vibrated inside her when he was near, when he touched her ever so briefly, when he brushed his lips against hers. She had no idea that a woman in her sixties could feel like a teenager.

She kept remembering what Vivian had said about mature love — that it was slower, sweeter, more tender and very fulfilling. Such thoughts made her shiver.

She had yet another long lunch with George planned for today. They were making the most of their time together before Aiden appeared for Thanksgiving week and Maureen concentrated on family again. When she heard the blast of a horn in front of Vivian's house, she was astonished. She went to the window thinking that it *couldn't* be George honking for her. He was, above all else, a gentleman. He was *debonaire.*

But there, sitting in front of the house, was Noah's old RV, and George was standing outside the door. Her mouth slightly open, she wandered out of the house.

"George, what's this?"

"What I really want to do is take you for another picnic, this time on the coast by the ocean, but it would be torture in this cold wind. So I volunteered to take Noah's RV for its weekly housekeeping — empty the lavs, load the potable water, all the stuff that has to be done regularly. He was more than happy to put me on that job since I've been using the RV as a hotel room. But I'll tell you the real reason I wanted to steal the RV — I'm going to take you to the ocean and we're going to have a picnic. But we'll sit inside, at the table next to the big window, and be nice and warm and comfy. And alone."

She grinned and knew it was a girlish smile. "I don't know if I ought to get into a vehicle that private with you."

"Well, you can be sure the neighbors won't talk! Now get your jacket and purse, lock up the house and let's get going."

"I'll just be a minute," she said. He was in the driver's seat by the time she got back. She climbed up and inside and sat in the seat beside him. While he drove the big vehicle down the street, she turned in her seat and craned her neck to take in the interior. "That's a cute little kitchen," she said. "What did you make us for lunch?"

"Takeout," he said. "I don't want to waste my time preparing food. How does it feel? Riding up here?"

She looked out. "I like it. It's wonderful

being high. I've been frustrated by all the big cars on the road. Big SUVs, trucks, vans and such. I've always hated being behind them and blind to what's going on up the road. This is nice."

"Not only is there a bathroom, kitchen, washer and dryer, master bedroom and living room, but a satellite for TV and radio reception, and storage underneath. And this is an old RV. I'm not much of a mechanic, so I hope it runs without any problems."

"Oh, George, what would we do if it broke down?" she worried.

"Call Noah," he said. "He'd come with his toolbox. He's been keeping this thing going for years. It's kind of nifty, don't you think?"

"I do," she said. "Is it hard to maneuver?"

"Not a bit. I could let you try it, if you like."

"No, thanks." She laughed. She ran a hand along the console. "But it's fun, George. I have to hand it to you — you're always fun."

"Why, thank you, Mrs. Riordan," he said. "Thing is, I've decided what I'm going to do next. I have to go back to the university, of course. Next semester, I'm cutting back my schedule. I need more freedom. I'm going to transition out, sneak up on retire-

ment. I'm going to get myself one of these!"
he exclaimed, smacking the steering wheel.
"Mary's sons are married and have children
— they're great kids, superior stepsons. One
lives in Texas, one in Florida. I'm going to
put my house on the market and retire by
the end of school, just in time to begin
traveling. I'm going to see this country one
state at a time, and I'm going to drop in on
those boys. They both have amazing wives.
One has three children, one has two — and
even though I'm a stepfather, they call me
Papa instead of Grandpa. I'm going to visit
them occasionally while I'm traveling, then
move on to other sights, then check back
in. What do you think of that idea?"

Her smile was alive. "It sounds wonderful.
You'll enjoy that. Maybe I'll even see you
now and then in Virgin River."

"Or, you could come along," he said. "You
have all those military boys all over the
place. We could check on them, as well. And
believe me, once a couple of them get married and have children, the others fall in
line. I've seen it a million times. As soon as
I get an offer on the house — which is a
good house and should bring a nice price
even in a depressed economy — I'm going
to start shopping for a quality RV. I've been
looking at pictures online. Maureen, you

have no idea how high tech these things have become! They now come with expandable sides, two people showers, freezers, big screens in the living room and bedroom, Whirlpool tubs — you name it! How'd you like to have a hot tub on wheels, Maureen?"

She looked over at him. He was so excited by his idea, he was actually a little flushed, and she found herself hoping it wasn't high blood pressure. If the moment ever presented itself, she'd ask about that. But after all his rambling about his future RV, all she could say was, "Come along?"

"A perfect solution for both of us," he said. "We'd have time together, we'd have fun together. We'd see the families, travel . . ."

"George, that's *outrageous*. We've had a few lunches —"

"And we'll have a few more! We'll also e-mail, talk on the phone, get together occasionally — in Virgin River, but also in Phoenix and Seattle. We'll spend the next six months figuring out if we fit as well as it seems we do."

"Long distance? Occasional visits?" she asked doubtfully.

"It'll give you time to look over my accounts to be sure you're not getting conned out of your retirement." He laughed at his own joke, slapping his knee. "Of course, with five brawny, overprotective sons you're relatively safe from a dangerous guy like me." He glanced at her and his expression was playful. "We're not young, Maureen. We should be sure we're attracted to each other and that we get along, but we shouldn't waste a lot of time. Every day is precious." He reached for her hand and squeezed it. "I'm very attracted to you. I'd love to get you alone in a fancy RV for a few years."

She laughed at him; she *hated* that she was behaving like such a *girl.* "Have you lost your mind?"

"I've been wondering what to do next. I've had a couple of fulfilling careers, but I can't go on preaching and teaching forever — I'll get bored. At a point I should retire again. When I lost Mary, I filled my time with activities — friends for dinner, going to the movies, attending a new play. I had a very nice life with Mary. I loved her deeply, as I'm sure you loved your Patrick. I miss her. But I also miss having a best friend to spend time with. Maureen, this is guaranteed *not* to sweep you off your feet, but you're the first woman I've met in years who could actually be that kind of friend! We have so much in common it's amazing!"

"You've slipped a cog," she said. "We have *nothing* in common! I'm Catholic, you're Presbyterian! I was almost a nun, you were a minister!"

"Almost a nun with five sons in ten years and, for your information, I'm *still* ordained."

"Phhhtttt," she emitted. "I like to play tennis, golf and bridge!"

"I jog," he said. "I could learn tennis. I've always enjoyed golf but bridge bores the crap out of me."

She burst out laughing. "Bores me, too," she said. "But the women gather for bridge and so I play with them. But, George, I'm not about to commit to a man I've known such a short time and —"

"Of course not, Maureen! Here's my proposal. Let's carry on! How hard is that? Let's communicate, visit, get to know each other and, even better, spend quality time together when we can. You'll want to visit that little granddaughter, and I have to keep tabs on Noah so he doesn't go astray! And six months down the road, we'll be more sure of ourselves, and of our relationship. And, believe me, six months is asking a lot of a seventy-year-old guy!"

She narrowed her eyes. "How's your health?"

"Excellent! After what happened to Mary by avoiding the doctor, I get a good physical every six months. I'm on cholesterol medicine, though. But I think it's a waste of time. My father lived to be eighty-eight."

"I'm on cholesterol *and* high-blood-pressure medicine."

"You don't say?"

"It's working." She shrugged.

"Isn't it amazing? My doctor says, as long as we can find and treat these things, we're going to be fairly hard to kill!"

Maureen shook her head and laughed. She would not let him get a foot in the door with this insane idea, but she knew, at once, she would have fun with him. *Piles* of fun. "I would have to run this idea by my priest," she said.

"Whatever works for you," he agreed. "But what idea are you talking about? The idea of getting to know me better, or the idea of joining me in the RV if it works out?"

She didn't answer. She chewed her bottom lip and thought about when she'd gone to her parish priest as a young mother and said she could *not* keep having babies — she just wasn't up to it! She wanted his blessing — the church's blessing — on birth control before she lost her mind and her body. He wasn't much help, and she'd already given natural birth control — timing her cycle, et cetera — two fair shots. They were named Sean and Patrick, Jr. She clicked her tongue without realizing it. That *was* more than thirty years ago and there had been progress on these matters in the church since. But she had to admit that some of the *rules* had been hard to take at that time.

"Forget I said that," she answered. "What did you get for take-out lunch?"

"Wonderful, fat deli sandwiches, coleslaw, sweet tea and brownies. How does that sound?"

She smiled at him. "Better than you know."

George pulled the RV off the road at a scenic outlook beside the ocean. They sat at the table and ate their sandwiches, talking about all the places in the United States they hadn't seen and would love to visit. Maureen lived in Arizona and had never been to the Grand Canyon; George wanted to extend his RV adventure into Canada and Alaska. It all began to sound like a fantasy, a dream trip.

"George," she said. "What if one of us gets sick?" she asked.

"We're not going to the wilds of Africa," he said with a shrug. "We can stop at a hospital. We'll see a doctor or —" But then he smiled at her. "But we should, if we feel like it."

"Should what?"

"Go to Africa. And maybe a long cruise . . ."

She sat back in her chair. "Have you been dreaming this up for years?"

He shook his head. "Just the opposite. I didn't know what I was going to do with myself. I'm not young — I have some years of travel in me, then I'll probably have to settle down a little and be happy with the occasional trip. You have longer, I suppose. But the truth, Maureen? All these fun ideas didn't even occur to me until I met you. Mary thought of stuff like this, but we were never able to act on them. You know what my late wife used to say? That it was her goal to have the grandchildren say, 'Anyone seen Grandma?' " He laughed at himself. Then he sobered. "I'm so sorry. It's probably such a faux pas, trying to tempt you with things my late wife said."

But Maureen loved it. It had been such a long time since she'd been tempted by *anything!* By a man, by living, by having fun, by risk and chance and *dare!* She would love to sell her condo, get rid of all that precious furniture she'd polished, pampered and protected for so many years — furniture that never managed to look good in that fancy condo! She'd love to give her sons the keepsakes she'd stored for them! The old school pictures, report cards and clay handprints. And the little china and crystal bric-a-brac her mother and mother-in-law left? What was she going to do with them after she was dead? Cart them with her to heaven? The boys could have all the Christmas ornaments from their childhood, their baby pictures, their school projects; their wives could have their great-grandmother's silver and dishes. It wasn't as though she sat up on lonely nights caressing that stuff! She'd much rather see the Grand Canyon!

She thought about drifting from grandchild to grandchild across the country, taking them on overnights in an RV, going on shopping trips and buying them presents from Europe, Asia, *Africa!*

Six months, George had said. Six months to see if they were really as compatible as they seemed. She laughed suddenly. She hadn't made Patrick, Sr., work at winning her for any longer than that!

"Funny? Did I offend you?" George asked.

She grabbed both his hands across the RV's table. "Not at all. I think I would have loved Mary. We would have been friends. In spite of the fact that she was Presbyterian!"

"That's what I think," he said. "But, Maureen, don't get the impression you're exactly like her. You didn't get my attention because you're anything like my late wife! In fact, you're very different in lots of ways. I'll tell you all about that another day. It's bad manners to discuss your wife with your girlfriend." He frowned slightly. "You have an odd look on your face. Does all this talk about her bother you? Does my suggestion about an RV upset you?"

"No, not at all," she said. She didn't intend to give him too much information too fast, but truthfully, she was looking forward to things. Fun, exciting, fantastic things that had never occurred to her before . . . and someone very wonderful to do them with. She suddenly realized that while she'd been content the past several years, she hadn't been excited about the future in a long time. In fact, she couldn't remember when she'd last felt that way.

FIFTEEN

The very day that George proposed the RV idea, Maureen was invited to have dinner with Vivian and Carl. In fact, the invitation was extended to George, as well, but Maureen was not quite ready for a double date — things were just too new. She had offered to cook *them* a nice dinner, but Vivian demurred. "Carl is a wonderful cook and he loves it. His kids have plans tonight and he's going to run by the grocery on his way over," she had said. "For once, just be a guest."

So after a couple of hours of playtime with Rosie, Maureen was back at Vivian's for dinner. Vivian and Carl were already in the kitchen; Carl was searing something at the stove and Viv was in charge of some slicing and dicing on the cutting board.

"Mo!" she said happily, turning from her chore and wiping her hands on a towel. "Here you are. Meet Carl. Dr. Johnson."

And as Carl turned from the stove and extended his hand, Maureen found herself face-to-face with a very tall, very handsome black man. "Carl Johnson," he said, as though she hadn't heard his name.

"How do you do," she said, taking his hand and looking up at him. Her first thought was that Vivian might've mentioned that he was black. In that kind of quandary, she blurted, "Johnson? You're Swedish!"

He threw back his head in a fantastic, deep, wonderful laugh. "Viv said I'd love you! African-American, Korean, Native American and Caucasian," he said.

"It's a pleasure. How long have you been in Eureka?" Maureen asked.

"Over twenty years. My late wife was from Fort Bragg and we ended up starting the practice here. It's a good place to raise kids — I have a boy and a girl."

"So Vivian told me," she said. "Can I help with dinner?"

"From what I hear about you, it will be hard for you to sit idle for even five minutes, but just pull a stool up to the breakfast bar and visit with us. You're going to love this," he promised, turning back to the stove. "How about a glass of wine?"

"Perfect," she accepted. "Something white and maybe dry?"

"Red is better for you," he said. "How about a merlot?"

"Office hours are over, Carl," Vivian scolded, getting out the glasses and pouring Maureen the same chardonnay that she had for herself.

When Maureen had her glass, she said, "Now, I want to hear all about how the two of you met."

Carl had a rumbling laugh that Maureen instantly loved. He was truly a beautiful man; his blended background gave his complexion the color of heavily creamed coffee and his large, dark eyes had a slight, almost exotic slant. He was well over six feet, perhaps as tall as six-four, while Vivian was a small average at about five-four. She was petite and he was large; he was dark brown and she was pale blond. And yet they seemed perfect for each other. They joked and bantered and shared quick affectionate pets and pats in the kitchen while they worked together.

"How we met is pretty boring. My partner hired Vivian. The practice was getting very busy and, rather than bringing in a fourth doctor, we decided on a PA."

"I worked for a women's health clinic in Santa Rosa for years before moving up here with Franci. I didn't think my chance of finding a good PA's position here was very good, given the size of the county. And it turned out I landed the best job at the best doctor's office in the entire state."

Carl turned from the stove and grinned. "She might be just slightly prejudiced about that. We have a nice little practice. We do some good work."

"So, your partner hired her, and then what happened?" Maureen boldly asked.

Both Vivian and Carl turned and gave her their full attention for a moment, as though it was curious she asked. Then Carl answered, "We had good rapport but, at the time we started working together, my wife was very ill, and shortly after that she died. Honestly, I couldn't focus on much else at the time. It was a year after my wife's death before I asked Vivian for a bona fide date. We've been dating since — a little over a year. But my wife has only been gone two years, and my kids, still under twenty, haven't adjusted very well. My nineteen-year-old daughter, especially. She really can't imagine me with a significant other and I'm giving her plenty of time." Then he smiled broadly, put his arm around Vivian and pulled her closer. "Plenty of time, but not forever. She's in her second year of college and soon we're going to talk about how everyone gets a life, not just the kids."

Carl prepared an astonishingly good goulash and they sat around the dining table long past dinner, visiting and laughing. Carl was the one to clear the table and serve slices of cheesecake with coffee, extending their good time. When it was time to clean up, Vivian and Carl wouldn't let Maureen in the kitchen. She was shuffled off to the living room to watch TV, read or do her needlepoint, and they promised to join her in just a few minutes.

While she sat in the chair that had become hers, she found herself thinking that even though she'd lived independently, happily, she'd somehow allowed her life to become too narrow. She had quite a lot of friends, but they were acquaintances really — people she'd known for years, but none of them felt as close as Vivian had become in just weeks. She'd been constantly busy — activities day in and day out, and yet nothing really got her motor running. She never took chances, never tried anything the least bit daring. She was stunned and embarrassed by her surprise to find Vivian in love with a black man, and how narrow was that?

Or how about an almost-nun traveling the country in an RV with a minister?

In the end it was what she heard in the kitchen that filled her with envy. When the water stopped running and she could hear the quiet sounds of conversation and soft laughter as dishes and flatware were being stored away, she longed for that in her life. A deep and romantic relationship, love and affection, laughter and adventure.

She heard Vivian giggle and Carl purr. Six months suddenly seemed like a very long time, and right then she offered up a promise to herself.

I'm in my sixties; it's late to become enlightened. I hereby vow to be relentlessly happy, ridiculously daring, outrageously open-minded and passionately optimistic.

At the onset of Thanksgiving week, specifically on Sunday at noon, Jack's Bar was full of people with bags and boxes filled with nonperishable food items. Jack and Preacher had been collecting the donations for Thanksgiving baskets for a couple of weeks. Jack liked the idea of presenting the food in a classy Harry & David type basket with a beautiful arrangement of food, but that was impractical for what they had in mind. Instead, he went to a shipping outlet and bought some sturdy boxes.

For the past couple of months Jack and

Preacher had had a jar on the bar with a sign on it that said Donations for Thanksgiving Baskets. They had collected more than enough money to buy nonperishable canned turkey and ham and some apples and oranges. In this, the first year of their project, they estimated they would deliver fifteen boxes of food to needy individuals and families. Noah Kincaid and Mel Sheridan had managed to come up with a list of folks who could use some help. If they had surplus after arranging these boxes of food, Mel would have no trouble coming up with more names; she was the one with the most experience in outreach.

Jack was supervising the stocking of the boxes — cans of vegetables, powdered milk, instant potatoes and rice, gravy mix, boxed stuffing, even canned cranberries. There were things that didn't really fit on the Thanksgiving menu that people would be happy to have if their budgets were tight — fruit cocktail, canned pork and beans, chili mix, lentils, black-eyed peas, chicken soup. "Cocktail weenies?" he asked, holding up a little can. "Who gives cocktail weenies to a needy family?"

"I mighta done that," said Hope McCrea, pushing her big black glasses up on her nose.

"The can is bulging," Jack said.

"Been a while since I had a yen for cocktail weenies," Hope replied, unrepentant.

Jack pitched the can in the trash. "Sorry, Hope. Can't take a chance on killing anyone our first try at this." He pulled out a bag from the Dollar Store that was filled with little can openers. He passed them out to his wife, Noah and Ellie, Preacher and Paige, Mike and Brie. George Davenport was on hand to help, of course. "Make sure one of these goes in every box. Mel, are you taking care of the boxes for families with babies? We've got diapers, formula and baby food."

"I'm on it," she said. "The neediest people Noah and I see are either families with small children or the elderly. Right, Noah?"

"Right," he affirmed.

"There's more than fifteen families who need help, huh," Jack said, and it wasn't a question. "We should've been doing this for years. Preacher, why didn't we ever do this before?" he asked.

"Because we do everything else," Preacher said. And this was true — wherever help was needed, they tried to pitch in. It wasn't unusual to see Jack and Preacher under the hoods of cars and trucks, or picking up groceries for widows and young mothers while they bought their bar stock. They helped Mel and Cameron at the clinic when asked, and of course they were on hand for any kind of search and rescue around the mountains. Last winter a school bus slid off the road and down the mountainside and all the men from town were there instantly, ready to assist emergency responders. Jack was the first one on the scene and Preacher was the second.

Noah laughed at Preacher's remark. "From all I can see, people in this town do a fine job of lending a hand wherever they can. My house is almost habitable, thanks to the neighbors. We might not be able to cook a turkey in it this year, but we'll be in there for Christmas. The kids are going to have Santa in their own house." He looked around the bar. "Who's on board to deliver these boxes of food?"

Every hand went up and Noah laughed again. "Then I guess the job gets done fast and easy! Just don't leave anything on a doorstep — you have to put it in the hands of an adult, otherwise wildlife could get into it. If there's no adult, we'll go back a second time. I know it's not Thanksgiving till Thursday, but I think it's practical to distribute now. Those who are able might try to save this for a holiday dinner they wouldn't otherwise have and those who are not able . . ." He paused. "Are not able to wait," he finally said.

"I'm a little embarrassed it took some city-boy preacher to get a project like this going in our own town," Jack said. "We should've been on this. We start for Christmas right away. And then we get going on holiday baskets for next year in July. And, Hope, don't be throwing any of your old weenies in the basket."

"You never know who's in the mood for a weenie," she said with a sparkle in her eye.

"I would give anything to see the inside of that mausoleum you live in," Jack muttered.

"It's filled to the ceiling with little cans of cocktail weenies," she said.

The door to the bar opened and Dan Brady and Cheryl Creighton came in. Dan was carrying a large box and Cheryl held on to two bags. "Are we too late to add to the Thanksgiving baskets?" Dan asked. "We meant to get this done sooner . . ."

"You're in time, no problem. In fact, if we figured right, you might be bringing us surplus, which means we can add a couple of families to our list," Jack said. He looked in the box Dan held and pulled out a jar of dark liquid. "Prune juice?" he said.

"I am not drinking that stuff. Ever," Dan said.

"Jack," Noah said with laughter in his voice. He put a hand on Jack's shoulder and gave a little shake. "Really, you can't be judging people's contributions." But he laughed some more.

"It's icky, but it's nutritious," Cheryl said. "Lotta vitamins in it. And I stopped in at the truck stop diner I used to work in and talked the owner out of some bulk-size canned goods — they're out in Dan's truck. You can probably figure out a way to use them in your food drive."

Jack was just standing still, looking at Cheryl with a smile on his face. "It's nice you're here," he said. "I don't know what possessed you to hook up with that lunatic," Jack said, smiling at Dan. "But it's real nice you're here. Thanks."

She threaded her fingers in Dan's, staking her claim, but she smiled at Jack. "No thanks necessary."

"Did you put that house of yours on the market?" Jack asked.

"I did. The Realtor seems to think it'll sell pretty easy. Dan made it beautiful."

"Will you come around sometimes after it's sold?" Jack asked. "Maybe let me buy you dinner?"

She laughed. During her drinking days, Jack wouldn't let her in the door. "You serve food in this place?" She slipped her arm around Dan's waist and he put his arm around her shoulders. "Yeah, I'll pop in once in a while, just to say hello."

"We'd like that, Cheryl," Preacher said. "Come Thursday if you don't have other plans."

"I work at the community college during the week."

Dan laughed and gave her a squeeze. "Not this week, honey. It's Thanksgiving."

She looked momentarily startled. "And you're open on Thanksgiving?" she asked.

"A few of us like to get together," Preacher said. "And I put on a real culinary show. You shouldn't miss it. Four o'clock."

Franci had been so busy over the past few weeks that she didn't give a second thought to T. J. Brookner. Sometimes when she was at the college, she thought about their brief period of dating and the harsh words from him at their parting, and thought, What a close call! She wondered how long she might've hung in there with T.J. ordering her dinner, telling her what to like and not like, if Sean hadn't turned up. She was just grateful it hadn't gone on any longer, especially having faced his incredible anger. That had been spooky.

And then, suddenly and accidentally, she stumbled upon a whole new dimension to the man.

After a brief workout in the college weight room and a shower before going home, a couple of female voices carried across the lockers, just as she was drying off.

"Gone, I hear," one said. "Suspended and likely to be fired. God bless the Internet, huh?"

"Was it like I heard?" asked another female voice. "Caught red-handed? By a nanny cam?"

"Literally with his pants down," said the first. "It must have been fantastic. How about that? All these years he's been claiming that just because he's marginally handsome and the girls flirt with him, he's been victimized by gossip. Poor, poor Professor Hottie, caught on tape with two naked eighteen-year-old blondes."

Both women giggled. Franci gasped and dropped her towel to the floor.

"The story is that this particular ménage à trois started in Cabo on his last diving trip. I suppose he thought he was in control of the girls and it turned out they were in the driver's seat! One of them had a hidden camera and put the movie on the Internet. From the comments on the site, they were hardly the first. This has been going on forever."

Franci wandered closer to the voices to hear better. Cabo? she thought. What about his "buddy system"? Sounded as if he had a couple of buddies, all right. He was supposed to have been Franci's boyfriend on that trip to Cabo. So much for that.

"I think he's scum, but what's the actual big deal? Is it against the law or something?"

"I dunno what's against the law — the word is they were all consenting, but the dean didn't appreciate him boinking the students on a field trip. There's policy about that sort of thing — no diddling the students. And the gossip has been pretty damning — he's been manipulating female students into sexually compromising situations for years. Old-timers around here say his wife left him because he couldn't keep his hands off the freshmen girls."

"He's not the first guy who likes younger women . . ."

The voices drifted off as the door to the locker room opened and the two women exited. And Franci thought dispiritedly, *I believed every word he said.*

Franci pulled on her jeans and sweatshirt.

She was in such a hurry to get out of there, she stuffed her bra in her purse and pulled on her boots without socks. She left the gym without drying her hair and went out in the cold with a wet head. Her stomach flipped and churned as images she just couldn't block came into her mind. Fresh young women, vulnerable students, taken advantage of by a man of forty, an instructor. Did he trade sex for grades?

You give me credibility, he had said to her. No one gossiped about him when he had a woman with looks and brains as his girlfriend.

So, there was a lot more about the whole relationship than just his controlling nature. She was nothing more than a decoy. She felt violated.

She drove home in a daze.

She drove too fast; she couldn't wait to get to Sean. It never even occurred to her not to tell him! When she walked in her house, Sean was sitting at the dining room table with the newspaper spread out in front of him. "Where's Rosie?" she asked, before she even said hello.

"My mom is picking her up and they're stopping at the store. Maureen's cooking to— Hey, you're white as a sheet." He stood. "What's the matter? Were you in an accident or something?"

She just stared at him for a long moment. She thought about spilling the whole story right there, but instead she just walked into his arms. "Close call," she said. "Hold me. I'll tell you all about it later."

"You okay?"

She nestled in closer. She realized uneasily that she hadn't really known as much as she should have about T.J., but she knew everything about Sean. She knew his strengths and weaknesses. He had never lied to her. When she first saw Sean a month ago, she thought he'd reappeared to screw up her life. She'd literally wanted to rearrange his face. Now, she ran into his arms for comfort and support. Her best friend. A man she knew she could trust. "I'll be fine now," she said.

Aiden arrived in Virgin River late on Tuesday, planning to stay until Sunday. He hadn't been there long before he realized the relationships in his family were changing quite a bit, and quickly. He found his scrappy older brother all soft around the edges, doting on his beautiful, sexy young wife, ever at her hand. If he saw her wrestling a full laundry basket into the bedroom, he took it from her. If she had the step stool pulled over to the cupboards to reach into the highest one for a platter, he lifted her down and got it for her. Aiden was anxious to have dinner with them to see if Luke cut Shelby's meat.

Aiden caught Shelby in a moment alone and asked, "When do you suppose you're due?"

"How did you guess?"

"I've never seen Luke act like this — hovering, protective, sweet."

"Annoying, cloying and paternal. I don't have a date — I haven't been to the doctor yet. But I suspect it happened on the wedding night, just as Luke planned."

Aiden laughed. "You're going to want to watch that. Unless you want six of them."

"Oh, I might have two, but not six." She grinned. "Snip, snip."

"Have to admire a forward-thinking woman," Aiden said with a grin. "Congratulations."

"I suppose there's no point in keeping it under wraps anymore, now that you and Sean both know. And if Sean knows, Franci knows. And if we don't tell Maureen soon, she'll feel left out."

"Speaking of Maureen, is she driving you crazy?" Aiden asked.

Shelby shook her head. "I feel so guilty

that she isn't staying with us here, but she's smart. Two women under the same roof for a long period of time will eventually have a power struggle. But not Maureen and Vivian — they seem to have a special bond. Luke says they're a couple of strange old broads," she said with a giggle. "Really, their living situation seems to be working out just fine."

"You can give the credit to me," Aiden said.

"Love your humility," Shelby said with a laugh.

"Seriously — my advice to her was to stay out of the way. I don't know much about mothers and daughters — maybe they do all right for extended visits. I can tell you that we all worship our mom — there's no woman I admire more — but I don't want to live with her for more than four days, tops. I wasn't that concerned about how you'd deal with her, Shelby. I was afraid Luke would strangle her after a few days."

"But why?"

"With everyone else in the world, Maureen is easy-going. She knows how to put people at ease, make them comfortable. But with her sons, she has high expectations. She's been trying really hard to keep a lid on it, but she eventually always has an opinion about how we should live our lives. Not a one of us has gone about things the way she'd like."

"What? But that can't be right! She's totally proud of you all!"

"Uh-huh." Aiden laughed. "Except for a few little things. Luke avoided commitment for too long after his bad marriage. Colin has had woman trouble of one stripe or another since he was fifteen. She was completely disappointed in me for marrying someone for only three months — she thinks I just didn't make an effort. Sean has a child because he refused to commit. And Patrick, her pride and joy and baby, is rumored to be thinking of marrying a girl who isn't just a non-Catholic — she calls herself agnostic. Did you know my mother almost became a nun?"

"I heard that, yes. That might explain some things."

"Believe me, I know nuns who are more liberal than Maureen . . ." He laughed and shook his head.

"Your brother is actually worried about her. He's planning to have a talk with you. Maybe you can help in some way. You seem to have the best rapport with her."

"What's up?"

"It could be nothing. I didn't even really

notice at the time. A nice friend of our local minister stopped to talk while we were all having dinner at Jack's and Maureen completely blew him off. He asked her out to dinner and she lied and said no, because she's recently widowed. He's a very nice man — handsome, funny, just a few years older than Maureen. Luke called her on it and she said she would absolutely never date, not even just to be social. Something about all that being for young girls."

Aiden's dark brows lifted in surprise. "Is that right? I never gave it much thought, but I assumed she went out occasionally and just didn't mention it to us. She's like that — she can be so private she's almost secretive. I didn't want to pry, but she was always busy enough that she had to be doing something. Maybe I just hated to think she spent all that time doing volunteer work at the church or hanging out with other widows. My mother is beautiful and she can be a lot of fun. I've always been a little surprised she didn't remarry. In the first couple of years after Da died, I admit I was relieved she didn't hook up right away."

"Relieved?"

"I didn't want to see her make an impetuous move like that out of loneliness and have it turn out to be a mistake. But after twelve years, it's becoming harder to see my mom all alone."

"She's not alone," Shelby said. "She has a million friends and lots to do, but she believes she's too old for romance."

He smiled. "I had a patient last year whose eighty-three-year-old mother just got married for the second time. She wore a lacy white gown." He chuckled. "And her orthopedic shoes. My patient said her mother was a little flushed for a month. True love. I'd prefer to think my mother was open to something like that than being closed off."

"Will you try to talk to her, then? Will you be delicate?"

"I have no choice but to be delicate. The only time my mother will discuss anything personal is if it's about one of us." He put his arm around Shelby and gave her a squeeze. "Don't worry about Maureen, Shelby. I think she's happy with her life. If she's avoiding how much more fulfilling it could be, at the end of the day it's her choice." And Aiden thought to himself that if she's not even aware of how much more life could give her, maybe she's the lucky one. For Aiden's part, he was all too aware what was missing for him.

On the day before Thanksgiving, Maureen

planned on baking at Luke's house. She drove to the grocery, collected all the supplies she needed and then went to Virgin River. Sean was keeping Rosie out of preschool and day care for the day so she could get acquainted with her uncle Aiden before the big dinner on Thanksgiving. Maureen would be doing what she loved most — spending time with her family and making them her special holiday treats. The only thing that would have made it better was if Paddy and Colin could have joined them, but neither one had managed to get leave. It would have been delightful to share Thanksgiving Day with George, but of course he'd be with Noah and his family.

When she pulled into Luke's cabin complex, Aiden was waiting on the porch, a cup of coffee in hand. She left her groceries in the car and went to him. He set his cup on the porch rail and wrapped his arms around her, laughing and hugging. "You look fantastic," he said. "I think being a grandmother agrees with you!"

She leaned away from him. "You have no idea, Aiden. She's absolutely wonderful."

"That's what I hear. She should be here before long. Sean called to say they were on their way. I'm surprised you beat them."

"I got an early start," she said. "I have

428

groceries in the car. Help me bring them in?"

"You're joking, right? Go inside and help yourself to a cup of coffee while I get them for you."

When all the supplies were unloaded onto the kitchen counters, Maureen and Aiden sat at the breakfast bar with coffee for a long overdue visit. It was just the two of them, a rare thing. Luke and Art were running an errand and Shelby was at school.

"Tell me about your visit so far," Aiden said. "How do things seem between Franci and Sean?"

She lifted an eyebrow. "You haven't talked to your brother?"

"Several times, but I was interested in hearing your take on things."

"If there's the slightest imperfection in their relationship, I can't imagine what it is, besides the fact they're not married. I take that back — the one flaw is that everyone is a little on edge, wondering where the air force will send Sean next, and when. Otherwise, they seem so happy."

"I'm facing transfer orders before long, too," he said. "Sean's overdue. Any day now he's going to get the word — and he doesn't want to uproot Francine and Rosie from their home and routine when everything could shift again in a month or two."

"And you, too, Aiden?" she asked. "What are you expecting?"

"I have no idea. I applied for a fellowship in high-risk pregnancy specialty, but I won't hear on that before spring," Aiden said. "For Sean's family, until they get a permanent assignment, Franci is best right where she is, in her own house with a job she likes and a mom who can help out with Rosie."

"Rosie's going to miss Sean when he goes back to Beale," Maureen said. "They spend every day together."

Aiden chuckled, shaking his head. "So much for the man who didn't want to be tied down to a child."

"The two most stubborn males in the family," she said. "Luke and Sean, the great playboys of the Western world. They always did make the rest of you look like choirboys, and the two of them have been completely tamed by pretty young women. They were in no hurry about it, either — I'm glad I lived long enough to see it. Patrick is young and I've heard the same woman's name mentioned more than twice, but I wonder about Colin."

"You might want to write that one off, Mom," Aiden said. "Another grunt in a Blackhawk — it would take a real special woman to domesticate him. He's pretty rough around the edges."

"More than Luke?" she asked, one brow lifted.

"You must have lit a million candles for Luke to run into Shelby. She's one of a kind."

"And you, Aiden?" she asked pointedly.

He sat back in his chair and took a breath. "I'm facing an interesting transition myself, Mom, and it has everything to do with women. You know I'm not avoiding commitment, but I'm ripe for transfer and the navy needs general medical officers on shipboard and I'm not inclined to spend two years on a big, gray boat, away from my specialty. And I'm not likely to find the right woman at sea. If they don't come through with a fellowship, I might have to look at my options."

"You can't retire," she pointed out.

"Correct, it's too soon. I can separate, however."

"And do what?" she asked.

"Medicine, obviously. Ob-gyn, of course. Maybe I'll do it as a civilian."

"Where, Aiden?" she asked.

"I have no idea," he said. "I'm just thinking about it at this stage."

"And there are no special ladies in your

life now?" she asked.

He leaned toward her. "No, Mother. Unfortunately. Now I believe we've covered almost everyone. Almost. There's you."

"Me?" she asked, startled, a slight flush moving up her neck. She could feel the heat rising to her face and damned her redhead's complexion.

"You. Luke mentioned the oddest thing to me. You apparently gave some perfectly nice, interested man the slip by claiming to be recently widowed."

"Oh, that," she said with a laugh, waving the subject off. "That was the Presbyterian minister's friend, briefly in town for a visit. I ran into him again and apologized for that. He was gracious, as I expected he would be. It's forgotten. But what concern is it of Luke's?"

"It's not just Luke's concern, Mom. I guess because you're always so busy, none of us even entertained the idea you weren't socializing with men at all, that you were deliberately avoiding them. Speaking for myself, I assumed you had a date now and then. By the time Da had been gone a few years, I prepared myself for you to find a man you wanted to marry — you were so young when we lost him. But what you said to Luke stirred the pot. It sounds as though you have no interest in even the most casual friendships with the opposite sex. Tell me what that's about."

"Don't be so ridiculous!" she said, fuming slightly. "I'm not talking to my son about that!"

"Any why not? You pry every sliver of information about women from each one of us."

"And you hardly throw me a bone!"

"That's because the kind of information available on that subject, until Luke and Sean were recently captured, is not intended for a mother's ears. You said it yourself — at least a couple of your boys were the playboys of the Western world. Details of their dating experiences would have had you gripping your heart."

"I knew it was bad," she said, shaking her head. "As if they were hiding anything from me. Sometimes I wonder who raised them!"

"But that's all old news. How about you?"

"What about me?"

"Do you refuse to date at all? Have you made some decision you'll never again meet a man? More to the point, have you decided not to even give the idea a chance?"

"Do you hear yourself?" Maureen asked. "Why in the world does that matter to you? Or to Luke, for that matter?"

"And Sean, and even Patrick. Only Colin is dense enough to have no interest in anyone's love life but his own."

"Tell me you're making that up!" she said, aghast. "You are *not* talking about my possible love life!"

Aiden leaned across the breakfast bar, toward her. "Mother, you are a very attractive woman in your early sixties. You're sharp and energetic and, as far as I know, in excellent health. And if anyone would know, I would — you pass the details of every doctor's appointment and blood test you have by me as I'm your official second opinion."

She made a face. "I listened to enough of your whining as you tried to pass your exams to have earned that right, haven't I?"

"I never once complained," he said. "I'm glad I know exactly what your cholesterol level and blood pressure are — someone in the family should. I'm committed to doing anything I can to support you living a full and happy life until you're extremely old. But, Mother, you're too young and vital to give up a normal heterosexual existence. You can still fully enjoy that part of life."

She blanched. "You did *not* just say that to your mother," she said in a whisper.

"I'm a woman's doctor. I say it to lots of

women in their fifties and sixties. And seventies, just in case you're curious. In fact, in a clinical situation, I'm much more direct, and I hope your doctor is, as well. Now, let's just retrench to the original question. Have you made some ridiculous and arbitrary decision that you won't even entertain the *idea* of dating?"

Right at that critical moment, the door to Luke's house burst open and Rosie came flying in, red curls bouncing wildly. "Gramma," she yelled, running to Maureen and throwing herself onto her lap. "We go fishing now?"

"You have fishing on the brain," Maureen said. "I thought you'd like to bake pies with me!"

"Fishing!" she said, squeezing Maureen around the neck.

"All right, all right. First, I want you to meet your uncle Aiden." She turned Rosie on her lap. "Rosie, this is Aiden. And Aiden, this is Rose."

"Wide Iwish Rose," she said with a grin.

Aiden laughed and stretched a hand out to her. "So I've heard. Nice to meet you."

"Fishing now!" she said. Sean came into the house. "Daddy! We go fishing now?"

"Let's get it over with, short stuff. It's all I've heard since I told her we were coming to Luke's for the day. Of course, her idea of fishing is tossing bread into the river for the trout. We're years away from hooking anything."

"I'll save some dough rolling for after you've had your fishing trip, Rosie," Maureen said. She eased Rosie off her lap and rummaged in a cupboard for some of Luke's bread, handing Rosie a few slices. "Remember, you only go near the river with Mommy or Daddy."

Aiden said he would go along and, while he fetched his jacket, Sean and Rosie were out the door and on their way. Aiden shrugged into his coat and said to Maureen, "We can continue this conversation later."

"I don't think so," she said. "You boys gossip worse than a bunch of old women and I think it's high time you mind your own bloody business."

He leaned toward her and kissed her cheek. "Yeah, good luck with that."

Sixteen

Thanksgiving had a special significance for John Middleton, known as Preacher to his friends. His mother passed away around this time when he was only seventeen, and for so many years after that, when the holidays approached, he just endeavored to get through them as best he could. He was always relieved when the whole season was over. But once he found Virgin River and his wife, Paige, everything in his life changed, and he looked forward to the holidays with excitement and spirit. He had a great deal to be thankful for.

Every Thanksgiving Preacher prepared a big turkey dinner and kept the bar open for anyone who wasn't otherwise occupied. It became the tradition at Jack's Bar to serve a big dinner free of charge to friends and any strangers who might wander in. Preacher could have used his new house to accommodate his Thanksgiving guests, but it just wouldn't be the same. Plus he liked the idea of being open to strangers who found themselves traveling or stranded on this very important day.

Mel Sheridan and Dr. Michaels were trading off holidays this year. Since Cameron and his wife had the new twins, they wanted to take a few days for family at Christmastime, so Mel and Jack were going to the Sheridan family home in Sacramento for Thanksgiving. But there would be no shortage of guests for Preacher's biggest dinner of the year.

He and Paige pushed the tables together in the bar into one long, wide table. Paige dressed up the table with a horn of plenty filled with gourds and colorful leaves. As well, orange candles provided soft lighting up and down the table. Each place setting had a construction-paper turkey created by her and her son, Christopher. When Preacher looked at the long table, he smiled and said, "You sure do class the place up, babe."

At four o'clock the turkey came out of the oven to sit for a half hour before carving. The side dishes were ready and the hors d'oeuvres were on the bar. A cabernet was breathing, a chardonnay was chilled, juice and sodas were cold for the kids and abstemious, the water glasses were all filled, coffee was ready to perk. Preacher looked around the room, puffing up a little in pride.

The first to arrive were Rick and Liz, helping Rick's grandmother, Lydie, into the bar. Next came Connie and Ron of the corner store and, for the first time, Connie's sister, Liz's mother. Joy and Bruce, good friends from down the street, arrived and, right behind them, Hope McCrea. Not long after, Cameron and Abby with babies, Julia and Justin, and enough baby gear to open a nursery. Preacher held on to his own little daughter, Dana Marie, and chuckled as he realized they basically *had* opened a nursery.

He beamed when the door opened again and Dan Brady and Cheryl came in. He'd hoped they would come, but he had no way of knowing if Cheryl was comfortable among them. It had taken her some time after adjusting to her newfound sobriety to get used to the idea that Virgin River folks didn't look down on her at all. The fact of the matter, Preacher knew, was that everyone was real proud of her.

Paige and Preacher passed around the hors d'oeuvres and drinks and, after about twenty minutes of visiting, there was a mad scurrying among the women to put out all the side dishes, settle small children in high chairs and find places for everyone to sit. Then and only then did Preacher bring out the noble bird on a large tray, surrounded by baked apples and parsley. He put it in front of his place at the head of the table and took in all the oohs and ahhs as he prepared to carve.

Right at that moment the door to the bar opened and a man stood in the entrance. His hair was too long and he looked a little on the worn side, his jacket collar frayed. "Oh, sorry. I thought you were open."

"Come in, come in," Preacher said. "You're just in time."

"Oh, no," he said, shaking his head. "I can see you're having a holiday dinner. And I have the family in the car. We're headed back to my in-laws in Trinity County and the car was sputtering, so we decided to stop for a while. But I'll take a look under the hood and we'll push on."

Dan Brady was on his feet. "Tell the family to come in, brother. Join us for a meal and then we'll have a look at the car. At least we'll send you off in good working order."

"I, ah . . . We have some sandwiches in the car for the kids —"

"It would be our pleasure to have you and your family join us. Please. No one pays for

440

a meal or drink, or even for car repair, on a special holiday like this one. This is a family day," Preacher said. "Come in and meet everyone. Join us. We'd be honored."

At the Riordan household, Luke had purchased a couple of long folding tables and foldable chairs for their Thanksgiving dinner. With Art's help, he rearranged the furniture to make room so the women could set up their dinner table.

"I'm not very good at this sort of thing," Shelby told her mother-in-law.

"What nonsense! You've stuffed the bird and he's roasting beautifully! You've done a fantastic job so far."

"My uncle Walt talked me through it — he's a great cook. We don't have enough dishes, so my cousin Vanni is bringing some of her mother's, along with some table linens. It isn't going to be fancy — all mismatched plates and flatware and —"

"Darling," Maureen said, putting a hand on her arm to still her. "I can't think of a thing you could do to make it more perfect."

Shelby smiled and leaned toward her to whisper, "I can think of one thing. You have to let Luke make his announcement, but I'll give you a tip. We're going to give Rosie a cousin."

Maureen pulled her into an embrace. "Congratulations, sweetheart. When are you due?"

Shelby shrugged. "The height of next summer, just as Luke planned."

"And you're feeling well?"

"Actually, I feel like crap. Oops," she apologized. "I mean, I'm kind of tired and have some morning sickness and, according to Luke, I'm not in the best mood. I might want to have a little consult with my brother-in-law after dinner."

"Good idea," Maureen said. "Maybe he'll have a suggestion or two. Now, let's get this house ready for the company!"

The first to arrive were Sean, Franci, Rosie and Vivian. Viv jumped right into the kitchen work with Maureen, while Rosie checked with everyone present to see if *anyone* was going fishing!

Next came Paul and Vanni with their little ones and a couple of boxes of additional dishes, linens and flatware. Right behind them were Walt and Muriel. Walt's son, Tom Booth, and his girlfriend, Brenda, were having dinner with Brenda's family but planned to arrive for dessert. The kitchen was full of women, talking and laughing, with the general trying to edge his way in to direct traffic.

■ ■ ■ ■

The house was full of people when Art quietly asked Luke how long it would be before dinner. When he was told it would be at least an hour — right around four o'clock — he slipped away and walked to his little cabin next door to grab his rod and reel. Art loved people, but large crowds stuffed into a small house made him a little jittery. All those little children! Art thought himself a little clumsy sometimes; he was afraid he might step on one of them!

Recently, Luke had given him a very nice watch for his birthday, and when Luke told him a time to be somewhere or do something, Art was *exactly* on time. He loved his watch! He did just as the Riordan brothers did — he'd check his watch and mark the time in his head. He never forgot. In his fantasy life, he *was* a Riordan brother. Brave and handsome and courageous.

Down at the river's edge Art walked upstream to his favorite spot where the river was shallow and most narrow. There were some flat rocks he could step on to get out into the middle of the stream and, from there, he would cast. Casting was still a little new to him and learning it hadn't been easy, but Luke had been patient and never made him feel stupid. Of all the things he loved about Luke, his favorite thing was that Luke always treated him like a man.

He stepped on the flat rocks — one, two, three — very slowly and cautiously. If he didn't go too quickly, not a drop of water would wet the tops of his tennis shoes. He went easy and lightly so as not to slip. Luke said he might get waders for Christmas and he was so excited about that.

Art stood almost in the middle of the river and threw his fly into the deeper part, reeling in slowly. If he caught a fish, they would put it in Luke's freezer for another day. Today was turkey day.

Contentment always washed over Art while he fished. Not only did it relax him, but when he pulled in a fish and gave it to Luke and Shelby, he felt as if he was contributing to the family. They ate fish for dinner about twice a week — almost always fish that Art had caught. Out of the corner of his eye Art caught a glimpse of something red. He turned and saw Rosie standing right at the water's edge. She had a fistful of bread and she was tearing off pieces, tossing them in the water, watching to see if the fish would come close to her. Her feet were wet and she didn't even have a coat on!

Just then, she threw some more bread in the water and she lost her balance!

"Rosie!" Art yelled.

She righted herself, standing in water over her ankles.

"Rosie, you're not supposed to be here all by yourself!" he yelled.

"I'm fishing," she said, completely ignoring Art's concern. She threw more bread and slipped again.

She was standing near a deep pool! It wasn't too deep for Art, but she was so little! If she fell in, she could drown! The current that ran near the shoreline wouldn't pull someone as big as Art downstream, but little Rosie might be helpless!

"You stay right there!" he yelled.

He dropped his rod right in the water, giving no thought to it, focused only on Rosie. He took two quick, giant steps, but on the third step he slipped on a large flat rock and the sole of his shoe slid off. He teetered and fell forward. He put out his hands, but there was too much momentum — he fell face-first in the shallow end of the river, hit his head on a rock and lay facedown in the river.

As the turkey came out of the oven ready for carving and Walt insisted on making the gravy, Franci went looking for Rosie — it was time to clean up and get her hands washed. She'd seen her just a second ago on the floor with Mattie and Hannah, Vanni's children, but right now she was nowhere in sight. She checked the bathroom and Shelby's bedroom, but she wasn't there. Franci looked up the staircase — would she have gone upstairs?

Franci ran up and peeked into the two bedrooms, but no Rosie. Running back downstairs she wondered if the little imp was hiding. "Sean," Franci called. "Where's Rosie?"

Sean looked around. "Bathroom?" he suggested.

Franci shook her head. Then she glanced into the kitchen. There, on the countertop, was a loaf of bread. But the plastic bag was open. No adult in this house would have left it like that; it was too close to dinner to be making sandwiches. She gasped and her heart fell with a thud.

"The river!" she yelled into the living room full of people. "Oh, God, she took bread to the river!"

Sean bolted out the door, Franci on his heels, both of them frantically running for the river. Franci could hear Rosie crying and she picked up speed. The river was close; she saw her little girl standing at its edge, clutching her sliced bread. Sean got to her first. He scooped her up instantly. "Sean!" Franci yelled, pointing at Art, facedown in the water.

There was the sound of running behind them — others had followed the alarm and several people came pounding down the trail.

Sean put Rosie back on her feet at the edge of the water and ran to Art. He was barely there before Luke and Aiden waded up to their knees in the icy water, pulling Art to the bank. They rolled him over and Aiden immediately straddled Art's waist and began pressing upward on his chest. "Someone call rescue — we'll need emergency transport," he said, pressing on Art's chest. A bubble of river water rolled out. "And blankets. Lots of blankets!"

There was a flurry of activity as Rosie was taken back to the house by Maureen, while others ran to use the phone and to hunt for towels and blankets. Aiden pulled himself off Art's midsection to kneel beside him and begin mouth-to-mouth.

Franci knelt on Art's other side. "I can spell you," she said to Aiden.

"I'm good," he said, pushing another breath into the big man. "Come on, Art!"

As if performing on command, Art coughed and spewed water into the air. He coughed again; he wheezed and gasped. Aiden and Franci together rolled him onto his side and, after a great deal of coughing and choking, he threw up a lot of river water. While Art struggled to sit up, Luke was shaking out a blanket and wrapping it around his shoulders.

"There we go," Aiden said. "Take slow breaths if you can, Art. Cough it out."

Art had a terrified look on his face and a big lump on his head. He had a hard time catching his breath enough to speak and was clearly panicked. Finally, in a voice he could barely use, looking around frantically, he said, "Rosie? Did she fall in?"

"No, buddy. You did. But you're going to be all right, I think."

That didn't seem to satisfy him. "Where's Rosie? Where is she?"

Luke knelt in front of Art and pulled the blanket around him, holding it tight. "Her grandma took her up to the house where it's warm."

"Luke," he said, his voice raspy. "I stepped too fast and didn't look."

"An accident, buddy," Luke said. "Were you trying to get to Rosie?"

He nodded and coughed. "She's not supposed to fish without Sean. Did she fall in?"

"She's okay. You were a close call, though. You scared me good, Art."

"Sorry, L-L-Luke," he said, teeth chattering.

The wet blanket was pulled away and a dry one wrapped around him. When he'd recovered enough to be breathing somewhat better, Luke and Sean made a chair out of their arms and carried him to the house so he could sit by the fire.

"I called Cameron," Walt said. "Once you had him breathing and sitting up, I canceled the helicopter transport. Cameron will be here faster, in less than five minutes. Luke, you can drive the Hummer for him so he can be in the back with Art." Then the general leaned close to Art. "Art, you're going to go to the hospital so they can check you over, make sure you didn't get a concussion or get too much water in your lungs."

"I don't want to," Art wheezed.

"I'll go with you, buddy," Luke said. "Right now I'm going next door to your house to find you some dry clothes."

"O-k-k-kay," he said. Maureen came close, holding Rosie, who was still gasping with barely subsiding sobs. Art looked up at her. He frowned at her. "No f-f-fishing without Sean," he said in a bit of a scolding tone.

She turned and buried her head in Maureen's shoulder for a second, then looked back at Art and asked, "Do I hab time-out?" Her breath caught pitifully and tears streamed down her cheeks.

"No time-out," Art said. "And no more fishing without Sean!"

She nodded her head and clung to her grandmother.

The front door opened and Cameron stuck his head inside. "Did I hear someone's been swimming in this cold weather?"

By seven that evening at Valley Hospital, Art had had a clean CT and good chest X-ray. The danger of developing pneumonia from nearly drowning was the risk, so Cameron wanted him to stay at the hospital overnight, on antibiotics for infection and breathing treatments to keep his lungs clear.

"I don't want to spend the night," Art said, his voice still gruff from the strain of coughing and choking.

"I'll stay here with you," Luke said.

"But I want Thanksgiving, Luke!"

"I'll make sure —"

Shelby popped her head in the room. She carried a covered tray. "Now, Art, would I let you miss Thanksgiving?" she asked. "Don't I know you like to eat better than anything?"

He grinned at her and she came into the room. She put the tray on his bedside stand. "I drove it over on a hot-water bottle, but if it's not warm enough, the nurses might let us borrow their microwave." She pulled the aluminum foil off the dishes. "Oh, I think you're going to like this!"

He dipped a fork in the mashed potatoes first and grinned. "It's good. Are you going to spend the night, too?" he asked her.

"Probably not," she said with a laugh. "If Luke is here with you, I can stretch out at home and have the whole bed." She leaned forward and gave Art a kiss on the head. "Be more careful," she said. "I can't stand the thought you might be hurt!"

Art glowed scarlet from the kiss.

"Knock, knock," someone said from the door. Sean came into the room with Rosie on his hip. "Some Wide Iwish Rose can't go to sleep tonight without seeing you. She's never been in a hospital before."

Right behind them Franci entered the room, saying, "And we brought . . ." Her voice trailed off as she saw Art with a generous Thanksgiving meal in front of him. "Pie." Within five minutes, Rosie was sitting on the bed beside Art, helping him eat his dinner, which he didn't seem to mind sharing with her.

Then Walt Booth's voice boomed from the hospital room doorway. "Aw, hell, I thought this was an original idea!" He brought in his own collection of leftovers and behind him Muriel laughed, holding a large serving of pie.

Next came Paul with still more pie. "Vanni sent this over," he said.

And right behind him, Preacher. "Heard there was a little excitement at the Riordan Thanksgiving dinner," he said, bearing a couple of take-out cartons from the bar.

And, finally, Aiden and Maureen crowded into the small room. "I guess it's a good thing we didn't bring food," she said. "We just wanted to check on you and make sure you had company, Art. But look at this — you have so many friends."

"I have very many friends," Art said. "Very many."

The day after Thanksgiving was bright and sunny, though very cold. Maureen told Vivian she had errands to run, but would be back in plenty of time to help with dinner at Franci's house. Tonight Shelby, Luke, Art and Aiden were all coming over for a family dinner before they scattered to the winds in a great exodus out of Virgin River and Eureka.

Maureen drove to Ferndale and back to the cemetery. She saw George's car parked by the side of the road and pulled up behind it. He was halfway up the hill, apparently reading a headstone. She walked up the winding stone stairs till she met him.

He turned and opened his arms and she walked right into his embrace. "Do you think it's a bad omen to meet in a cemetery?" she asked him.

"I have a special fondness for this place," he said. "This is exactly where you completely lost control, threw yourself at me and passionately kissed me. I like it here."

"I think I surprised myself more than you," she said.

"Impossible. I thought I'd have to chase you for years before I got a kiss." He stroked her hair back over her ear. "Are you ready to go?"

"As ready as I'll ever be. You?"

"I'd rather not," he admitted. "But I have responsibilities. The upside is, I'm going to get those things taken care of quickly so I can get the next part of my life under way. I'm looking forward to this next stage."

"And you'll be back here for Christmas?"

Maureen asked.

"Didn't I promise you?"

"I suppose I can trust you to keep a promise," she said. Then she wrapped her arms around him and hugged him tight. "Are you still planning to leave tomorrow?"

He nodded. "I'll drive for a day and have Sunday to get myself organized before classes. I think I might drum up the hardest end-of-term exams in the history of the world. I want to be remembered for something."

"George, you'll be remembered. Who could forget you?"

"Hopefully not you!" He kissed her forehead. "Will you please give me a call when you get home? Just so I know you're safe?" They had spent one of their lunches plugging numbers into each other's iPhones. She had numbers for him on his cell phone, at the university and at home.

"Of course. Once I get rid of Aiden."

"Don't be grumpy," he said, giving her a squeeze. "You'll have a very pleasant drive with him. It's nice of him to look after his mother."

"He's not being nice, George, he's being over protective and nosy. He's got this idea we have to have a heart-to-heart talk about the fact I haven't been dating! He brought it up, you know — apparently, my sons have been concerned about me being alone. More to the point, they're all concerned that I'm *determined* to be alone!"

"Shame on you, Maureen! Tell the young man you're not going to be alone!"

"No! It's none of his bloody business!"

"You're just being stubborn. If he's worried, it might put his mind at ease."

"I'm not ready to talk to Aiden about you. Besides, once you tell one of those boys, they'll all know. They're worse gossips than a bunch of girls. Nothing is sacred with them. No way I'm confessing to any one of them."

"Could be a very long drive," George observed.

"I'd counted on driving alone. I like to drive. And I had looked forward to being alone with my thoughts. I have a lot on my mind, you know."

"I know," he said with a laugh. "Plus, you need time to check in with your priest, see if you can trick him into giving you a blessing."

"I'd like your opinion about something," she said, smiling slyly. "I mean, I do realize your education in the religious arts is spotty compared to a Catholic priest's . . ."

"Indeed?" he said with laughter in his voice.

"But do you suppose, at my advanced age, God would trust me to make my own decision about you?"

He threw back his head and laughed. "Maureen, have you ever heard the story about the Lutheran who went to heaven?"

"I don't believe I have . . ."

"Well, let's see if I remember it correctly. As I recall he wasn't a real bad sinner, as Lutherans go, and made it to heaven based on his good works. Saint Peter was giving him a little tour. They walked through magnificent gardens, past glorious mansions, beside breathtaking waterfalls and rainbows. There was a group of people in a fabulous park and Saint Peter said, 'Those are the Baptists — no dancing or card playing over there.' They walked farther and passed what appeared to be a big celebration, a roaring party, and Saint Peter said, 'Methodists. Anything goes.' And a little farther along there was a gathering of folks visiting, chatting and laughing, having a good time, and Saint Peter said, 'Shhh, be very quiet.' When the Lutheran asked why, Saint Peter said, 'Those are the Catholics. They think they're alone up here.' "

She laughed and gave him a playful slap

on the arm.

George grew serious. "Maureen, you have to follow your heart. You're a good woman and God loves you." He smiled almost shyly. "And, I think, so do I."

"It's going to be a long month before I see you again," she said wistfully.

"You'll miss Rosie, won't you?"

"Dreadfully. And you'll miss Noah and Ellie."

"And the children. Even though I'm not Noah's father, I feel like one — I've never seen him happier. It's not so hard to be away from him, knowing how much he loves life right now. But it will be hard to be away from you." He kissed her deeply, lovingly. "Travel carefully, sweetheart. Don't be too hard on Aiden."

During the month of December, Maureen was kept busy getting ready for a very special Christmas. While she shopped for gifts for Rosie and a new Riordan baby, gender still unknown, she kept thinking, *This is what Christmas is all about — children!* She talked to Rosie on the telephone a couple of times a week and made plans with her, getting her all wound up and excited. "When I come to California, we will shop together and go look at Christmas lights," she had told her granddaughter. "I'll help you buy presents for your mommy and daddy, if you like. And we can bake Christmas cookies together for the whole family."

Maureen had talked to Sean; he was spending approximately four days a week — just three nights — at Beale. He had enough long weekends in Eureka with Franci and Rosie for it to almost seem as though he wasn't gone at all. He was scheduled to have the Christmas holidays off. And, he reported to his mother, Franci was now wearing his engagement ring, wedding plans to follow soon. She couldn't have worked that out better herself.

She heard from Colin and Paddy — they were going to make it to Virgin River for at least a few days over Christmas. Colin was coming from Fort Benning, Georgia and Paddy from Virginia.

She talked to George on the phone, too, even more often than to anyone in her family, and he had new ideas for big travel plans on a daily basis. According to George, Noah and Ellie and the kids had managed to make enough progress on their new old house to move into it in time for Christmas. George, however, was planning to use the guest room over the Fitches' garage that Ellie had just vacated. "I'm sure I'll be spending most of my time with Noah and the family, and with you when I can wrestle you away from your granddaughter, but according to Noah his house still has a long way to go and they don't have a place to put me except on a lumpy sofa."

"When will you arrive in Virgin River?" she asked him.

"I'm coming early. As soon as I'm done at school, I'll head down to Virgin River. Noah can probably use my help with the house. And, Maureen, I've put my house on the market."

"Have you!" she exclaimed. "You're really doing it, then!"

"I'm really doing it. Check your e-mail — I've sent you pictures of RVs! And when we see each other, I'll show you brochures from my recent shopping trip."

"But you haven't made a commitment yet, have you?" she asked.

"Not until the house sells. And I want to finish up the next semester. And, of course, your opinion matters to me. After all that, anchors aweigh!"

Since Christmas Eve would fall on a Friday Maureen was planning to arrive in Virgin River on the Saturday before. She had agreed to meet Aiden in Sacramento and drive with him the rest of the way. She decided that, on this visit, she would stay with Luke. Because it was a holiday week the cabins were not all full. It hadn't taken too much arguing to convince Luke that a couple of his brothers could stay with him in the house and Maureen could have her own space in one of the cabins.

When Maureen had driven home from California right after Thanksgiving with Aiden, he had returned to the subject of her refusal to date. She assured him nothing could be further from the facts — that if she met someone she liked, she'd most certainly keep company with him. Then she'd said the subject was closed!

The trip from Sacramento back to Virgin River was going to be much more interesting.

When she arrived in Sacramento, her son was waiting. He'd gotten there first, taken care of the car rental and was waiting for her in the baggage area at the airport. Once they were under way and zooming north, traffic rather sparse, she said, "I have a couple of things to tell you, Aiden."

"Shoot," he said, giving her a glance and a smile.

"I'm thinking of selling my condo. I might put it on the market after Christmas. I'd divvy up all the furniture and keepsakes I've been polishing, dusting and storing for over forty years, of course. Is there anything in particular you'd like to have?"

"Wait, wait, wait," he said. "You're getting rid of everything?"

"Not everything," she corrected. "But definitely the furniture that came from Illinois, the crystal and china that was left by my mother and your father's mother, and absolutely all the things from your childhoods that I've kept safe. I think it's time you boys take charge of your own fifth-grade report cards and prom pictures."

"I see," he said warily. "And what are you going to sit on? Sleep on?"

"Well, that's a rather long story, but the short version is that I haven't refused to date at all. In fact, I've had quite a few dates with a gentleman friend I met in Virgin River. George Davenport — that nice friend of Pastor Kincaid's who Luke accused me of brushing off."

Aiden was quiet for a moment. "Are you getting married or something?" he asked cautiously.

"No." She laughed. "That would be premature. I've only known him for a short time. Although I've talked to him every day since before Thanksgiving, and we had several long lunches when we were both in

California."

"All right, let's back up a little bit. You didn't brush him off, after all, and —"

"Oh, but I did! I was rude, in fact, and I apologized, and we had lunch and began to get to know each other. And I found out I actually liked him. He's very nice. We have a lot in common, it turns out."

"But you're thinking of selling your condo," Aiden said. "What are you planning to do?"

"Travel," she said. "We got to talking about how spread out our families are. He has a couple of grown, married stepsons who have children — children who consider him their grandfather. And my sons are all over the country. Sean and Luke might be more or less in the same place right now, but that's temporary. And with Rosie and a baby on the way . . . But that's only part of it — getting around to see all the grand-children. There are so many things I've never seen — from the Grand Canyon to Yellowstone! I'm not getting any younger, you know."

"And you're planning to travel with this *George?* This man I've met *once?*"

"I plan to introduce him to everyone over the Christmas holiday," she answered calmly. "He'll be in Virgin River, visiting

Noah's family, and all you boys will be around to meet him again."

"How nice, Mother," Aiden said sarcastically. "You're going to introduce him, and then you're going to take off with him? To see the sights? This man we don't know at all and you *barely* know?"

"Please, don't be ridiculous." She laughed. "I thought maybe Sean or Luke might overreact, but I thought you, who lectured me about the part of my life that's not over, would remain calm and curious."

"All right — here's calm and curious. You're planning to introduce us to this man and then go traveling with him?"

"Not exactly. We've only known each other for a little while. What I'm going to do is continue to get to know him. I'll visit him in Seattle and he'll visit me in Phoenix and we'll meet in Virgin River a time or two. He's a professor, you know, and he's finishing out the term. We also e-mail and talk on the phone. If, at the end of the term in June, we haven't changed our minds, then we'll do some traveling together."

"I see," Aiden said calmly. "*Then* you're getting married?"

"I don't exactly know," she answered. "It's something to think about, but really, Aiden, I don't feel in a big hurry to make that kind of commitment right now. However, I do think he has a point — we're getting a little too old to put off doing the things we've always wanted to do — like travel. And there are practical considerations — like Social Security benefits, pensions, that sort of thing. I'd have to give it a lot of serious thought." Then she shrugged. "I might not have made up my mind about that by June. I might want to test the waters a bit. You know? See if our rapport is as good when we spend a great deal of time together. As good as the visits, phone calls and e-mails."

Aiden's face was getting red. "So, you're going to sell your condo, give away your furniture and go traveling? And if it doesn't work out?"

"I suppose I'll have to say, sorry, it didn't work out. And then I'll find an apartment or small house near one of you boys. I'm trying to stay flexible. I've gotten a little tired of being such a stick-in-the-mud."

"I see. You're going to spend your life savings on plane tickets? Hotel rooms?"

"No, Aiden," she said with a laugh. "George is buying a nice, new RV. He's been looking around, sending me pictures of the various models. He's bringing brochures to Virgin River. These new RVs? They're every bit as big and modern as the condo I'm living in!"

"Mother! Have you lost your mind?"

"Well, actually, once I started thinking about this adventure, I decided I'd lost my mind by closing myself off so much. I've just been marking time for the past twelve years. I stay very busy, you know, but there hasn't been much excitement in my life. I haven't really looked forward to much. You boys are wonderful about visiting when you can, but it hasn't exactly escaped my notice that you each have a three-day limit. I haven't been as excited as this in *years!*"

"I don't know what to say, Mother. This is sudden, it's a little crazy, and —"

She looked at her watch. "We have four hours for you to get right with the idea. I'm not the only one who will have six months to find out everything about George I want to know — so do you and your brothers. I'm sure he'll be more than happy to answer any of your questions."

"Great." Aiden sulked.

"There's a reason I wanted to talk to you first, Aiden. You've always been the voice of reason in our family. I think you get that from my father — he was like that. So, we're about to have one of the best holidays ever! Our first with Rosie, a new baby coming in the summer, Luke married, Sean engaged,

465

all my boys together. I'm not going to have that ruined with a lot of high drama from a bunch of overprotective pups who can't be bothered to spend more than a long week-end with me, anyway. I'm ready for some company! I'm ready for some fun! Get to know George to your heart's content, ask anything you like, but I'm hoping you can keep your brothers from going off the deep end." She reached over and touched his shoulder as he drove. "I'm counting on you, Aiden."

He grumbled something. And grumbled and grumbled.

"What's that, sweetheart?" she asked.

"I said, you've gone from the nun wannabe prude who wouldn't have a *date* in twelve years to a crazy woman who plans to take off in a Winnebago with an old man none of us knows and live in sin, and all he has to recommend him is that he's the friend of some Presbyterian minister! And you expect me to sell this idea to my brothers?"

She couldn't help it, she burst into laughter. "Nun wannabe prude? I guess I'll have to live with that, though it sounds pathetic. And George isn't just a friend of a minister, Aiden. As it turns out, he's an ordained minister, as well. Presbyterian."

Aiden checked his rearview mirror, turned on his signal and pulled onto the freeway's shoulder. He put the car in Park and turned toward Maureen. He looked at her for a long moment. And then he said, "Who are you and what have you done with my mother?"

Sean arrived at Franci's house on December 23 at about ten in the evening. He had called at four, said he was finishing up his out-processing at Beale Air Force Base and would be on his way as soon as possible. The front door was unlocked when he arrived and he walked in, tossing his packed duffel on the floor just inside the door.

In seconds, she was in his arms. "Are you okay?" she asked him.

"I'm okay," he said. "I got everything done. I don't have to go back to Beale at all. On January 15 I leave for Iraq out of San Francisco. But we're so lucky, Fran — a six-month deployment, then a year at Air Command and Staff College. It could've sucked way worse than this. Have you told anyone?"

She shook her head.

"Not even Rosie?"

"We should do that together."

Sean got his orders a week ago and the

first person he told was Franci. He would go to Iraq to fly a U-2 on a UN peacekeeping surveillance mission. He'd relieve one of the aircraft commanders who had been there since July. Then, his alternate position for the Air Force Air Command and Staff College had been upgraded and he'd have a year in residence in Alabama — a very hard slot to get. All things considered, it was a gift. He could've been sent to Iraq for a year; he could've lost that ACSC slot altogether. He almost felt as if he was stealing.

"The movers came, put everything from my house in storage," Sean said. "The Realtor has instructions to try to sell it, and if after ninety days passes with no sale, the property management division of her company will rent it. There's nothing for you to do. Except, have you thought about —"

"Yes," she said, nodding. "Let's get married before you go."

"I don't want it to be sad," he said. "It's not sad — it'll be the happiest day of my life. But if you don't have time to plan a pretty wedding . . ."

"I bought a dress," she said, smiling broadly. "I bought a dress, made a list, called that minister in Virgin River and swore him to secrecy. Tomorrow at breakfast we'll tell Rosie about your orders, about our wedding."

"You're sure? I'm not suggesting this because I'm afraid something will happen. Nothing will happen — I'm going to be flying one of the safest, most protected aircraft in that part of the world. But if I step in front of a jeep and get myself killed, I want the air force to take care of you and Rosie."

She rubbed her fingers along the dark blond hair at his temple. "I'm not worried about anything happening to you. I'm not afraid. I just want to be your wife." She grinned. "I want the piece of paper."

"My mother will be ecstatic," he said.

"Your mother is turning the family upside down," she told him. "I can't wait to fill you in. All your brothers are here and she has plans that they —"

"Oh, I already know," he said. "Aiden called and filled me in. We're under strict orders not to screw up Saint Maureen's Christmas with Rosie by acting out about her new plans. Besides, I don't want to talk about my mother or my brothers tonight," he said, pulling her against him. "I want to go kiss Rosie, make sure she's sound asleep and then get you alone. All alone, with the door closed."

■ ■ ■ ■

Colin and Patrick arrived in Virgin River on
the twenty-third and did a little grumbling
about Maureen's proposed adventure, even
suggesting once or twice that she'd officially
lost her mind completely. But early on the
twenty-fourth George paid his first visit to
Luke's house, and it didn't take them long
to begin joking about this nutty idea, this
idea that no one was going to take with
complete seriousness until certain things
happened — like the sale of the condo, the
purchase of an RV, the solidification of these
crazy plans. The quick acceptance of George
came not so much because of George's
natural wit and charm, but because Maureen was so different when he was around.
He gentled her; her smile was almost girlish, and the Enforcer had turned into a
woman in love. After a couple of hours of
general comradery, Colin shook George's
hand and said, "My man, we should have
hired you years ago to soften up the old
girl."

"I *heard* that," Maureen said from the
kitchen.

The next day when everyone was milling
around in Luke's house Rosie burst through

the door, coat open and curls flying. She looked around at all the people, hunting for her grandmother. When she spotted her in the kitchen, she squealed and ran to her. "Gramma Mo-ween! Mommy and Daddy is habbing a wedding! And then Daddy's going to Iwack! It's *bery* important!"

Dead silence hung in the air. The men in the living room all slowly stood.

Maureen smoothed Rosie's curls. "Is that right?" she asked.

"Uh-huh. And before he goes to Iwack, we're getting us a cawendar and I will make a *X* on ebry day till he comes home. He's going in his plane — 'member his plane? The big plane? It's a *bery* important job!" She stopped talking for a moment and looked around at the room full of people. Softly, she asked her grandmother, "Is that the uncles?"

"They are," Maureen said. "And very anxious to meet you." She laughed softly. "You always enter a room with flair, Rosie, I'll give you that."

The door opened and Franci preceded Sean into the house. They took in the still, silent crowd, Rosie with her arms locked around Maureen's neck. Sean smiled. "Well, I guess you got the news," he said. He hooked an arm around Franci's shoulders.

"Having a daughter like Rosie is better than a town crier. If you can stick around a few extra days, there's going to be a wedding."

On December 27 there was a notice on the door of the bar that said that Jack's would be closed at 5:00 p.m. for a private party. Paige and Preacher worked all day to prepare a wonderful prime-rib dinner with all the trimmings. Preacher worked his art on a beautiful, two-tiered white wedding cake. Maureen and Shelby were at the bar promptly at five, putting out centerpieces they'd made themselves — pine boughs strung with holly and white roses. The Riordan brothers made a special run into the valley for wine and champagne to add to the bar stock, while Ellie and Noah Baldwin showed up with rolls of wide, silver ribbon, white paper doves and strands of small twinkling lights to decorate the bar and buffet table. The bar was transformed for a wedding reception.

At a little before 7:00 p.m. people started to gather around outside the bar, bundled up in their finest outdoor suits, coats and capes. By the time Jack turned on the Christmas tree lights at exactly seven, there were sixty people holding small lit candles.

With precision timing, Noah took his

place in front of Virgin River's very special tree — decorated in red, white, blue and gold, adorned with military unit patches. He had his Bible in hand, standing before a formidable group of Riordans, friends and neighbors. George held Maureen's hand and Vivian looped her arm through Carl's. For this unusual wedding there were no chairs; the ceremony wouldn't be long and the setting was perfect. They made a wide semicircle around the tree, about five rows deep.

First out of the bar doors came Shelby and Luke; Luke wore his wedding suit while Shelby was decked out in a lovely new mauve-colored knee-length coat with black fur trim and black boots. She carried a bouquet of holly and white roses. Next came the bride and groom and flower girl. Franci wore a beautiful full-length white coat with white fur collar and cuffs and a matching fur hat that completely covered her super short hair; she carried a slightly larger bouquet of holly and roses. On her feet were white high-heeled boots. Rosie had a matching short coat and little white boots. Sean was resplendent in his air force dress blues, complete with hat.

Holding hands with Rose, the bride and groom walked down from the porch, over to the front of the magnificent tree, and stood between Shelby and Luke. They bent, one at a time, to put a little kiss on Rosie's cheeks before she was moved to the side to stand with her aunt Shelby. And that left Sean and Franci facing each other, holding each other's hands in front of a tree that was decorated to pay homage to the men and women who were in service to their country.

Right on cue, a light snow began to fall, the flakes glittering down to the ground in candlelight.

Noah said, "Dearly Beloved, we are gathered here together to join a very special man, woman and child in holy matrimony. . . ."

ACKNOWLEDGMENTS

I am deeply grateful for the continued and dedicated early readings and fantastic suggestions made by my friend Michelle Mazzanti of the Henderson District Public Libraries. I count on you more than you'll ever know.

Kate Bandy and Sharon Lampert, my dear friends, my right arm and my left, thank you for early reads, traveling with me on book business and staking out bookstores to hand sell books.

Colleen Gleason, you scary-smart writer you, my deep appreciation for critiquing, brainstorming, reading early drafts and making the most fantastic suggestions.

I have the most wonderful team assisting and keeping me straight, giving moral and professional support, and I'd be so lost without you. Thank you Nancy Berland of the Berland PR Agency, Liza Dawson of Liza Dawson Associates, Inc., and Valerie

Gray, Executive Editor of MIRA Books. You are true goddesses.

Thanks to Jeanne Devlin of the Berland Agency and Cissy Hartley of Writerspace. com. I reap the benefits of your many hours of creative work. I am so lucky to have you in my camp.

It is with humble appreciation I'd like to thank the entire Harlequin team. I know that I have the fun job and you do all the heavy lifting and I am profoundly grateful. Thank you from the bottom of my heart for this fabulous opportunity to spend every day in Virgin River.

Thanks to the men and women who gather at the virtual Jack's Bar online — your enthusiasm is often the bright light on a cloudy day. You're like family and I enjoy your company so much. Special thanks to Ing Cruz, the brain power behind Jack's — you are a gem!

And finally, to the thousands of readers who have written with comments and suggestions, with your personal stories and encouragement, I am indebted to you. I take each e-mail very seriously and you'll never know how much it means to me that you take the time to write.

Bless you.
Robyn Carr